Manor of Buried Secrets

Manor of Buried Secrets

Mason O'Connor

CATALYST PRESS
El Paso, Texas

Published by Catalyst Press.
www.catalystpress.org

Cover design by Karen Vermeulen
Author photo by Rosie du Toit

In North America, this book is distributed by Consortium Book Sales & Distribution, a division of Ingram. Phone: 612/746-2600
cbsdinfo@ingramcontent.com
www.cbsd.com

In South Africa, Namibia, and Botswana, this book is distributed by Protea Distribution. For information, email orders@proteadistribution.co.za.

First edition, first printing
1 3 5 7 9 8 6 4 2

ISBN 978-1-960803-26-9
Library of Congress Control Number 2025936342

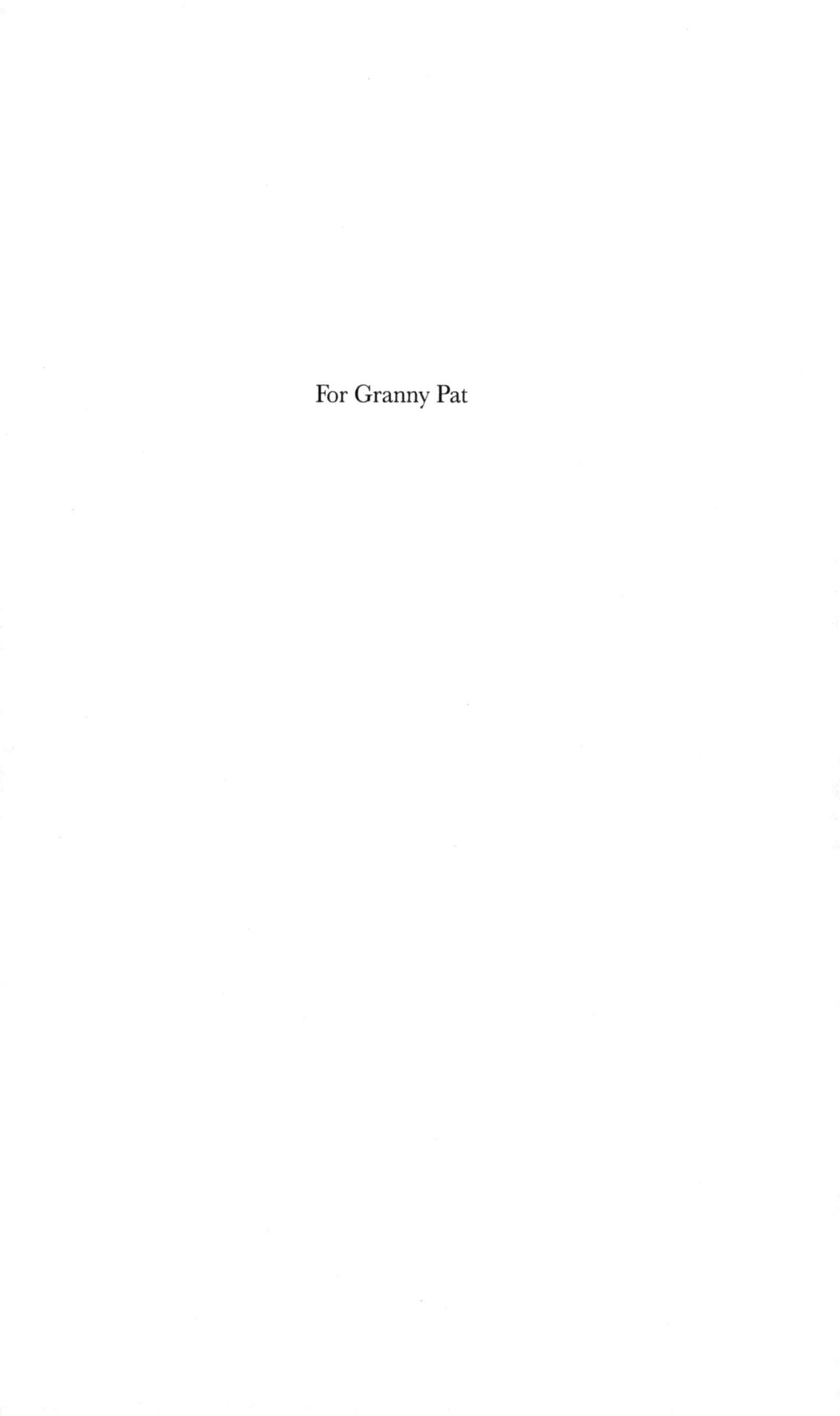

For Granny Pat

Prologue

Thulani Msimang sat on his haunches to inspect a few castor bean plants that seemed to have been chopped down when a voice called his name. He turned to see Vuyo, the new butler, striding out toward him.

"Yes?" Thulani called back. "What is it?"

Vuyo didn't reply immediately. He looked terribly uncomfortable striding through the garden in his uniform. Only once he had reached Thulani did he speak again in a hushed voice. "Miss Woodwright wants to see you," he said, looking at the ground. "She is in the library. I think it is important."

Thulani waited for more of an explanation, but Vuyo wasn't giving him one. He glanced around to see if someone else was nearby to warrant the hushed voice—they had a lot of visitors around at the moment—but nobody was there. A few workers were busy out in the fields and some children were playing near the house, but they were all far away. With a sigh, Thulani eventually stood up and followed Vuyo back to the house at his own walking pace.

Vuyo held the door open for him, and Thulani removed his hat and hung it on the coat rack. The house was refreshingly cool after being out in the sun all morning.

"Morning, Thulani," Brian said pleasantly as he passed them in the hall. "Will you be joining us for breakfast then?"

Brian was Patricia Woodwright's great-nephew, which in his mind somehow made him the de facto manager of the farm.

"No," said Thulani, "just coming to see Patricia."

"Oh?" said Brian. He was about to say something else but stopped himself and turned to Vuyo. "Vuyo, the Neethlings have just arrived; could you please see to them and make sure they have everything they need."

Vuyo nodded and hurried off down the passage, and Brian turned back to Thulani. "How's she doing?" he asked in a lower voice.

Thulani shrugged. "You know as much as I do."

"What are you seeing her about?"

"I don't know. She asked to see me."

"What does she need you for? Perhaps I should come too …"

"She only asked for me," said Thulani. He left Brian watching him as he headed up the stairs.

The third floor was quiet, darker; the air had a certain stale quality about it, with the scent of old wood and leather.

He opened the door of the library and found Patricia hunched over the desk, writing in a book. Her skin hung loosely over her hand as she clutched the pen. She looked thinner and paler every day.

"Ah, Thulani," she said in a weak voice, then paused to cough. "Close the door, will you? I'm almost done."

Thulani obliged, then stood patiently next to the door until a soft breath of "alright" summoned him closer. Patricia carefully tore out the page on which she had been writing, then reached down to one of the bottom drawers of the desk and took out an envelope, a stick of wax and a stamp. "I need you to deliver a letter for me," she whispered, and not just because her voice was weak—she seemed on edge. She folded the page and put it into the envelope, then lit a match and melted some wax onto the envelope before stamping it with her seal. "This letter needs to go to Ms.

O'Sullivan in Pietermaritzburg," she went on, holding the envelope up for Thulani. He tried to take it, but she held onto it and looked him dead in the eyes. "You must hand it to her personally. Nobody else can see it. It is for Ms. O'Sullivan and Ms. O'Sullivan only. Don't tell anyone else where you're going, Thulani. I don't know who I can trust around here anymore. Even now, I fear someone may be watching."

Thulani narrowed his eyes. He was quite sure her family wasn't out to get her, but all this secrecy was making him uncomfortable. He nodded solemnly. "I will get it to Ms. O'Sullivan."

"Thank you," she said, and released the letter. "As soon as you can, if you don't mind. I don't think time is on our side. But first, would you help me back to my bed?"

With great effort she raised herself out of the chair, reaching for Thulani to support her. Thulani bent down to allow her arm around his neck and, with his arm round her back, slowly helped her out of the room. She stopped briefly to place the book in which she had been writing back on the shelf before Thulani led her down the passageway to her bedroom. Her health had been deteriorating over the last few years—inevitably, given her age—but her mind was still sharp, so Thulani found it very odd that she had become increasingly paranoid recently. She wasn't forgetful or confused, just paranoid. This wasn't the first time she had voiced concerns over not knowing who she could trust.

He helped her onto her bed and was about to turn away, but she took his hand.

"Thulani, wait," she said. "Look at me one more time."

Thulani looked at her, and she examined his face like an old photograph. It might have made him uncomfortable had he not known her so well. She then sighed and looked him in the eyes.

"Thulani, if anything were to happen to me, I want you to remember something: the lion has a tail that goes in its mouth."

"A … I beg your pardon?"

He wasn't sure he had heard her right.

"It once belonged to a very dear friend of mine," she said as she closed her eyes and rested her head back. "Your father repurposed it for me."

He stared at her closed eyes for a moment, wondering what she could possibly be talking about. Of all the cryptic things she had said to him over the years, this was definitely the strangest.

It was a long drive to Pietermaritzburg in the heat. Thulani then had to navigate the lunchtime traffic and eventually arrived at O'Sullivan and Woolfe a little after noon. The building was a relic of Pietermaritzburg's history as the administrative capital in an otherwise uninspired city. He climbed the stone steps and was let in through wide glass doors to a cool and spacious foyer where he found the receptionist busy at work.

"Good afternoon," he smiled.

She looked up from her computer. "Good afternoon," she replied without a smile. "How may I help you?"

"I have come to see Ms. O'Sullivan."

"Do you have an appointment?" she asked impatiently, as though she knew the answer.

"No, no appointment; I'll be quick."

"I'm afraid you need an appointment to see Ms. O'Sullivan."

Thulani detected a hint of condescension.

"I just need to give her a letter." He held up the envelope to provide evidence.

She reached her hand out. "I can take that for you."

Thulani didn't move.

"I need to hand-deliver it to her. This is very important."

"What is this in connection with?"

"That is confidential."

The receptionist sighed. "Ms. O'Sullivan is not here," she said defiantly, hand still outstretched.

"When will she be back?"

She checked the computer. "She is in court until at least six o'clock," she said, and looked up again, smug. "Would you like to come back tomorrow?"

Thulani sighed. Later today would be better than tomorrow, but he couldn't wait around for that long. "Will she come back to the office after court?"

"Yes."

"Okay, could you please give her the letter?" he said, and held it out reluctantly.

"Yes, I can." She took the letter and threw it on a pile of papers in a pigeonhole labeled "O'Sullivan." "Thank you for stopping by," she said, and was already back to working on the computer.

Thulani hesitated. "Please," he said earnestly, "this is very important. Could you make sure she gets it as soon as she's back?"

"Of course," she said with a brief glance at Thulani, and was again back to work.

"And could you let me know once she's received it?"

"Mhm."

"Thank you," he said, unconvinced.

After running a few more errands, Thulani finally made the long drive back to Woodwright Manor. He decided he'd better tell Patricia that he hadn't been able to give Ms. O'Sullivan the letter in person. He went inside and started heading up to Patricia's room, but passed Tony, one of the visiting family members, coming down the stairs.

"You going up to Patricia?" Tony asked.

"I am."

"She's asleep. Gideon was just up there."

Thulani checked his watch. He may as well wait until he's heard from Ms. O'Sullivan and report to Patricia tomorrow; no need to wake her unnecessarily.

He left the manor and ambled down past the dam and up the hill to his house where Ngesihle, his wife, was starting to prepare dinner and their grandchildren were at the kitchen table writing in workbooks. He greeted them as he removed his jacket and tie.

"Mkhulu, can you help me with studying?" said the eldest.

"Studying? I thought you were on holiday?" He went to give Ngesihle a kiss on the cheek.

"I have entrance exams for high school coming up."

"Of course I can help," Thulani said, checking his watch, then picked a sample from the pot on the stove to taste.

"Did you speak to Brian about tuition?" Ngesihle said quietly so the children wouldn't hear.

Thulani shook his head while his mouth was full. "Not yet. I'll speak to him tomorrow." He checked his watch again.

"Why do you keep looking at your watch? What are you waiting for?"

"I'm expecting a call from Ms. O'Sullivan. I had to deliver a letter to her today. She should have received it by now."

"You have her number. Call her."

"She might still be in court."

"If she doesn't want to answer, she doesn't have to. You can still call."

Thulani nodded. He was starting to get anxious about it—he should call to make sure. He took out his phone and dialed her number.

"Olivia O'Sullivan," she answered.

"Hi, Ms. O'Sullivan, this is Thulani Msimang from Woodwright Manor. I came by your office today to deliver a letter from Patricia. Your receptionist assured me she would give it to you—I'm just phoning to check that she did?"

"She did not. But I'm still at the office—let me check if she left it for me."

Thulani waited.

"Thulani, I don't see anything here from Patricia."

"It was in an envelope. She had written your name and address on it."

"Perhaps the receptionist put it in the wrong pigeonhole."

"No, I saw her put it in yours—it should definitely be there."

He heard the ruffling of papers on the other end of the phone.

"Thulani, I'm afraid it's not here."

"Did the receptionist perhaps take it to give to you later? I did ask her specifically to make sure you got it."

"I doubt it—she's not the type to go above and beyond. I can ask her tomorrow."

Thulani felt his anxiety building. "I apologize, Ms. O'Sullivan, but I'm afraid I must press the issue; this is urgent."

"What is it about?"

"I don't know the contents, but Patricia stressed that it was important, and very confidential. I was supposed to deliver it to you in person, but you were in court the whole day. She was afraid someone might be watching and was very concerned about keeping it secret."

"Do you know why?"

"She didn't say. She didn't want to say too much in case someone could hear. So you can understand why I need to make sure you get it."

"It's probably about her Last Will and Testament. But all this secrecy is very odd. I'll call the receptionist to see if she knows what happened to it."

"Thank you."

Thulani waited while he heard Ms. O'Sullivan dial a number into an office phone.

"Hi, Thembisa, my apologies for calling after hours. A letter from Patricia Woodwright was delivered for me today by Thulani Msimang, which I'm told you received for me. Do you know where the letter is? … Yes, that's correct … No, I have checked and double checked the pigeonhole, it is definitely not there … Is there no chance you moved it by mistake? Or that it got mixed up with some other mail? ... I see. And did anybody else go through any of the mail? ... That's alright. In the future, if a client hand-delivers anything and says it's urgent, you need to notify me. You could have given it to me when I was back at lunch … I understand. Thank you, Thembisa, I will see you tomorrow … Goodbye."

Thulani heard the headpiece being placed back down.

"Thulani, are you still there?"

"Yes."

"You must forgive my receptionist—every client thinks their matter is urgent, and normally they're not. But I'm afraid she has no idea what could have happened to the letter. According to her, it should still be in the pigeonhole. I think we need to inform Patricia as soon as possible."

"She is asleep now; I will tell her first thing in the morning."

"Get her to call me. I assume she was trying to avoid that for fear of being overheard, but the cat is out of the bag now."

"I will. Thank you, Ms. O'Sullivan; I apologize for this mess."

She must have heard the stress in his voice. "Thulani, you've done nothing wrong. Get Patricia to call me in the morning and we can sort this all out. For now, get some rest."

The next morning Thulani got ready as quickly as possible, with a horrible anxiety hanging over him. It wasn't often he had to tell Patricia that he had let her down.

He marched down the hill from his house and up toward the manor, preparing himself for how he would break the news to her. But when he went inside, he could tell something was different. For a start, there was absolutely nobody downstairs, which was odd. None of the visitors getting breakfast in the dining room, no children running and laughing—completely empty.

He made his way upstairs toward Patricia's room, and that's

where he found everybody else, filling up the passageway toward her room. Some were crying, some speaking very seriously in hushed voices.

"What is going on?" Thulani asked.

Some of the faces turned to look at him, then turned away again as though they could not bear to be the one to tell him. Then Brian stepped out from Patricia's bedroom.

"Thulani," he said, "Patricia has passed away."

Chapter 1

A few days earlier

Peter Brewer was woken by a knock on his door.

"Pete, are you up?" came his mom's voice.

It took a moment for his consciousness to come into focus. He felt like he should be in a good mood about something, but right now it was being disturbed by the annoyance of having been woken up.

"Pete?" his mom repeated.

Peter groaned to let her know that he was awake, but not happy about it.

"Come on, Pete, time to get up!" She sounded more encouraging than commanding, which was odd. "I'm making breakfast," she added. He heard her footsteps leaving down the stairs.

He opened his eyes. A streak of familiar Durban sunlight was beaming in through a gap in the curtains; the neighborhood was already alive with the hum of lawnmowers somewhere over the hedge and the occasional dogs' barking at mailmen and joggers. It was later than Peter would normally be getting up for school.

That's where the good mood was coming from: the school holidays had just begun! He sat up with a smile and a stretch before hopping out of bed and heading down the stairs in his pajamas.

"Morning, Dad," he said as he passed through the lounge.

His dad briefly glanced up from his Sudoku and muttered a sullen "Morning, Pete."

Peter tried to peek at the Sudoku over his dad's shoulder, but his dad covered it with his hand.

"Don't even think about it."

Peter left him alone and went through to the kitchen, where his mom was making breakfast.

"Morning, Mom," he said.

"Oh, good, you're up!" she exclaimed, suspiciously upbeat as she rushed around the kitchen. "Breakfast won't be long. Would you like some tea?"

Odd that she would offer tea when she's already making breakfast.

"No, thanks."

His dad didn't notice him come back into the lounge and spy the Sudoku for a few moments.

"That's a two, that's a two and that's a two," he said, leaning over his dad's shoulder to point at the squares.

"No! Stop it!"

"Which makes that a seven, and that a three …"

His dad snatched the paper away. "Do your own Sudoku!"

Chuckling to himself, Peter went to sit down at their piano and began to play softly while they waited for breakfast. Normally the roles were reversed: his dad, Martin, was usually the one in the kitchen making breakfast while his mom, Gill, got ready for work. What's going on today?

A gleeful shriek interrupted his thoughts from the other end of the passage, followed by quick footsteps, and then the full weight of his nine-year-old sister landed on his back.

"Hello, Peter!"

"Morning, Rebecca," Peter grunted.

"Guess what!" she said. "Our cousins are coming for tea!"

Peter stopped playing. "What? Which cousins?"

"The Van der Westhuizens," his mom said from the kitchen,

still trying to sound enthusiastic. "Just Carol and the boys. Tony's in town on business and he'll come and fetch them afterwards."

So *that's* what was going on. Peter buried his face in his hands, frustrated at the way she was throwing their names around like they were familiar when they really weren't. His dad gave him a sideways glance that said *you and me both.*

"Why?" Peter whined.

"Because they're our family and we haven't seen them in two years," she said. "Now come and set the table. Breakfast is nearly ready."

Peter groaned and got up to set the table.

"Remind me why they're in this part of the world?" his dad asked.

"Oh, they're visiting Patricia," she said. "She's been very ill recently."

His dad gave a wry laugh under his breath as he turned back to his newspaper.

"Could've guessed," he muttered.

Patricia was something like Peter's great-great-great-aunt—it was hard to remember exactly—who lived out near Underberg in what was often described as a mansion. He had vague memories of her visiting them when she used to go to the sea, and he remembered liking her. Of course, she hadn't been for some time now; her age had caught up with her over the last few years. The last time they had seen her was at a big family gathering they had had at her beach house five years ago, for her hundredth birthday. That was the last time the entire extended family had been together. He remembered thinking then that her age was starting to show, but he nonetheless marveled at the fact that she was now one hundred and five years old.

After breakfast, Peter was ordered upstairs to go change as the Van der Westhuizens would be there soon. There was an unspoken implication that he should dress smartly, which he wasn't wild about; collared shirts only accentuated his thin neck and skinny body. He could see his dad was also grumpy about having to dress smartly, and his mom was doing her utmost to keep the mood harmonious. Rebecca, on the other hand, clearly had no concern for the unspoken dress code, all in pink with her curly golden locks bouncing freely as she skipped around with a huge grin on her face.

At eleven o'clock the bell rang, and Peter reluctantly followed his parents outside to welcome the Van der Westhuizens. The two boys were even taller than Martin now. He remembered they were big on rugby and thrived on being the center of attention. They each wore a tight shirt to show off their muscles, and expensive-looking sunglasses to compensate for everything else their personalities probably lacked. They each carried a large suitcase and backpacks, full to the brim, while their mom strode alongside them with her handbag. She had a bob of dark hair that bounced as she walked, and an air about her that made Peter think she might ask to see the manager at any moment.

"Gill, Martin, good to see you," Carol said with her arms out. Rebecca ran up and hugged her around her waist, which made everyone laugh. "You remember the boys, Jesse and Daniel."

Jesse and Daniel each stepped forward with confident smiles to give Gill a very well-rehearsed hug and a kiss before shaking hands with Martin.

Peter had never given anyone a kiss, greeting or otherwise, and he wasn't about to start now. "Hi, Aunty Carol," he said, and gave her an awkward hug. He then turned to Jesse and Daniel, who towered over him.

"Howzit, bru," they said in turn as they each squeezed his hand much tighter than necessary. They made very deliberate eye contact.

"Howzit," Peter replied, and looked away.

Gill invited them all inside and brought out the tea and cake she had prepared while everyone made themselves comfortable in the lounge. Carol wasted no time in catching everyone up on all the family gossip.

"... and of course Karen still stays in touch with Jacky because Megan and Katie are good friends, but now Kim contacts me regularly, which is fine, but it's like she's trying to make sure nobody forgets about her, and I'm just like calm down, you don't have to prove you're part of the family ..."

Peter couldn't remember who these people were, except that Megan and Katie were girls about his age.

"... I mean, honestly, those two never got along, but ever since Walter died it's gotten worse, like a competition of 'who has more claim to the family'..."

She continued for at least half an hour with very little punctuation and barely a breath between sentences. It was only when she excused herself to go to the bathroom that the conversation finally opened up a little. It didn't make much difference to Peter, of course, because he never contributed much to conversations with more than two people. He was a little shy, but he also just didn't feel the need to say anything most of the time. He sat quietly and listened to Jesse and Daniel dominate the conversation: Jesse had finished school now and was going to Stellenbosch University next year, mostly to play rugby; Daniel would be in matric the coming year, first-team rugby captain, and hoping to get into the Blue Bulls Academy after that; Tony, the currently absent father, was an attorney, bogged down with work, and had an urgent meeting that he couldn't get out of; and the reason for all the luggage, it turned out, was because Jesse and Daniel were in fact not joining their parents to visit Aunty Pat, but were on their way to Ballito Rage, and their lift was coming to fetch them soon.

"Which reminds me," Daniel said to Jesse, "do they know where to pick us up from?"

"Ja, I dropped them a pin on WhatsApp," said Jesse. "They should be here soon."

Martin frowned as he did the math in his head. "Now, Daniel," he said slowly, "are you going with to Ballito?"

"I am."

"But ... aren't you still seventeen?"

"Ja," Daniel said with a grin, "but I'm tall enough that they generally don't ask me for ID at clubs."

"Oh." Martin raised his eyebrows and gave a quick glance toward Carol, who didn't seem to be paying attention.

Then, much to Peter's surprise, Jesse turned the conversation to him.

"So, Peter, what grade are you in?"

"Oh, um, I'm going into grade eleven now."

"Okay, nice. And do you play much sport?"

"Ja, mostly rowing," said Peter, "but I play rugby and soccer as well."

"Oh, you play a bit of rugby?" said Jesse. "You enjoy it?"

The honest answer would have been "no, because I'm not very good at it," but he figured that that answer wouldn't have flown with this crowd.

"Ja, it's cool," he said.

This brief exchange was about the total of his contribution to the conversation as the Van der Westhuizen boys then started talking about rugby to Martin, who wasn't an avid rugby watcher but had a passionate interest in how well the Boks were playing and at least kept tabs on the Sharks.

Soon the bell rang, and Jesse and Daniel stood up. "That's us," Jesse announced, and they very politely thanked Gill and Martin for the tea and said goodbye to everyone.

"Peter, would you mind letting them out the gate?" his mom said, handing him the keys with the remote.

Waiting for them outside the gate were a guy and two girls,

with an open-roof beach buggy and music blaring that Peter's dad would've frowned at. The guy was wearing a sombrero and a floral shirt with the buttons undone, red in the face as though he had been in the sun the whole day. The two girls were almost carbon copies of one another, with platinum-blonde hair, short skirts and crop tops. They looked as though they might have just stepped off the beach, except their perfectly straight hair and untouched make-up gave them away.

"Boys, boys, boys!" the guy in the sombrero shouted.

"Gazza, what's happening, bru!"

"Ow, Dan the Man!"

None of them even noticed Peter standing there. The guy was too inebriated to notice anything, and the girls couldn't seem to look any further than Jesse and Daniel. They threw their bags on the back, then gave Peter a casual wave as they got into the buggy, and were soon speeding off down the road. Peter could still hear the music for a while as they drove through the suburb, but it gradually faded and all he could hear from the driveway were a few upset dogs. He closed the gate and went back inside to rejoin the others.

As he approached the living room, something made him hesitate. Carol was speaking, her voice little more than a whisper, a sense of urgency in what she was saying. Paused at the door, he realized that only his mom and Carol were in the room.

"... but it isn't the first time she's said something like this."

"Honestly, Carol, the woman is a hundred and five years old; I think she's just going a bit batty."

"That's what I said, but my dad doesn't think so."

"She doesn't know who she can trust? That seems a little extreme. None of it makes any sense."

"My dad thinks it might have something to do with the inheritance."

"You don't think maybe she's coming to realize that she's on her deathbed, she doesn't have any children to inherit the estate, and she's just getting a bit paranoid about where it's all going to go?"

"Perhaps, yes, but ..."

Peter heard a door open and Rebecca's voice babbling on about something to their dad as they re-entered the room, which put an end to the whispering and that topic of discussion.

Eventually, Tony arrived—not a moment too soon, as far as Peter was concerned—and they all went out to greet him in the driveway. He lit up a cigarette while they had a very short catch-up, then threw it on the ground and stomped it out as they said their goodbyes. Soon he and Carol were off toward Underberg, and Martin was closing the gate behind them.

"I trust you enjoyed seeing your cousin?" Martin said to Gill as they went back inside.

"Yes, it was actually really nice. We don't get to catch up often. We used to be quite good friends growing up, Carol and I."

"What did you get to talking about while I was out the room? I got the sense the discussion ended when we came back in."

"Oh, this and that." She gave him a quick glance. "Patricia," she added, trying to sound nonchalant.

Martin grinned. "A favorite topic of theirs," he said.

Gill smiled too. "Yes, well, this time it does actually sound quite interesting."

Chapter 2

The beginning of the holidays went pretty much exactly as planned for Peter: late mornings, a lot of lounging around, and not much being accomplished in general. But after a few days of piano, books, and the odd crossword puzzle, he was starting to get a little bored; so when his dad announced he would be going up to Pietermaritzburg for some business and asked Peter to come along and help carry boxes, Peter was almost relieved. Of course, he was careful not to let on to this fact. "But there's nothing to do in Maritzburg!" he whined.

"Yes, well, I'm not asking you to come because I think it'll be good for your Instagram; I'm asking you to come because I need your help."

"I don't have Instagram, Dad."

"We're leaving in half an hour."

"How do you even know what Instagram is?"

But his dad wasn't listening anymore. Peter went to get dressed.

Pietermaritzburg wasn't humid and clammy like Durban; it was dry and dusty, baked by the sun. There was only a handful of buildings higher than three stories, and they were all very block-shaped and unimaginative.

"So where are we going?" Peter asked as they drove into the city.

"I have a meeting in the center of town first," said Martin, "It won't be long. But after that we're going to a law firm called O'Sullivan and Woolfe. That's where I need your help."

"What am I supposed to do while you're in your meeting?"

"You're just going to have to wait for me, I'm afraid. I could drop you off at the museum, if you want? Or the art gallery? They're nearby."

Peter looked up at the ceiling and sighed.

"Decide quickly, because they're coming up," said Martin.

"Whatever's easiest," said Peter.

Martin pulled over to let Peter out of the car. "This is the art gallery," he said. "The museum is just round the block there; you won't miss it."

He gave Peter some money, then re-entered the traffic and was off.

Peter looked around. The buildings here were drastically different from what the rest of the city looked like. They were old and beautiful, with red brick and stunning architecture, adorned with gardens and a few statues of old people who were probably once very important.

Across the road was the town hall—a big building with intricately carved detail in the walls and a high tower with a timepiece on each side, all of which read quarter-past-twelve. Peter checked his phone; the time was in fact 11:35. He turned to look at the building in front of him, the Tatham Art Gallery, but decided instead to walk round the block to the museum.

His dad was right: he couldn't miss it. It was another beautiful old building, but immediately more interesting because giant insects made of iron looked as though they were crawling on the wall around the entrance. He went in, paid his entrance fee at the counter and started strolling around.

The first few rooms on the ground floor were dedicated to birds; each room was covered wall to wall in taxidermy displays of different birds behind glass windows. After the birds were primates, and then a great hall of other African mammals. He spent a while moseying about each room, trying to identify which animals he recognized from their various holidays and camping trips, before making his way into a smaller room that was obviously the inspiration behind the decorations outside: rows upon rows of insects inside glass casings, with everything from dung beetles and rhino beetles to long-horned beetles and cicadas. There were four cases completely devoted to butterflies that were indigenous to the Pietermaritzburg area, all pinned neatly in rows with their Latin names underneath.

He spent a good while examining the insects and was about to head out when he looked up and stopped in his tracks: three women had just entered the room. One of them had white hair and wrinkles and looked about his grandmother's age. The second had blonde hair, tied up with an air of professionalism, and looked about his mother's age. And the third, smiling as she chatted softly with the others, had dark, wavy hair flowing freely to below her shoulders. She wore a loose top that wasn't trying to prove anything and a skirt that was confident without being showy. And she looked to be about Peter's age.

His heart promptly lost all sense of rhythm. He tried to remain casual as he walked past, but he couldn't help glancing at her. Of course, at that precise moment, her gaze flicked from the butterflies up to him, and their eyes met. In a blind panic, Peter quickly looked the other way. He immediately wished he hadn't, but it was done now. All he could do was just look straight ahead and walk out the room as quickly as possible.

He hurried upstairs, heart still beating, and wandered distractedly through a section made to look like scenes of the early 1900s, with a blacksmith's shop, gravel roads, and a post to tie horses to. He was barely paying attention. He kept thinking about the girl he had just seen downstairs, and how he wished he hadn't looked away so quickly. Out of embarrassment, he wanted to avoid them but somehow found himself glancing around every now and then in the hope of seeing her.

He walked under an arch with the word "Freedom" printed above it and into a section about the entire history of people in KwaZulu-Natal, starting with the San, who lived in caves in the Drakensberg thousands of years ago. The first African farmers arrived in 400 AD, and then the first Nguni-speaking farmers in the mid-eleventh century. The Voortrekkers came much later, in 1835, followed by the British in 1843.

He was busy reading about the Anglo–Zulu War when a soft voice behind him broke the silence.

"Visiting museums all on your own. How very grown-up and sophisticated."

Peter turned around. It was the girl from the butterfly room. His heart started losing its rhythm again.

"I'm just waiting for my dad," Peter said. "He's in a meeting."

The girl looked at him for a moment, nodding slowly. "You should've pretended you were sophisticated," she said, and then turned her attention to the displays, strolling slowly with her hands behind her back as she read their signs.

Peter didn't know if he should say something or carry on reading in silence. He moved on to the next period, titled "Chief Langalibalele and the Hlubi resistance of 1873." The girl continued strolling until she reached the same place and stopped to read it next to him.

It was about how the English wanted the Hlubi people to register their guns. Chief Langalibalele refused so the English put out a warrant for his arrest. He fled into the Drakensberg mountains but was ultimately captured, and the people who remained of the Hlubi tribe were forced to work as laborers for English farmers who claimed the land. Langalibalele was released years later but died soon afterwards and was buried in the mountains.

"Imagine …" the girl said next to Peter. It was more of a whisper; he wasn't sure if she was talking to him or just thinking out loud.

"Um … ja," he said. Like an idiot.

"Imagine growing up on that land, like your family had done for centuries, and then some people arrive with guns, arrest your chief, and force you to work for *them* on the land that *you* grew up on."

Peter glanced at her awkwardly. "Ja, sometimes I'm ashamed of my English heritage," he said thoughtfully.

She nodded. "Me too."

He glanced at her again. He didn't want to say anything insensitive but she very clearly wasn't white. He quickly realized he was being dumb and that the other women were probably her mother and grandmother, but she had already caught the look on his face.

"I also have English heritage," she said with a grin.

Peter nodded. "Ja, no, I actually just worked that out," he said, embarrassed.

"It's a bit weird for me," she said, "having heritage on both sides. When I read stuff like this I automatically relate to the victims. I have to remind myself that I'm as white as I am black."

"Makes sense," he said. "Although, I'm about as white as they come, and I wouldn't say I relate to either group from so long ago."

Her grin turned into one of the most captivating smiles he had ever been subjected to, and she put out her hand.

"I'm Larissa, by the way."

Her eyes were golden brown.

"Peter," he said as he shook her hand.

She then turned her attention back to the displays and continued slowly moseying along. Peter tried to follow her example.

"So, your dad goes to a meeting and you get dropped off at the museum," she said in a ponderous, offhand kind of way as she looked at a picture of King Cetshwayo.

"Well, actually he dropped me at the art gallery, but I decided to walk here instead."

"Oh, so there was actually some choice involved?" she said, now looking at a piece about Mahatma Gandhi getting thrown off the train. "I guess that is quite sophisticated."

Peter thought about that. "And if I had decided to go to the art gallery?" he asked.

She shrugged. "Maybe a little more pretentious, but, yes, also quite sophisticated."

Without looking at him, she slowly strolled across to a section about the Natives Land Act of 1913.

Peter followed close behind. "How can it be sophisticated to come here instead of going to the art gallery, if it would have been sophisticated to go to the art gallery as well? That doesn't make sense."

She didn't answer immediately, apparently lost in thought. Eventually she seemed to come back to the present and looked up at him.

"It doesn't matter what you did," she said. "The point is you had a choice and made a decision. In some way, it's something that you wanted to do. And wanting to do something sophisticated makes you sophisticated. Or at least more so than if you were just dropped off with no choice at all."

As he was trying to think up a response, Peter's phone started vibrating in his pocket. "Sorry, my dad's calling me."

"Saved by the bell," she said with a smirk.

"Hi, Dad," Peter answered. "No, the museum ... In five minutes? Umm, alright ... no, that's fine, I'll see you there in five ... okay, bye."

He hung up the phone. Larissa was looking at him.

"I need to go. My dad's coming to fetch me."

"Just think," she said, leaning against the wall with her arms folded, "if you had pretended to be sophisticated from the start, you could've acted like that was a business call or something. That would've been really smooth."

"You definitely wouldn't have believed me if I pretended it was a business call."

"No, I would've known you were making a joke about me calling you sophisticated. And that would've been smooth."

Peter nodded. "I'll remember that for next time."

There was a brief silence, and Peter knew that this was the moment to ask for her number.

She smiled. "It was nice meeting you, Peter."

But he buckled.

"It was nice meeting you too," he said. "Bye."

With that, he begrudgingly walked out of the room, cursing himself all the way down the stairs and out of the museum.

They arrived at O'Sullivan and Woolfe to be informed by a very sassy receptionist that Martin's contact was in court. She looked extremely unimpressed when Martin explained that she herself could show them to the boxes they needed to carry. As Peter and his dad carried a large box down the stairs to their Fortuner parked on the street, Peter thought about Larissa; what she had said, and what he *wished* he had said. Futile now, though, because he would probably never see her again.

A woman came up through the entrance and saw him and his dad. She had gray hair and some wrinkles, and spectacles from a bygone era; but behind the spectacles her eyes were keen and sharp.

"Hello, Martin!" she said. "Sorry, I've been in court all day. But I see you've gotten started. Thank you so much for doing this!"

"Not to worry," said Martin. "I was in town for a meeting anyway. Oh, this is my son, Peter. Peter, this is Ms. O'Sullivan."

"Hi, Peter," she said as she shook his hand firmly; "It's a pleasure to meet you."

"Pleasure to meet you too," said Peter.

Ms. O'Sullivan checked her watch. "Unfortunately, I must run," she said. "Martin, thank you once again, we really do appreciate it, and thank you, Peter, for your assistance. I'm sure I'll see you soon. Goodbye!"

As soon as she had left, a man emerged from a nearby room and approached the receptionist while Peter and his dad fetched another box. As they carried the box out, Peter watched the receptionist ignore him at first, then suddenly sit up straight with surprise after he cleared his throat. "Sorry, Mr. McKenzie! What can I do for you?"

When they came back in for the next box, the receptionist had gone and the man was behind her desk, looking through some papers on the shelf behind. He picked up an envelope, turned it over to look at both sides, then slipped it into his pocket. On their next trip down, the man was gone.

The day after their trip to Maritzburg, Peter and the rest of the family waited at the table for Martin to serve dinner. Rebecca giggled as she tried to play with Peter by putting random inedible things on his plate, like the salt cellar lid and the wine cork. He didn't want to give her any satisfaction, so he just took them off without saying anything, but she kept putting things back as fast as he was taking them off. He was nearing the point of shouting at her when the phone rang, and their mom got up to answer it.

"Stop it, Becca!" he said in a hushed voice while their mom was on the phone. But she just giggled some more and put the bottle opener where he had just removed a candle.

"Becca, that's not how we behave at the table," their dad said as he came through from kitchen with a pot of curry.

She stopped putting things on his plate, but she was still giggling when their mom came and sat back down.

"Who was that?" Martin asked. He stopped serving and Rebecca stopped giggling as they read the expression on Gill's face.

"That was, um ..." she started, trying to gather her thoughts. "That was my mother."

They all looked at her, waiting for an explanation.

"Aunty Pat died last night," she said.

Everyone was silent.

"I'm sorry to hear that," said Martin.

Gill nodded. "I am too."

"From her illness?" Martin asked.

"I guess so," she said. "And old age."

Martin said nothing, but took Gill's hand and held it gently.

The rest of dinner was very quiet. Even Rebecca was silent. Peter had lots of questions, but kept them to himself for the time being.

Chapter 3

Dear Gill and Martin Brewer

Our beloved Patricia passed away on the night of the 7th of December. It is a sad time for all of us, and all we can do is be present for each other and take comfort in each other's company.

The funeral will be held on Sunday, the 13th of December, at Woodwright Manor, as per Patricia's wishes. Ms. O'Sullivan, Patricia's appointed executor of her estate, has agreed to come to Woodwright Manor for a reading of the will, but will only be available on Friday, the 18th of December. We therefore invite you to spend the week at Woodwright Manor with the entire family and a few special guests for a "week of remembrance" in Patricia's honor, from the 12th of December before the funeral until the 18th after the reading of the will.

Please let us know if you will be able to attend.

Sincerely,
Brian Kingsbury
Woodwright Manor

Peter watched the trees flash past from the back-seat window of the Fortuner, his head resting against the glass. Behind the trees, hills upon hills of farmland stretched as far as the eye could see—which had been the case for a while now. His mom was driving; his dad was working on his laptop in the passenger seat; Rebecca was fast asleep next to him, and on Rebecca's other side their grandmother, Beverly, was also fast asleep. No one had said a word since Bulwer.

The letter had arrived the morning after the phone call. His mom had tried to sell it to him as a getaway, but he was not excited about the prospect of a week-long family gathering. His cousins generally got along with each other better than he did, especially the ones from Joburg. Most of them also had siblings of a similar age. Peter, on the other hand, had a sister seven years younger than him who was mostly just annoying. So he had a week of that to look forward to.

The road curved around a hill and gave them a great view across the valley to the little cluster of buildings and trees that was the small town of Underberg. Beyond, the Drakensberg mountains started to take form as they got closer, carving the horizon into a dramatic skyline.

"Are we nearly there?" Peter asked.

"We're just going to stop for some flowers in Underberg," said his mom. "Not much further after that."

In the town, they pulled into a small shopping center and parked outside the florist. Once they had all gotten out and had a stretch, Gill got out her purse. "Here, Pete, why don't you get us some snacks from next door," she said, handing Peter some money.

Next door was a farm stall, stocked mostly with homemade jams, honeys, and other local products. Peter found some choc-chip cookies and freshly cut biltong and took them over to the counter.

"Durban, eh?" said the old woman behind the counter, glancing out the window at their car. "On your way to visit the Drakensberg?"

"No, actually, it's my great-aunt's funeral tomorrow," he said.

"Oh, Patricia Woodwright?" she said. "Great loss. She'll be missed."

"Did you know her?" Peter asked.

"Are you kidding?" she said as she started scanning the items. "Everybody knew her. The whole town went into mourning when we heard. Anyway, she's in a better place now. Maybe we'll finally find out what happened to all that money, eh?"

"What money?"

"You know, the Woodwright fortune."

"I don't know anything about that," Peter said as he paid for the snacks.

"Have you never wondered where it all came from?" she said. She handed Peter his slip and leaned on the counter. "That huge house, all that land; it's certainly not from their modest farming practices, I can tell you that much. No, the Woodwrights came from immense wealth. Practically royalty, the story goes. But somewhere along the way they lost it all, and nobody knows how. Patricia didn't like to speak about it."

"I've never heard any of that," said Peter.

"Well, now you have," the woman smiled. "And don't be surprised if you hear more about it over the next few days—I dare say that's why a lot of people are coming. Goodbye!"

Peter left the shop, wondering what she meant by that. He met his parents coming out of the florist with a bunch of flowers.

"That lady knew Aunty Pat," he said as they climbed back into the car.

"I'm not surprised," said Gill. "Most people around here know her. It's a small town."

"She said something about a missing fortune," said Peter. "Do you know what she was talking about?"

His dad glanced up at his mom, who gave a big sigh, and his grandmother muttered "Oh, nonsense!" under her breath. Rebecca, on the other hand, got very excited.

"A missing fortune? Like treasure?"

Peter caught a glimpse of his mom's tired face in the rear-view mirror and wished he hadn't asked. She took a deep breath before she answered.

"Somebody once started a rumor that they had found 'the missing fortune' at Woodwright Manor," she said. "It was just a hoax, but it made everyone think that there actually *was* a missing fortune. Nobody really believes it anymore; it's just one of those legends that has been passed down. That's all they were talking about."

"Why start a rumor like that?" said Peter. "And why would anyone believe it?"

"I don't know," said Gill. "They said the Woodwrights were once very wealthy, but no one knows if even *that's* true, and—"

"No, no, that much is true," Beverly cut her off.

Peter could see his mom rolling her eyes and shaking her head.

"Charles Woodwright owned a big mining company," said Beverly. "He was extremely wealthy. He used to have tea with the King."

"You don't know that, Mom," said Gill.

"I certainly do know that!" said Beverly.

"So, then what did happen to all of the money?" Peter asked, but his question was met with silence. Beverly looked stubbornly out of the window.

"Mom?" he asked.

But his mom just shrugged. "I don't know, Pete."

Silence took over again. Peter gave up and rested his head against the window, his mind filled with the thought of missing treasure.

Soon they turned off the tar road and onto a gravel road with a pair of large iron gates. The gates were mounted on great stone walls curving outward from the entrance, and large iron letters spelled "Woodwright Manor" across each wall. Welded on each of the gates was the Woodwright family crest—a lion on a shield—

and perched at the top of the walls, one on either side, were two large lion statues, both sitting upright as though guarding the gates from intruders.

From the entrance, sycamore trees lined either side of the road as it curved through the fields, slowly circling round a grassy hill on their right. On the left, the land was covered by different crops and sloped gently downward to a small stream in the valley. Further ahead, Peter could see the glistening water of a large dam.

And there, straight ahead as they came round the last bend, was Woodwright Manor. It looked more like a small castle than somebody's house, surrounded by gardens with giant oak trees and tall yellowwoods.

Peter's mom caught a glimpse of the wonder on his face in the rear-view mirror and smiled. "Do you remember this place, Pete?"

"Hmm, not really," he said, looking around.

"I don't remember it," Rebecca said conclusively.

"You weren't born yet the last time we came here," said Beverly. "I'd be surprised if you did."

Peter gazed out at the fields and hills lined with fences and trees. There were stables and barns, and all manner of farm equipment; horses out in the fields and sprinklers over the crops. A small house sat atop the hill on the other side of the dam, and up on the near hill to the right stood an old stone chapel.

"What's going to happen to all this now that Aunty Pat has died?" he asked.

"Well, that's what we're going to find out," said Gill. "They're going to read the will on Friday. Normally it would go to her next of kin—unless she's stated differently in her will. But she didn't have any children of her own so it's not clear where it all might go."

"I don't suppose we're going to get anything?" Peter asked, more sarcastically than actually hopeful.

His mom laughed. "No, I'm afraid it has to go through about three generations before we see any of it. But that's not why we're here; we've just come to pay our respects. And there isn't that much money anyway. This manor is about all that's left."

"So, who's going to get the manor?" Peter asked.

His mom shrugged. "I'm not sure. Possibly Phillip D'Arcy, because he's 'first in line,' so to speak, although he's quite old. Brian Kingsbury has been managing the farm recently, so it might go to him."

They pulled into a large parking area among the tall yellowwoods where a few cars were already parked. Two ridgebacks and a Dalmatian came bounding up to the car, barking excitedly with their tails wagging. As the car came to a stop, two men were there to greet them: one larger in smart clothes, slightly older, and the other a thinner, younger-looking man in a butler's uniform.

"Mr. and Mrs. Brewer, welcome!" the older man said with a big smile as they stepped out of the car. He had a strong Zulu accent and an air of authority about him. His hair was thick but neat, his beard well trimmed, and his shirt tight around his big chest and arms. "No, Trixy, stop that!" he said to the Dalmatian as it tried to jump on Gill. The dog obediently came to his side.

"Hi," Gill smiled, and Martin went to shake his hand.

"My name is Thulani Msimang, in case you've forgotten me."

"Of course we haven't forgotten you, Thulani, we're not as old as we look," said Beverly while Gill helped her out of the car just as Peter was thinking he had never met this man in his life.

Thulani laughed. "It's good to see you, Ms. Higgs," he said as he went round to take over from Gill, and they exchanged a hug and a kiss. "I'll show you to the guest hall, where everybody is waiting. Vuyo will take your bags to your rooms." He gestured to the butler, who looked like he was still getting used to the smart attire.

They followed Thulani from the parking area down some stone steps and along a path through the garden, the three dogs panting happily alongside them. Peter looked up in wonder as Woodwright Manor towered above them. Ivy covered the bottom of the old stone walls and looked like it had done so for centuries. The gardens around the manor were vast and magnificent: an array of beautiful flowerbeds, shrubbery, and tall trees, with the occasional water feature hidden in between the hedges and along the various footpaths. In front of the entrance was a square lawn with a large fountain, water cascading down from each level to the next.

The entrance itself was a set of massive oak doors, with steps leading up to them and large pillars on either side. A lion on each door held a heavy iron knocker in its mouth.

Thulani pushed the doors open, letting them through into the entrance foyer. The interior seemed only slightly less medieval than the outside, but immediately warm and homely. A big carpet covered wooden floorboards, worn thin from years of being trodden on. Two old coats hung on a coat rack and a couple of boots stood neatly against the wall, where the floorboards had been rubbed smooth, next to a barrel with wooden canes and walking sticks. A great old grandfather clock ticked away tirelessly in the corner. Everything looked like it had been there for years.

"This way," Thulani gestured to a door on the left with voices mingling inside.

They passed through into a room full of people talking quietly to each other.

"Beverly and the Brewers! Good to see you all!" a man greeted them as they walked in. "Thank you for coming."

Peter remembered him. He was a rather large man, both in height and girth, older than Peter's dad; his once dark hair was almost completely gray, and he had wrinkles around his eyes and strong frown lines.

"Good to see you too, Brian," said Beverly and they exchanged a kiss.

"We're sorry about Patricia," said Martin as they shook hands.

"Yes, we all are," said Brian. "Although I'm sure she was more than happy to move on. A hundred and five years is a hell of a good run." Then he turned to Peter with a smile. "And Peter, is it? You're a lot taller than the last time I saw you!"

Peter smiled politely. "Hi, Uncle Brian."

"I'm Rebecca!" Rebecca said with a huge grin.

"I know exactly who you are," Brian laughed, and he picked her up and gave her a kiss on the cheek. "Can we get you all some drinks?" he said as he placed her back down. "Some brandy perhaps? We also have some wine open ..."

Just then some more people walked in the door behind them.

"Ah, more guests," he said. "Sizwe here will help you with your drinks," he motioned to another gentleman dressed in the same uniform as the other butler. "Please feel free to ask either myself or any of the butlers if you need anything." With that, he smiled and turned to greet the new guests. "Jane, thanks for coming ..."

As Sizwe led them to the drinks table, Peter absentmindedly turned to see the people coming in and nearly tripped over his own feet. It was a family of four: a grandmother, a mother and father, and a daughter about his age. She had dark, wavy hair, golden brown eyes, and a smile that radiated confidence.

"My name's Larissa," he heard faintly as he watched her lips move.

It was the girl from the museum! Heart racing, he quickly turned away and pretended he hadn't seen them. What were the chances of *her* being there?

To avoid making premature eye contact, he kept his back firmly towards Larissa as they got their drinks. He then had to constantly fight the urge to look at her and tried to concentrate as he followed his parents around to greet the rest of the family, which usually entailed saying "hi" and then standing by quietly while the adults spoke and Rebecca occasionally blurted things out. He knew he had met all these people before, but he didn't remember any of their names or how they were related; except for his great-grandfather, Oupa Tim, of course. They went on to greet the Le Rouxs, the Ulbrichts, the Greenacres, a few Croxfords, one or two Kingsburys, and Peter promptly forgot all their names as soon as they had been introduced. They met a relative who was a priest and introduced himself as Father Ian, and of course the Van der Westhuizens were also there; Jesse and Daniel were polite as always and did a great job of commanding the conversation to come across as adults. Carol delighted in not-so-subtly pointing out Kim Kingsbury-Ellis's extravagant hat, and Tony excused himself for a cigarette outside.

"Alright, well my glass is empty," Peter's dad said after they had finished speaking to the Neethlings—a family with two girls, Megan and Michelle, who seemed to think the conversation wasn't worth their time and kept checking their phones. But just as they were about to make another trip to the drinks table, another voice stopped them: "Excuse me, I don't believe we've met."

They turned round to see Larissa's family.

"No, I don't believe we have," said Peter's mom with a smile. "I'm Gill."

The grandmother's name was Jane, and the parents were Richard and Martha. Then Larissa stepped forward.

"Hi, I'm Larissa," she said with a delightful smile, first shaking Beverly's hand, then Gill's, and then Martin's.

"Well, aren't you a radiant young thing," said Beverly. "And how old are you, Larissa?"

Peter wanted to cover his face.

"I'm sixteen," she said. "Seventeen in a few months."

"Oh, that's the same as Peter!" said Beverly, grinning at Peter with very little tact.

"Really?" said Larissa with a grin of her own, turning her attention to Peter.

"Yup," said Peter, managing half a smile.

Her eyes narrowed, then widened as she finally recognized him. "Hey!" she said. "You're Peter from the museum!"

Peter nodded with lips pressed together. "Well, I'm not *from* the museum, but, yes, I met you there."

"Oh, my word!" she laughed. "What a coincidence!"

"You two know each other?" Martin asked.

"Not really," said Peter.

"We met at the museum last week," said Larissa.

"Oh, really?" said Martin, eyebrows raised in a slightly amused way that Peter knew to mean *perhaps you owe me for dragging you off to Maritzburg ...*

Peter just nodded without looking at him.

"So how do you all fit into the picture?" Beverly asked. "Not family, I presume? I'm sure I would recognize you if you were."

"Yes, you seem to be a rather close-knit family," Jane laughed. "No, my mother was very good friends with Patricia before she died. Before my mother died, I mean. And I guess I just stayed in touch with Patricia after that."

They spoke for a short while and Peter, true to form, remained mostly silent. Larissa, on the other hand, had no issues including herself in the conversation, and spoke with a certain conviction that made everyone want to listen to her.

"Well, it was great meeting you," Richard said once the polite conversation had run its course. "I'm sure we'll get to know each other over the next few days."

They all agreed, and Larissa flashed Peter one more effortless smile before turning away and walking off with her parents.

"Family and friends," called a loud voice, "can I get everyone's attention quickly?"

The room quietened down as everyone turned to face Brian at the front.

"I'd like to extend a warm welcome to everybody; thank you all for coming. It's a sad time for all of us, but amid the sadness it is nice to have all the family together again, along with close friends of Patricia's. Just to keep everyone up to speed, the ceremony will take place tomorrow morning at ten in the chapel, after which we will proceed with the casket to the graveyard outside, where Patricia will be buried alongside her sisters. Father Ian has graciously offered to officiate the ceremony—oh, that reminds me," he turned to Father Ian, "I've got the chapel keys for you; I'll bring them to your room."

Father Ian nodded and Brian resumed addressing everyone. "As you know, Patricia was always an advocate for celebrating life rather than mourning death, and one of her favorite things to do was to braai down at the dam. So we thought it would be nice if we then spent the afternoon at the dam for a late lunch braai; I think she would've liked that."

There were murmurs of agreement around the room.

"On to more pressing matters," he continued, "dinner tonight will be served at seven-thirty. That's in ..." he looked at his watch, "about an hour and a half. In the meantime, myself, Thulani and the butlers will come round and escort you to your rooms; please feel free to unpack and make yourselves at home. Now, we never thought we'd be pushed for space in this house, but it turns out we're rather a big family, so we've got all the boys bunking together in one room and all the girls together in another. Hopefully, you kids can all get to know each other. Lastly, there are a few renovations underway so I'm going to ask that everybody stays out of the west wing on the third floor. That's all for now; we'll see you at dinner."

Peter's mom ruffled his hair as the hum of chatter resumed around the room. "Hear that, Pete? You're going to be bunking with the other boys. It'll be fun!"

Peter was less than enthused.

The crowd started thinning out as, one by one, the guests were taken to their rooms. Soon Thulani came to fetch the Brewers. He led them back out through the entrance foyer and into a large hall where a staircase curved up to the second floor, and another staircase continued the spiral up to the third floor. Doors and passageways led off in all directions; artwork and old tapestries covered the walls, while the space was filled with furniture and old brass equipment that had become purely ornamental.

Thulani led them up the stairs to the second floor and down a long passageway with many doors on either side and paintings in all the gaps. Eventually they stopped at a door, which Thulani opened before standing aside. “Ms. Higgs,” he said with a smile and gestured for Beverly to go in.

“Thank you,” she said, “and please, Thulani, it’s Beverly.”

Thulani then opened the next door along. “Mr. and Mrs. Brewer,” he said with the same gesture.

“Okay, kids,” their dad said, “we’ll see you at dinner. Don’t be late!”

They disappeared inside, and Thulani smiled at Peter and Rebecca. “Now if you’ll follow me, you two will be staying on the third floor.”

He led them back down the passageway, up the stairs to the third floor and then down another passageway that looked almost exactly like the last one.

They came to the girls’ room first. Some girls were busy unpacking their bags; some were chatting, others were on their phones.

“Here you go,” Thulani said to Rebecca, cheerfully as always. “Your bed is over there by the window.”

Sure enough, there her bag was on top of a neatly made bottom bunk. She stepped forward slowly, her head bent down slightly as she looked around the room with wide eyes. She then looked back at Peter, nervous and unsure. The spirited exuberance was gone from her usually bright face; his pesky little sister was now shy and vulnerable. She was one of the youngest there and didn’t know any of them. Peter wanted to stride into the room and command that all the girls be accommodating and kind to Rebecca; but just as the emotion was building, Larissa appeared.

"Hi there, Rebecca," she said with a comforting smile. "Let's take you to your bed." She took Rebecca's hand and immediately Peter could see that his sister relaxed. Larissa looked over her shoulder and gave him a friendly wink before leading Rebecca off to her bed.

"She'll be fine," Thulani said knowingly. "She's in good hands. Now if you'll come with me, your room is just down here."

He led Peter a little way down the passage, and already Peter could hear that the boys' room was more noisy.

"Your bed is just there," Thulani said, pointing to one of the top bunks where Peter's bag had been placed neatly.

The boys in the room were laughing loudly. Two of them were passing a rugby ball between one another. Nobody even turned to look when Peter came in. He made his way to the bed Thulani had pointed out, but just then somebody yelled, "Dibs on the top bunk!", ran across the room, and leaped onto Peter's bed. Without a second thought, he grabbed Peter's bag and dropped it onto the bed below, where there were now two bags.

Peter didn't know what to do and looked around the room for someone to back him up. Still, nobody noticed him.

"Umm, excuse me," he said, perhaps a little too softly because the boy paid absolutely no attention. "Sorry," he said louder, "I think that was my bed."

The boy turned to him with a cheeky grin. He was a lanky boy with blond hair and freckles, his grin mischievous but friendly.

"Well, quick!" he said. "Grab another one before all the good ones are gone!"

The rest of the boys heard this, and suddenly there was a mad scramble for beds! Peter grabbed his bag as everyone started pushing and shoving, laughing all the while, tossing bags across the room as they all clambered for the top bunks. He threw his bag onto the next bed, but Daniel pushed him aside before he could jump up. Jesse then pushed Daniel aside, and Peter took the opportunity to quickly climb onto the bed, then laughed with the others as they watched Jesse and Daniel play-wrestle it out.

There were nine boys staying in their room. Jesse van der Westhuizen was the oldest, and there were two others around Daniel's age: the lanky, blond-haired boy with freckles and a shorter, stocky boy with dark hair. The other four boys were younger than Peter.

For the rest of the evening before dinner the older boys all sat on their beds or on the windowsill, chatting. Peter just lay quietly on his bed and listened.

"Sorry, bru, remind me where you're from?"

"I'm from Joburg."

"Oh, is it? What school?"

"St. Stithians. Going into matric next year."

"Ja, me too. Can't wait to be done."

"You from that side as well, hey?"

"Ja, St. Johns."

"Just remind me your name quick?"

"Sorry, I'm Daniel."

Daniel briefly lifted himself out of his chair to shake hands, holding his cap with his left hand.

"Howzit, bru; Kyle."

Kyle was the stocky boy with dark hair.

"Are you out of school then?" Kyle said to Jesse.

"Ja, just finished."

"Epic, bru! Did you go to Rage?"

"Ja, we actually came straight from there."

"Ja, I also went," said Daniel. "It was insane."

"Is it, hey? I wanted to go as well, but I didn't get a passport in time."

"Austen, did you go? I don't think I saw you there."

"Nah, I was on cricket tour."

Peter stopped paying attention. He gazed out the window at the bright orange clouds set ablaze by the sun dipping behind the

Drakensberg. The mountains really did look majestic up close. Down the hill, the dam reflected the light of the evening sky. The air was still warm, though starting to get cooler. He pulled the blanket up over his shoulders and his mind wandered to the image of Larissa winking at him ...

When he opened his eyes it was almost dark outside; there was just a faint glow of light over the horizon, silhouetting the mountains. He must have dozed off for more than half an hour. The rest of the boys were still talking, but the topic had changed completely.

"No, that's not what I heard," Daniel was saying. "Apparently they used to be super wealthy. My dad reckons there's no way they would have lost all that money."

"So, what does he think happened to it?"

"He reckons it's still around."

"What, and Patricia's just been sitting on all that dough for years and hasn't spent it? Hasn't even said anything? Nah, bru, I don't back it. It's definitely not still around. And think about it: there were three daughters. It would have been split between all of them. Then they had their own families, and it got spread even more. It's trickled down through the generations and been spent along the way."

"I'm telling you, by the time their old man died, there was barely anything left. Something happened before he passed away, and the daughters never saw any of it."

"Well, you can't say they never saw *any* of it; they were all wealthy."

"Ja, okay, whatever; you know what I mean. He lost most of it."

"You reckon he was a gambler?"

"Ja, maybe. I mean, that would explain how he lost it all."

"I also heard that Patricia never got along with her pops. Maybe that's why. Because—"

A knock on the door made everyone immediately fall silent,

looking over their shoulders to see who it was. Vuyo, the butler, stood in the doorway. He looked from boy to boy for a moment as they all stared up at him, before simply stating: "Dinner is served."

Just like that, the topic was dropped like contraband. There were a few mentions of "thanks" as the boys all got up to follow Vuyo from the room, and already the conversation had moved on.

"We should get a game of touch rugby going tomorrow by the dam."

"Ja, that'd be awesome!"

Peter walked down with a boy called Steven Greenacre, who had just finished his first year of high school—the only boy in high school younger than Peter. He had short, spiky hair, and paid very close attention to everything Peter said.

"Who's going to get all of Aunt Patricia's stuff?" he was asking, clearly still fixated on what the other boys had been talking about.

"Normally it would go to her next of kin," Peter explained, as though he hadn't just been asking his parents the same thing. "But she didn't have any children so it'll probably go to Brian."

They followed Vuyo to the dining hall on the ground floor, where a feast had been prepared. Rows of dishes were laid out on heating trays alongside a variety of drinks and glasses. The table itself was immaculately laid, with candles spaced along its length on a white tablecloth decorated with leafy wreaths. A large chandelier hung from the center of the ceiling. Around the side of the room were a number of cabinets for glassware, crockery, and the like. They clearly had no trouble catering for so many people.

Once Peter had found his parents and sat down, Brian stood up from the head of the table at the other end. "Good evening, everyone," he said in a loud voice to get everyone's attention. "May we say grace, please? Just right where you are, no need to move."

The room fell silent as everyone bowed their heads.

"Lord God, thank you for bringing all the family here safely as we mourn the death of our dear Patricia. We also thank you for Patricia's life, and the time we got to spend with her. Please now bless this food unto us, and us in your service. In the name of Christ, amen."

There was a chorus of "amen" across the room.

"Now," said Brian, "the butlers will serve everyone shortly. Please do start eating once you have your food—we don't want it to get cold. If you would like a second helping just come and help yourself." He gestured to the dishes on the warming trays.

By now everyone was in their seats and the butlers had started bringing plates of food around. The one upside to these sorts of family gatherings was the food; it was always good, and there was always plenty of it: slices of lamb and beef, roast onion, pepper, and butternut, a cheesy potato bake and creamy spinach. The room filled with the hum of voices and the clinking of silverware, while the butlers made their way around the table offering a choice of red or white wine.

Peter was seated in between his dad to his right and a rather old man to his left. His dad chatted to other people across the table, so Peter ate silently for a while until the old man to his left attempted to strike up a conversation. "I'm sorry, I don't recall whether we've met," the old man said in a very posh English accent, enunciating each word clearly, "What's your name?"

Peter desperately tried to chew and swallow the food in his mouth before he could answer. "Peter," he finally said.

"Peter who, if I may ask?"

"Brewer."

"Ah, yes," said the old man. "So, you must be from the Croxford side of the family?"

"Yes, that's right," said Peter.

"It's nice to meet you, Peter. My name is Phillip D'Arcy."

Sizwe came round with the wine, which he offered each of them. Peter said no, but Phillip had his glass filled nearly to the brim with white wine.

"You don't want to have a glass of wine with an old man?" said Phillip.

"I'm only sixteen," said Peter.

"Ha, alright then," said Phillip. "Now tell me, Peter, are you from Gregory's or Timothy's side of the family?"

Peter had to think about that for a moment.

"Umm, my great-grandfather is Timothy Croxford."

"Okay, I see," said Phillip, between sips of wine. "Yes, Timothy is my cousin. We used to see quite a lot of each other; him and his brother Greg. Greg passed away in 2006, of course, but we spent a lot of time together growing up. That was before our family moved down to our farm in the Western Cape. Always been big on farming, our family has; ever since Charles Woodwright moved down here from England in the 1800s and built this house. He was a right visionary, that man. You know, before he moved down to South Africa, they say he used to have tea with Prince Alfred, Duke of Edinburgh ..."

Phillip carried on about their family history for what felt like ages, hardly pausing except to sip his wine and occasionally nibble on his dinner. Peter tried to be polite by responding every now and then with an appropriately timed "oh, really?", but in all honesty the man didn't need to be prompted; and he was burning through topics so quickly it was hard to keep up. Peter looked up to the other end of the table and saw Larissa and her family chatting with the Van der Westhuizens, all in fits of laughter. Daniel was the one speaking, and clearly it was well received. Larissa was giving a genuine eyes-closed, head-back kind of laugh. At least they were having a good time. He also noticed that both Daniel and Larissa had a glass of wine in hand. He felt like a child for having refused any.

While he was looking up, he saw Vuyo come into the room and lean down to say something into Brian's ear at the very end of the table. Whatever had been said, Brian looked concerned. He considered it for a moment before giving a two-word response that sent Vuyo hurrying back out of the room. He then promptly started laughing along with the people around him as though he had been there for the joke. Nearer to Peter, Thulani had also watched the whole exchange, unsmiling.

Dinner wrapped up, and after tea and coffee everyone headed to their rooms. There were two bathrooms on their floor, one at each end of the passageway. Naturally, one was dedicated to the girls and the other to the boys. Calls of "dibs!" among the boys determined the shower schedule, decided more by who spoke loudest than by who spoke first, and there was some banter around the room as they all waited for their turn. Jesse and Daniel did most of the talking, assisted by Austen and Kyle, until everyone had showered and the chatting finally died down. Eventually their first day at Woodwright Manor had come to an end, and Jesse turned off the lights.

Chapter 4

Peter was woken the next morning—along with the rest of the boys—by Carol van der Westhuizen.

"Come on, boys, up you get!" She strode into the room, her bob of hair bouncing up and down, and pulled the curtains open with vigor. Light flooded in and everyone tried to roll over in their beds to turn away.

"Up, up, up!" she said again. "It's already eight o'clock. You all need to have breakfast and get dressed before the service at ten."

Peter didn't groan in protest as some of the other boys did, but he was on board with the sentiment—not a chance would it take two hours to get ready.

Once he had had breakfast and got dressed into his suit, he met his parents, his sister and Granny Bev in the hallway and together they made their way out to the chapel. All the families, dressed very smartly and mostly in black, slowly headed out in their own time—except for Phillip D'Arcy, the old man, who for some reason was coming in rather than going out. He greeted Peter as though they were friends now after their chat at dinner the night before.

"Good morning, Peter; you're looking smart!" he said.

"Good morning," Peter said, and he stood back to allow Phillip through.

"Sorry," said Phillip as he passed, "I just need to fetch my ... umm ... I'll see you in the chapel!"

Outside, the sun shone brightly, the sky a deep blue, with barely a cloud in sight. They had been in such a rush to be ready in time that they were now too early for the service. In an attempt to stall themselves, they took a slow amble through the garden, admiring the flowers. Trixy the Dalmatian trotted around, excited by all the activity, while the two ridgebacks sat and watched curiously as everyone came past. Even more cars filled up the parking area now; people who were just arriving had to park their cars down the road before joining the procession of black suits and dresses making its way slowly on the cobbled path up the hill to the chapel. Here the grass grew freely on the hill, long and uneven. The chapel was old stone; older even, it seemed, than the manor itself. It had been built on the slope so that the entrance was at ground level, but the rest of the chapel was elevated above a stone retaining wall. The windows were stained glass, faded from old age but beautifully intricate with their different colors.

Flowery wreaths hung on the walls of a small vestibule where Sizwe handed out funeral programs to everyone who came through. Inside, it was very similar to the church they sometimes attended back home: wooden pews on either side formed an aisle that led to the front, where a pulpit stood to one side, a lectern on the other, and an altar behind, all decorated for the occasion with white roses and candles.

In the front, right in the center and adorned with a great arrangement of white lilies and roses, lay the closed casket. On a small table next to it was a tall candle and a black-and-white picture of Patricia from when she was about thirty, smiling happily.

Peter and his family filed into one of the empty pews and sat down quietly. Larissa and her family were sitting a few rows ahead of them. In one of the pews at the very front Peter saw Thulani sitting next to a lady whom he presumed was his wife, and either their children or grandchildren sitting next to her. Peter then did a double-take—Phillip D'Arcy was there too! Surely Phillip hadn't come past them? How on earth did he get there before them?

His train of thought was broken when the Van der Westhuizens arrived and joined Larissa's family in their pew, and he somehow wasn't surprised to see Daniel slide in next to Larissa. No sooner had they all sat down than Tony was standing again and heading back up the aisle and out the door, reaching for his cigarettes.

By ten o'clock the chapel was almost full. Everyone waited patiently, talking in whispers; neither Brian nor Father Ian were anywhere to be seen. Wondering if they were going to start any time soon, Peter became aware of something from outside: a sound, distant at first, but getting louder.

It was singing. One voice sang one line, loud and clear, and then an entire chorus of voices replied in perfect harmony. Then the one voice sang again, followed by the entire chorus. It was all in Zulu and Peter couldn't understand a word of it, but it was slow and melancholic and beautiful.

A few people turned their heads as the singing got closer and closer, trying to see where it was coming from, and soon a huge crowd of people—the workers of the farm and other locals from the area—marched slowly through the doors in time with the singing and filled the back rows. There was barely enough space for everyone, so they remained standing, their voices ringing loudly through the chapel. They swayed as they sang, some of them with their hands up to the heavens, some with tears in their eyes; Patricia must have meant a great deal to them.

At half past ten Father Ian finally came through the doors, wearing a black cassock, followed by Brian in a suit and reading glasses, carrying some papers and a Bible. The whole congregation stood up as they walked down the aisle and took their place side by side in front of the altar. The singing died down and there was complete silence.

"Dear friends and family," Father Ian said in a loud and commanding voice, "we gather today to mourn the death of our beloved Patricia Woodwright, but also to celebrate her life. May the Lord hear our prayers as we say our final goodbyes."

He put out his hands, then looked around at everybody with a routine smile before saying loudly, "The Lord be with you!"

Almost everyone answered immediately, "And also with you."

"Let us pray."

The congregation bowed their heads in unison and silence fell over the chapel once more.

"Oh, God, whose mercies cannot be numbered, accept our prayers on behalf of your servant Patricia Woodwright ..."

It didn't take long for Peter to lose focus and let his mind wander. Who were all these people in the chapel and what reasons did they have for being here? For himself and the rest of the family it was almost an obligation, though in all honesty he barely knew her. There were some who had arrived that morning—the ones in smart cars who walked carefully on the gravel road to avoid getting their shoes dirty—and he got the sense that they wanted to be seen to have had a connection with Patricia. But then there were the likes of Thulani at the front, along with Phillip D'Arcy, and almost everyone at the back who had come in with the singing, for whom it seemed like this actually meant a lot to them.

His attention was brought back just quickly enough to join in the chorus of "amen" with everyone else. Father Ian then asked them to be seated and called for the first reading. A woman got up from one of the front pews, looking rather self-important as she made her way to the lectern. When she got to the front, she faced the casket and signed herself with the cross before going to the lectern, opening her Bible, and saying in a very serious tone, "The first reading will be taken from Isaiah chapter twenty-five, verses six to nine."

Peter noticed Kim Kingsbury-Ellis, who had another extravagant hat to match the occasion, roll her eyes and lean over to whisper something to her husband. Jesse and Daniel were both fidgeting restlessly. Larissa was sitting dead still with a look of utmost concentration. He then noticed Phillip in the front turn his head to check if anyone was looking, before slipping a hipflask out from the inside of his jacket and sneaking a quick sip. He put it back, looked forward, and pretended nothing had happened. Thulani glanced at him, then looked pointedly back at the woman reading, breathing in deeply.

When the reading was over and the lady had sat back down, Father Ian stood up.

"Please stand for the singing of our first hymn, 'How Great Thou Art,' which you will find in the program."

On the program it was actually supposed to be the second hymn; they had obviously given up on the first one when the Zulu singing was going on. There was no music; Father Ian led the singing, and everyone else followed as best they could. It was dull and flat, and, frankly, Peter thought they would be better off with more Zulu singing. As it was, the Zulu contingent of the congregation provided most of the volume.

After the hymn, Father Ian asked for the second reading. Kim Kingsbury-Ellis with the fancy hat, who had rolled her eyes at the first reading, then got up and sauntered over to the lectern to give her reading with an air of *this is how it's supposed to be done.*

Once she had strutted back to her seat and Father Ian had led them in another dreary hymn, he made his way up into the pulpit and asked them to stay standing for the reading of "The Holy Gospel of our Lord Jesus Christ according to John."

After the reading, he asked them to be seated, then paused dramatically in what Peter guessed was supposed to come off as thoughtful silence.

"You know, it's funny," he said. "Patricia was never very religious. She was, as you know, raised Anglican, and I'm sure she attended church and said her prayers, but I don't think she took it very seriously. However, on the eve of her death, she reached out to me, and she reached out to God. I came to see her here at Woodwright Manor, and she said to me, 'The one thing I still need to do is to make peace with the Lord.' And, as the Lord said, 'whoever comes to me I will never turn away.' So, I sat with her, and we prayed; and when she died not four days later, she was at peace ..."

Not being particularly religious himself, Peter found himself once again struggling to concentrate. Eventually Father Ian closed with a prayer, and Brian stood up and made his way to the lectern.

"Good morning, everyone," he said, more conversationally. "For those of you who don't know me, my name is Brian; I am the grandson of Patricia's eldest sister, and I will be giving a brief eulogy today. I may not have known her quite as well as some of her friends and older members of the family, but I have done my best to give an honest account and be true to who she was."

People around the chapel nodded as he paused to gather up his papers. He was easy to listen to—confident and laid-back.

"Patricia was not always the old and wise matriarch that we all knew her to be," he continued, squinting down at his pages through his reading glasses. "She, too, was once a young girl—but that was long before any of us here were alive.

"Patricia Jane Woodwright was born on the first of October, 1910." He looked up from his notes. "It sounds amazing when you say it like that, doesn't it? *Nineteen-ten*." He looked back to his notes. "She was the daughter of Harold and Goldie Woodwright, and sister to Margaret and Elizabeth. She was the youngest of the three siblings, born in Grey's Hospital in Pietermaritzburg, and grew up here on this farm.

"She was home-schooled by her mother, along with her sisters and some of the local children, until she was old enough to be enrolled at St. Dianne's College in Hilton, where she was said to have an exuberant personality and keen spirit ... not to mention a bit of cheek. Apparently, at her first interview for a place at the school, after her sisters had been Head Girl and Dux respectively, the headmistress said that having older sisters can sometimes put pressure on the girls, but not to worry about it. She said, 'Pretend we don't even know that you have any sisters, and tell us about yourself,' to which Pat promptly replied, 'Okay, well, my name is Patricia, and I have two sisters.'"

The chapel echoed as everyone laughed on cue.

"She loved her sport," Brian continued, "and joined the school hockey team and the shooting team, for which she won second place at a provincial tournament in 1926. Her main passion, though, was horse riding, which she practiced predominantly here on the farm. In fact, it's largely due to her that we have these stables with such magnificent horses now. She was also rumored to have a bit of a knack for trouble." (Brian had a grin now.) "Her father received numerous letters concerning disciplinary issues, for reasons such as 'night swimming' and 'leading her peers on a Golden Mile.'"

There were a few laughs around the chapel by people who knew what he was talking about. Peter saw Larissa laughing, her eyes wide with surprise, and Daniel asking what it was all about.

"As I'm sure those of you who attended the school will be aware," Brian continued, looking up at everyone now, "the Golden Mile has become something of a tradition whereby, once a year, the girls sneak out of their houses at night and run a lap around the school in the nude."

All caught up on the joke, the rest of the congregation joined in on the laughter. Peter had to admit, the thought of his sweet old Aunty Pat leading her friends on a naked charge around the school was quite amusing.

"Once she had finished her schooling," Brian went on, "Pat came back to the farm. Her father was desperate for her to get married and organized all kinds of meetings with potential husbands and their families—not that she needed the help, by all accounts! She was said to be quite the heartthrob of the town in her day, and received invitations to every ball and social gathering in the province, just about!

"But our dear Aunty Pat was looking for nothing more than a reason to dance. She enjoyed the gregarious lifestyle, but none of her suitors was ever successful. Unlike her sisters, who got married and moved elsewhere, Patricia never found love; she was always perfectly content just being herself. After her mother's untimely death in 1931, she took over home-schooling the local children, which became something of a vocation for her until her father fell ill and she had to look after him and help to manage the farm. I'll never forget coming to visit when we were young boys; running a farm had always been seen as a man's job, but there was Pat in her gumboots, riding up and down the farm on horseback sorting out farm equipment and tending to the livestock, not to mention looking after her bedridden father. I thought she could do anything.

"When her father died in 1962, Phillip came to help manage the farm," he gestured to Phillip in the front row who gave a polite nod, "and she went back to teaching children, which she did well into her later years.

"For most of us here, however, I think she will be remembered for her unfailing cheerfulness and her great compassion—of which we have all been on the receiving end at some time or other.

"Above all, she loved her family. Although she never had children, she treated each of us like her very own. I must say, I think it's quite impressive that, five generations down from Charles Woodwright, we're all still in contact and still very much a family; and I think it's largely because of Patricia." (Peter saw his dad smile quietly to himself.) "She made sure we all spent time together, for Christmases and other holidays. To be quite honest, I think we have her amazing beach house to thank for that." (A few laughs and murmurs of agreement.) "But I think she would've been very happy, despite our mourning, that her death brought us all together one more time. Although, I think if she were here to see us, in fact, she would've rolled her eyes and told us to liven up; that there's no time to waste on mourning the death of someone who is happy to have moved on. In her own words—this is something she said to me earlier this year, just a few months ago: 'I'm a hundred and five years old and, take it from me,' she said, 'life is short; so, if you're lucky enough to be with the people you love, don't waste a second of it.'"

He paused. For the first time, Brian's eyes were starting to glisten behind his glasses. "Aunty Pat," he said, only just managing to keep his voice stable, "life is going to be very different now without you. But I'm so grateful to have had you in my life until now and truly honored to have been a part of yours. Farewell."

Brian walked back to his seat, dabbing his eyes under his reading glasses with his handkerchief. Peter saw Phillip's shoulders bobbing up and down in the front row, holding his own handkerchief over his nose and mouth, and Thulani put his arm around him to comfort him.

Father Ian then stood up and walked to the lectern.

"Thank you, Brian, for those words. After the commendation, I will ask the pallbearers to come forward and lead the procession to the graveyard outside, where Patricia will be buried. Everyone is invited to shovel some sand onto the grave as a final goodbye, after which you are free to leave in your own time—take as long as you need. For those of you who are attending the reception afterwards, we will commence with the braai at two o'clock. Let us go forth—"

A voice from the back rang out and interrupted Father Ian mid-sentence. He stood paused with his hands awkwardly out in front of him, wondering what was happening, and then the entire Zulu congregation followed with another melancholic hymn. Even Larissa's dad joined in. Eventually Father Ian seemed to accept that this was happening, and he gestured for the pallbearers to come forward.

Among the pallbearers were Phillip, Brian, Oupa Tim, Granny Bev's brother Michael, and, to Peter's slight annoyance, Jesse and Daniel. Probably a good thing, actually, because Phillip and Oupa Tim were not so much carrying the casket as hanging on for support. Father Ian led the procession down the aisle to the sound of the Zulu chorus and everybody followed from their pews, out of the chapel and into a small graveyard on the grass outside. Rebecca somehow made her way to the front, picked up the shovel, and no sooner had the casket touched the ground than she was shoveling mound after mound of sand on top of it. With a laugh, Brian stopped her and told her that everyone needed a turn, so she gave him the shovel and dusted off her hands like she had just finished a hard day's work.

Soon a line formed as everyone waited for their turn. Peter, in no rush, leaned against a gravestone embedded in the retaining wall. The gravestone had a lion's face on it but no names, so it was safe to assume he wasn't being disrespectful to any dead people.

He watched mound after mound of sand being thrown into the grave as the line slowly inched forward, thinking to himself that they had probably underestimated the number of people who would be here when they decided to do this. Father Ian was speaking the whole time, but no one could hear him over all the Zulu voices singing.

As Peter gazed around, he spotted a woman he recognized in the crowd: Ms. O'Sullivan, from the O'Sullivan and Woolfe law firm in Pietermaritzburg, with her gray hair and spectacles. She had spotted them too, and came over to greet them.

"Good morning, Martin; good morning, Peter," she said, straight and to the point. Peter was surprised she remembered his name.

"Ah, Ms. O'Sullivan," said Martin. "I should have known you'd be here! This is my wife, Gill, and my daughter, Rebecca."

"Pleasure to meet you both," she said, first shaking Gill's hand and then Rebecca's with equal vigor.

"How did you first get to know Patricia?" Gill asked.

"Oh, I've known her for a very long time. She used to give me music lessons."

"Ms. O'Sullivan is now the executor of Patricia's estate," Martin explained. "Quite a job you've got on your hands, I'd imagine?"

"Oh, Martin, you don't know the half of it," she said, shaking her head solemnly. "They want to have a reading of the will on Friday; well, I don't know if that will happen, but we've got a lot of work to do before then. Unfortunately, I'm not at liberty to discuss it, but you'll find out soon enough."

"I'm guessing Patricia hasn't made things easy?" said Martin.

"Her wishes were simple enough, but now we're running into all sorts of problems with the document. Quite a fiasco."

"All to keep a dead woman happy …" said Martin.

"She didn't even *want* a will!" said Ms. O'Sullivan. "When her sisters died and she inherited the farm, I had to come here to persuade her to write one; she was very apprehensive. I was glad when I thought we were finished with it, but it turns out we're far from! Anyway, I'd best join the queue; I need to get going soon. Good to see you, Martin; good to see you, Peter, and lovely to meet you, Gill and Rebecca."

Chapter 5

Now that the formalities of the day were over, the jovial atmosphere of the boys' room returned as everyone got changed out of their formal attire. The usual four boys dominated the conversation, Jesse the undisputed leader with his willing confederates Daniel, Kyle, and Austen chiming in, while Peter remained largely silent. Steven didn't say much either but made a big effort to laugh at everything they said.

"Kyle, I saw you nodding off during the service; what was happening there, mate?"

"Bru, that guy was putting me to sleep with his monotone!"

"Yoh, he could've put anyone to sleep. 'She reached out to me, and she reached out to God!'"

Everyone laughed at his impression of Father Ian.

"Ja, and my mom reckons Aunty Pat didn't reach out to him at all; he just pitched up unannounced."

"You serious? What a clown! Wait, is anyone related to him?"

"Nah, he's our mom's cousin."

"Megan and Michelle's uncle. He doesn't have any children."

"Which are Megan and Michelle?"

"The two sisters."

"The pretty ones?"

"Whoa! Easy there, mate, those are your cousins."

Everyone laughed.

"Okay, first of all, they're like my third cousins or something, and second of all, I'm not trying to flirt with them or anything; I'm just saying objectionally."

"Yoh, that's a slippery slope."

"And the word you're looking for is 'objectively.'" This was the only thing Peter said, and, to his delight, he got a laugh out of everyone.

"Ja, you clown! You're not gonna pull your cousins with that kind of English."

"Have you guys checked that Larissa girl?"

"Ja, she *is* quite hot."

"Surely not your type though, Kyle? She's not even family."

To be fair to him, Kyle laughed as much as everyone else.

"But I reckon Daniel's been laying some foundation work there."

"Nah, bru, just been chatting." Daniel said this with such a childish grin that everyone laughed and Jesse punched him on the shoulder. Peter turned away and busied himself with folding his towel into his bag.

"How come she's here if she's not family?"

"Her folks were mates with Aunty Pat or something."

"Weird to think Aunty Pat had mates."

"Some of those stories of Aunty Pat were quite a laugh though, don't you rate?"

"Ja, bru, I reckon she was good banter back in her day. I've actually heard of the Golden Mile; it's a thing!"

That was Daniel speaking, and Peter immediately thought back to how he had asked Larissa what was going on while Brian was telling the story. He chose not to say anything about it.

"Why do you think she never married?"

"No idea. Jesse, you got the rugby ball?"

"Ja, boet, in my bag."

"Aweh."

Peter once again found himself walking with Steven as they joined the steady stream of people leaving the house. They headed along a little garden path, through a small gate and down an old farm track to the dam, with the three dogs bounding alongside excitedly. A couple of gasoline-half-drum braais had been set up in the shade of some trees, where a few of the dads eager to assert themselves as braaimaster were busy making the fires. Everyone else was spread out on the lawn next to the dam on picnic blankets and the odd camping chair.

Peter and Steven found their parents sitting together, along with Kyle and his family—it turned out they all shared a great-grandfather in Oupa Tim—and Steven quickly dropped Peter's company for Kyle's. Ellen, Kyle's sister who was about a year younger than Peter, seemed friendly enough, greeting them both cheerfully as they arrived. She was sitting with Rebecca, smiling kindly while Rebecca rambled on about the sorts of things that are interesting to nine-year-olds and no one else. Her patience with his sister immediately made Peter like her.

The adults were talking about the service, saying in rather more polite terms much of what the boys had been saying earlier about Father Ian's sermon.

"Bit odd that Father Ian wanted to officiate, don't you think?"

"Ag, I think he just wanted to be helpful."

"Why's it odd?" Steven asked.

"Priests usually don't officiate funerals of their own relatives," his mom said. "They also need time to grieve."

"But old Father Ian seems to have quite a high opinion of himself, doesn't he," said Kyle's dad. "Reckon he relished the opportunity to be at the center of everything."

"Kim was even worse! Did you see her doing her reading like she was in drama class?"

"And Karen as well! Heavens, you'd have thought they were competing for a part in the school play!"

"Ja, ever since Walter died …"

Peter sat with Oupa Tim while the rest of the adults continued to gossip about other members of the family. Oupa Tim asked all the usual questions about school, to which Peter gave all the usual responses of "Fine, thank you," "Yes, thank you," and "No, I finished primary school three years ago." His eyes wandered while they spoke, and he spotted a small rowing boat next to the jetty in the dam. His first thought was that it would make a convenient getaway when he wanted to be alone. He could see a line of trees on the other side where the stream entered the dam and wouldn't mind going to explore it. His gaze then fell on the track and followed it over the dam wall and up the next hill where Thulani and his wife were coming down from what he presumed was their house at the top. He watched them cross the dam wall and join everyone on the lawn, where they inevitably found Larissa's dad and started chatting away like old friends.

Before long, two of the younger boys were in their swim trunks and jumping into the dam, followed by two more kids and not long after that Rebecca was saying, "Mom, look! Emma and Shannon are swimming! Can I go swim with them?"

Peter knew it was only a matter of time before the rugby ball came out, so he decided on the spot that this would be a great time to try out the old rowing boat.

"See you just now," he announced to his parents as he stood up and started making his way to the jetty.

But then he hesitated. Larissa was in her bikini, walking toward the dam for a swim with Megan, Austen, and Katie. For a moment he contemplated going to join them, show her that he's one of the lads, maybe get a few jokes in … on the other hand, he'd rather not show off his pale, skinny body. He carried on to the rowing boat instead, playing out scenarios in his head where Larissa asked him to come and swim with them.

The boat was not like the long, thin sculls he was used to from school. It was short and wide, made of wood rather than fiberglass. There was a plank across its width to form the seat, with an oar at either side. Another plank at the back formed a seat for a second person, which Peter thought was ambitious—the boat was old and splintered and looked like it had seen its fair share of weather out here on the dam. He wasn't convinced it could even hold one person.

He stepped in cautiously, fearing his foot might go straight through into the water below, but was surprised to find it was actually quite sturdy. He sat down; the seat was solid too. He took hold of the oars and slowly pushed himself out into the deeper water until he could row properly. With each stroke, he watched the people on the bank get further and further away, and heard the voices get fainter. He could see Larissa taking tentative steps into the cold water and could only just hear her laughing as the others urged her on. Daniel, whose muscles looked even bigger without a shirt, ran and jumped into the water right next to her, splashing her and everyone else. Now they were all laughing, and Daniel pulled Larissa into the water. Peter looked away and told himself he was glad he hadn't joined them.

He pulled up on the sand the other side of the dam and jumped out into the shallow water with a splash. He pulled the boat up onto the bank and started up the stream.

In the cover of the trees, the water rushing in the stream took over the noise from the braai; kids' shouting and Trixy's barking gave way to the wind through the leaves and the birds singing.

He picked his way carefully from rock to rock as the surrounding thicket closed in around him, getting denser and denser the further he went. On the other side of the dam, the trees looked curated , but this was all natural, indigenous forest, wild and thriving. It had almost gotten to the point where it was too dense to go any further and he thought about turning around and heading back, but then he noticed something odd: a few trees and bushes with stumps where branches had once been. The wood of the stumps was flat but had slowly been covered by gnarled bark; definitely cut by a human, but a very long time ago. The ground here had less vegetation than the rest of the forest, and it created a vague clearing. This used to be a path.

He followed it. He had to step over some shrubbery and duck under a few branches, but there was no doubt. It was an old path that had not been used for many years, overgrown and forgotten, but still held its original secret quite intact. After climbing over logs, pushing through leaves and dodging spider webs, Peter came out into a small glade in the forest next to the stream, just big enough for some sunlight to come beaming through and catch the water rippling over the pebbles. In the center of the glade, slightly out of place but equally beautiful, was a big, majestic weeping willow, its branches dangling low over the running water.

It would be almost impossible to reach this little haven from any other direction. He sat down on the bank of the stream and leaned against the tree, his bare feet in the water, reveling in the satisfaction of having found this spot. But the tree against his back was uncomfortable, bumpy and uneven. He turned round to see what the problem was and found that a patch of bark had been removed to reveal the bare wood underneath. The wood had been engraved with the letters *M + P*. This spot had once belonged to someone else.

Eventually Peter became accustomed to hearing nothing but the running water and the gentle breeze, and decided he had been there long enough; food would probably be ready soon. He slowly got up, dusted himself off, and looked around the little glade once more, taking it all in before heading out. He picked his way back along the overgrown path and down the stream, pushed the boat back into the water, and started rowing back across the dam.

But he had miscalled it. The two ridgebacks sat eagerly by the braais, watching the self-appointed braaimasters throwing some meat on the grid while they chatted with beers in hand. The Dalmatian leaped and splashed in the shallows of the dam, barking excitedly at the few children still swimming, and, although most of the older kids were out of the water, Peter saw a rugby ball being passed around.

In an attempt to avoid any sort of request to join their game, he tried his best to circumnavigate the crowd of people near the dam and spotted Father Ian, who had changed out of his cassock, near some trees. He looked from one tree to another, looked at the base of the tree, then up at the branches, then the ground around the tree … what on earth was he doing?

"Have you lost something?" Peter asked, looking around on the ground as though to help. Anything to get out of playing rugby.

"Excuse me?" He was startled. "Oh, no! No, I'm just looking at the trees here. Love these willow trees."

"Oh … Alright then …"

Without knowing what else to say, he left Father Ian alone to look at his trees, doing his utmost not to come across as withering. When he glanced back, Father Ian had his ear to a tree and was knocking on it with his knuckles.

Peter surreptitiously made his way back to his parents and brushed off the inevitable exclamations of "Where have you been?" with a casual "Just looking around." He saw the older boys congregate with the rugby ball in hand and tried to camouflage himself among the adults, but, just as he feared, he soon heard Austen call out to him.

"Hey, Peter! Join us for a three-V-three, surely?"

Austen probably thought he was being nice. He weighed up refusing to play and chilling by himself against accepting the invitation out of courtesy and risking embarrassment. The other boys were all watching him, waiting for a response, when another voice came from behind them.

"I'll play!"

They all turned around to see Larissa strolling confidently toward them. Hesitating and unsure of what to say, they turned back to look at Peter. Peter got to his feet, having just decided in that moment that he would play as well.

"Umm, but now we've got odd numbers," said Kyle.

"Katie will play as well. Won't you, Katie?" Larissa looked hopefully at Katie lying on her towel, reading a book.

Katie looked up at Larissa, took a moment to register what had been said, and then also seemed to decide in the moment that a game of touch rugby would be fun.

"Sure!" she said cheerfully, putting her book down and jumping to her feet.

"Umm, alright," Kyle said slightly uncomfortably, glancing at the others.

"Cool," said Jesse, taking charge. "Four-V-four. Pete, you in?"

"I'm in," he said as confidently as he could, in stark contrast to how he was feeling.

"Okay, let's do it!"

"How are we doing teams?"

"Jesse and Daniel are the best," said Austen, "so they should be on opposite sides."

"And we're the worst," said Larissa, "so we should also be on different sides."

"And the youngest should be with the oldest, so Steven with Jesse."

"Right," said Jesse with authority, "myself, Kyle, Steven, and Larissa, versus Dan, Austen, Pete, and Katie."

"Awesome!"

"Let's do it!"

"How many touches? Three?"

"No, one touch."

"Are we kicking off?"

"Ja, kick to start."

They all took their positions on opposite sides of the lawn and, once everyone looked ready, Austen lobbed a dropkick into the air. Jesse caught it and passed it gently to Larissa, who promptly fumbled it.

"No worries, no worries!" said Jesse, picking up the ball and throwing it to Austen while Larissa and Katie both laughed with embarrassment.

Austen tapped the ball with his foot and popped it to Daniel, who then passed the ball so hard to Peter that he also dropped it.

"Unlucky, unlucky!" was Daniel's apology as the ball was once again handed back to the other team, and Katie and Larissa laughed even more.

There were a lot more calls of "no worries" and "unlucky" before they started getting into a good rhythm, and then the calls tended to be more along the lines of "run straight, Peter, run straight!" and "mark the channel, Steven, not the player!" The girls' laughter proved to be a constant throughout the game.

Dodging Trixy became another constant of the game as she desperately tried to play with them—and seemed well convinced that she was doing exactly that, tripping people up and chasing any loose balls. Peter found that he could avoid too much embarrassment by focusing on defense, marking the channels and not being easily fooled by fancy footwork. Larissa was especially easy to touch, having the confidence to run straight at him but neither the speed nor agility to get past. Every time he touched her she would laugh and cry out in exasperation as though she couldn't understand how he had got her.

"I swear I'm gonna get past you soon," she said.

"Ja, I mean your tactic of running straight at me is bound to work eventually," Peter teased, which made her laugh and raised his confidence a healthy dose.

Although Daniel scored the most tries, Austen was their stand-out player as far as Peter was concerned; almost all of their tries came from his passes. At one stage he quickly pulled Peter aside during a turn-over and said quietly, "Start on my left and switch with me; I'll dummy to Dan and play you inside." The dummy was so convincing that even Peter was surprised when the ball suddenly landed in his arms! Jesse, Kyle, and Steven were all sent the wrong way and Peter had a clear gap. Larissa chased but couldn't catch him. When he turned back to the applause of his team and the few bystanders who were watching, he caught Larissa's eye.

"Don't get cocky; that was luck," she teased.

"Ja, I know," said Peter. "And I wasn't even running straight at you ... weird that I managed to get past ..."

He could still hear her chuckling when he returned to his side and got a clap on the back from Austen.

The undisputed highlight of the game came later, once they had more of an audience. Larissa received the ball and tested the ill-defined boundaries of the field by straying slightly into the shallows of the dam. Daniel gave chase, but slipped in the mud and dove face-first into the water, giving Larissa the chance to get around him and score. Both teams erupted with cheers, along with everybody else watching, and Daniel was left to try to wipe the mud off his face—not to mention the shame—while everyone applauded Larissa's try.

After that, the game strayed more and more into the shallows of the dam, and the touch rule was pretty much abandoned as full-on tackles in the water became commonplace. Peter pretended to go down whenever Larissa got a hold of him and was legitimately flattened by Jesse a few times.

It soon became noticeable, however, that despite all his earlier advice on "marking the channel," Daniel was now doing a superb job man-marking Larissa. He would tackle her into the water whether she had the ball or not, and she would shriek with laughter.

Megan and Michelle eventually felt like they were missing out and jumped into the fray, followed by Ellen, after which the game descended into chaos. The ball was soon forgotten—along with the teams—and the object of the game became dunking everyone else.

Peter managed to dunk Steven a couple of times, but that was about the extent of his success. His attempt on Austen backfired, and he was too shy to try on any of the girls. Unsurprisingly, Jesse remained undunked for the longest. Everyone inevitably began teaming up on him, and once they had succeeded in their combined effort to submerge him underwater, they all cheered and the game came to a unanimous end.

"Food's ready!" one of the dads called as they dried themselves off.

Perfect timing. The ridgebacks remained almost unmoved since Peter had come back from his walkabout, still staring longingly at the men who were now taking trays of meat to the tables and unwrapping the tinfoil from the garlic bread. The tables had been laid with various salads and bread rolls. Vuyo and Sizwe carried a large metal tub filled with drinks and quickly melting ice.

Once Peter had his food, he went back to sit on the picnic blanket with his parents. The other boys, however, all regathered once they had their food. He knew perfectly well that nothing was stopping him from getting up and joining them if he wanted to, but he couldn't help feeling a little left out. He stubbornly stayed exactly where he was and ate his food in silence.

Unbeknown to everyone, the weather started changing. Clouds gathered from the south, steadily building above them. Peter was comfortably into his second helping before he noticed the sky getting darker. Soon everyone had caught on to this development and started packing things away in anticipation of the inevitable downpour.

The thunder came first, echoing over the Drakensberg mountains. They felt the first drops, and everybody hastened their efforts to fold blankets and towels and pack books away into bags. Peter quickly ran to the table to get a third helping before it was all taken away and devoured it as fast as he could.

The rain picked up and attempts to pack everything away were swiftly abandoned. With chairs in hand and blankets under arm, they ran back up the track toward the house. A few flashes of lightning lit up the dark sky, the thunder roared around them, and within minutes the rain had become a relentless downpour.

Chapter 6

Everyone was soaked by the time they reached the house, laughing as they removed their wet shoes and tried to dry themselves.

Brian turned briefly to Thulani. "Thulani, could you get us some towels?"

He hadn't even looked Thulani properly in the eyes, and was already back to laughing with the others again.

A menacing glint in Thulani's eye made Peter think he was about to flip out, deeply offended … but it only lasted the briefest moment, and then Thulani was calm and composed.

"Of course," he said. "In the meantime, you can gather everyone's wet clothes and usher them into the guest hall where there is more space. I will ask Vuyo or Sizwe to start cleaning this up."

"Sorry?" Brian started saying as he turned around again, not having fully registered what Thulani had said; but Thulani's calm yet uncompromising stare quickly brought him back to reality. "Oh, yes, yes, of course …" He cleared his throat. "Alright, everyone," he said loudly, "let's all move through to the guest hall."

Thulani turned to Peter, who was nearest him. "Could you help me grab a few towels, please?" he said.

Peter followed him out of the entrance foyer and through to the other end of the hall. The wall beneath the stairs was dark wood, with a gap in the center that made a narrow passageway with cupboard doors on either side. Thulani opened one of these doors to reveal a walk-in closet. Various cleaning equipment and detergents filled the shelves on one side, and blankets, bed linen, and towels the other. He handed a pile of towels to Peter, took a pile for himself, and they went back to the guest hall to hand them out.

The room was filled with excitable chatter to accompany the sound of the rain and the occasional rumble of thunder outside. Slowly it got quieter as, one by one, people peeled off to take a shower and change into dry clothes. Peter was pleasantly surprised to find that his bed had been made for him, as had everyone else's, and the entire room had been tidied up.

They reconvened through the same narrow passage under the stairs to a large and spacious sitting room on the other side with plenty of seating, and decor in much the same Victorian style as the rest of the house: paintings on walls, ornaments on antique cabinets, and a pair of eland horns hung above the fireplace. Vast windows offered a view of the dam (and, in better weather, the mountains) and glass doors opened onto a patio outside.

Peter returned from his shower to the dismal news that there would be no dinner because apparently everyone else reckoned lunch had been big enough and late enough not to warrant any. Cheese and crackers were being served instead—a pretty bleak substitute, in Peter's opinion.

He found all the older kids congregated on one side of the room around a couch occupied by Megan, Katie, and, of course, Jesse and Daniel. He quickly grabbed a wooden chair from the other side of the room and pulled into a spot between Austen and Ellen while Jesse was recounting the day's activities.

"Yoh, Austen was *stepping* ous today! And your passing was on point!"

"Nah, Dan was just making me look good."

"Bru, you were making all of us look good," said Dan, which was annoyingly modest.

"Can we all just take a moment to appreciate how Larissa absolutely rounded Dan?" said Jesse, and everybody cheered.

Daniel tried to laugh it off but couldn't help looking a little embarrassed.

Larissa patted him on the knee. "Next time, maybe just put your dignity in a safe place so you don't lose it again," she said. There were howls of laughter from everyone, which got a few looks from the adults.

Peter didn't say much. He laughed along helplessly at Daniel's jokes that all seemed to be aimed at Larissa, but never made any jokes of his own. The longer he sat there, the more he felt like a spectator. It was basically a Jesse and Daniel two-man show with assistance from Austen and Kyle; Larissa, Megan, and Katie were the active audience. Peter, Steven, Michelle, and Ellen might as well have not been there.

He soon lost interest in the conversation and instead watched through the windows as the rain slowly eased off and stopped. The air cleared and he could see the mountains again; the last of the sun even peeked through under the clouds. The earth was wet and glistening.

As the light faded from the sky and a distinct chill started creeping into the air, he decided it would do him some good to take a walk to get a sweater, and perhaps continue on to somewhere else after that. Helping himself to his last few crackers, he quietly got up and left the circle, deliberately leaving his chair where it was so as not to draw attention to the fact that he had no intention of returning. He had no idea if anyone even noticed him leave, but, if they did, he guessed it would be of little concern to anyone.

The din coming from the sitting room got fainter as Peter walked up the stairs and down the passageway to their room. He fetched his sweater and began moseying back along the passage with no real direction in mind but quite determined not to find himself back in the sitting room. He wandered around, gazing at all the art on the walls and old ornaments and collectables on small tables and shelves—china plates, figurines, and the like. On the landing at the top of the stairs he took his time to examine a few black-and-white photographs on a table. There were family portraits from different generations, and one of a young Patricia and another woman in ball gowns, laughing. Peter then noticed a familiar sight and picked up a photo of two important-looking men standing on a pier in Durban harbor, but from a very long time ago. There were no tall buildings around, no Millennium Tower on the Bluff, and fewer people on the docks than there were now. The ships in the harbor were old steam ships, with tall masts and smoke billowing out of their funnels. Anchored just behind the two men in the forefront was a ship with the name 'R.M.S. *Durham Castle*' painted on its side, and a line of men carrying crates down the gangplank.

He carefully placed the picture back on the table and continued his amble down the passage. It was darker this side, and slightly eerie with all the old paintings of even older people staring down at him. It slowly dawned on him that this was the part of the house that they had been asked to keep out of. As he went round a corner, he found a door that stood ajar. It creaked as he gently pushed it open to stick his head through and have a look inside, but it was completely dark. He pushed the door open further and fumbled around for a light switch on the wall next to the door. When he eventually found the switch and turned it on, a dim, yellow light illuminated the room, revealing bookcases, a vintage vinyl record player, and, at the back against the wall, an old upright piano.

Peter went over to the piano to have a look at it. It was a dark, mottled brown, beautifully carved with candleholders on the front panel, and completely covered with dust. As gently as he could, he lifted the lid and, with a light *thud* that echoed through the piano, rested it against the back. The ivories were an off-white, stained from having been played so much, but otherwise as clean as though they had been wiped yesterday.

He gave a few of the keys a test. To his surprise, it sounded alright—slightly out of tune, but definitely playable.

He pulled the stool out, gave it a wipe with his sleeve, which sent a cloud of dust into the air, and sat down. He held down the soft pedal to minimize the noise and played a few chords.

Looking around, he noticed that a lot of the books in the bookcases were music books. He stopped the chords and went to look for some interesting sheet music. After paging through a few books in which most of the music was too advanced for him, he came across Beethoven's "Moonlight Sonata." He had learnt it a while back but couldn't fully remember it—might as well give it a go. He folded down the music rack, placed the book onto it, and began playing. The first few chords came back to him quickly; by the second page he had to refer to the music a lot, stopping and stuttering and replaying bars he got wrong, squinting at the music the whole time. Once he had stumbled through to the end, he played the last few lines again now that he had the hang of it and it came out a lot more smoothly. He held the final note, satisfied with himself, and then let go.

"Wow."

Peter jumped up and spun round with a gasp.

"That was amazing."

Larissa was standing in the room, the door closed behind her, with an impressed look on her face. "You're really good," she said.

"Umm ... thank you," said Peter.

"That really was amazing."

Peter frowned. "Actually, it was kind of horrible. I don't think I got through a single line without a mistake."

"Nonsense," she replied, walking toward him. "It was beautiful." She sat on the table with the record player, next to where he was sitting, and looked at him with genuine interest. "How long have you been playing?"

"I don't know, like, ten minutes?" said Peter. "Could you hear me playing from outside?"

Larissa smiled at him delightfully. "No, I came up to fetch my charger and I heard you from the top of the stairs," she said. "But I meant how long have you been a piano player?"

"Oh! Um, since I was about seven."

She nodded. "You're very good," she said again.

"Thank you," said Peter, more earnestly this time.

"Could you play something else for me?"

Peter looked around the room at the bookcases. "I was looking for music to play, but this was about all I could find that was within my skill set."

"Okay, let's see," said Larissa, hopping off the table. She strolled around the room, eyeing out all the books, sometimes taking one out and paging through it before carefully replacing it. With nothing but contentment, Peter watched her perform the exact exercise he had just performed not five minutes ago. "These books all seem very old," she commented as she removed one from the shelf.

"Luckily music hasn't really changed in the last hundred-odd years," said Peter.

"Tell that to Taylor Swift."

"I meant the notation."

"Ooh! Look here!" she exclaimed.

Peter got up to look at what had caught her attention, and she

turned the book for him to see. It was an old jotter, college ruled, with extra hand-drawn lines ruled across it to use as musical staves, and handwritten music scribbled across it. The title "Under the Willow Tree" was written at the top. Odd to see music written in a notebook rather than on staff paper. Larissa then pointed Peter's attention to a little inscription under the title that said "Patricia Woodwright."

"Hectic," said Peter. "I never even knew she played. Is everything in there written by her?"

Larissa turned the page. The next page had been torn out, and the page after it had the name "Olivia O'Sullivan."

"Doesn't look like it," she said. She turned back to Patricia's piece. "Try play it?"

Peter looked it over. The notation was quite messy and difficult to read, especially given that it wasn't on normal manuscript paper, but it seemed simple enough.

"Okay, we'll give it a go," he said.

He replaced "Moonlight Sonata" on the music rack and studied the music for a moment before attempting the opening chord progression. Larissa leaned on the chair and watched over his shoulder, which didn't do wonders for his nerves, but once he got the hang of the repeating melody he was soon playing smoothly. He disregarded the crescendos to avoid playing too loudly but otherwise found the music to be pretty and nostalgic.

"That was beautiful," Larissa said when he had finished. "Patricia wrote that?"

"Ja, looks like she did," said Peter, picking the make-do music book up to examine it. "I never knew she was so musical."

Larissa stared at the page over his shoulder, shaking her head in awe. "It's crazy to me that you can just look at that page of scribbles and somehow make music out of it," she said.

"It's the same as reading any language," said Peter. "Only the symbols represent notes on the keyboard, not letters in the alphabet."

"What do these things mean?" she asked, pointing at the beginning of the lines.

"Those are called clefs," said Peter. "So, the right hand plays in the treble clef, and the left hand plays in the bass clef."

"And these letters above here?" said Larissa. "Are those the notes?"

"No, those are the chords," said Peter. "You don't really need those if you can read music; it's just so you can see at a glance which chords are being used."

"What are chords?"

"Uh …" It was a difficult thing to explain to someone who didn't know anything about music. "Here, let me show you."

He put the book back down on the rack again.

"So, this first one is B-flat major, which sounds like this."

He played two octaves of the chord with both hands.

"And then C minor, which sounds like this."

He played two octaves of C minor. When he did, he suddenly frowned and squinted at the music again.

"Hang on," he said, "that's not supposed to be C minor."

He quickly played the opening two bars again.

"Ja, that's definitely supposed to be C major. So, she got that wrong. Anyway, the next one is D major … wait a minute, that's also wrong! What's going on with these chords?" He looked over the entire piece with a puzzled frown. "They all seem to be the correct root note, but she's just thrown on a major or a minor at random. Some of these chord changes aren't even noted. Maybe she didn't actually know what she was doing."

"Well, the chords look like they were written with a different pencil," said Larissa. "Maybe it wasn't her. Might have been someone else who didn't know what they were doing."

"Ja, could be," said Peter. "Anyway, you get the idea of what a chord is."

"Cool!" said Larissa. "Let's find something else to play."

"No, I think that's enough for tonight," said Peter, closing the lid. "Besides, I don't think we're supposed to be here."

"What makes you say that?"

"Well, partly just the feeling this place gives me ... but also because they explicitly told us to stay out of this part of the house."

"What are you talking about?"

"Yesterday, they said we must stay out of the west wing on the third floor. That's exactly where we are."

"We're on the second floor."

"What? No, we're not!"

"It goes ground floor, first floor, second floor. We're on the second floor."

"I don't think that's what they meant. In fact, I don't think there *is* even another floor above this one."

"Well, that's not our fault; we can't be expected to just *know* what they mean."

"But ... we *do* know what they mean."

"Why do you think it's off limits anyway?"

"Not sure; I think they said renovations."

"Have you seen any signs of renovations since we've been here?"

Peter had to admit he had not.

"Come on," she said, "if you're not gonna play anymore, let's go find out what they're hiding."

He wasn't thrilled by the idea, but Larissa was already walking toward a door between two bookcases and he wasn't going to be the one who chickened out. He opened the piano stool, dropped the book inside, and followed her to the next room.

They could not immediately find a light switch, but the light coming through from the piano room revealed a desk with a desk lamp. Larissa turned it on and it shone down onto some books and papers spread out on the desk, but was enough to illuminate the rest of the room as well.

It was a sort of library, lined wall to wall with bookcases. An archway led through to an extension of the room, also lined with bookcases. Almost all the books on the shelves were big, leather-bound tomes, usually in series of identical-looking books, with titles like *Principles of Geology, Volume III*.

Larissa picked up some of the papers on the desk, paged through them, then put them down and picked up a book that lay open.

She read aloud: "In this case, the entire estate will be inherited by the descendants of the parents. The descendants inherit *per stirpes* by representation."

"What are you reading?" Peter asked.

"No idea," said Larissa. "It was underlined."

She fanned through a few pages. "Other things have been underlined as well," she said, stopping on another page, and read aloud once again: "A will that is still in existence but has been revoked by the testator may be revived by the testator by means of a subsequent reviving document."

"Yawn!" said Peter pointedly, looking around the rest of the room.

"I actually find law quite fascinating," said Larissa, looking through a few more of the pages. "I wonder if these are to do with Patricia's will?"

Peter hadn't even thought about that. She was probably right. "Ja, maybe," he said. "Although, don't the lawyers normally just deal with that kind of stuff? Why would they be reading up about it here?"

"Literally no idea," said Larissa. "Although ..." Her voice trailed off in thought as she started reading another passage that had been underlined. "This one is talking about not being able to find the will," she said. She paged back to the first passage. "And this is talking about what happens if there is no will ..." She paused thoughtfully. "Do you think they couldn't find Patricia's will?"

"That would be a laugh," said Peter, thinking about what his dad would say if it came out that she didn't have a will. "Hey, check this out!"

He had just walked through the arch to the other section of the room and found a set of double doors with large glass panels leading to a balcony. Larissa put the book down and followed him as he went to try the doors.

"Locked," he said.

"You're blind," said Larissa.

She unhooked a set of keys that Peter hadn't seen hanging right next to the door and tried them in the keyhole. The key turned and they opened the doors to the cool night air. They were standing on a small balcony that must have been directly above the patio, looking out over the dam and toward the mountains, which were nothing but black shapes against the starry sky. It was completely dark now; some light escaping from the sitting room cast shadows across the garden. They could see the lights from Thulani's house on the next hill. Shining far in the distance was evidence of neighboring farms and the nearby township.

They both walked to the edge of the balcony to look down. The ivy on the walls had crept all the way up to where they were standing.

"I reckon I could climb up here," said Peter, eyeing out a gutter down the corner between the balcony and the main house.

"Oh, wow!" Larissa said sarcastically. "You must be so strong and brave!"

Peter laughed. "No, I'm just saying—"

"No, I know," said Larissa; "you just want me to know how cool you are."

Peter shook his head and gave up.

"So, are you from Maritzburg?" Larissa asked.

"No, I'm from Durban," said Peter. "I was just in Maritzburg that day because—"

"Your dad had a meeting, I know," Larissa said with a grin. "You made that quite clear at the time."

Peter nodded. "And you?"

"Well, Hilton actually, but ja."

"I saw you laughing when Brian spoke about the Golden Mile," Peter said. "Do you also go to St. Dianne's?"

Larissa turned to look at him. "You were watching me?" she asked.

"What? No! I was just ... I mean ..."

"Relax!" she laughed. "I'm just teasing. Yes, I go to St. Dianne's. And you?"

"Southcliff," said Peter.

They stood looking out into the night sky for a moment. In the quiet, Peter became aware of a thumping bass faintly echoing over the hills. "Can you hear that?" he said with a finger to the air. "Where's that coming from?"

Larissa listened for it. "Oh, ja," she said; "probably the township."

"On a Sunday?"

"Why not?" Larissa shrugged. "And there were a lot of people at Patricia's funeral today; it's probably some kind of 'after tears' thing."

"What's that? Like a party?"

Larissa pursed her lips in a smirk and looked at him with big eyes in a 'shame, you're cute' kind of way.

"Ja, I suppose it is like a party," she said. "As the name suggests, it's after the mourning has happened. Then everyone gets together to celebrate."

Peter turned toward the thumping where the lights of the township sparkled. "Straight after the funeral?" he said. "Seems a bit … I don't know …"

Larissa raised an eyebrow. "A bit what?"

"Soon," said Peter.

"Does it?" she said. "It was only an hour or so after the funeral that we were braaiing and playing rugby in the dam. Or are you going to tell me that's different?"

Peter thought about it for a moment before conceding the point. "No, I guess you're right," he said. "It's just not something I'm used to." He leaned on the balustrade. "What's it like?"

"What, After Tears? I wouldn't know; I've never been. My dad would never let me go to something like that."

"Really? Why not?"

Larissa laughed. "So many reasons! After Tears is not exactly traditional. It's quite a recent trend, mostly with younger people. A lot of elders don't approve."

"They don't?" said Peter. "Why?"

"I think because it can get quite raucous and it's no longer about the person who passed away or their family. Sometimes the family is still grieving and people are just wondering in and out of their house having a jol. It can be disrespectful."

"While the family is still grieving?" said Peter, raising his eyebrows in a cheeky expression. "So, I guess one might even say that it's … a bit … soon?"

Larissa laughed. "Ja, but you knew nothing about it when you said that! You were just making a judgment based on the music. And, like I said, the loud music and stuff is a recent trend. Sometimes it can still be a respectful gathering of people for the family of the deceased."

"No, I know, I'm just kidding," said Peter.

There was another moment of silence as Larissa grinned into the night and Peter had the thought to exchange numbers; but he got the same nervous feeling in his stomach and hesitated.

"Come on," she said, "it's getting cold. Where to next?"

Without waiting for an answer, she turned to go back inside, and Peter followed her. They locked the doors behind them, turned off the desk lamp and went back through to the piano room.

Despite her earlier confidence that they were doing no wrong, Larissa carefully peeked her head round the door and looked up and down the dark passage to make sure the coast was clear before they snuck through.

They opened the first door they came across, turned on the light, and found themselves staring into a storeroom. They stood in the doorway for a moment, looked around, then switched the light off and closed the door.

Peter was about to try the next door when Larissa tapped him on the shoulder and pointed down to the door at the end of the passageway. They made their way as quietly as possible down the passage, checking nervously over their shoulders as they went, and then stopped to listen when they came to the door at the end in case someone was inside. Satisfied that nobody was there, they slowly opened the door.

It was a master bedroom: a great four-poster bed in the middle with two bedside tables, art on the walls, and big windows with a view toward the mountains. A dressing table stood to one side with a large mirror, and a large chest of drawers at the foot of the bed. A row of cupboards completely covered the opposite wall.

They hesitated at the door, thinking they were busy intruding on somebody's bedroom, but then they noticed the bed had no linen, and there was a thin layer of dust on the wooden surfaces.

"I think this was Patricia's room," Larissa whispered.

"I think you're right," said Peter.

They stood in silence for a short moment.

"Should we go in?" Peter asked, looking at Larissa for affirmation.

Larissa looked down the passage one more time, then responded by stepping decisively into the room. Peter followed and shut the door behind them.

They walked slowly around the room as if it were a museum, looking at all the old trinkets and artefacts.

"There are a few photos with Aunty Pat here," said Peter, looking at some frames standing on the chest of drawers. "Nothing to conclusively prove this was her room, though."

"Well, it definitely belonged to a woman," said Larissa, perusing through the various objects on the dressing table. "An old woman. These things are ancient."

"It could have been shared by a man and woman," said Peter. "My mom has a dressing table with all her make-up stuff in their room."

"Good point," said Larissa. "Did Patricia ever have a husband?"

"No, didn't you hear Brian at the funeral today? She never got married."

"Oh, ja; I had forgotten about that. Check the drawers—see what kind of clothing is in them."

"That's a little intrusive, don't you think?"

"Oh, but snooping around the room is perfectly fine," Larissa retorted, rolling her eyes. "And if it is Patricia's, I can promise you she doesn't care."

Peter conceded and started going through the drawers while Larissa tried the cupboards.

"Yup, all woman's clothing in here," said Peter.

"Here as well," said Larissa.

She stopped at the cupboard door on the end with a frown on her face. "That's odd," she said, looking at the floor, and then the cupboard, and then back to the floor.

"What is?"

"The rug is worn a lot more in front of this cupboard than any of the others, but the cupboard is empty," said Larissa.

Peter came over to check what she was talking about. She was right. It had no shelves, just a rail with nothing on it, but the rug was definitely thinner there than anywhere else. He opened the next cupboard to compare, and it was full of cloaks and gowns.

"Maybe she used to keep something in there that she used a lot," he suggested.

"Maybe," said Larissa, "although the rest of the room seems pretty untouched. Why would they leave everything else and move the stuff from this cupboard?"

"Ja, look, I have no idea," said Peter, "I was just making suggestions."

After a moment's silence, Peter spoke again. "My gran also has a row of cupboards like this, but one of them leads to an en-suite bathroom. You wouldn't know just from looking at them."

"Nope," said Larissa, looking into the cupboard, "definitely solid wall behind here."

To prove her point she gave the wall at the back of the cupboard a good knock, and was surprised to hear a hollow, wooden sound.

They both looked at each other. Without a word, Peter tried the next cupboard and gave the back wall a knock; it was decidedly solid.

They looked at each other again, and then Larissa gave the wall another knock to make sure they had heard properly the first time; the same hollow sound echoed behind the wall.

"Do you think it's been boarded up?" asked Larissa.

"Or it's a door," said Peter, already searching for some kind of handle.

Larissa immediately joined in the hunt. They both groped around the back wall and the sides of the cupboard for some kind of latch, but they came up short. Larissa tried her luck at giving it a push, but it was in vain. They stood back, puzzled, looking at the cupboard.

"Well," said Larissa, after a long while, "I'm beat."

"Hang on ..." said Peter.

He stepped forward and grabbed the rail at the top. After trying to wriggle it this way and that, he found he could turn it, and then push it in toward the back wall. There was a loud *click!* and the door swung open.

Chapter 7

On the other side of the door was a small room, just big enough for two bookcases against the far wall, another cupboard against the near wall, and, fitting snugly between them, a desk and a chair. The desk was tidy, with a small pile of papers stacked neatly to one side, along with a lamp, a typewriter, and a box of old trinkets. On the wall behind the desk was a cork pinboard with a few old pictures and newspaper cuttings pinned to it. The shelves of the bookcases held a variety of books, files, boxes, and the odd bit of stationary, in no apparent order and gathering layers of dust. It looked like somebody's office from a long time ago.

"This is amazing," Larissa said as they gazed around the room.

They took a few tentative steps, taking it all in. Larissa tried the cupboards while Peter read some of the newspaper cuttings. After finding the cupboard to be completely empty, Larissa joined Peter at the desk.

"Hey, look!" she said, eyeing one of the papers on the wall. "You're on here!"

Peter looked to see what she was talking about: it was a diagram of their family tree, with somebody called Charles Woodwright at the top, going all the way down to Peter's generation. Peter's name was there under Gill and Martin Brewer.

"Becca's even on here," said Peter. "This is quite recent."

"Not that recent," said Larissa, pointing at Patricia's name where the year of death had not yet been filled in. "Ha, you come from a whole line of younger siblings! That explains so much."

"My mom was an only child, so she's not a younger sibling."

"She's the youngest by default."

"Shame, look at this," said Peter, changing the subject. "Brian's wife and his brother died in the same year. And they weren't even that old."

"Yoh, that's quite rough," said Larissa. "What are those all about?" She pointed to the newspaper clippings Peter had been reading.

"Not sure," said Peter. "That one's about a Harold Woodwright meeting with someone from the Royal Family; that one's about a big storm, where they had to fix the chapel afterwards; this one's about some guys getting hijacked on their way to Woodwright Manor, and one of the workers was arrested ... I think they're just times that the family made the news."

Larissa started going through the box of trinkets, which were mostly old jewelry—rings, necklaces, and the odd bracelet—none of which seemed particularly expensive. Peter started looking at the stuff on the shelf, checking inside one or two of the boxes and leafing through a few of the loose pages.

"Anything interesting?" asked Larissa.

"Not really," said Peter. "That side?"

"I mean, these are nice," said Larissa, "but I don't know why they're locked up in a secret room." She was looking at a strange metal object, turning it over in her fingers. "What do you think this is?" she asked.

"Hmm ... Looks like a key," said Peter. "With a flame on the end. Like a candle."

"A candle? Ja, maybe. Except the flame is bigger than the stick."

"Okay, not a candle; an old flame torch."

"Could be." She put the jewelry back in the box and went to look at the things on the shelf with Peter. "What's in the boxes?" she asked.

"Mostly just papers and things," said Peter.

Larissa leafed through a few pages. "Woodwright-Jefferson Mining Company ... Gold prices ... more Woodwright-Jefferson ... mining restrictions ... nothing very interesting here," she finally concluded.

"I think these ones are from when she was at school," said Peter, peering into another box.

Larissa picked out an old piece of paper, unfolded it, and read it aloud.

29 August 1927

Dear Mr. Woodwright

I regret to inform you that your daughter, Miss Patricia Woodwright, was caught out of the house after lights-out last night. She and a group of girls were found in the swimming pool in the nude at around half past twelve. Furthermore, it is believed that Patricia was the one to have instigated the whole ordeal and encouraged the rest of the girls to follow her in breaking the rules. This rebellious behavior is unacceptable and will not be tolerated. Unfortunately, disciplinary action is going to have to be taken against her.

Sincerely

Miss D.L. Andrews

"Hectic!" Larissa folded the letter up and put it back where it was, already looking for something else to read. "What about this box?"

"I don't know; haven't checked it."

It was an old shoe box. Larissa picked it up and removed the lid to reveal two piles of envelopes, each tied neatly in a bunch with a string. She placed the box on the desk and took out one of the bunches of envelopes.

"Mandla Sithole, Woodwright Manor, Underberg, Natal," said Larissa, reading the address on the back. "Any idea who Mandla Sithole is?"

"Nope." Peter picked up the other bunch, and found underneath it an old, well-used sheet of paper with a handwritten Morse code alphabet. "Apparently she used to dabble in a bit of cryptography," he said.

"I wonder what on earth for," Larissa said.

Peter untied the string around the bunch of letters he was holding. He took out the top letter from the pile. "This one is addressed to … Miss Patricia J. Woodwright, St. Dianne's College, Hilton, Natal."

"To Patricia while she was at school?" Larissa said excitedly. "Open it!"

"You really have no regard for other people's privacy," said Peter.

"Again, I don't think Patricia is too concerned right now," she replied, untying her bunch of envelopes.

Reluctantly, Peter took the letter out, unfolded it, and held it out for them to read together.

17 April 1924

Dear Miss Woodwright

I should not have left it until so late to write you—I have been longing to speak with you again since the moment you left Woodwright Manor three months ago. Working on the farm without the prospect of your company to look forward to is so much more tedious.

I am eager to hear about your new school and what you do there. I do wish that I could go to school as well. Please tell me everything!

Mostly I am eager for your return; to see you again and to speak with you. When are you due back at Woodwright Manor?

Yours with sincerity

Mandla

Peter and Larissa each reread the letter before looking at each other.

"So Mandla must have been a friend of hers," said Larissa.

"That must be her response," said Peter, nodding at the letter Larissa was holding. "Open it; let's see."

"Oh my gosh," Larissa said sarcastically, "you've got no respect for other people's privacy."

Peter rolled his eyes as she neatly slid a finger under the envelope to open it, unfolded the letter, and also held it out for them both to read.

5 May 1924
My Dearest Mandla

I was absolutely delighted to receive your letter! I apologize for taking rather a long time to respond but, in answer to your question, school has been very busy!

We have been learning English, History, Mathematics, and Geography, as well as needlework and Religious Studies, and I have taken dancing as an extra class. Needlework is an absolute bore, but the other subjects are interesting—it helps that Mum had already taught us a lot of what we're learning now. I had a slightly skewed notion when we did school at home that perhaps I was quite smart, but I'm afraid I have been forced to concede that I am not one of the top students. Some of the girls here are very clever indeed. Although I dare say you would outshine the brightest of them!

Some of the girls are quite nice, but it must be said that the majority of them are rather a snooty bunch. All they can talk about is the upcoming elections, and they love to sound like they know what's going on. I get the distinct impression, however, that we only ever get the benefit of their fathers' opinions. A lot of people seem to think Jan Smuts is going to lose to the National Party—I don't know much about it, but I think Mother will be furious!

I have befriended a girl named Alice, with whom I spend most of my time; we get along very well. You would like her. She's quite amusing. I do wish you could be here with me too! I would love to have a friend from home.

There are so many rules here; I am finding it difficult to adjust! Elizabeth had warned me, of course, but one doesn't take heed of advice for which they have no context. Miss Andrews, our Lady Warden, does not seem to have taken a liking to me the way she did Elizabeth and Margaret.

I will return for the holidays in June—I am so looking forward to it! I can't wait to play in the fields, and in the stream, and to talk to you in earnest. I miss home, and I miss you!

Your friend
Patricia

Once they had read the letter, Peter flicked through the rest of the envelopes. "Are those all to the same address?" he asked. "Because these are."

"Yup," said Larissa, doing the same.

"Oh, wait," said Peter, looking at a particularly fat envelope, "this last one doesn't have an address."

"Ja, same here," said Larissa. "But open the next one. Let's do them in order."

20 August 1924

Dear Miss Woodwright

Seeing you during your holidays was the most fun I have had in months! It's only been a few weeks and already I wish you were back here.

I have finished reading the books you lent me—thank you for introducing me to Dickens, I thoroughly enjoy his writing! I have returned the books to your mother and she has graciously allowed me to borrow a few more. Whenever I'm not working in the fields, I am reading a book under our tree (my new favorite reading spot).

Please tell me everything about school; I love hearing about what you're doing there!

Your Friend
Mandla

"Who do you think this Mandla guy was?" asked Larissa, almost as soon as they had finished reading the letter. "I mean 'Mandla' is a Zulu name, and by the sounds of it he worked on the farm; but his English is phenomenal!"

"I must say," said Peter, "for a Zulu gent in the twenties, this man can spin a phrase."

"And his handwriting is *beautiful*!" said Larissa, while opening the next letter.

6 September 1924

My Dear Mandla

If you insist on calling me "Miss Woodwright" one more time, I shall refuse to answer any more of your letters!

I'm glad you're enjoying Charles Dickens. Some of his language is beyond me, but I thought you'd appreciate it more than I.

School is even busier now than it was in the first semester, as we're preparing for our exams at the end of the year. I have also started playing hockey, which I am enjoying, and I have joined the school's shooting team. Unfortunately, I can't do any horse riding here, tho' that is probably a good thing because I already have so little time. I imagine I shall be too busy to write you any more letters.

I look forward to seeing you in December when I return!

Your loving friend

Patricia

"Not exactly inviting a response, is she?" said Peter.

"Well, she's busy," said Larissa. "It's understandable."

"I don't know," said Peter, "I kind of get the feeling that this is a bit of a one-sided relationship."

"Not at all!" said Larissa. "You're reading too much into it."

Peter didn't answer and opened the next letter.

19 May 1925

Dearest Patricia

I hope that you are well and that your schoolwork is not too overwhelming. I trust that you're still partaking in hockey and shooting and that it's keeping you reasonably content.

We have had an exciting month here, and I thought I must tell you about it. Firstly, we experienced the biggest storm I have ever witnessed! I'm sure you would have caught some of it in Hilton, but I doubt whether to the same extent. The dam was overflowing, which I have never seen before, and trees were uprooted. We had to repair part of the chapel roof. You will see it all for yourself when you return.

Secondly, my sister, Jabu, got married to Siphiwe last week. My brothers came from Johannesburg for the wedding, and we made umqombothi. Jabu is very happy; it was a wonderful day!

Your father is planning to take his bull to the Royal Show and I will most likely need to help him, so there is a chance that I might see you in Pietermaritzburg in early June. Until then, I wish you all the best and, as always, can't wait to see you.

Your Friend

Mandla

20 June 1925

Dearest Mandla

Once again I apologize for my tardy response. I have hardly had time to think, what with all the excitement around here!

I am very happy for Jabu—I assume you're talking about Siphiwe Msimang? I always liked him; he is a real gentleman.

I'm sure you must have been aware of when Edward, Prince of Wales, arrived in South Africa nearly two months ago. Our entire school huddled into the hall to listen to the radio broadcast of his arrival speech, only to instead be tuned into a telephone conversation between a man and woman talking about their holiday plans! Everybody was mightily angry, tho' it is rather funny in hindsight. We caught enough of the speech at the end to hear what he sounds like!

I gather you were there when Father met him at the opening of the Royal Show last week? I saw him later that day—Father took me out of school for the day. He is ever so handsome! (I'm sorry I never got to see you—most unfortunate timing.)

The night before, Father took us all to see the famous Garda Hall perform her final concert. One of Margaret's friends knew her from school days, and we got to meet her! I thought she was lovely, and her singing was beautiful.

This past Wednesday I was ever so jealous when there were three balls in Pietermaritzburg and I couldn't attend any of them because I am too young. Both my sisters went to the Grand Ball at the Town Hall where Prince Edward was Guest of Honor, and Elizabeth says she met him but I think she is lying. Apparently, he graced all three balls with his presence over the course of the evening. Almost all the 6th form girls went to at least one of the balls, and some of the younger girls snuck out as well. They say he is a very good dancer, and was dancing with whomever he pleased. Oh, how I wish I could have gone! On Thursday, there were rumors that two or three of the girls were lucky enough to have danced with him, and by Saturday half of the school was claiming to have been amongst the lucky few! Nonetheless, it has been a very exciting few days!

I am afraid to say that I will be accompanying my father to Cape Town in July, so I will not likely see you until December. We are going to meet some family from England, and do a bit of sightseeing. I will tell you all about it in a letter when I return.

Your loving friend
Patricia

24 August 1925
Dear Patricia

You have left me wondering how your trip to Cape Town was for almost a month now! Please do tell me about it. I would be fascinated to hear about the Cape of Good Hope.

There is not much news from this side, I'm afraid, other than that we've had a lot of snow, and the hills and mountains were all white for a few days. I'm sure you would have seen it from Hilton.

There is one other thing I thought I should tell you. I returned some books to your mother and asked if she would mind lending me a few more, to which she said I should come up to the library to choose some for myself. I was hesitant but did not want to appear ungrateful so I accepted the offer. When your father saw me in the house he became angry and told me to get out. Your mother tried to explain but he would not hear it. He has been keeping a closer eye on me since then. I don't think he likes that I read, and I think he has been giving me extra work so that I cannot read as much. I do not wish to create a spectacle; I just thought you should know.

Your friend
Mandla

5 September 1925
My dear Mandla

I am very sorry to hear about what happened with my father, and I would like to apologize on his behalf. You know how he is. However, I doubt very much that he would be giving you extra work to keep you from reading; that seems preposterous.

Cape Town was absolutely amazing! The journey by train was rather long and tedious, and the landscape was dry and dull, tho' quite beautiful in its own way. Cape Town itself is wonderful. There are great mountains right next to the sea, and beautiful beaches. We visited a few of the beaches and even attempted swimming, but the water was much too cold to be in it for more than a minute or two. We also climbed up Table Mountain, and the view from the top was incredible! I wish I could have taken a photograph to show you. Apparently, they're going to build a cable-car in the next few years so that anyone can get to the top, which seems ridiculous to me!

I feel like I have so much to tell you, and couldn't possibly fit it all into a letter. I can't wait until December when we can see each other again for the first time in almost a year!

Your loving friend
Patricia

9 April 1926

Dear Patricia

I should like to tell you that I enjoyed this past January possibly more than any other time of my life. The only problem with having you around is that the days seem to pass so much more quickly!

You will be pleased to know that I took a machete from the shed and cleared the path to our tree. I try to go there as often as I can. Since you convinced me to sneak into the library from the balcony, I have been back a few times for more books. I have also started reading a few of your father's Law books for the intellectual stimulus. It was that or Geology.

What news from school?

Your friend
Mandla

24 April 1926

My dear Mandla

I must say, I have become rather fond of this little tradition of ours whereby we write a letter to one another each semester; indeed, I have begun to always look forward to them! I almost wrote you a letter about a week ago but then decided that I would surely receive a letter from you very soon; and I did!

It is quite nice to not be one of the young girls anymore. We have a lot more freedom now. Of course, Miss Andrews still berates me about not trying to attain a "Red Girdle," which is awarded for deportment and some other nonsense. Mandla, if I ever come home with a Red Girdle, please see to it that some sense is beaten into me and that the girdle is burned.

I recently went with Alice, my good friend, to watch the rugby at Hilton School for Boys. Alice has a brother there, and she introduced me to a few of the boys. Before we left, one of the 6th form boys, Jeremy Paxton, invited me to their formal dance next month. I'm a tad nervous, but very excited! Alice is also going, so we should have a lot of fun. All of the 6th forms who have been before say that it's a lovely evening, and some of them say they were kissed there for the first time, something which I have yet to do!

Schoolwork is difficult and plentiful. Mathematics is particularly troublesome. You were always so good at it; I was wondering if I should maybe bring a textbook home over the holidays and see if you can help me with it.

For the meantime, keep our path clear, and more than ever I look forward to seeing you in June!

Your loving friend
Patricia

Just as Peter began reading the next letter, Larissa stopped him. "Look here," she said, pointing at the date on her next letter. "I think this one comes next. It looks like there was a bit of a falling out."

18 August 1926
Dear Mandla

I have been thinking about the very harsh things that you said to me. You made me feel guilty and ashamed. But I should like to point out that I did not choose to be white. I did not choose for you to be black. And most of all, I did not choose for things to be the way they are, where I can go to school and you cannot. If I could change it, I would. You are one of the smartest people I know, and you deserve to go to school more than most. I would trade places with you if I could. But I can't, and that is the way of things; and it is no reason for me not to take advantage of the opportunities afforded to me.

Now, if you like, I could stop telling you about my life at school, but, need I remind you, you were the one who always asked me about it. And school makes up the majority of my life at the moment, so if I cannot talk about it then, frankly, there is not much for us to talk about.

Sincerely
Patricia

30 August 1926
Dear Patricia

Firstly, I never said that I did not want to hear about your school. That has got very little to do with what I was talking about.

Secondly, if you truly believe that not talking about your day-to-day life means that we have nothing to talk about at all, then perhaps you're right, but certainly not for lack of subject matter!

Lastly, you need not lecture me about "the way of things." I dare say I am more cognizant than you are of the ways in which your being white advantages you and my being black hinders me, and of how little there is to be done for it. I cannot go to school, regardless of my aptitude. I cannot have a career in the field of my choosing, but am confined to those jobs that are of the most benefit to the white man. And if I fall in love with a girl whose skin is a different color to mine, I must accept that our lives exist in separate worlds and that those dreams can never become a reality.

Believe me, Patricia, I am well aware of "the way of things." There are many injustices that I have had to accept. But you will excuse me for not smiling graciously about it.

Sincerely
Mandla

8 September 1926
Dear Mandla

I never presumed to lecture you on the way of things, and you would do well to realize that. I only pointed out that your anger toward me was misplaced and not appreciated. And you say now that you were not talking about my school life, but I must contradict you and point out that you most certainly were talking about it; unless, as it seems to me, there is another issue entirely at the heart of all of this, in which case you must speak your mind and speak it plainly. Do not use my being white as an excuse to not say something when in fact you are just too shy.

And lastly, if you want to believe that a black man and a white woman cannot be together, then that is your business. But I do not believe it for a second.

Sincerely
Patricia

17 September 1926
Dear Patricia

I will speak to you in person when you return in December.

Sincerely
Mandla

Peter and Larissa looked at each other.

"This is getting too spicy!" exclaimed Larissa, hurrying to unfold the next letter.

"Bit of a redundant letter, don't you think?" said Peter. "If he was only going to speak to her in December, why not just wait until December?"

Larissa sighed. "Obviously, he didn't want her to think he was ignoring her. He did the right thing."

"What he did was waste an envelope and whatever it cost to send the letter."

"You don't know anything. Now check the date on that letter—which one comes next?"

10 February 1927
Dear Mandla

I have been contemplating why we even send letters, and Father Stewart agrees that it is up to the person who reads it to decide if it holds any value. Some of these words might be a waste of time. I write these letters, full of such meaningless phrases, but seldom do the words I use have any real purpose. I sign off conventionally, "With love, Patricia," regardless of which emotions I experienced when writing to you. I record the date, only to reveal how many of my words are wasted before one actually means something. At the heart of the issue is that, like most things, writing letters is an attempt to express myself, but ultimately it is then yours to interpret. Whether or not you do so correctly is always going to be up to you.

With love
Patricia

Peter and Larissa both stared at the letter in bewildered silence.

"What in the nineteenth-century hell was that?" said Peter.

"Did we miss something?" said Larissa. "What on earth is she on about?"

"It's probably in response to something they spoke about in person."

"Ja, must be. Also, because she normally waited for him to send a letter first. Bleak. I honestly thought this was going somewhere."

"Ja … Wait, what do you mean 'going somewhere'?"

"You know, like … I thought *they* were going somewhere …"

"Going somewhere? Going where?"

"Oh, come on, Peter, wake up!" said Larissa. "He liked her from the start—that much was obvious. I wasn't sure if she liked him back, but in the letter where she said he must man up and say what's on his mind, she was *clearly* telling him to make a move. I thought he would have! I thought the next letter would be after they got together."

"Nah, I think you're getting a bit ahead of yourself," said Peter.

"No, man, you can't be that oblivious! They definitely liked each other."

"Oh, ja? So why doesn't the letter say anything about it?"

"I have no idea. But I'm very interested to see what Mandla's response to that cryptic letter was. Have you got the next one?"

Peter didn't respond. He had started rereading the letter to make sure there were no signs of romance he might have missed but had got distracted. Despite how weird it seemed, there was something strangely familiar about it; about the style it was written in … almost like …

"It's a riddle!" he said.

"What do you mean?"

"Look!" said Peter. "… *it is up to the person who reads it to decide if it holds any value … it is then yours to interpret … whether or not you do so correctly is up to you* … Those sound like hints that he has to decipher it."

"Decipher it? How?"

"I'm not sure," said Peter, "but look here: *these words might be a waste of time … full of meaningless phrases … I sign off conventionally … I record the date* … It all makes it sound like she's just writing a letter for the sake of it and her heart's not in it; but then she also calls it *an attempt to express myself* and says *it is then yours to interpret* … What if she's actually trying to say it *appears* like a normal letter, but there's more to it—that it's not what it seems at face value!"

Larissa frowned at the letter, running her finger under each line as she scrutinized it.

"You might be onto something," she said. "But what? What does it mean?"

Peter shook his head as read it one more time, trying to figure it out. After a moment, he pointed at another line: "Meaningless *phrases* … the *words* have purpose … I think it's got something to do with individual words, rather than the full sentences."

"*Seldom* do the words have purpose," said Larissa. "That sounds like the words *don't* have purpose."

"No, I think it means only *some* words," said Peter. "Not every word. Because look here: *some of these words might be a waste of time*."

"Oh, ja, you're right!" said Larissa.

They both read the letter again, eagerly searching for more clues.

"She mentions words again," said Larissa: "*I record the date, only to reveal how many of my words are wasted before one actually means something.*"

Peter reread the line. "*Reveal how many of my words are wasted …*" he repeated.

Larissa could see Peter's mind working. "What do you think it means?" she asked.

"Hmm … What's the date—the tenth … okay, hang on, let me try something …"

He began counting each word from the beginning.

"One–two–three–four–five–six–seven–eight–nine–ten–*Father*–one–two–three–four–five–six–seven–eight–nine–ten–*reads*–one–two–three–four–five–six–seven–eight–nine–ten–*these*–one–two–three–four–five–six–seven–eight–nine–ten–*letters*."

Larissa gasped.

Peter looked up with a grin. "Cracked it."

"That's why she's writing in code!" said Larissa. "What does the rest of it say?"

Peter decoded the message: "*Father … reads … these … letters … I … love … you … my … heart … is … yours … always.*"

"HA! I knew it!" Larissa shouted.

"Shh!" Peter scowled at her. "We're not supposed to be here, remember!"

"I was right!" she said, struggling to keep her voice down. "I *told* you they got together!"

"Okay, okay, you were right," said Peter, looking at the previous letters again and wondering how he missed it.

"But Patricia obviously realized Mandla was going to write her another letter, like he always did, so she had to tell him not to say anything discriminating, and she had to do it *without* letting her father know! She's a genius!"

"It is quite impressive that she thought of that," said Peter. "The question is: did Mandla pick up on it?"

4 March 1927

Dear Patricia

Thank you for those very wise words. Indeed, a clever man once suggested that I should leave letters a long time before responding, both for my sake and for your sake, and then only return to them after consideration to not misinterpret their meaning. Look once, but only answer upon returning to it later. Your premise is correct: the beauty of letters is inferred, and one can only fully embrace it if they know you.

Your friend
Mandla

"Well, I have no idea what he just said but it sounds like he was picking up what she was putting down," said Larissa. "Let's see what he really said ..."

She began counting the words as Peter had done.

"One–two–three–four–five–six–seven–eight–nine–ten–*man*–one–two–three–four–five–six–seven–eight–nine–ten–*before*–one–two–three–four–five–six–seven–eight–nine–ten–*then* ... Hang on, this doesn't seem right ..."

"He would've used his own key," said Peter.

"What do you mean 'key'?"

"That's what it's called in cryptography. Patricia's key was ten, because that was the date on her letter. The date on his letter is 4—try that."

"You mean ... only count every four words?"

"Exactly."

"One–two–three–four–*very*–one–two–three–four–*clever* ... That's it! Okay, *very clever*, then let's see: *I ... long ... for ... your ... return ... to ... look ... upon ... your ... beauty ... and ... embrace ... you*! Aww!" she held the letter to her heart, "that's so romantic!"

"Not exactly Jane Austen," said Peter.

Larissa looked sideways at him. "You read Jane Austen?"

"I mean, I *have*; I wouldn't say I *do*."

Larissa looked back at the letter. "But he wrote it in code!" she said.

Peter didn't say anything.

"And think about it," said Larissa, "nowadays we have phones; we're constantly texting the people we're flirting with, and, let's be honest, there's normally more than one."

"Totally," said Peter.

Larissa grinned. "But they wouldn't see each other for *months*," she went on, "and these letters that came once or twice a semester were their only communication …" She gazed at the letter with dreamy eyes. "I can just imagine what it would have been like to be in boarding school back then, thinking about a boy all semester, wondering if he's thinking about you, and then you get a letter like this …"

Peter took the letter, nodding in admiration. "He had moves."

"He did not have *moves*!" Larissa said incredulously. "They were childhood friends and they fell in love! In fact, she had to *tell* him to make a move!"

"Call it what you want," said Peter. "My man had game."

"He's not *your man*!" Larissa snatched the letter from his hands. "Get the next one!"

"You have the next one."

"Oh. Right."

8 May 1927

Dear Mandla

I am glad that you have understood what I was saying. On to more pressing matters, I have invited Alice over for the holidays—I have told you about her before, she's a good friend. Alice has a hand-held camera; she's one of about ten girls at school. I hope Father gets us one, they're terribly fun!

Inside this envelope, with the letter, you will also have found an old key. I don't think it does anything, but it is quite pretty and could, I thought, be used for adornment, like a necklace. I don't know what the other girls would say, but the girl next door to me also wears a necklace like that with a key. I want you to have it. The shape makes me think of you: like a lion.

With love
Patricia

"Looks like they're done writing in code," said Larissa.

"I wouldn't be so sure …" said Peter, already counting out the words.

"Really?" said Larissa. "It looks like a much more standard letter."

Peter read out what he had decoded so far: "*I have told Alice about us.*"

"Oh! Anything else?"

Peter took a minute to decode the rest. "*The key is for the door with the lion.*"

"The door with the lion?"

"That's what it says," Peter shrugged.

"Do you know of any doors with lions?"

Peter thought about it. "The gates have lions," he said. "The front doors have lions. I've actually seen a few lions around this place."

"Okay, I don't think she's talking about the front doors, because she would've just said 'front doors.'"

"Ja, look, I'm not sure," said Peter. "Could be anything. Maybe the next letter talks about it."

16 August 1927
My dear Patricia

I have managed to arrange with the postman that I deal directly with him when sending and receiving post, so we no longer need to worry about what we write.

It was lovely to meet Miss Rutherford when she was visiting; please do give her my regards. I thoroughly enjoyed the time we all spent together and look forward to seeing the photographs she took once they have been developed! I only wish that I could have spent as much time with you as she did when you were in the house, or out horse riding. That is not to say I was jealous; merely that I am mindful of every precious moment we are together, and every moment we are not.

Yours adoring
Mandla

Larissa suddenly looked away with a frown, trying to remember something.

"Nothing about a door with a lion," said Peter. He looked at Larissa. "What is it?"

Larissa looked thoughtfully at the letter for a moment before answering. "I think ..." she began slowly. "I think her friend Alice might have been my great-grandmother."

Peter's eyes widened. "Are you serious?"

"My great-grandmother's name was Alice," said Larissa, "and she was very good friends with Patricia. She's the reason our family is here now. She died when I was quite young, so I don't really remember anything about her, but when I thought of the name 'Alice Rutherford,' it rang a bell. I knew her as Alice Brookes, but I think Rutherford might have been her maiden name. She must've been about the same age and I'm pretty sure she was from the same area. I'll ask my gran tomorrow."

"Umm," Peter said hesitantly, "maybe don't mention that we've been going through these letters."

"Obviously," Larissa said as she unfolded the next one. "I'm not an idiot."

2 September 1927
My dear Mandla

"Miss Rutherford" returns her regards, and kindly requests you refer to her as Alice.

If you are not the jealous type, as you would have me believe, it should not affect you to know that last week all of the 6th form girls decided to have a bit of daring fun: after lights out, when the house mothers were asleep, we gathered in the common room, removed all of our clothes (yes, all of them), and snuck out to run around outside completely naked! We then all ended up jumping into the swimming pool for a midnight swim in the nude.

Unfortunately, Miss Andrews somehow caught wind of what we were doing and came down to discover us all in the pool. Luckily, they can't expel the entire grade, but we've all got three detentions, and letters are going out to all of our parents to let them know. Father will not be very impressed with me, especially because I've been accused of "inciting the others," which isn't strictly true but I don't mind. The other girls will be in less trouble if I take the fall for it.

I don't know whether Father will punish me, but it might prevent us from seeing one another for a while once I return. Although, even if he does, I feel now as though I could just sneak out at night to come and see you.

With love
Your Patricia

19 September 1927
My dear Patricia

After your last letter I will have to concede that I do in fact feel jealous from time to time. At the risk of being improper, I dare say there is little that I wouldn't give to have been there with you. However, my trepidation is not only that your father might punish you, but also how *he might punish you. I fear that it will almost definitely limit the amount that we can see each other.*

A new Act was passed recently called the Immorality Act: relations between people of different races is now illegal. People already didn't approve, but now they will have legitimate cause to report us to the police. We will have to be extra careful.

I realize that this puts you in a quandary. Your life would certainly be a lot easier if you were not with me. I do not mean to put pressure on you, but it is my opinion that you should think properly about what you want and make a decision.

For what it's worth, I have already made my decision: I love you, you have always been my best friend, and being with you is worth any risk.

The decision is therefore yours.

W*ith love and sincerity*

Mandla

P.S. Good luck with your final exams.

"Aww! He's adorable!" said Larissa.

"Yes, I'm sure when he was writing about his grievances as a black man under a racist government, his deepest ambition was that he came across as 'adorable,'" said Peter.

"*His deepest ambition*," Larissa mimicked him as she unfolded the next letter. "Look who's trying to sound like they're from the 1900s!"

9 November 1927

My dear Mandla

I began writing a letter reprimanding you for even considering that I might choose not to be with you, but then I realized the seriousness of what you were saying and how selfless you were actually being, and it makes me love you even more.

I don't want you to think that I just responded without properly thinking about it. I have thought about it thoroughly. But I have arrived at the same conclusion as you: I love you, and to be with you is worth any risk.

I'm afraid my father wrote me to inform me that he had received word from the school about my escapades (the girls are calling it the Golden Mile) and that he will indeed be punishing me when I return. He told me not to invite any friends over, so I think it is safe to assume I will be grounded.

Yes, I had heard about the Immorality Act. Alice told me. She made out as though it was exciting that we might be breaking the law. She referred to you as the "forbidden fruit." Of course I told her not to be ridiculous; that we had done no law breaking and that the matter is to be taken seriously.

But I'll tell you what: the first night I'm back, on the 7th of December, once everyone is asleep, I'll sneak out from the library balcony. Meet me at the dam, and we can have our own Golden Mile.

With love
Your Patricia

By the time they were reading the final paragraph, Larissa was excitedly hitting Peter on the arm.

"Yes," said Peter, "I read it as well."

Larissa's jaw hung open with a disbelieving grin. "Your Aunty Pat was one spicy lady!" she said.

Peter cringed. "I keep forgetting that it's my great-aunt whose letters we're reading."

"Well," said Larissa, "that's the last of the letters with addresses."

"What do you reckon these big ones are?"

Larissa was already opening hers. "We're about to find out."

Inside each of them was a collection of smaller notes rather than actual letters. Larissa took them all out from her envelope and leafed through them. "The first one doesn't have a date, but the rest are in order," she said.

"I think you go first," said Peter, looking at the first note in his envelope.

Dear Mandla

I once again apologize for the things my father has said and done. I'm afraid we are going to have to meet in secret from now on. Meet me tomorrow night at ten o'clock under our tree.

If you can't make it tomorrow night, leave a note for me in the hole under the tree.

Love

Patricia

12 May 1930

Dear Patricia

Thank you for getting a note to me; this is a great idea!

Unfortunately, I cannot meet tonight; I am going into town to see my brothers from Jo'burg. I am sorry you had to walk down here in the dark for no reason. I can meet tomorrow at the same time, or any night after that. Leave a note to say when you'd like to meet and I'll check tomorrow afternoon when I'm back from town. When we meet we can make arrangements for the next time.

Love

Mandla

P.S. Leave a date on the note so I know when you left it.

12 May 1930

Dear Mandla

Tomorrow night after you're back is fine by me. I'll see you then.

Love

Patricia

18 July 1930

Dear Mandla

I am afraid I cannot meet tonight like we planned—my sincere apologies. Let me know when next you can come and I shall check tomorrow. I have left paper and a pencil here in this tin so we do not need to keep bringing paper down with us.

Love

Patricia

18 July 1930
Dear Patricia

I can come tomorrow.

I've left this sheet of Morse code for you. Take it and learn it. If I go to the top of the hill I can see your window, and we can communicate with flashlights at night.

Love
Mandla

"That's where the paper with the Morse code comes from!" said Larissa. "They communicated with flashlights!"

Peter picked up the sheet of Morse code again and looked at it, this time seeing it as almost a hundred years old. He imagined a young Patricia sitting at her window with a dim candle and the sheet of Morse code in hand, watching for the flashes of her lover in the dark. "Pretty cool," he said.

They skimmed through the other letters, most of which were more plans to meet, apologies for not being able to make it, the occasional request for books, and clarifying some miscommunications that were apparently made with Morse code—until Larissa came to one worth mentioning. "Look at this," she said, pulling two notes out from the others and holding them out for Peter.

24 March 1931
Dear Mandla

My mother has fallen very ill and we are taking her to the doctor in Pietermaritzburg. I don't know how long we will be gone, but I will not likely be able to see you for a few days. You will probably see us return, but I will leave a note to let you know when I can see you again.

Love
Patricia

29 March 1931

Dear Mandla

My mother has passed away. I must see you at once.

Love

Patricia

"Shame," Larissa said after a long silence. She checked the next note. "The next one is a whole month later, so he obviously managed to see her."

"Look at this one," said Peter.

3 May 1931

Dear Patricia

I need to see you sooner than we agreed. My brothers want me to go with them back to Jo'burg in a few days. I want to talk to you about it before I make any decisions. If you get this in time, please meet me tonight or tomorrow night. If you do not get this in time, I'm afraid I might have decided to go with them to Jo'burg.

Love

Mandla

Larissa checked the date and looked for a response in her pile.

3 May 1931

Dear Mandla

I can't meet tonight but I can meet tomorrow night.

Maybe I could come with? I really want to get away from here.

Love

Patricia

"She wanted to leave!" Larissa repeated.

"Well, they carried on sending letters to meet up, so I don't think it happened," said Peter.

They skimmed through more notes, still mostly plans to meet, until Larissa stopped them again.

16 July 1931

Dear Mandla

I can meet tomorrow night. We need to talk about how we can run away together.

Love

Patricia

There was no immediate response and they skimmed through the last few notes, almost to the end, before Peter stopped them again.

21 August 1931

Dear Patricia

I have received word from my brother in Jo'burg to say that we could stay with him for a while, but that we'll need a plan. We will also need money before we go, and maybe you should bring your rifle for safety. Let's meet to discuss this. I can meet any night this week.

Love

Mandla

22 August 1931

Dear Mandla

I can meet tonight.

And I'm afraid my rifle is only ornamental now; it's no longer functional.

Love

Patricia

There was one more note from Patricia, and the last two were from Mandla.

5 September 1931
Dear Mandla

I think I might have a plan. Pack all your things and be ready to leave in two days' time. Check for another letter from me first thing in the morning the day after tomorrow.

Love
Patricia

6 September 1931
Dear Patricia

I have packed and I am ready to leave when you give me the word. I will check for your letter first thing tomorrow morning.

Love
Mandla

Then, finally: *The police are coming—I don't know why, but if they search my house and find these they'll know what we had planned, so I'm giving them to you.*

Peter and Larissa stood in silence for a long time.

"I don't understand," Larissa eventually said. "What do you think happened?"

Peter shrugged and shook his head.

"What happened to that last letter he was waiting for?" she asked and checked her pile of letters again to make sure she hadn't missed it. "Do you think they ran away together?"

"I'm afraid I know as much as you do," said Peter. "Except Brian didn't mention anything about it during the eulogy, so I'm guessing not."

"Brian didn't mention *any* of this during the eulogy! Maybe it was just another part of her life that he conveniently left out."

Peter considered that. "Maybe," he said. "Although, they were trying to keep their relationship a secret, so maybe he just didn't know about it."

"And maybe he just didn't know that they ran away together!"

"I don't know," said Peter, unconvinced. "I mean, it's one thing keeping a relationship secret, but if you run away from home, people are going to notice you're gone. And it's the kind of thing that would've been mentioned in the eulogy."

"Maybe Brian didn't want everyone knowing that she had a relationship with a black guy! Maybe he was ashamed of it, or he thought the family wouldn't approve."

"Okay, now you're just being silly," said Peter. "Nobody would have had a problem with Patricia having a relationship with a black guy."

"You don't know that," spat Larissa. "And don't call me silly! A lot of white people try to act like they're not racist, but on the inside they'd never actually consider being with a black person."

"You just want to believe they ran away together, but honestly I don't think they did."

Larissa gave Peter a look not far off disdain, then turned away and started putting the letters back into their envelopes in silence. He got the distinct impression that she was not pleased with him. "Look, I'm not trying to argue with you," he said. "I'm just telling you what I think."

Larissa didn't respond. She checked her phone and sighed. "It's late. People are going to be wondering where we are."

She carried on putting letters into envelopes. Reluctantly, Peter did likewise.

Once they had put all the letters back into their envelopes and tied the envelopes into two bunches, Larissa put them back in their box, placed the box back on the shelf and turned to the door without looking at Peter. Peter followed her out and closed the secret door behind them. She seemed much less concerned about being seen now than she had been earlier that night and almost stomped down the dark passageway.

When they reached her room, Peter attempted a feeble "Good-night."

Larissa didn't respond and closed the door behind her.

Chapter 8

Peter woke the next morning with an uneasy feeling. The way the previous night had ended hung over him like a bad dream.

They had all been allowed to sleep in today. Peter looked around; most of the other beds were already empty. The air was crisp, the sky a deep blue, and the mountains bathed in sunlight. He tried to take it in as he got dressed, but he couldn't shake his anxiety. What was he going to say to Larissa when he saw her?

He made his way down to breakfast, half expecting to see her around every corner, and not altogether relieved when he didn't. He eventually did see her when he entered the dining room, sitting with Megan, Austen and, of course, Daniel. He tried not to look at them and made his way straight over to the food, passing Kim Kingsbury-Ellis in yet another hat—it seemed as though she had a different one for every occasion—talking to some of the other adults.

"... and did you see the way she signed herself with the cross as though she's actually religious?" Kim was saying. "Who's she kidding? Everyone knows she goes to church about twice a year ..."

Peter shook his head as he piled food onto his plate.

"Good morning, Peter."

Ellen had just arrived and also started helping herself to toast and scrambled egg.

"Morning, Ellen," said Peter, trying to match her calm tone.

"So where did you disappear to last night?" she asked.

"What?"

"Last night? We were all in the sitting room and you just disappeared."

"Oh," said Peter, "I was, umm, just looking around the house. Exploring a little."

"Cool," said Ellen. "Find anything interesting?"

Peter hesitated. "I found a piano," he said.

"Do you play?"

"I do."

"That's cool," she said. "Are you coming to sit with us?" She had finished serving herself and was ready to walk off.

"Oh, um, ja, sure," said Peter.

She politely waited for him to finish putting a few pork sausages on his plate, and together they walked to the table and joined the others.

"Good morning, everyone," Ellen said as they arrived.

They all returned the greeting except Larissa, who glanced up, saw Peter, then carried on talking to Daniel.

Soon Katie joined them as well and put her plate down next to Megan's. "Jeepers, Meg, your mom and Kim do *not* get along well," she said as she sat down.

"Ja," said Larissa, "what's up with that?"

"Ugh, it's *so* embarrassing!" said Megan. "They're so childish!"

"Aren't they, like, stepsisters or something?" Katie asked.

"They're half-sisters," said Megan. "My granddad had my mom, then divorced my granny, remarried and had Kim."

"So how come they don't get along?" Larissa asked.

"It's literally the stupidest thing!" said Megan. "My granddad used to tell us that he once found hidden treasure in, like, some secret passageway or something stupid—he was a bit of a nutter, to be honest. Then he died, and my mom was actually bleak that he never told her where the treasure was." She rolled her eyes dramatically in exasperation. "I think she was expecting something in his will or something, and I was, like, you didn't seriously *believe* him, did you? And then it turned out Kim was *also* bleak that he hadn't told *her* where the treasure was, and then they got into a big fight about *who he would've told*, and I'm just like calm down, clearly he was never gonna tell either of you, because it's not even true!"

They all laughed, and the conversation moved on to Patricia's will and who they thought was going to get the estate.

When there was a lull in conversation, Katie spoke up again. "Does anyone want to go for a walk past the dam?"

"Nah, not for me, hey," said Daniel.

"I'm keen," said Larissa.

"Ja, actually it could be cool," said Daniel.

Austen nodded. "Ja, why not," he said.

"Ellen?" said Larissa.

Ellen smiled politely but shook her head. "No, thank you."

"Alright then," said Larissa, standing up, "should we go change, meet at the front door in ten?"

"Wait," said Austen. "Um, Peter, are you keen to come as well?"

Peter hadn't failed to notice how eager Larissa was to get going without him. He glanced up at her; she was staring in the opposite direction.

"Thanks, but I think I'll pass this time," he said.

"No stress," said Austen. "Next time then?"

"Next time," said Peter.

"Cool," said Larissa, "let's get going."

The five of them got up and took their plates to the kitchen, leaving Ellen and Peter alone at the table. Peter turned back to his food, much less hungry now than he had been when he served himself. He glanced up: Ellen was looking at him with a mixture of pity and understanding. "Do you want to come horse riding?" she asked.

"Horse riding?" said Peter.

"Ja, I spoke to Uncle Brian yesterday and he said he would take me horse riding today. You can come if you want."

"I'll be honest," said Peter, "I'm not the biggest fan of horses. They scare me."

Ellen's face broke into a smile. "They're very gentle," she said, almost laughing. "Come on; it'll be good for you!"

Peter was apprehensive, but at this stage it was either horse riding with Ellen or wallowing in self-pity on his own. He decided Ellen was right.

The stables were behind the garage, at the bottom of the hill near the chapel. Brian had given them each a pair of special horse-riding pants he called jodhpurs and told them to wait for him there.

"Do you do a lot of horse riding?" Peter asked Ellen as they made their way through the garden past the garage.

"Nope!" said Ellen, quite cheerful.

"Have you *ever* been horse riding?" Peter asked.

"Twice before," said Ellen. "Once when I was very small—they kind of just sat me on the horse and walked it around a bit—and then about two years ago at a friend's farm I got to ride one properly. It was so much fun! And I've always loved horses." She looked at Peter. "Have you?"

Peter shook his head. "Nope."

Ellen smiled. "You'll love it," she said.

Peter wasn't entirely convinced, but Ellen said it with so much happiness that he was becoming quite excited to try. He remembered being scared before trying to ride a bicycle for the first time as well, and now it was the most normal thing in the world. Perhaps this wouldn't be so bad.

The stables smelled of horses and old hay. Ellen went from one horse to the next, patting their noses and feeding them hay from her hand. Peter followed her but steered clear of the horses.

"Come feed them," said Ellen, holding some hay out to him.

"Have you seen how big they are?" he said. "If that thing wanted to hurt you, you wouldn't stand a chance!"

Ellen laughed. "But you don't want to hurt anybody, do you, my baby?" she said to the horse, stroking its nose.

Brian arrived in his gumboots and took them into a small room at the near end of the stables with the words "Tack Room" carved into the wood above the door.

"First," said Brian, "you'll both need to wear a helmet." He handed them each a helmet, then picked up a few more things. "Can you manage this?" he asked Peter, handing him a saddle. It was a little heavier than it looked, but easily manageable. "And these," he said, adding two more things that also looked like saddles, which confused Peter a little. "And these." He added another two saddle-looking pieces of equipment, though these were spongy and much lighter. "And, Ellen, if you could take these, my darling?" He handed her an assortment of leather straps with metal bits. "And I'll bring these," he grabbed a few more things, "and we're good to go!"

He led them back to the horses and opened the first horse's door. "This is Bella," he said, leading Bella out of her stall. She was a very dark brown, almost black, with a white mark on her forehead. "Ellen, my darling, I think you should ride Bella."

He handed the lead rope to Ellen, who looked absolutely delighted and began stroking Bella's nose.

"And for you, Peter," said Brian, now leading them a few stalls down, "I think you should take Rusty."

Rusty, who had clearly been named for his color, was a fair deal bigger than Bella.

"Rusty is our fastest horse!" said Brian as he handed Peter the lead rope, then laughed when he saw Peter's face. "Not to worry," he said, "he is also our calmest and most obedient horse."

Peter was slightly relieved, but not by much.

"Now I'll tack up Rusty, because I can see Peter is a bit skittish," Brian said, giving Peter a wink. "And, my darling, if you could just watch me and do the exact same with Bella."

"I sure could!" said Ellen.

"Right," said Brian, "first thing we're going to do is put the saddle pad on."

He took the spongy things from Peter, handed one to Ellen, and placed the other onto Rusty's back.

"Other way," he said to Ellen. "That's it. Just behind her shoulders. Yip, just like that."

He then took the other saddle-looking things from Peter and handed one to Ellen. "These are half pads," he said, placing it on top of the saddle pad, then waited for Ellen to do the same. "Then take that saddle and just put it on nice and gently; yip, there we go."

He showed Ellen how to put on a breast plate, then the girth strap, and then the bridle and reins. Finally, the horses were all tacked up.

"Now bring them outside here where there's a mounting block."

Brian led them out to what was basically a miniature step ladder with only two steps.

"Alright, Ellen, you first, my darling. Bring her round here so you can get up on her left side. Okay, up on the block. Bring the reins in a bit and hold them with your left hand so she doesn't run off. Now, put your left hand at the bottom of her neck; yip, just there. Grab a bit of mane if you have to; then put your right hand on the other side of the saddle. That's it. Now, left foot in the stirrup, knee facing forward, knee facing forward; now lift yourself up—there you go!"

Ellen couldn't stop grinning, bobbing up and down on the horse as it walked slowly out of the way.

"Alright, Peter, you're up!" said Brian. "Up on the block."

Peter could feel his heart beating faster. He was beginning to have second thoughts.

"Don't be scared," said Brian.

Sound advice.

"Now, take the reins with your left hand. Bring them in a bit more; there you go. Hold the bottom of the neck, right hand on the saddle, no no, other side of the saddle; that's it. Now, left foot in the stirrup. Good. Knee facing forward. And lift yourself up!"

Peter hoisted himself up onto the horse, terrified that it was going to run off before he had even sat down properly. But then he was seated, and Rusty was still standing perfectly still. This actually wasn't as bad as he thought.

"Excellent," said Brian. "Now, hold the reins with your thumbs on top; there, look how Ellen is doing it; yip. Alright, so, to make the horse go, you squeeze with your heels. Pull the reins to stop. Pull on the right to go right; pull on the left to go left … And that's all you really need to know. Okay, enjoy!"

"Thanks, Uncle Brian!" Ellen waved and started walking her horse away from the stables.

"Wait, what?!" said Peter. "Are you not riding as well?"

"Oh, no, I'm much too old for that!" Brian laughed. "And I don't think any of the horses would appreciate having to carry me!"

Peter was quite sure that there must be more to the lesson before they were left to their own devices, but suddenly his horse was moving, and in that moment he became fully aware that this was going to be *nothing* like riding a bicycle; he was mounted on a large, powerful creature with a mind of its own. He hadn't even wanted the horse to start moving, but here he was, following Ellen and Bella toward the hill. He realized he was so tense that he was squeezing his legs without even knowing it. He tried to loosen them, and noticed Rusty relax a little.

"How cool is this?!" Ellen called to him over her shoulder, but he didn't feel like he was in a position to answer her.

"Let's trot," she called, and next thing Bella was trotting.

Before Peter could protest, Rusty had also started trotting, as though this was some sort of competition. Peter was bouncing up and down uncontrollably, genuinely concerned that he might fall off at any moment.

Ellen looked back over her shoulder to see Peter and Rusty coming up on her flank. Giggling, she gave Bella another little kick and they broke into a canter.

Rusty followed suit. Peter decided this was too much for him and tried to pull the reins to stop, but Rusty was having none of it. Soon they were passing Ellen and Bella, and Peter could do nothing but hold on for dear life. Ellen, enjoying herself immensely, kicked it up another gear into a full gallop. Peter watched helplessly as Bella started getting ahead of Rusty; he knew what was coming next. Sure enough, Rusty didn't enjoy being left behind and they immediately broke into a gallop as well, easily passing Bella and Ellen, who laughed but could do nothing to keep up with them. The stables were out of sight, as well as the house, and the grass beneath them was whizzing past in a blur as they rounded the hill.

Rusty seemed content to carry on running at full speed regardless of how far behind Bella and Ellen were, and with no consideration to Peter's comfort or safety, until suddenly they had come to the entrance gates of Woodwright Manor. Finally, Rusty started to slow down, and Peter pulled on the reins. Satisfied that he had successfully outrun Bella, Rusty came to an amenable stop.

"Wow, that horse is *fast*!" Ellen said when they finally caught up a few moments later.

Now that Peter was sitting still again, no longer fearing for his life but with the adrenalin still pumping, he couldn't help breaking a smile; soon he and Ellen were both laughing. That was possibly one of the most thrilling things he had ever done!

"Not bad for your first time riding," said Ellen. "That was epic!"

"That was completely insane!" said Peter, still laughing.

"You know, for someone who claimed to be scared of horses, you weren't shy to push him to full speed," said Ellen.

"Are you kidding me?" said Peter. "I tried to stop while we were still walking; I had absolutely no control over this thing!"

Ellen burst out laughing again. "You were obviously doing it wrong!"

They walked their horses slowly down the gravel road from the entrance gate. With a bit more perspective now, Peter saw that the road actually headed away from the house before bending round the hill back toward it.

"I never realized the road took such a detour," he said as they bobbed gently on their horses. "It's so much quicker to the house round the other side of the hill."

"Ja, cool," said Ellen. "So what happened with you and Larissa?"

"What?" Peter's heart started racing again and it had nothing to do with the horse. "What do you mean?" he asked.

"You weren't the only one who disappeared last night," said Ellen. "And when I asked her where she had been, she said pretty much exactly what you said."

Peter remained silent, trying to think what to say.

"And," Ellen went on, "she didn't seem very keen for you to go along with them today. In fact, she didn't even seem happy to see you at breakfast."

Peter was still silent.

"And *you* didn't seem very happy about *that*," she finally added, with a quick peek at Peter's facial expression.

"You reckon?" said Peter, trying to sound nonchalant.

"I do reckon," said Ellen. "So, what happened?"

Peter sighed. "To be honest," he said, "I'm not really sure. We were just walking around, looking at stuff. One minute everything was fine; then I must have said something, because she pretty much just stormed out."

"What did you say?"

Peter didn't want to say exactly where they were and what they had been talking about. "I think it was because I disagreed with her about something," he said. "I didn't think it was a big deal."

"But she obviously did."

"Well, she shouldn't have. We were trying to guess how something had happened; she made a few suggestions, and I just didn't think she was right."

"Ah," said Ellen, "I see. I think she probably felt like you didn't value her input."

"Well, then she's an idiot."

They walked for a little while in silence before Ellen spoke again. "Look," she said, "I don't have a horse in this race, so to speak, but the way I see it, you could either mope around for a week not talking to each other, or you could just suck it up and apologize. You'll enjoy the rest of your time here a lot more if you do."

Apart from a light breeze rustling the leaves, the only sound for a few moments was the horses' hooves on the gravel and their loud breathing.

"What about you?" Peter asked. "Any boyfriends?"

Ellen had a playful smirk. "I've got options," she said. "But, no, no boyfriends. I'm still young; what do I need a boyfriend for? I'm more worried about figuring out what I want to do with my life."

"Bloody hell," said Peter, "you don't think you've got that a bit backwards? You're too young to worry about the rest of your life, but you might as well have some fun in the meantime."

"Is Peter Brewer trying to give me life advice?" she teased, and Peter laughed.

"Alright, fine," said Peter, "so what have you decided you want to do with your life?"

"Not sure," she said. "Something with people. Maybe a psychologist."

"To be fair," said Peter, thinking about it, "you read me like a book this morning."

Ellen smiled. "Yes, I have a knack for that."

Next thing, she was standing up in her stirrups. "Come on," she said, "time for another trot!"

"Whoa, wait a second, why don't we just take—"

But both horses had already taken off. They ran down the road toward the house until Ellen turned off toward the dam. Without Peter doing anything to steer, Rusty followed.

They passed the dam and ran up the next hill, where they were at an incredible vantage point and could see for miles in all directions: the mountains, the valleys, neighboring farms and distant plantations. They carried on through the fields, walking as much as Peter could convince them to and running whenever Ellen and Rusty felt like it.

Eventually they had completed a long loop that encircled the house and, just as Peter was starting to get the hang of riding, they found themselves approaching the stables once more. Brian was there in his gumboots to see them in.

"Have a good ride, did you?" he called as they came in. "You were out long enough!"

"It was amazing!" said Ellen. "Thank you so much for letting us ride, Uncle Brian—it was so much fun!"

"I'm so glad you enjoyed it, my darling."

He helped them to dismount their horses. "And you, Peter?" he asked. "Did you enjoy?"

"It was definitely an experience," said Peter. "I find it hard to believe Rusty is the most obedient horse."

"Did I say that?" said Brian, acting surprised. "Oh, I must have misspoke." He gave Ellen a wink.

"Come on, man, you loved it," said Ellen.

"Let's just say, once I get over the trauma, I'll look back at this day and it'll probably be a good memory."

Brian and Ellen laughed, and Peter finally cracked a smile. They finished untacking the horses, thanked Brian again, and headed back to the house.

"By the way," Ellen said as they reached the doors, "if anyone else asks, horse riding was the best time ever."

"Umm, okay," said Peter. "Why is that?"

Ellen lowered her voice. "Because Larissa told me she also loves horses," she said with a sneaky grin. "It'll make her jealous and she'll regret not talking to you." She smiled at Peter, very pleased with herself, and headed inside.

"Even so, I still think it's weird—Ah, Peter, there you are! We haven't seen you the whole day!"

The afternoon was passing into dusk, and Peter found his parents sitting out on the patio overlooking the garden and the dam.

"How was the ride?" his mom asked.

"Well, I'm alive," said Peter as he sat down, "so that's good. What's weird?"

"Oh, nothing," said his mom. "Your father's just being cynical."

"I'm being genuine," said Martin. "For someone her age, and in her condition, most of the time—"

"Martin," Gill cut him off, "that's enough!"

They looked at each other, clearly communicating something that Peter didn't understand.

"What?" said Peter. "What's going on?"

His mom sighed. "We just found out that an autopsy was performed on Patricia after her death. I don't think it's a big deal, but your father seems to think it's strange."

"I don't understand," said Peter.

"Autopsies are only performed if there's any doubt as to how the person died," his dad said. "Patricia was a hundred and five years old, and not very well. There shouldn't have been any doubt as to how she died, but the fact that they performed an autopsy suggests that there was."

"We don't know that it was a forensic autopsy," said Gill. "There wasn't a doctor present when she died, and it's not unusual to do one in those cases."

"Yes, but why keep it a secret?" said Martin. "*That's* what's weird about this. Why are we only hearing about this now through Carol?"

"Because it's not a big deal!" said Gill.

"What was the result of the autopsy?" Peter asked.

Gill shrugged. "Nothing conclusive," she said. "Most likely a natural death."

"Well, there was fluid in her lungs," said Martin.

"Yes, but that's not uncommon in elderly people," said Gill.

"And hemorrhages on some of her organs," said Martin. "And she hadn't really shown any previous symptoms ..."

Gill sighed and shook her head, giving Peter the old you-know-how-your-father-gets look.

"Oh, by the way, Peter," she said, changing the topic, "tomorrow we're going for a hike in the Drakensberg."

"Okay, cool," said Peter, suddenly standing up. "I'll, um ... I'll see you later!"

He had just spotted Larissa walking by herself through the garden, and in that moment decided to heed Ellen's advice and go speak to her. She was strolling slowly among the bushes with her hands out, letting the leaves brush them as she passed.

Peter jogged to catch up with her. "Hey, Larissa," he said.

She turned around. "Oh. You."

She turned back and continued with her slow amble.

"Look," said Peter, "I wanted to apologize."

She stopped and looked at him again, as though deciding whether he was worth her time.

"About last night," he went on.

She just glared at him.

"I ... I'm sorry," said Peter. "I didn't mean to call you silly. I was just trying to be honest with you."

Larissa shrugged. "Fair enough," she said, then turned around and carried on walking.

"Fair enough?" said Peter. "Is that all you're going to say?"

She nodded. "Pretty much."

Peter followed her, but she started talking to a farm worker who was busy in the garden.

"Good afternoon," Larissa said politely. Peter was quite sure she was just doing this to not have to speak to him.

"Good afternoon," the man replied with a smile.

"May I ask what you're busy with?" Larissa said pleasantly, leaning over to see what he was doing.

"I am taking out these castor bean plants," he said, holding up some stems that he had already uprooted. "I don't know if maybe the children were playing here or what, but they have been chopped down; so now we are going to remove them."

"Aren't those used to make castor oil?" asked Larissa.

"Yebo," said the man, "but they are not indigenous; so now we are going to plant something that is indigenous."

He handed a packet of seeds to Larissa with a picture of pretty orange flowers on the front.

"Oh, Red Hot Pokers? Lovely, those are beautiful!" said Larissa. "Tell me, now that Patricia is gone, who decides what to plant? Is it Brian?"

"No, no, Mr. Msimang tells me," he said.

The man could see the next question in Larissa's expression, so he pointed to Thulani's house on the hill.

"Oh, Thulani?" said Larissa.

"Yebo."

"Oh ..."

Larissa suddenly paused and turned round to look at Peter with a stunned look on her face.

"What?" said Peter.

She looked at the gardener, then at Peter, then back at the gardener.

"Um ... thank you," she said.

She then grabbed Peter by the arm and pulled him round some other bushes so that they were out of sight, apparently forgetting that she wasn't speaking to him.

"In the letters we read last night," she said in a hushed voice, "didn't Mandla say his sister married somebody Msimang?"

Peter thought about it and nodded.

"Ja, I think you're right," he said. "How on earth did you remember that?"

Larissa ignored the question. "Thulani is probably related!" she said. "Maybe he knows more about what happened with Mandla!"

"Those letters were from, like, the thirties," said Peter. "Thulani's not *that* old."

"Well, he might know *something*. We could at least ask."

"Oh, ja," said Peter, "that'd be a great conversation: 'Hey, Thulani, we were snooping around the dead lady's room, you know, on the third floor where we weren't supposed to be; anyway, do you know anything about her secret affair?'"

Larissa was giving him the same look she had given him the previous night just before she stopped talking to him, and he quickly changed his tune.

"But you're right," he said. "It's worth a shot."

Her face lit up with a smile, and a wave of relief rushed over him.

"Good," she said. "Let's try to find Thulani and ask him if he's got some time to speak to us—preferably in private."

"Cool," said Peter.

Together, they started walking back up to the house. About halfway up, Larissa stopped and looked at Peter. "Thank you for coming to apologize," she said.

Peter just nodded, and they carried on walking.

Chapter 9

They found Brian coming down the stairs and asked him if he knew where Thulani was.

"Why do you need Thulani?" Brian asked. "Perhaps I could help you rather?"

"Oh, um ... no, thank you," said Larissa. "We just want to ask him some things."

"I assure you there's nothing Thulani can help you with that I can't," said Brian.

"No, we don't need help with anything," said Larissa. "It's personal stuff."

"Alright, if you're sure," said Brian. "I would assume he's at his house. But it's a bit late now, I'm afraid. Dinner will be ready in about half an hour—you'll have to speak to him another time. Say, you haven't by any chance seen Phillip, have you? I'm supposed to give him his medication, but I can't find him anywhere."

"No, I don't think so," said Larissa.

"Not to worry," said Brian. "See you at dinner."

Peter waited until Brian had disappeared through the narrow passage under the stairs before speaking. "Did I understand correctly that Thulani won't be having dinner with us?" he asked.

"I guess it makes sense," Larissa shrugged. "He's got his own house and his own family."

"Feels a bit weird," said Peter. "He's basically part of this family."

Larissa nodded her agreement. Just then, Phillip came strolling out from the narrow passage Brian had just gone through, carrying his hipflask.

"Oh, hi there, Mr. D'Arcy!" Larissa said just as he had taken a sip, which startled him, and he hurried to put the hipflask away.

"Oh, uh ... hi there, umm ..."

"Larissa," she reminded him with a smile.

"Larissa!" said Phillip. "That's right!"

"Did Brian find you?" she asked.

"Excuse me?"

"Brian," said Larissa. "He was just looking for you. Did he find you?"

"Oh, no, I haven't seen Brian," said Phillip.

"Oh," Larissa frowned. "He just went that way." She pointed back the way Phillip had come.

"Oh, well, you know ... big house," said Phillip. "Anyway, cheerio."

And with that he walked off in the other direction, reaching for his hipflask again.

Larissa looked at Peter. "That was a bit weird, wasn't it?" she asked.

"Ja, it was a bit," said Peter. "Although I'm never quite sure with that old man."

Larissa nodded, still watching where Phillip had gone; then she sighed and returned her attention to Peter.

"So, what now?" asked Peter.

"You heard Brian; we'll have to go after dinner," said Larissa.

"That's ... not exactly what he said."

"I'm gonna go shower in the meantime. See you later."

At dinner, everybody was seated in roughly the same places as on the first night. Peter was once again in between his parents and Phillip.

They were served a wonderfully creamy pasta dish, which Peter lapped up while Phillip narrated more accounts of their family history. When Vuyo came round with the wine this time, Peter was sure to have a glass. His dad eyed him curiously but didn't say anything. Phillip, on the other hand, was delighted that they would be having a drink together.

Once again, Peter stole a peek to the other end of the table, and, once again, Larissa and Daniel were having a fat chat. He tried not to let it bother him and resisted the urge to look up again.

By the time dinner was wrapping up, it was nearly eight o'clock and completely dark outside. Peter was about to help himself to another bowl of ice cream when Larissa came to find him.

"I think we should go see Thulani soon, before it gets too late," she said.

"You don't think it's already too late?"

"Worst-case scenario, he tells us to come back tomorrow."

"Worst-case scenario, we wake him up and he shouts at us for coming so late!"

"He's not asleep yet," said Larissa. "His lights are still on."

She pointed out the window to Thulani's house on the hill. Peter couldn't argue with that. They agreed to quickly get ready and meet outside the front door in ten minutes.

"And I think it would be easier if we didn't have to explain ourselves to too many people," said Larissa, "so try not to be seen on your way out."

Peter went to brush his teeth, put on some shoes and grab a sweater, then made his way down the stairs. Some people were having a conversation in the doorway to the dining room, so he slipped into the bathroom until he heard their conversation was over, then hurried out the front door before anyone else came.

"Took you long enough," Larissa said when he found her waiting on a bench out of sight from the front door.

They made their way through the garden in the dark, went through the little garden gate and closed it quietly behind them, and then they were on the track that led past the dam to Thulani's house.

"So, how are we going to broach this topic without telling Thulani that we were going through those letters?" asked Peter.

"I've been thinking about that," said Larissa. "The best I've come up with is that we say my great-grandmother had told me more about Patricia that wasn't mentioned in the eulogy, and we try steer the conversation toward Mandla somehow."

"So, is your great-grandmother the Alice from the letters?" Peter asked.

"Ja, I asked my gran; she used to be Alice Rutherford."

"Okay, that could work," said Peter. "If he knew her as well. But if we have to explain the tenuous connection before we even bring Mandla into the conversation, it could just raise more questions."

"I'm sure they would've met," said Larissa. "How long has Thulani been on the farm?"

"I don't know," said Peter. "If he *is* related to Mandla, then he's probably been here a while. If not … well, then it's going to beg the question why we came to visit him at all—let alone this late at night."

They passed the dam in the moonlight and climbed the hill to Thulani's house. Peter, in front, went to knock on the door, but hesitated. "I'm still not sure that I'm entirely comfortable with this," he said.

"Oh, come on!"

Larissa shoved past him and gave the door two knocks. A few moments later the door opened and a rather surprised and confused-looking Thulani was staring at them. His large figure took up the entire doorway. "Yes?" he said. "How can I help you?"

"Good evening," Larissa said politely. "Sorry to bother you so late, we were just hoping we could chat to you quickly?"

Thulani, no less confused than when he had first opened the door, looked from Larissa to Peter, then back to Larissa, then peered into the darkness behind them as though it might provide some answers. "Just the two of you?" he asked.

"Um ... yes," said Larissa, glancing at Peter.

Eventually Thulani just shrugged. "Alright," he said, standing back to allow them through. "Ngesihle, we have visitors."

Ngesihle was busy in the kitchen. It was small, just big enough to squeeze in a table with four chairs.

"This is Peter and Larissa."

"Very nice to meet you," Ngesihle said with a smile. "Can I make you some coffee?"

"Please!" said Larissa.

"Any chance I could have some tea?" said Peter.

"Of course!"

Thulani sat down and motioned for them to do the same. "I'm afraid we have to speak quietly," he said. "The grandchildren are asleep in the next room."

"Not a problem," Larissa said as she and Peter sat down.

"So, Peter, was that you I saw on a horse this afternoon?" Thulani asked.

"Oh, yes, it was," said Peter. "Me and Ellen."

Larissa looked at him with an expression somewhere between shock and jealousy.

"That's good," said Thulani. "These horses don't get out as much as they used to. Did you enjoy it?"

"Oh, ja, it was the best!" said Peter, remembering what Ellen had said. He could see on Larissa's face that Ellen had been right.

"That's good, that's good," Thulani laughed. "I used to enjoy riding as well, you know."

"Enjoy?" Ngesihle said as she joined them at the table and handed each of them their cups. "You were scared of the horses!"

They all laughed as they took their drinks.

"To be honest, I'm also scared of horses," said Peter. "Ellen coerced me into riding."

"You get used to them the more you ride," said Thulani. "I used to ride around the farm a lot."

"How long ago was that?" Larissa asked innocently, with a pointed glance at Peter.

"Let's see …" said Thulani, leaning back to think. "I'm about sixty now …"

"Mmhm," Ngesihle called him out, pulling her cheek in a sarcastic expression.

Thulani's smirk suggested he had rounded down generously.

"It must be about ten years now since I rode a horse," he said.

Larissa gave Peter another glance as though this was somehow significant, but as far as Peter was concerned this didn't tell them anything. Thulani being on the farm ten years ago didn't necessarily mean he knew Alice—or Mandla, for that matter. He turned to Ngesihle. "He used to be scared?" said Peter. "How long ago was that?"

A smile broke across her face, and she looked at Thulani, reminiscing. "When he was learning," she said. "Shame, he was so bad!"

"Unamanga! I was good!"

"He thought all the girls were smiling at him, but we were just laughing at him!"

"But now you have married me, so it worked!" Thulani said smugly, and they all laughed.

"So, you both grew up here?" said Larissa.

"Yes, we grew up in the village," said Thulani, pointing somewhere over his shoulder. "Our ancestors have lived on this land for many generations, long before the white man arrived."

"And you've lived here your whole life?"

"No, no," Thulani shook his head. "We lived and worked in Joburg for many years. Then we came back here, I don't know?" He looked at Ngesihle. "Maybe thirty years ago?"

Ngesihle nodded. "Yebo."

"What made you come back?" Larissa asked.

"Patricia," said Thulani. "She asked me to come and work for her. I think it was always her plan. She sent me to study agriculture at Cedara College, where I was one of the few black people they had ever seen, and then, when Phillip was getting old, she contacted me and asked me to come and help on the farm. And I've been managing the farm since."

"I thought Brian was managing the farm?" said Peter.

Immediately the atmosphere became frosty. Thulani shrugged awkwardly.

"Ya, but nobody asked him to come," said Ngesihle. "He just arrived."

"Ngesihle, ngicela," said Thulani, raising his hand to ask for silence. He then smiled at them to change the subject. "So, what was it that you actually came to talk about?"

Peter and Larissa exchanged a look.

"Okay, well," Larissa said slowly, trying to find the right words, "we wanted to talk about Patricia. We wondered if, perhaps … there were some parts of her life that weren't mentioned in the eulogy yesterday."

"She lived for a hundred and five years," Thulani said, a curious frown creeping onto his face. "It would be difficult to include everything in a ten-minute eulogy. What did you think was left out?"

"Well … what did she do when she left school, for example?"

Thulani dismissed any thought of intrigue with a shrug. "As far as I know, she came back to the farm. She taught the local children, like my father, and then me, and she managed the farm until Phillip came in about the seventies."

"Is that all?" Larissa asked. "There were never any stories of her, like … running away, or anything?"

Thulani's eyes narrowed as he shook his head. "Not that I know of," he said. "Why? Do you have reason to believe that she did?"

Larissa glanced nervously at Peter again. "No, no, I just thought, maybe …"

"Perhaps you should be asking someone else these things," said Thulani. "Phillip, maybe. He would know better than me."

"The thing is, my great-grandmother knew Patricia very well," said Larissa. "Better than anyone, probably. Perhaps you knew her—Alice Brookes?"

Thulani considered the name and nodded thoughtfully. "Yes, I met her a few times," he said. "Jane's mother?"

"Yes, exactly!" said Larissa. "She told me a lot about Patricia, but I feel like we're missing pieces of the story. The reason we came to you is because she also mentioned Jabu Msimang, and we thought you might be related?"

Thulani frowned. "Jabu Msimang was my grandmother," he said. "What did she have to do with anything?"

Larissa gave Peter a quick, excited glance. "Alice, my great-grandmother, told me about a boy," she went on. "One of Jabu's brothers. She said Patricia became very close to him. We thought you might be able to tell us more about him. A boy called Mandla …"

She let the name hang in the air to see if Thulani recognized it.

Thulani stared at her, not giving anything away until eventually he spoke. "That," he said slowly, "is a name I have not heard for a very, very long time."

Larissa resisted exchanging another look with Peter. "So … what do you know about him?" she asked.

Thulani raised his chin. His entire demeanor had gone from relaxed and curious to stiff and guarded. "What do *you* know about him?"

"Only what Alice told me," she said. "She made it sound like they had been … in love."

Thulani eyed Larissa for a long time before nodding slowly.

"Yes, that is what my grandmother told me as well."

"Which is why I wondered if they ran away together?" said Larissa.

Now Thulani shook his head solemnly. "No, they never ran away together," he said.

"Are you sure?" she pressed, getting a little too excited. "Because it seemed like—from what Alice told me, I mean—it seemed like they wanted to?"

"I can't say what they wanted to do," said Thulani, "but I know that they never ran away."

"But then what happened to Mandla?" said Larissa. "Why do we never hear about him?"

Again, Thulani eyed her for a long time. "You don't know what happened to Mandla?" he said.

"I don't even know who Mandla is," said Larissa. "I thought we were going to hear about him in the eulogy, but all Brian said was that Patricia never found love, which is rubbish!"

"I don't think Brian was being purposefully deceitful," said Thulani. "I think he didn't know about Mandla. Not many people do. In the village there used to be lots of stories about him, but that was a long time ago. No one remembers anymore."

"Do you remember the stories?"

Thulani nodded while taking a sip of coffee. "My grandmother and my father also told me about him," he said.

"So, who was he?" Larissa asked. "How did Patricia meet him?"

Thulani took another long sip of coffee before he answered. "He was a local boy from the village, like me," he said. "Patricia met him in homeschool. Patricia's mother homeschooled some of the children from the town, as well as some of the local children. Mandla was a few years older than Patricia, but they were taught together. That's how they became friends. But everyone knew of him. He was tall and handsome and charismatic. And they say he was very clever. *Very* clever. There was no high school for black children, but he would steal books from the Woodwrights and teach himself. He taught himself about law, championed black workers' rights on the farm. There were lots of stories about how he helped this and that person when they were mistreated, or in trouble, and how he stood up to the white man. Harold Woodwright—that's Patricia's father, who owned the farm at that time—he never liked Mandla because he wasn't as ... *compliant* as the other workers and made his life difficult. So Mandla made quite a name for himself. Everyone in the village knew him and respected him, even though he was still only a young man."

He paused to take a sip of coffee.

"So, what happened to him?" Larissa asked.

Thulani told her with his hand to slow down while he drank his coffee.

"First," he said after he swallowed, "Patricia came back to the farm after she finished school, and the two of them used to see each other in secret. You must understand, it was unheard of for a white woman to be with a black man, so they only met at night and didn't tell anyone about it. But parents are not stupid. Patricia's father found out about Mandla. You can understand how furious he was. Not only was she going behind his back to see a black man, but it was the one man whom he liked the least. He wanted Mandla gone. So maybe they did want to run away. I could believe that."

"What makes you so sure that they didn't?" Larissa asked.

Thulani looked at her with a stern gaze as he took another sip from his coffee cup.

"Because one day the police arrived to arrest Mandla," he said. "The night before, some men had been on their way to Woodwright Manor, carrying something very valuable, when they were hijacked. All of their belongings were stolen. Harold

Woodwright used this as the opportunity he had been waiting for. As soon as he heard about it, he phoned the police and accused Mandla. The police came immediately. Mandla was put into handcuffs and taken away. He told his family not to worry, that it was just a mistake and they would release him soon. Later that day, the Woodwrights were informed that Mandla had attempted to escape, a struggle ensued, and Mandla was shot."

Larissa covered her mouth with her hands. Peter sat frozen in shock.

Thulani used the silence to take another sip of coffee. "But my father was there that day," he said, putting the cup down. "He was only a young boy at the time and didn't understand what was happening, but he said he remembered it clearly. Mandla had been home the entire night. They had heard about the hijacking, and in the morning when they saw the police coming, he quickly took out a shoebox with a bunch of letters, wrote a short note on a scrap piece of paper, and told my father to take them to Patricia, but not to let anyone else see him. My father ran off just before the police got there, and that was the last time he saw Mandla.

"So was there actually a struggle? Had he actually tried to escape? My grandmother did not think so. She said Mandla was a calm and rational man, and he knew the law. He would never have tried to escape when he knew they would have to let him go. Everyone in the village was sure that it had been arranged by Harold Woodwright."

He took one more conclusive sip of coffee. "That is how I know they did not run away together."

There was long silence as Peter and Larissa tried to gather themselves.

"That is horrific," Larissa eventually said.

Thulani shrugged. "That was South Africa in the thirties."

Peter looked around at their small kitchen and the basic items they had in it. Soon he would go back to the manor that the

Woodwrights had built on the land they had taken from Thulani's ancestors. The manor that Harold Woodwright had once lived in. And Peter was his direct descendant. He would climb two flights of stairs and get into a bed that had been made for him by a maid whose name he didn't even know, but whose ancestors were probably also from the area and had been displaced, if not by the Woodwrights then by one of the neighboring farms.

Larissa cleared her throat and gathered herself. "Brian didn't mention *any* of that in the eulogy," she said.

Thulani pulled his cheek in a callous shrug. "Brian has only been here about five years," he said. "He didn't know her very well. There are lots of things he didn't mention about her."

"What else wasn't mentioned?" Larissa asked.

"No major life events that I know of," said Thulani, "but she had a lot of hobbies that were a major part of her life. She liked gardening. She liked puzzles and riddles. She knew Morse code."

"And she played the piano," said Peter. "She taught Ms. O'Sullivan."

Thulani was taken aback.

"You know Ms. O'Sullivan?" he said.

"My dad does," said Peter. "We did some work for her last week. That day we met at the museum, actually," he added, turning to Larissa.

"Oh, so you didn't go all the way to Pietermaritzburg on a Monday just to look at the museum," Larissa teased. "Not so sophisticated after all. Good thing you never tried to pretend you were having a business call."

"Well, technically, when my dad called me it actually *was* to help him with business, so—"

"Hang on," Thulani interrupted. "Did you say you did work for Ms. O'Sullivan on Monday?"

"Umm, ja," said Peter, quickly making sure he had remembered correctly.

"Where?" Thulani asked with a slight raise of his head.

"At her office; what's it called? The O'Sullivan and something law firm."

"Woolfe," said Thulani, still eyeing him.

"Woolfe, that's the one. O'Sullivan and Woolfe."

"And did you see Ms. O'Sullivan?"

"Ja, she came in briefly and left almost immediately," said Peter. "I think she said she was in court the whole day. Why?"

"Because I was also there on Monday," said Thulani. "I was delivering a letter to her, but she wasn't there, so the receptionist convinced me to leave it with her. When I phoned her that evening to check that she had received it, the letter was gone. She never got it. I watched the receptionist put it in her pigeonhole, but she checked the pigeonhole and it wasn't there. The receptionist doesn't know what happened to it."

"What was it about?" Peter asked. "Was it important?"

"I don't know what it was about, but Patricia said it was very important. And very confidential. She was concerned that somebody else might try to see it."

"And then it went missing?" said Larissa, shocked.

Thulani nodded solemnly.

"Do you think … someone took it?" she said.

Thulani shrugged. "That seems to be the only explanation."

"And what did she say after it had been taken?"

"Unfortunately, it was the day before she died. I never got to tell her."

"But wait a second," said Peter. "Who could have taken it? How did anyone even know about the letter?"

"Patricia was very worried that someone was watching her, even when she gave it to me. Perhaps she was right."

"Watching her? Where?" said Larissa, fearing she already knew the answer. "Here? At Woodwright Manor?"

Again, Thulani nodded solemnly.

"Who could it have been?" Peter asked. "Who was here at the time?"

"Lots of people," said Thulani. "Patricia was sick and a lot of people were coming to see her. It could have been anyone. But ..." he paused, peering out of the window into the darkness. "Everyone who was visiting was family. And everyone who was here then is still here now."

Peter and Larissa exchanged wide-eyed glances. Ngesihle stared at Thulani with a scared expression. The room was quiet.

"But listen," said Thulani, looking at Peter and Larissa with concern, "the only other people who know about the letter are Brian and Ms. O'Sullivan. Brian wants us to keep this strictly confidential until we know what is going on. You have to promise me that you won't tell anyone about this—not even your parents."

"Absolutely," said Larissa.

"We promise," said Peter.

Thulani nodded, then glanced out of the window again. "It's very late now," he said. "I think it's time for you to go back."

They thanked Thulani and Ngesihle for the tea and coffee, and Thulani let them out.

"Wait," Thulani said just as they were leaving. They both turned round to look at him. "Your great grandmother, Alice ... did she ever mention anything about a lion's tail?"

Larissa stared at him blankly. "What do you mean?"

"Something Patricia told me the day before she died: 'The lion has a tail that goes in its mouth.' I don't know what she was talking about. But she said it used to belong to a dear friend of hers. I thought perhaps that friend might have been Alice. She never mentioned it?"

Larissa shook her head. "No. Sorry."

"What do you think that lion tail thing is all about?" Peter said as they made their way down the hill by moonlight once more.

"I don't know," said Larissa. "I'm still a bit rattled by that story about Mandla. And someone taking the letter and everything."

"To be honest," said Peter, "I don't think he was telling us the full story."

"What do you mean?"

"Today, my parents found out that an autopsy had been performed on Patricia after she died. My mom didn't think it was a big deal, but my dad said it was strange to perform an autopsy on a sickly hundred-and-five-year-old unless there was a reason for it. And it was especially strange that they didn't tell anyone about it."

"What are you saying?"

"Don't you think it's weird that this letter to her executor gets mysteriously intercepted and then she dies the next day? I mean, my mom told me the inheritance won't be worth that much, but maybe she's wrong. Maybe someone knows something the rest of us don't."

Larissa looked up at Peter. "Are you saying you think this person killed her? You realize it's someone in the family?"

"My mom reckons the autopsy was inconclusive, so I don't know," said Peter. "But just the fact that they performed an autopsy means I'm not the only one. I think that's why they didn't want anyone going down that passage on the third floor—it's basically a crime scene."

Larissa pulled her cardigan tighter around her and folded her arms against her chest. "Suppose you're right," she said, "suppose someone did kill Patricia ... who could it have been? I mean, think about everyone who's here—no one exactly seems like the type, do they? But it could be anyone."

"Well, it can't be *anyone*," said Peter. "It had to be someone who was already staying here before she died. So that at least rules my family out."

"Mine too," said Larissa. "Who all were here at the time?"

"No idea. Thulani couldn't even say for certain."

"I think Megan said they had been here for a while already."

"The Van der Westhuizens were also here," said Peter, remembering when they had come for tea.

"But, I mean … surely they couldn't do something that awful? They seem like such nice people! Megan's parents as well; sure, they bicker about Kim and everything, but they wouldn't … you know …"

Peter shrugged. "We don't know for sure that someone did kill her," he said, but even he wasn't convinced by his words. Larissa didn't say anything.

"Jesse and them will probably still be up," said Peter, changing the subject. "Are you going to join them?"

"No, I'm tired," Larissa sighed. "And, to be honest, after that whole conversation I'm not really in the mood for their banter. Besides, that'll just raise too many questions about where we've been."

They reached the little garden gate and made their way in silence to the front door.

Larissa paused to take a nervous breath. "Do your best not to be seen," she whispered, and took the door handle.

But the door just rattled slightly and didn't move. She tried again; it was definitely locked.

"Dammit!" she said through her teeth.

She craned her neck to look around the side of the house. "Maybe there's another way in …"

"I don't think it's such a big deal," said Peter. "Let's just knock for someone to let us in; it's not the end of the world if people know we went to speak to Thulani."

Larissa stared at him incredulously. "Clearly you don't have African parents," she said. "I can't just go wandering around at night! With a boy, nogal! I'll get the hiding of my life."

"Just tell them we went to see Thulani. He can back us up."

Larissa laughed humorlessly. "You think my dad is going to wait for an explanation? No. If he sees me, I'm done. Also, Thulani made us promise not to tell anyone what we were speaking about. And we can't tell anyone why we went there in the first place. So really, the less people know, the better."

"Ellen noticed we disappeared last night," said Peter. "She'll probably have noticed again tonight. And she might not be the only one."

"Ja, well, Ellen can think we've been making out for all I care—she's not the one who's about to give me a hiding."

She started looking around as though there might be another entrance they could use.

"I'm pretty sure if this door's locked, they're all locked," said Peter.

Larissa sighed. "Okay, fine," she said. "We'll knock. But quietly—I don't want to alert the whole house."

Peter took one of the lion knockers and gently tapped the door. He wasn't sure it was loud enough for anyone to hear, but soon enough the key was turning in the door and then Brian was staring at them, as surprised and confused as Thulani had been when they knocked on his door.

"What in heaven's name are you two doing out there?" he said.

"We went to visit Thulani," said Peter. "We told you, remember? Before dinner?"

"So late?" said Brian. "Come inside, quickly! It's not safe."

Larissa gave Peter a curious glance, but before they could ascertain why Brian would say that, Larissa's dad appeared.

"There you are!" he shouted, and Larissa's face fell.

He proceeded to berate her at a volume loud enough to attract some attention, and although the words were Zulu, the tone was pretty universal. While she was being chastised, Peter's dad stuck his head round the door to see what all the commotion was about. "What's going on?" he asked Peter.

"Nothing, Dad, I promise! We just went to visit Thulani; nothing's going on!"

"Alright, slow down," his dad said. "I'm not accusing you of anything. What were you doing visiting Thulani? And so late?"

"Nothing!" said Peter. "Larissa's great-gran knew him, so she just wanted to ask him about her."

"Okay, okay," said his dad. "But, Peter, you know it's irresponsible to go off at night without telling anyone."

"Ja, I guess."

They watched Larissa's dad shout something with his hand pointing up the stairs, and Larissa skulked off, hanging her head.

"You'd best get to bed as well," said Martin. "We don't want to cause any more trouble. And, Peter?" he added as Peter began to turn away, "no more wandering around at night, okay?"

Peter nodded, then followed Larissa up the stairs. He caught up to her by the third floor.

"I'm sorry," he said. "I feel partially responsible for that."

"No worries," said Larissa. "Nothing I'm not used to by now. I actually got off lightly."

"I guess that means no more sneaking off at night for the two of us," said Peter.

Larissa stopped at her door with the slightest hint of a sneaky grin.

"We'll see," she said, and went into her room.

Chapter 10

Next morning, the boys were once again woken by Carol van der Westhuizen. "Come on!" she said. "The sun is shining; it's a beautiful day! Up, up, up!"

They all moaned and groaned and turned over in their beds.

"Don't be lazy!" she said. "Jacky tells me the girls are all up already. Come on; quick breakfast and then we're going to the Drakensberg!"

Slowly the boys started getting up and getting dressed, and eventually made their way down to breakfast.

Larissa was sitting between Katie and Megan, and Daniel made it his business to sit directly opposite her. Peter sat at the end again, and Larissa gave him a smile.

"Larissa, where'd you go last night?" Daniel wasted no time asking what had clearly been on his mind.

"Wouldn't you like to know," she said casually, chewing a piece of bacon.

Daniel didn't know how to respond and dropped the subject. Ellen looked at Peter with a smirk, and he quickly looked back at his food.

After breakfast they all got ready with walking shoes and rain jackets in case of another afternoon thundershower and helped pack the cars with picnic blankets and camping chairs. The

Greenacres shared a lift with Peter's family, and all piled into their Fortuner. Frank Greenacre was an ecologist and spent the drive telling them about the Drakensberg's geology, the vegetation, and which animals they might see if they were lucky.

They drove back through Underberg, then turned off onto a gravel road that took them through plantations and dairy farms. Soon they passed through a gate with a sign that read *Cobham*, stopped to sign in at the office where Frank bought a map of the area, and then parked in the day visitors' parking under a large oak tree.

"Alright," Frank called to everyone once they had all parked and were out of their cars. "There are two options: for the smaller kids, and anyone else who wants to take it easy this morning, there's a short walk to a nice waterfall that way." He pointed down one of the paths leading away and across the river. "And for the older kids, and anyone up for something a little more strenuous, there is some really neat San rock art up the valley."

He seemed to be pointing more to the top of the mountain than just up the valley.

"I think I'll go with the smaller kids," Megan started saying.

"Oh no, you don't!" Larissa pulled her back into the group with the older kids.

Only three of the adults joined for the hike to the rock art; everyone else opted for the shorter hike and an early lunch. The older kids, however, were not given an option.

Jesse led the way, setting off at a brisk pace. They went through a little riverine woodland of small shrub-like trees, and then out into the open grassland, always within hearing distance of the water running over the boulders in the riverbed.

It was at least five minutes before Jesse and Daniel had their shirts off, claiming it was too hot in the sun. Peter admitted to himself that if he was that well built, he would also find any excuse to take his shirt off in front of girls.

He hung back from the other boys in the hope that Larissa might catch up to him, but when he glanced back, she was far behind with Megan and Katie, chatting and laughing and in absolutely no rush to catch up with anyone.

At one point, he stopped and looked back the way they had come, but the picnic area where they had parked was already hidden behind a hill. He slowly turned, and for miles in every direction he could see nothing but the mountains and the valleys, blue sky and green slopes, meandering rivers with boulders and pools.

"What are you doing?"

Ellen caught up to him while he was standing in the middle of the path.

"Look," said Peter, "you can't see a single man-made thing anywhere."

Ellen slowly turned around as Peter had just done. "Oh my gosh, you're right!" she said.

For a few moments the two of them stood quietly, admiring their surroundings, until Peter finally started walking again and Ellen broke the silence. "So ..." she said, as though they were moving on to business now.

Peter laughed. "I know what you want to talk about."

"Is it?" said Ellen. "So, what do you have to say for yourself?"

"It's not what you think."

"Oh, ja? And what do I think?"

"You know what you think."

"Yes, obviously *I* know what I think. But do *you* know what I think?"

"Yes, I do," Peter laughed. "But there's nothing going on between us."

"I think it's cute," said Ellen.

"Again," said Peter, "it's not what you think."

"So you apologized to her?"

"I did."

"Good on you. And did you tell her about horse riding?"

"Sort of," said Peter. "I told someone else so she could hear."

"Really?" Ellen said with a put-on impressed tone. "Perhaps there's hope for you after all."

They walked together for about half an hour until they heard Frank call out from the back for Jesse and the other boys up front to stop and wait where the path passed between the river and a huge boulder.

"I think this is a good spot for a quick rest," Frank said once everyone had gathered there. "We've got a big climb after this, so have a drink here and refill your bottles."

"Where are we supposed to fill our bottles?" asked Michelle.

"Just from the river," said Frank.

Michelle looked at him like he was a lunatic. "You're not being serious?" she said. "We can't drink river water!"

"It's perfectly safe," Frank said with a bit of a laugh. "In fact, this is some of the cleanest water you'll ever drink."

"But ... it's from a *river*!" said Michelle.

"Where do you think that spring water you buy comes from?" Austen chimed in.

"From a spring!" said Michelle.

"And where do you think *this* water comes from?"

"From ... I don't know ... the ground, or something!"

"Ja, you're right ..." said Austen, pretending to think about it. "I wonder if there's a word for that ..."

Jesse and Daniel proceeded to put their faces in the water and drink straight from the river. Michelle eventually conceded the point and dipped her bottle into the water, then inspected it carefully for any bogies before taking a very cautious sip.

Once they had all filled their bottles and rested for a little while, Jesse carried on leading the way, and soon Frank was telling them to turn left up the slope. It didn't take long before Peter was gasping for breath, taking slow, sluggish steps and using his hands to push off the rocks whenever he could. Luckily, he wasn't the only one. Almost everybody seemed to be struggling. Jesse and Daniel had powered on up ahead, keen to show off their fitness, and Austen, Katie, and Larissa appeared to be coping just fine. Everybody else seemed to be secretly hoping that Frank would tell them to stop for a break any minute now.

They reached the top of a great plateau, and then it was the final ascent to their destination: a layer of sandstone in the mountainside that made a cave-like overhang, and all along the sandstone walls, in inks of charcoal and ochre, were some of the last signs of an ancient people who used to live in these mountains.

"Wow," said Megan.

She reached out to feel it with her hand, but Frank stopped her.

"Please don't touch it," he said. "This rock art has been here for hundreds of years, and if everyone started touching it, it would rub off within a couple of months."

"Do you know how old it is?" Karen asked.

"I'm not sure about this particular site, but I think most of the rock art in the Berg is from the last thousand years," said Frank. "I think the oldest site is about two and a half thousand years old."

There were paintings of humans and animals and other human-like figures that made them all wonder what kinds of things the people had seen back then. They walked the length of the wall looking at all the art, trying to guess what the different scenes were attempting to portray, and discussing why they thought the San painted them.

Peter, still drenched in sweat from the climb, sat down to look out over the plain and at the mountains, and downed half his bottle of water. The escarpment rose out of the earth like a great wall, stretching far into the distance in both directions. He could see the famous Rhino Peak away to the south, and the two peaks of the Giant's Cup towering above them.

"Quite a view," Larissa said as she sat down on a rock next to him.

Peter was suddenly very conscious of how sweaty he was.

"The Zulu name is 'uKhahlamba,'" she said. "It means 'barrier of spiers.'"

"Pretty apt," said Peter, and for a while they just sat in silence, taking in the grandeur of the mountains. "Sorry about last night," Peter eventually said. "I never realized, you know …"

"No, you have nothing to be sorry about," said Larissa. "I knew the risks I was taking. We'll just have to be more careful from now on."

"From now on? But … we already found out what happened with Mandla—he was arrested and killed, so they never ran away together."

"But why?" Larissa turned to him. "Why was he arrested? And what happened to the last letter he was waiting for from Patricia? I feel like there's more to this story. Not to mention," she lowered her voice, "the things Thulani told us about that person who intercepted the letter to her executor."

"What exactly are you suggesting?"

"Not sure," said Larissa. "We could try that secret room again. We didn't check everything in there; there could well be things that'll give us more clues."

"You want to go back to the place that's off limits because it's probably a crime scene, even after we've already been scolded once?"

"If it's off limits, it's because there's something to find."

"Larissa, I think you're being a bit cavalier about this! If it *is* a crime scene, that means someone here—*someone among us*—did that to her … I don't think they'll be too chuffed to find a couple of kids poking around!"

"Peter, if someone did this they need to be caught!"

"I don't think that's our business," said Peter. "I'm more worried about our safety. You saw how concerned Brian looked last night—"

"Hey, Larissa!" Daniel's voice interrupted them. "Come look at this!"

Larissa gave Peter one more straight-faced glare to let him know she didn't agree before she got up to go see what Daniel was looking at, leaving Peter to turn his attention back to the view of the mountains.

The walk back was much easier, being almost entirely downhill or flat. Daniel, who had successfully asserted his dominance by being the first one up the mountain, now hung back to talk to Larissa. Peter couldn't help thinking that she would still be walking with him if it wasn't for Daniel being so eager; he blamed himself for not being more assertive. The walking helped take his mind off it: he got into a rhythm and let his mind wander as he walked. He thought about what Larissa had just been saying, and about the first time they went sneaking around the third floor the night of the funeral, with all the letters; and then last night when they had gone to see Thulani ...

And then he suddenly realized something—something that Thulani had said.

Peter stopped dead in his tracks and turned around to look for Larissa, but she was still with Daniel. Should he interrupt them the way Daniel had just done when Peter was speaking to her? No, he would have to wait for a better time.

They arrived back at the picnic site to cheers from everyone else. The waterfall hikers had returned a while ago, and lunch was already on the go. Peter quickly found his parents and sister and dived right in. He kept glancing up at Larissa, waiting for a chance to tell her what he had thought of, but she was always busy talking with someone else: if it wasn't Megan, it was Katie, and if it wasn't Katie, it was her parents. No matter who she was talking to, Daniel was always only a few feet away.

After lunch, everyone changed into swimsuits and headed down to the river. Steven, who had been to Cobham before, led the older kids across the rickety old swing bridge and a short way up the path to a spot where the river made a sharp turn, with a ledge and a deep pool below, perfect for swimming. Daniel was obviously the first one in the water.

"How is it?" Kyle asked.

"It's beautiful, you ous have to get in."

As if anyone wasn't going to get in without his encouragement. It's only the reason they came here.

"Looks a bit nippy," said Austen.

"Bru, trust me."

He wasn't wrong. The cold water was a relief after walking in the sun the whole day; Peter could feel his core temperature dropping as he wallowed in the water. Steven then jumped in off the ledge, and of course they all had to line up and take turns jumping in after that. They reveled in the water for so long that they actually got cold, and needed to get out to soak up some sun, laying their towels out on flat rocks. Daniel didn't even attempt to be subtle about spreading his towel out next to Larissa's. He lay on his side on one elbow, and the two of them chatted and laughed for the better part of their remaining time there. He seemed to be in his element whenever his shirt was off, which was most of the time. Peter looked around for Ellen, but she was with Michelle, so he just closed his eyes, listened to the river, and felt the sun on his back.

When Frank Greenacre arrived to tell them it was time to pack up and leave, Peter had almost fallen asleep. Slowly everyone started getting up and dusting off their towels in no real rush. Peter saw the opportunity and tried to catch Larissa's eye. Eventually, she looked at him, and he raised a subtle hand to tell her to wait. She seemed to get the message because she started wasting even more time than everyone else.

"What's up?" she asked once the others had all started to leave.

"I've been thinking about what Thulani told us about Mandla," Peter said in a low voice as he started leading them away from the river, far behind everyone else. "About the day he was arrested."

"Ja?" said Larissa.

"He said that Mandla took a bunch of letters and wrote a note, and then sent them to Patricia with the young boy—Thulani's father."

He glanced back and Larissa nodded.

"Those were obviously the letters we were reading," said Peter, "and the note was the very last one. That's why Patricia had both sets of letters."

"Ja, I actually managed to work that out on my own," said Larissa. "I thought it was kind of obvious."

"It *was* obvious," said Peter. "Hence my use of the word 'obviously.' I'm not done."

"Oh. Sorry."

"Two things," said Peter. "Firstly, you might remember that in the final note he said something like *they'll know what we had planned*."

Larissa gasped as she realized Peter was right.

"Do you think it *was* them who hijacked those people?!" she asked. "As part of their plan to run away?"

"Well ... I don't know," said Peter. "Thulani said Mandla had been home the entire night, but—"

"But he could've been lying," said Larissa. "Or his dad could've been lying when he told him the story. Or maybe he's just remembering wrong because it was so long ago, and he's started believing what he wants to believe."

"I mean, any of those things are possible," said Peter, "but it doesn't make any sense. I can't remember exactly what the note said, but it didn't give me the impression that they were expecting the police to get involved."

Larissa thought about it. "Ja, you're right," she said. "Is there any way we could try to find out?"

"I don't know about *that*," said Peter, "but I did think of something else."

They heard voices from the river as they approached the bridge and they both fell silent. Some of the younger children were giving their parents a hard time, not wanting to leave the river, and their parents were dragging them away by their hands. Peter and Larissa stopped once they had crossed the bridge to let the others get ahead, waiting in the cover of a few small trees.

"You were saying?" said Larissa.

"Patricia and Mandla had been planning to run away for a while, and it sounded like they were about to do it. Mandla was just waiting for one more note to tell him when and where, which he never got, and then he got arrested so it never happened."

Larissa nodded.

"And they communicated by leaving letters for each other in a secret hiding place; some kind of tin in a hole under some tree," said Peter.

Larissa nodded again.

"*Except*," said Peter, "for the final note, which Thulani told us was in fact *delivered* to Patricia. It was never left in the tin."

Larissa looked at him quizzically. "So …?"

"What if Patricia *did* actually leave Mandla one last letter," said Peter, "only he never got it because he was arrested before he could go look? What if the final letter is still there in their secret hiding place—in the tin in the hole under the tree?"

"Yoh, that's quite a long shot," said Larissa. "And, anyway, how does that help us?"

Peter hesitated. "Because I think I know where their hiding place is."

They were interrupted by someone calling them.

"Peter! Larissa! We're leaving!"

"Okay, you're gonna have to tell me the rest of the story when we get home," said Larissa, "but I want to know everything!"

They emerged from the bushes and made their way back to the cars.

"Sorry, we just got caught up chatting!" Larissa told their concerned-looking parents.

Rebecca piped up with "Peter and Larissa, sitting in a tree!"

"Shut up, Becca!" Peter snapped at her, but Larissa just laughed.

Peter could tell he was blushing, so he got in the car as quickly as possible, trying not to look at Steven.

They arrived back at Woodwright Manor and the dogs came to greet them.

"Now I want you all to be showered and clean before dinner!" Carol called to all the kids while fending off an excited Trixy.

This time Larissa was the one trying to catch Peter's eye as everyone was getting out of their cars, and she gestured for them to go into the garden to talk. They found a bench next to a bird bath among some azaleas.

"You were saying you found their hiding place?" said Larissa.

"Well, I don't *know* that it's their hiding place," said Peter, "but I'm pretty sure. When we had the braai at the dam, I went for a walk up the stream, and I found an overgrown path that led to a little clearing with a tree in the middle—just like they talked about in the letters. And it had the letters 'M' and 'P' carved into the wood."

"Mandla and Patricia? That's definitely the place!" said Larissa. "I don't know if you're right about a letter still being there, but I'm keen to go check it out anyway."

"There won't be enough time to go now before dinner," said Peter. "We'll have to go another time."

"Let's go after dinner," said Larissa.

"After dinner? You're not serious?"

"When else could we go?" said Larissa. "We can't go during the day; it'll be too obvious. And, besides, the sooner the better."

"So, after what happened last night, you want to sneak out again?"

"We'll be more careful."

"Okay," Peter shrugged, "your funeral."

"Don't be so dramatic; I'll make a plan," she said. "Come, let's go back inside."

They started winding their way through the garden back to the front door, when they heard two voices behind a hedge.

"... you *must* know where it is!"

"Even if I did, I would be under no obligation to share that information."

They saw Thulani first, towering over the bushes. They rounded the hedge, and saw he was speaking to Father Ian.

"He drinks too much, Thulani, you know he does!" Father Ian was saying. "And I guarantee you he's there now. If we found him there, we could help him!"

"How much he drinks is completely up to him," said Thulani.

Just then Thulani noticed Peter and Larissa and looked greatly relieved to see them.

"Hi there, you two!" he exclaimed loudly. "How are you doing? How was the Berg?"

"Oh, the Berg was lovely!" Larissa replied, realizing what he was doing. "We went on a long hike to some rock paintings, swam in the river; you would have loved it! Why didn't you come along?"

"I have been many times," said Thulani. "I do love it. But we had things to do around here, unfortunately."

"Well," said Father Ian, smiling at all of them, "I had better go back. I'll see you all at dinner."

Once he had left, Thulani sighed with relief. "Thank you," he said, "that man is very persistent."

"What did he want?" Larissa asked.

"Oh, nothing; just to be let in on some of Woodwright Manor's well-kept secrets," Thulani said with a wink. "So, you say the Berg was good? You were there a long time?"

They didn't fail to notice the hasty change in topic and sensed he wasn't going to tell them any more about what Father Ian wanted. They dropped the subject and spoke about the Berg as Thulani inspected a few plants around the garden.

"You're quite passionate about gardening?" Larissa observed.

Thulani chuckled. "It's a hobby I picked up from Patricia. Except, I pay more attention to indigenous plants. She wanted whatever looked nice and didn't worry too much about where it came from. But there are enough beautiful plants that occur here naturally. I eventually want to remove all the exotic plants and replace them with indigenous species."

"Because it's better for the environment?"

"It is better for the environment," said Thulani. "Exotics can ruin the ecosystem. But it's more than that. For me, it almost feels like a link to my ancestors. When the colonizers came and appropriated these lands, they brought with them their own plants and trees to make it feel like the land they were used to. But when I walk on the land of my ancestors, I want to walk among the same plants that my ancestors did. Like this …" he said, lifting the leaf of an aloe with his finger. "Umhlabana. It was used to make muti for childbirth."

"You should've been an ecologist or something," said Peter.

Thulani smiled, still looking at the aloe leaves. "Yes, I would've enjoyed that," he said. "But in our culture, we have a duty to look after others in our family. The community cannot afford the luxury of someone with a tertiary education becoming an ecologist."

Peter didn't really know what to say and just nodded. But Thulani was already pointing out the next indigenous species he had planted, and slowly they ambled back to the house together, looking at plants.

Chapter 11

Dinner that night was much the same as the previous nights, except that Phillip had swapped places with a man named Greg. Greg was in his early thirties and one of the only people in the family older than twenty who was not yet married. He was completely bald and hilariously funny. He did most of the speaking around their part of the table, engaging everyone with enough banter to keep them all laughing, and even included Peter a couple of times, which Peter appreciated because it made him feel like one of the adults. For the first time since they had been there, he thought Larissa and Daniel were the ones missing out. He glanced up at their end of the table, feeling no disaffection when he saw them enjoying a chat. He also noticed Phillip trying to persuade the people next to him to have another glass of wine with him, and he felt a little bad for Phillip. He felt bad for even thinking it to himself, but he was glad that Phillip and Greg had swapped places.

When Peter went for another helping, still smiling to himself about some of the things Greg had been saying, Larissa once again found him at the serving table.

"Also getting seconds?" she said cheerfully.

"Um ... thirds, actually," said Peter.

"So, listen," she said in a slightly lower voice.

"You don't want to go anymore?" Peter guessed.

"No, I definitely still want to go!" she said scornfully. "*But* I think it would be best if nobody else knew."

"Wasn't that always the plan?"

"No, I mean nobody can even know that we're missing," said Larissa. "I don't even want Ellen to notice. Not just because of my dad, but after what Thulani was telling us about that letter that got intercepted, and what you were saying about the autopsy ... the more I think about it, the more I think something's up. Something weird. So, the less people know about us digging around in Patricia's affairs, the better."

"I've been thinking the same thing," said Peter. "So, what do you propose?"

"I propose we wait until everyone has gone to bed, and then we sneak out. We obviously can't use the front doors, though, because they lock them."

"I think they lock all the doors."

"Except the doors to the library balcony," said Larissa. "The keys for those are hanging on the wall right there."

Peter stopped what he was doing and looked at her. "The balcony?" he said. "On the third floor? Are you being serious?"

"You were talking a big game earlier," said Larissa. "It's how Patricia used to sneak out to see Mandla."

Peter went silent. He couldn't really talk himself out of that one. And, more to the point, he couldn't think of any alternative.

"Alright," he finally said, turning back to the food. "So, we wait until everyone has gone to bed and then sneak out from the balcony. Got it."

"Right," said Larissa, a little smug. "I think we should hang out with everybody this evening after dinner, and we should go to bed the same time as everyone else, which will probably be sometime before eleven. At twelve o'clock, we sneak out of bed and meet in the library; everybody should be asleep by then. But we don't want to go walking around outside in our pajamas, and we also don't want to be making a noise looking for clothes and getting dressed when we're trying to sneak out; so straight after dinner we should go get a change of clothes and hide them in the library. But not at the same time."

"Wow," said Peter, "you've given this some thought."

"I have," she said, quite chuffed with herself. "So that's the plan. I'll see you after dinner."

Back at the table, Peter was quickly distracted from the anxiety of their midnight plans by Greg regaling them with stories of his university days. Soon dessert was wrapping up, tea and coffee were being served, and some of the adults were starting to get up from the table while others swapped places to talk to different people.

Peter noticed the likes of Kyle and Austen gravitating toward Jesse and Daniel, soon followed by Megan and Michelle. Heeding Larissa's advice, he decided to join them. Sure enough, Ellen, Katie, and Steven soon joined as well so that the whole crew was there.

"I'm coming back now," Larissa announced at one point as she got up to leave, "I'm just going to charge my phone."

She left the room and, when she arrived back five minutes later, she gave Peter a quick look. He waited a few moments before getting up to leave without explaining himself.

Back in the boys' room, Peter quickly took some clothes out of his bag. One of the younger boys was busy getting into bed, so he tried to be as inconspicuous as possible. He hoped the boy didn't notice him walking out with a bundle of clothes and some shoes, or at least that he wouldn't think anything of it if he did.

He made his way quickly down the passage and past the stairs, rounded the corner of the next passage and went through the piano room to the library.

Larissa's clothes weren't visible anywhere; she must have hidden them well. Keen to do the same, he took out a few books that looked like they hadn't been touched in over a century, placed his clothes behind them, then put the books back to cover them up. On his way out, he listened at the door of the piano room to make sure nobody was coming up the passage, then quickly left and headed down the stairs as fast as he could without looking suspicious.

When he arrived back at the dining room, the others were all getting up to leave.

"Come on," Ellen said to him, "we're going to play a board game."

"Cool," said Peter, "what game?"

"It's called Heist," Austen told him. "You'll love it, bru."

Austen quickly ran upstairs to fetch the game from his bag while the others made themselves comfortable in the lounge.

"It's only for five players," Austen said when he got back, "so we'll play in teams of two and one team of three."

"I'll be with Jesse," Steven said eagerly.

"Why don't we do boys with girls?" said Katie.

"Ja, but no siblings," said Megan. "I'll be on Austen's team."

"Cool, I'll be with Larissa," said Daniel.

Peter teamed up with Ellen, Katie with Kyle, and Jesse, Steven, and Michelle made up the team of three. Austen then set up the board and explained the rules.

Heist turned out to be a really good time. They had to put pieces strategically around the board to "rob" places for money, but it was all about guessing what the other people were going to do and avoiding the police. With Peter's strategy and Ellen's ability to read people, Peter and Ellen made a great team. The only people enjoying the game more than him and Ellen were Larissa and Daniel, who seemed to be having a great time fooling around and not taking it very seriously.

After playing for nearly two hours, Peter and Ellen emerged as the winners, which, to Peter, was a small consolation for losing the real game that was going on. By now it was late and people were beginning to yawn, so they packed up and headed upstairs to bed, still discussing different strategies of the game and what they should have done differently.

Jesse turned the light off in the boys' room and everyone else was asleep within minutes. It had been a long day in the sun, and they were all exhausted. Peter knew that if he closed his eyes, even for a second, he would fall asleep instantly. He played on his phone to keep himself awake, under the covers so nobody else would notice the light, but even that was difficult and he had to pry his eyes open.

Eventually he checked the time and it was 23:55; good enough. He quietly got out of bed, climbing down as gently as he could so he wouldn't wake the boy in the bottom bunk, and crept out of the room to the sound of a few boys snoring. Luckily, the day in the sun had affected everyone and nobody even stirred as he slowly opened the door and closed it behind him.

The passage outside was completely dark and quiet; he couldn't see a thing. He felt his way along the wall, trying to let his eyes adjust to the darkness, very aware of every little sound he made. Rationally, he knew that nobody else would be up, but he was still somehow terrified that somebody might catch him.

Suddenly a dark figure appeared in front of him and he jumped with fright! But it was just Larissa. She muffled her laughter behind her sleeve, and Peter could do nothing but stand and soak up the embarrassment at his own skittishness.

"Are you quite done?" he whispered.

"Alright, alright," Larissa said, still giggling. "Let's go."

Together, they crept down the passage through the darkness, past the stairs, round the corner, and through the piano room.

Once they had turned on the light in the library, it somehow felt okay to talk.

"Wow, I nearly fell asleep," Larissa said as she got her clothes out from one of the bottom drawers of a little cabinet next to the desk.

"I know, me too," said Peter, taking the books out to get his clothes from behind them. "Honestly, I'm surprised I didn't."

"Should we take the keys with us?" Larissa asked as she unbuttoned her pajama top and took it off. She had on a white bra underneath. "Or leave them here? Peter?"

"Hey? What?" He shuffled round to the other side of the room so she wouldn't see him changing.

"I'm saying we could either lock the doors behind us and take the keys with us, or we could leave the keys here and leave the door unlocked."

"Nah, if we locked the door and then dropped the keys somewhere, we wouldn't be able to get back in," said Peter. "Rather just leave it unlocked."

"But what if somebody wanders through here and thinks the door has been left unlocked so they lock it?"

"It's the middle of the night," said Peter. "Everybody's asleep. Nobody's wandering through here."

Once they were changed and ready, they turned off the lights and, using their phone flashlights, unlocked the doors to the balcony.

The night air was cool and fresh; a light breeze swept their hair. The dam far below glistened in the moonlight. There were no lights from the house casting shadows on the lawn this time, but the moon appeared bright enough to cast shadows of its own.

Peter went over to the gutter he had eyed out last time, suddenly not so confident now that he actually had to use it to climb down. The climbing itself still looked easy enough, but they were three stories high if something went wrong.

"The best thing to do if you're nervous is to not think and just do it," Larissa said, as though reading his mind. "Otherwise, you just psyche yourself out."

Peter then realized she was talking to herself. She breathed deeply and looked at him.

"This was my idea," she said, "so I'll go first."

He tried to protest but she had already put one leg over the balustrade, and then the other. Slowly and carefully, she started climbing down, while Peter watched with clenched teeth.

Soon she was at the bottom, safe and sound; now it was Peter's turn. Having seen her do it, his nerves were put at ease somewhat, but he could still feel the adrenalin. He lifted himself over the balustrade and carefully climbed down to join Larissa at the bottom.

"That was scary," she whispered excitedly, also feeling the adrenalin.

They made their way round to the front where they once again went through the little garden gate onto the track leading to the dam.

Larissa was walking close to him, her arms tightly folded against her body, glancing this way and that in the darkness. Suddenly she grabbed Peter's arm, looking behind them. "Peter!"

Peter spun round and saw a large figure coming quickly toward them. He heard its paws on the ground, then its panting, and soon he could see the spots. Trixy, the Dalmatian, wagged her tail happily, hoping to be petted.

"Look who's skittish now," said Peter as he petted the dog.

Larissa buried her face in Peter's shoulder and laughed with embarrassment. She was more at ease after that, with Trixy to guide them, but he noticed she didn't let go of his arm when they carried on.

"So where is this place?" she asked when they reached the dam.

"Umm ..." Peter hesitated, realizing he hadn't fully explained this part to her. "It's on the other side of the dam," he said.

Larissa looked across the vast expanse of water glistening in the moonlight, then back at Peter with an expression he could only guess was disbelief.

"Peter," she said, "it's going to take us the whole night to walk around the dam! Is it even possible?"

"We're not going to walk," said Peter. He glanced at the boat next to the jetty, still right where he had left it after the braai.

Larissa looked at the boat, then at Peter.

"Surely we're not going in that?" she said.

Peter nodded.

"Is it even safe? What if it sinks?"

"It won't sink," said Peter, trying to convince himself as much as he was trying to convince her. "I used it before, when we had the braai; it's very sturdy."

He was glad it was dark and Larissa couldn't see just how old and fragile the boat actually looked. He got in, took hold of the oars, and waited for her to join him. Trixy then jumped in, which Peter hadn't anticipated. He just hoped the boat would be able to hold all three of them. She wagged her tail and looked eagerly at Larissa. Reluctantly, Larissa stepped into the boat; one foot first to test if it was sturdy, then the other. She sat down slowly and carefully, as though any sudden movements might tip the boat over. Eventually, Peter pushed them away from the jetty and began rowing.

It was a lot heavier now with an extra person and a Dalmatian, and it took a lot more effort to get the boat moving.

"This is actually quite cool," Larissa said once she was satisfied that the boat wasn't about to capsize or break in two. "It's a beautiful night!"

"I told you it would be fine," said Peter, trying not to sound out of breath.

They reached the other side and came to a stop in the sand. Trixy jumped out at once, splashing in the water, then ran ahead to sniff the trees.

"Hold on," said Peter, "I'll pull you up."

He stepped out into the water and, with a lot more effort than when he was by himself, heaved the boat high enough up the bank so Larissa could step out without getting her feet wet.

"Thank you, kind sir," she said as he helped her out. "Now which way do we go?"

"It's up here," said Peter, and he led them to the stream.

The sound of the running water was barely audible over the cacophony of insects and frogs. Hardly any moonlight reached them through the trees, and the further they went the darker it got. Soon they had to pull out their phones again.

"Now, this is going to be tricky," said Peter. "Last time I hopped along the rocks up the stream, but last time was broad daylight."

"I'm sure we'll manage," said Larissa, and she held Peter's hand for balance as she stepped from one rock to another. She then kept hold of his hand while she waited for him to follow. Slowly they made their way up the stream, hand in hand, while Trixy splashed on up ahead.

Peter had been wondering whether he'd be able to find the spot where they needed to turn off, but just as he was beginning to think they might have missed it already, they found Trixy sitting next to the stream waiting for them. Behind her, Peter recognized the once-cleared pathway.

"This way," he said.

They clambered through the sticks and bushes and over logs until eventually they came to the small glade.

"Wow," Larissa said as she slowly stepped out and looked around. "This is beautiful."

The moonlight shone through onto the gurgling stream; the willow tree swayed gently in the breeze.

"Well, this is the tree," said Peter.

"This is exactly what I pictured when we were reading the letters," said Larissa.

"And over here," said Peter, going over to the side of the tree, "is how I know it's their spot."

Larissa ran her hands slowly over the letters carved into the wood. "That's amazing," she whispered.

Unfortunately, there was no immediately obvious hole under the tree. They scratched around its base, raking the leaves away with their hands, until suddenly some sand gave way. They quickly dug it out and, sure enough, revealed a hole that had slowly been filling up with sand and leaves over the years.

With his phone in one hand and his face almost against the ground, Peter peered into the hole. "It's in there," he said. He could make out the shape of the old tin.

Larissa lowered her head to look in as well. "Didn't see that coming," she said. "Let's see if anything's inside it."

They dug a bit more until Peter could reach in and pull it out.

If the tin once had any color, it didn't anymore. It was old and completely rusted—all the way through in a few spots. The lid was stuck from the rust, and it took both of them to pry it open. Eventually, with a *scratch* and a *pop*, the lid came off.

Inside the tin, apart from the dirt and mold, was a pencil that seemed to be in working order, a little stash of paper completely soiled and unusable, and, folded in half with Patricia's handwriting on it, one final letter.

Larissa threw her arms around Peter's neck and hugged him tightly. "I don't believe it!" she said. "You were right! I honestly wasn't expecting to find anything here!"

Larissa couldn't see it, but Peter's cheeks had gone bright red.

But the letter was so old and bug-eaten that it was almost impossible to read. They went through it word by word, trying to make out what it said and having to guess a lot of it.

7 September 1931
Dear Mandla

We need to leave ... as possible.

... S. Durham arrived yesterday ... rode out to Pietermaritzburg to meet ... they showed me the ... took it from their motorcar during the night without

them noticing ... said I'd see them at Woodwright ... arriving later tonight ... in the wine cellar for now ...

But as soon ... realize it's gone, and Father ... snuck out to meet ... figure out that I took it.

Meet me by ... at sundown. We can ... if we ride through the night.

Love

Patricia

They reread the letter a few times before they could make any sense of it, and even then they were still quite confused.

"So, it seems to me," said Larissa, "that somebody called S. Durham arrived in Pietermaritzburg, and Patricia rode out to meet them without her father knowing. Then she took something from them and wanted to leave with Mandla before they figured out that she had taken it."

Peter was thoughtfully silent. "That name," he said after a while, "S. Durham—it sounds really familiar. I've definitely heard it before."

"I don't think I've ever heard it," said Larissa.

"Could you try google it?" Peter asked. "I don't have any data. But if we can work out who S. Durham was, we might be able to work out what they had that was worth stealing."

"Even if I did have data, there's absolutely no signal here," said Larissa.

For the time being, they weren't going to figure anything else out, so Larissa pocketed the letter and they made their way back along the path, then hopped down the stream, with Trixy leading the way.

Peter let Larissa and Trixy get in before pushing the boat back into the water, then got in and began rowing out into the dam once more.

"Who do you think this S. Durham person might be?" Larissa asked.

"I don't know," said Peter, "but I'm sure it's relevant or she wouldn't have mentioned them by name."

"What I don't get," she said, "is that it sounds like, whatever she took from them, she took it without them knowing. But she was still going to see them later at Woodwright and was just hoping they wouldn't notice by then. That's hardly the hijacking Thulani told us about."

"Ja, the stories don't really match up," said Peter. "What do you think she took?"

But Larissa didn't respond. Something had caught her attention.

"What is it?" Peter asked.

She didn't answer immediately, but stared into the darkness. "What's that?" she finally said, pointing behind Peter.

Peter stopped rowing and turned round. Somewhere in the distance there was a dim light moving slowly through the darkness, changing colors as it went.

"I have no idea," said Peter.

Larissa stared at it. "Let's get a closer look," she said.

Peter carried on rowing, and soon they pulled up next to the jetty. They got out and started heading up the track toward the light.

"It's coming from the chapel," said Peter; "through the stained-glass windows. Somebody's in there."

Larissa checked her phone. "It's after one in the morning," she said. "Who would be in the chapel at this time of night?"

"I have no idea."

"Come on," she said, "let's go check it out."

They let Trixy through the garden gate and closed it behind her so she couldn't follow them, then headed up toward the chapel.

Under the cover of the large oak trees in the parking area they felt quite safe, but they paused at the bottom of the hill where the path started. From there to the chapel on the hill the path was completely exposed. If someone happened to look out while they were on the path, they would definitely be seen.

"I think we just need to run up the path as quickly as possible," said Larissa.

"Quietly," said Peter. "We don't want them to hear us either."

They hurried along the path as quickly and quietly as they could, then pressed themselves against the wall of the chapel. The light was coming from a window a little further down, and they could just hear someone moving around inside. They crept along the side of the wall, crouching below the windows, until they reached the window with the light inside. They could hear furniture being scraped across the floor and things being shifted and moved around inside.

"What are they doing in there?" Larissa whispered.

Peter shook his head and shrugged. They listened for a few moments but couldn't discern anything else from the sound.

"I'm going to take a peek," said Larissa.

Peter's heart started racing. As she began lifting herself, he grabbed her arm. She stopped and looked at him.

"What?"

"Just … be careful," he whispered.

She nodded and raised her head until her eyes were just above the bottom of the window. Peter watched nervously, tensing all his muscles, waiting for something to happen …

When nothing happened, he slowly relaxed, and eventually raised his head as well to have a look.

The stained glass was nearly impossible to see through. There was a candle in the room, and they could make out the figure of a person pushing things around. They appeared to be looking for something, and they seemed to think it might be under a cabinet or the pulpit, or behind the altar. Peter and Larissa watched them check a few of the same places at least twice. Whatever they were looking for, they weren't having any success.

Suddenly the person stopped moving. After a few moments, they took a cautious step in the direction of the window. Peter and Larissa realized that the person was looking at them, and they immediately dropped down.

Larissa grabbed Peter's hand. "What do we do?" she whispered.

Peter's heart was pounding but he tried to stay calm. "I don't think they could actually see us," Peter whispered. "Just stay still."

Then they heard footsteps, and saw the light leave the window and then light up the next window, and then the next, getting closer to the door, the footsteps getting quicker and quicker.

"Scratch that," said Peter. "Run!"

They both sprang up. Larissa was about to make a break for the path, but Peter grabbed her and pushed her in the other direction.

"That way!" he said, pointing toward the stables.

They jumped down the retaining wall and ran as fast as they could down the hill through the long grass, hardly able to see where they were going, stumbling as they went, but they didn't slow down. They had no idea whether the person was chasing them, or if they had even seen them, but they weren't going to hang around to find out. They ran all the way to the bottom of the hill and quickly ducked behind the garage and then into the garden among the bushes.

Once in the safety of the garden, they stopped to catch their breath. When it became apparent that they hadn't been chased, they snuck through the garden to a spot where they could get a glimpse of the chapel. There, next to the chapel, right where they had been crouching only moments ago, was the single orange light of the candle held up by the dark figure of a man.

"Who is that?" Larissa asked.

"I saw as much as you did," said Peter.

"Do you think he saw us?"

"I don't think he saw our faces. If we couldn't see him through the glass, he couldn't see us."

"What was he doing?"

"Obviously looking for something," said Peter, "something he doesn't want anyone to know he's looking for."

The candle suddenly went out.

"Come on," said Peter, "let's get up to the library before he gets back."

They ran round the back of the house to the gutter, and both climbed up at the same time. Once they got back into the library and locked the door behind them, they used their phones to find their pajamas and got changed in the dark.

"I'm not going to be able to sleep," Larissa said. "I've got too much adrenalin. My heart is beating out of control!"

"You and me both," said Peter.

"Let's just stay here until we've both calmed down?" she said.

Peter couldn't tell her how much he really wanted to do that, but he knew it would be too risky.

"I don't think that's a good idea," he said. "Even if we just lie awake in our beds for hours, we can at least pretend we're sleeping. Here, we might get caught."

"Ja, you're right," said Larissa. She sounded disappointed, but he might have imagined that.

They snuck back to their rooms as quickly and quietly as they could. Without speaking, Larissa hugged Peter tightly, and lingered for a moment with her arms around him before letting go and slipping into her room.

Chapter 12

Peter woke up the next morning to the sound of light rain. He leaned over to look out the window: gray clouds covered the entire countryside.

He lay back in his bed, still exhausted, and checked his phone: 9:10. It had taken him at least an hour to fall asleep, and they had only got to their rooms at about 2:00 in the morning. He had had less than six hours of sleep.

He sat up and looked around the room. He was the only one still in bed.

The fear and anxiety of the previous night abated in the daylight—albeit dim and gray. Despite everything that had happened, the thing his mind fixated on was the way Larissa had hugged him before she went to bed. He couldn't stop thinking about it.

"Morning, Pete." Austen came in and started rummaging around in his bag, looking for something.

"Morning," said Peter. "What's everyone up to today?"

Austen shrugged. "Nothing much," he said. "Weather's bleak. Brian's going to drive us to Underberg a bit later to get a DVD; that's about it at this stage."

"Underberg?" said Peter. "What time?"

"Probably in about twenty minutes," said Austen. "Wanna come?"

"Can I?"

"Ja, we're taking the Landy; there should be space."

Peter knew better than to ask who else was going. Besides, he could work it out: if Austen was going, it was probably because Daniel was going; if Daniel was going, it was almost definitely because Larissa was going.

That was enough for Peter. He made his way down to the dining room, where he was the only one having breakfast. A few of the adults were sitting having tea and chatting.

He placed his bowl of yoghurt and muesli down quietly at the other end of the table, but he could still overhear them. Karen Kingsbury was speaking, and Peter didn't have to do any guesswork to know she was talking about Kim.

"... and have you seen those *ridiculous* hats she wears? Who's she trying to impress?"

Katie then stuck her head through the door and saw Peter.

"Oh, Peter, there you are!" she said.

She looked at Karen, who was still going on about Kim, and looked at Peter with raised eyebrows in a *yikes!* kind of expression. Peter knew exactly what she meant and nodded his agreement.

"Austen tells me you're coming with to Underberg?"

"If that's alright," said Peter.

"Ja, of course! But we're leaving in like two minutes so you might want to hurry up."

"I'm on my way!"

Peter quickly guzzled down the last of his food and took his bowl through to the kitchen before heading out to the parking area, where everybody was waiting.

Jesse, Daniel, and Austen squashed into the seats in the middle while Megan, Katie, and Larissa took the seats at the back. Peter found himself in the front seat, next to Brian.

Daniel spent the drive with his head turned, leaning over the seat to speak to Larissa and the other girls behind him, and Austen and Jesse were in a deep discussion about rugby, so Peter was forced to make conversation with Brian. Luckily, Brian was easy to speak to and did most of the talking.

"So, you enjoyed your horse riding the other day, did you?" he asked as they headed off down the long driveway.

"I did," said Peter. "Thanks again for taking us. Although I was expecting a bit more of a lesson before we were left to fend for ourselves."

"Experience is the best teacher, I always say!" Brian chuckled. "Besides, you handled yourself just fine!"

"I mean, I managed to hold on," Peter laughed, "but I had absolutely no control over the horse."

"Yes, he has a mind of his own, does old Rusty," said Brian. "But he's very comfortable with having people ride him, so at least he wouldn't buck you off. Anyway, it's good that they got a ride. I managed to get some of the others out when I took Megan and Michelle about a week ago, so they've all had a run recently."

"When last did you ride?" Peter asked.

"Oh, no, those days are long behind me," said Brian. "I haven't ridden for about fifteen, twenty years. I might have kept it up if I had known I was going to end up on the farm here, but it's not something I did much of in the Cape."

"Oh, you're from the Cape?" said Peter. "When did you move here?"

"Twenty-ten," said Brian. "I've been here five years now, going on six."

Peter remembered their not-too-dissimilar conversation with Thulani, and how it seemed like Thulani and Ngesihle weren't very impressed with Brian suddenly finding himself at Woodwright Manor. He had to ask.

"Why *did* you end up on the farm here?"

Brian stared ahead at the road and nodded thoughtfully before he answered. "My wife died," he said. "Cancer. It wasn't sudden, but still tough to deal with. I had my brother there to help me through it, but then he also died the same year. And he *was* quite sudden."

Peter immediately felt bad for assuming the worst. He had even seen the family tree—he should've known!

"The death of the two people closest to you can be rough," Brian went on. "And I had no more family around me to help. My parents were long gone, my daughters had long since moved to Joburg, and Phillip was here at Woodwright. I stayed for a while—almost a year—but it was too much for me. So I came here." He glanced at Peter with a smile. "I could've gone to live with my daughters, but they have their own lives; I didn't want to be a hassle. And I've never been much of a city person. Farming is all I've ever known. I wanted to still be useful, you know? Anyway, Patricia was great—she took me in and made me feel right at home."

"I'm really sorry," Peter said.

"No, it's all in the past now," said Brian. "Lillian and Walter were both in their sixties. They had good lives."

Peter started piecing a few things together. "Walter," he said, "is he … Megan and Michelle's grandfather?"

"Yes, that's correct."

"Did he … start some kind of rumor about a missing fortune here at Woodwright?"

Brian chuckled. "Yes, he used to say that, old Walter. I think he was having us all on for a laugh—although he was quite persistent at times. He could be a bit odd, to tell you the truth."

"Did he ever speak to you about it?"

"All the time, when we were kids," said Brian. "He used to say he had found hidden treasure in the wine cellar. He had a knack for these kinds of stories. But this one he told me all the time, almost like he was taunting me. Aunty Pat eventually got so tired of his lies that she forbade him ever to speak of it again, and that seemed to be the end of it—for a while, at least. Then, much later, when we were all grown up and you would think those stories were behind us, it came up again somehow, and he still insisted he had found treasure in the wine cellar. Most of us just had a laugh about it. And, of course, the more he told the story, the more farfetched it became. Soon it wasn't just a wine cellar but an entire secret passageway underground, and he said Aunty Pat hushed him up about it because she didn't want others to know. Then we would ask him where this mystery wine cellar was, and he would pretend he couldn't find it. Sometimes I couldn't tell if he was getting genuinely upset with us for not believing him or if that was all part of the act."

"So, there's no wine cellar then?" Peter asked, trying to sound casual.

"No, no, it was all made up," said Brian. "No wine cellar, no secret passage, and definitely no treasure."

"But his daughters believed him, didn't they?" said Peter. "Kim and Karen?"

"Oh, no, I don't know if there's any truth to that," said Brian, but he shifted awkwardly in his chair.

Peter waited in silence for him to continue, and eventually he let out a sigh. "There was a rumor," he went on, "that he told his children everything he could remember, and he swore that, once he figured out where it was, he would tell them how to find it. So some people thought they believed it and wanted to find it. But that was a long time ago, and I don't think there's any need to propagate rumors like that."

"Quite a story," said Peter.

"Yes!" Brian laughed. "But what's a family without a bit of drama?"

Peter couldn't tell if Brian knew more than he was letting on, but he laughed in agreement and dropped the subject.

They arrived in Underberg and Brian dropped them off at

the video store while he went to attend to some business. Peter wondered if the video-store owner in the quiet little town of Underberg had ever had to deal with such a rowdy bunch of teenagers. Megan, Katie, and Larissa had been tasked with getting a movie for the younger kids, and were giggling at movie titles as they looked through their options. They had to talk loudly to compete with Austen, Jesse and Daniel, who were each looking in different sections and would shout their suggestions out to each other across the room, with no apparent preferences and without getting any closer to some kind of consensus.

"Guys, what about *Pirates of the Caribbean*?"

"I could always go in for some Jason Bourne!"

"Ah, *Iron Man*! Surely?"

He tried his hardest not to notice, but out of the corner of his eye Peter saw Larissa sidle up to Daniel so the two of them could giggle at movies together. Determined not to let it bother him, he moseyed around quietly by himself, looking for any half-way-decent film. It was quite difficult with the limited selection, and he guessed it was futile anyway because his opinion probably wouldn't count for much.

His heart suddenly soared when Larissa skipped over to him.

"What you looking for?" she asked.

Peter shrugged. "Preferably something I haven't seen before, but I'm not too fazed."

Larissa looked at the shelf in front of Peter and picked up one of the DVDs. "*Hitch*," she said, reading the title, then turned it over and read the back: "*Meet Hitch, New York City's greatest match-maker. Love is his job and he'll get you the girl of your dreams in just three easy dates, guaranteed!*" She looked up at Peter. "Looking for tips, are you?"

"You wish," said Peter. "I was actually looking at these."

Larissa looked a few rows down to where Peter was pointing.

"*Pride and Prejudice*," she read. "Oh my, sophisticated, aren't we!"

Peter's phone started vibrating in his pocket. He gave Larissa an unimpressed look and took his phone out. "Hello?" he answered.

It was his mom, asking him to go and buy some shampoo for her.

"What kind? ... Well, how am I supposed to know? ... Okay, but you're getting whatever I give you ... Okay, bye."

"What was that all about?" Larissa asked.

Peter put his phone in his pocket, then looked at her. "Business call," he said, and turned to walk out the shop.

He heard her laughing behind him, but kept looking straight ahead to make sure she couldn't see the smug look on his face.

As he crossed the road, Larissa caught up with him.

"Following me, are you?" he said.

She was still smiling at his business-call joke. "I'm coming to get some data," she said.

"Oh, good idea!" said Peter, "We can google S. Durham."

"Pass your phone here," said Larissa.

"Why?'

"Just pass it."

Peter reluctantly handed his phone over. She typed her number in and saved it under "Someone cooler than me." She then phoned her phone to get his number and handed Peter's phone back to him.

"Just in case, you know ... we ever need to get hold of each other."

"Makes sense," Peter said as casually as he could manage.

He left her at the tills and went to get the shampoo, then bought some data of his own for good measure.

He found Larissa outside, leaning against the wall under the veranda, phone in one hand and some biltong in the other.

"Did you google S. Durham?" he asked.

"Ja, I'm busy looking," she said while chewing. "Here, have some."

"Find anything?" he asked as he took a few pieces of biltong.

She shook her head. "There's a street in America ... a county in America ... Oh, here we go! Oh, no, never mind; they died in 1859."

"Maybe add 'South Africa' to the search," said Peter.

She typed it in, but carried on shaking her head when she started scrolling through the results.

"Another street in Pinetown ... a cottage in Grahamstown ... nothing here vaguely of any interest to us."

"That's so weird," said Peter. "I'm sure I've seen that name somewhere."

"Maybe you saw the street name in Pinetown," Larissa suggested.

"Possibly," he said, "but that doesn't seem right."

"When we read the letter, I definitely didn't recognize the name."

"Oh, that reminds me. Didn't the letter say something about a wine cellar?"

"Mmm, ja, possibly," she said, reaching into her pocket. "I've got it with me ..." She took the letter out, quickly skimmed over it, then read aloud, "*... in the wine cellar for now ...*"

She looked up at Peter with a curious frown. "Is there a wine cellar at Woodwright?" she asked.

"Well, that's the thing," said Peter. "I was chatting to Brian in the car on the way over here, and he told me the story about Megan and Michelle's grandfather, Walter, and how he claimed he found treasure in the wine cellar, but no one believed him. Brian said there *is* no wine cellar."

"Strange ..." Larissa started saying, but just then they heard their names being called.

"Peter! Larissa!"

They turned to see Austen coming toward them.

"What are you guys doing here?" he asked.

"I just came to get some data," said Larissa, "and Peter needed some …" She glanced at the bottle in Peter's hand. "Shampoo, obviously, for his … dry and damaged hair. Biltong?" She held the biltong out for Austen.

"Thanks." He took some. "Come on, we're leaving. Brian's here."

On the drive back Peter learnt that, in a rare moment of maturity (and to much protest from Daniel), Jesse had rented *Dead Poets Society*, because apparently "it's a classic." Peter had seen it before, but he was more than happy to watch it again. Daniel, however, didn't appear very happy at all. Partly because of the movie choice, but mostly because of the way Jesse had pulled rank on him.

They pulled back into Woodwright Manor and the dogs all came bounding out to greet them as always. Peter might have been imagining it, but Trixy seemed particularly happy to see him after their little moonlight stroll the night before.

There was a TV room down the passage from the hall, in which the flatscreen TV provided a nice contrast to the Victorian decor of the rest of the room. Many of the adults joined them, making themselves comfortable on the chairs while the kids had to make do with cushions on the floor. Daniel took the best spot in the middle, right in front of the TV, then eagerly looked up to see where Larissa was sitting. Peter took a spot near the back. He was a lot more subtle about it, but also secretly hoped Larissa would take the spot next to him. Larissa, however, sat between Megan and Katie without giving it a thought.

Ellen and Michelle came through carrying trays of hot chocolate for everyone, and, once they had handed them out, sat next to Peter at the back. Soon they were all settled in and sipping their hot chocolate as the movie began.

Dead Poets Society was a lovely film about a group of boys at a boarding school whose English teacher encourages them to "seize the day." Peter could relate to the boys in the movie; in a lot of ways, staying at Woodwright Manor and rooming with the other boys was quite similar to staying in a boarding school. In the first class, the teacher takes the boys to the school's trophy room, with photos of old clubs and sports teams, and tells them to "peruse some of the faces of the past." Woodwright Manor had a similar sense of history, only the cabinets were filled with collectables rather than trophies, and the photos were of old family members rather than alumni.

Something about the old black-and-white photographs and that sense of history made Peter think of the name S. Durham.

About half an hour in, the boys in the movie all snuck out of their rooms at night to go find a cave in the woods. Larissa turned to look over her shoulder at Peter, her lips curled into a little smile. He knew she was thinking about their own adventure the night before. She gave him a wink, then turned back to the movie.

Suddenly, Peter realized why the old photos had made him think of S. Durham! This couldn't wait. He quietly got up and left the room as inconspicuously as possible, then took his phone out, searched his contacts for "Someone cooler than me," and sent a message.

Wait a few minutes then come meet me in the next room. I need to talk to you.

He went to wait in the next room, which looked like it was once either a bedroom or a study but was now pretty much just a storage room. An old rifle caught his eye, perched on a stand that had a small brass plate engraved with the words *Patricia Woodwright*. He went over to have a look at it; he didn't know much about guns, but it didn't look like it could still fire a bullet.

The door opened and Larissa came in. "What is it?" she asked. "I was enjoying that."

"Look—it's Patricia's old rifle," said Peter.

Larissa glanced at the rifle, unimpressed. "Please tell me you didn't call me in here just to show me an old rifle—"

"Oh, no, sorry ... I thought of something: do you remember those newspaper clippings on the pinboard in Patricia's secret study?"

Larissa nodded.

"One of them was about a hijacking," said Peter. "It must have been the same hijacking that Thulani told us about."

"Oh my gosh, you're right!" she said. "Do you remember what it said?"

"Not really," said Peter, "but I think it might have been where I saw the name S. Durham."

"That would make sense," she said. "Should we go back and have another look?"

"I think we should," said Peter.

"People might wonder where we are."

"I don't think anyone will notice. And even if they do, it's much less suspicious during the day than at night."

"Okay, but let's hurry."

They headed quickly up the stairs, down the passage and round the corner, glancing back over their shoulders as they went. Soon they were in Patricia's room, closing the door behind them and opening the secret door to the hidden study behind.

They paused at the doorway to survey the scene: things had been moved, boxes had been taken down, papers were all over the place, and the little box of trinkets had been emptied out onto the desk. Someone had been looking for something.

"Let's be quick," said Peter, going straight over to the pinboard. "Someone's been here and they might come back."

There was a photo of two men and a police officer next to a police car. Peter read the names underneath but none of them sounded even remotely like S. Durham.

Two tourists were held up and robbed near Bulwer on their way from Pietermaritzburg to Woodwright Manor on Tuesday evening.

Mark and Henry Jefferson, relatives of the esteemed Harold Woodwright, had allegedly stopped to take a break when four men armed with knives appeared and forced them out of their motor car. They made their way back to Bulwer on foot, where they contacted Woodwright, and Woodwright contacted the police.

The Jeffersons informed police officers that all their belongings had been taken with the car. Most valuable among the stolen goods were personal items being delivered to Woodwright, the particulars of which they refused to disclose.

Police Officer Hendrik van der Merwe reports that Mandla Sithole, a worker on the Woodwright estate, has been taken in as a suspect, but that the Jeffersons' car and belongings have not yet been located.

"So that is when Mandla was arrested, but absolutely nothing about an S. Durham," said Larissa.

"That's frustrating," said Peter. "I was sure I remembered seeing it in one of these photos."

"And this says they were robbed by four men with knives," said Larissa, "so definitely not Patricia."

Suddenly a loud buzz made both of them jump with fright! A cellphone they hadn't even noticed lit up next to the typewriter.

"They left their phone!" Larissa gasped.

Peter picked it up to look at it.

"They just got a message from a 'McKenzie,'" he said, and looked at Larissa. "McKenzie?"

Larissa shrugged.

He pulled the message down on the lock-screen display. As he read it, he put his hand over his mouth.

"What?" said Larissa. "What does it say?"

In a low voice, Peter read it aloud.

You're overthinking this. Nothing else to implicate you. If someone's onto you, destroy all evidence

Peter and Larissa looked at each other.

"Destroy all evidence?" said Larissa. "What on earth—"

She was interrupted by the phone buzzing again.

If you can't find the exit in the chapel force it out of the old man

"Must be the person from the chapel last night!" said Peter.

"Force what out of the old man?"

Before Peter could answer, it buzzed again.

What did the kids see? How much do they know? Do they need to be dealt with?

Larissa gasped. "They saw us!"

"Maybe they didn't see our faces," said Peter. "Maybe they could just see that we weren't adults."

"What do they mean *need to be dealt with*?"

Another buzz.

Forget about the lion tail. Focus on finding the Will. The paper should help. I'll drop the letter off tomorrow

"Again with the lion tail!" said Peter. "What does it mean?"

"I have no idea," said Larissa. "Maybe we should tell someone about this."

"Who would we tell? If we tell the wrong person, they'll find out we're on to them. They'll destroy all the evidence before we even know who *they* is. And, even more concerning, *they'll* know who *we* are."

"They might already know who we are."

"All the more reason to keep a low profile," said Peter. "Come on, let's get out of here before they come back for their phone."

She didn't argue with that. They left the secret study, checked through the keyhole of the bedroom door to make sure nobody was coming, and headed quickly down the passageway and back down the stairs to the TV room. Larissa went back in first, trying not to look suspicious, and Peter followed a little while after her. Ellen gave him a look but didn't say anything.

Peter paid absolutely no attention to the rest of the movie. He stared at the screen, but the only thing on his mind was the message. He eyed everybody, seeing them in a new light now. Was it someone here? Or was it someone who *wasn't* here, snooping around while everybody else was occupied with the movie?

When the movie finished, Katie got up to take out *Dead Poets Society* and put in *Frozen*. "Who wants to stay to watch the next one?" she asked.

Everybody put their hands up with calls of "yes" around the room.

"Ten-minute bathroom break?" said Carol. "Maybe get a snack?"

Everyone agreed. They all started getting up and stretching, heading out toward the bathroom or the kitchen.

When Larissa left the room with Katie and Megan, Ellen turned to Peter. "So, Peter, how did you enjoy the movie?" she said with a smirk.

Peter had to bring himself back to the present. "I actually think it's a really good movie," he said. "I really like it."

"Hmm, that's interesting," said Ellen, "because you only saw about half of it."

"I've seen it before."

"Oh, ja? And what about Larissa? What did she think of the movie?"

"I have no idea," said Peter. "You'll have to ask her." He quickly got up to avoid any more questions, leaving Ellen snickering to herself as he followed some of the other boys toward the kitchen.

"What an epic movie," Daniel was saying as though he had been on board when Jesse chose it. "I wish we had a teacher like that. All our teachers are boring."

Peter's phone vibrated in his pocket.

Come upstairs to the girls' room, nobody's here.

It was Larissa. He knew she wasn't trying to be suggestive, but he still felt a flutter in his stomach. He left the others and made his way upstairs.

Larissa was sitting on her bed, staring out the window. Peter had to knock on the door to get her attention.

"Hey, Pete, come in," she said.

Peter hesitated, looking around.

"Oh my word ..." Larissa rolled her eyes and got off the bed. "Nobody's here."

She grabbed Peter's hand and pulled him inside, then shut the door behind them.

"I don't feel like watching the movie," she said as she sat back down. "I can't concentrate. I'm too worked up."

"I know, me too," said Peter, and he sat down on the bed next to her.

"We need to do something," said Larissa. "We need to stop them."

"We don't even know who 'them' is." said Peter. "Or what they're doing."

"Well, I've been thinking about that," she said. "That message said something about dropping off 'the letter.' What if it's the same letter Thulani told us about—the one that went missing?"

"Could be."

"As for what they're doing," Larissa went on, "the message also said 'focus on finding the will.' They must be talking about Patricia's will. That's what they were looking for."

"You think that's what the were looking for in the chapel?"

"No, in the secret study. I don't know what they were doing in the chapel. It was a different message."

Larissa's phone buzzed. She looked at it and sighed.

"Megan's wondering where I am."

"Don't answer," said Peter.

"I won't, but maybe we should head down," she said, standing up. "She might come looking for me."

Peter agreed and followed her from the room.

"What we need to do is find out who else was here at the time," said Larissa as they started down the passage. "The day that letter went missing."

"The day Patricia died," Peter added.

"I'm sure Megan and Michelle will remember most of the people who were here, and we can ask around to fill in the gaps."

"We can't be too blasé about asking people," said Peter. "If we're asking too many questions, they might catch on—"

Peter cut his sentence short. As they rounded the corner they caught a glimpse of Vuyo exiting the passage to Patricia's room and hurrying down the stairs. They both stopped and looked at each other.

"Did he just come from Patricia's room?" Larissa asked.

"Looked like it. I don't know what else is down that passage."

Larissa hurried over to the top of the stairs to try to see where he was going, and Peter hurried after her. But she shook her head.

"Missed him," she said. She turned to look down the passage. "I wonder why he was in such a hurry …"

Her voice trailed off as something caught her eye. She went to it, and Peter turned to see what it was.

"Look at this!" she said.

A few old photos in frames stood on a table, and she picked one up. It was of a young Patricia and another woman wearing ball gowns. Peter had looked at these photos before.

"My gran has a photo just like this at her house," she said. "This is Alice, my great-grandmother!"

Peter looked it over. "She was pretty."

"They both were."

He glanced at the other photos on the table, and one in particular caught his eye—one of two men at Durban harbor.

"Larissa ..." he said.

"What?"

"*This* is what," said Peter, and he handed her the photo.

Larissa frowned, not sure what she was supposed to be looking at. "I'm confused," she said.

"This is where I had seen the name before!" said Peter. "I knew it was in an old photo! It wasn't *S.* Durham; it was R.M.S. *Durham*!"

Peter watched Larissa's face as she realized that behind the two men standing in the foreground was a ship in the harbor with a line of men carrying crates and boxes down a gangplank; on the side of the ship, in great, white letters, was the name R.M.S. *Durham Castle*.

She pulled the letter they had found the night before out from her pocket and reread it.

"You're right!" she said. "These must be the people she went out to meet!" Then she frowned. "But hang on; aren't they ...?"

"The same people from the photo in that newspaper clipping," Peter finished for her.

"But that doesn't make any sense!" said Larissa.

Peter shrugged. "She must have met with them before they got hijacked," he said.

"Who do you think they were?" asked Larissa. "What do you reckon she took from them?"

Peter didn't have time to answer; they heard footsteps coming up the stairs and turned to see Brian. He stopped suddenly when he saw Peter and Larissa.

"What are you both doing here?" he asked, looking from one to the other with slightly narrowed eyes. Peter noticed him glance down the passageway toward Patricia's room, then quickly look back at them.

"We're just looking at some of these old photographs," Larissa said pleasantly. "Peter was showing me this one." She held the photo out for Brian, but he didn't look at it.

"Why aren't you watching the movie with everyone else downstairs?" he asked.

"We're going there now, I just had to charge my phone," Larissa said casually, still holding the photo out for him.

Brian looked down at it skeptically.

"Why are you looking at these photos?" he asked.

"Umm ..." Larissa started.

"Oh, I recognized that this was Durban," Peter jumped in. "But from a long time ago. It looks completely different now. Interesting to see how it's changed over time."

Brian's expression softened as he looked over the photo. "Oh, yes, so it is," he said.

"We were wondering who these two men might be," said Larissa.

Brian squinted at the photo. "I'm afraid I don't know," he said. "I know I'm old, but this looks like it's a little before my time. Sorry," he smiled.

"Alright, no worries," said Larissa as she put the photo back on the table. "Anyway, we're gonna go watch the movie now. See you later!"

"Alright, cheerio," said Brian.

Peter gave him a nod, and they headed down the stairs. Out of the corner of his eye, he saw Brian head down the passage and round the corner toward Patricia's room.

He turned to Larissa as soon as Brian was out of earshot. "Why do you think he's going down there? You don't think it was his phone that we saw in that room, do you?"

"The thought crossed my mind," said Larissa. "I'm not gonna lie, I was getting creepy vibes; I wanted to get away as quickly as possible."

"Ja, no, me too," said Peter. "You're really good at that, by the way."

"At what?"

"Acting natural under pressure," said Peter, "defusing the situation."

Larissa smiled. "I do drama. That probably helps. And thanks for jumping in there about Durban and how it's changed, that was quick thinking!"

"Thanks," said Peter, and his face went a little red. A compliment from Larissa felt like a kiss on the cheek.

"Unfortunately," said Larissa, "that photo doesn't really help us. We're still no closer to finding out who those people were. All we know now is that they were the same people who got hijacked. And, I mean, if Brian doesn't even know them ..."

Peter suddenly stopped and looked at her. "Brian doesn't, but I might know someone who does," he said. "I usually sit next to Phillip at dinner, and he loves to talk about our family's British history. And if they came on the *R.M.S. Durham*, they must be British. If anyone knows who they are, I'll bet he does!"

Larissa didn't answer. She looked at Peter thoughtfully.

"What?" said Peter.

"Do you ... do you ever get the feeling that Phillip knows something the rest of us don't?" she said after a moment.

"What do you mean?"

"Remember when Brian was looking for him but couldn't find him? And then he turned up out of nowhere and we didn't understand how Brian could've missed him?"

"Ja?" Peter said slowly.

"And he was drinking from a hipflask," said Larissa.

Peter nodded.

"He must keep a stash of alcohol somewhere," said Larissa. "Somewhere others—like Brian—don't know about."

"Probably," said Peter.

"What if there *is* a wine cellar. Phillip might know where it is."

Peter thought about it. She might have a point.

"Actually, now you mention it," he said, "the morning of the funeral I also noticed him turn up out of nowhere with a hipflask … at the chapel!"

"So … not the wine cellar?"

"No, listen! When Brian told me the story of Walter, he said Walter claimed it wasn't just a wine cellar; it was a secret passage. And in one of those messages we just saw, it said something about finding the 'exit in the chapel.' The wine cellar has a passage through to the chapel!"

"That's what we saw them looking for!"

"Exactly!"

"Except …" the excitement faded from her voice, "they couldn't find it, and I reckon they probably know more about it than we do."

"But not more than Phillip," said Peter. "Maybe we can get him to show us."

"Phillip?" said Larissa. She sighed. "Peter, people who keep a stash of alcohol hidden aren't usually too keen to show off their stash to everyone else."

"No ..." said Peter, "but I might have a plan."

Chapter 13

Larissa followed Peter to the dining room, where he peeked in to make sure nobody else was there before striding across to the wine cabinet on the other side of the room. He opened the cabinet and surveyed the wine inside.

"What are you doing?" Larissa asked. "What's the plan?"

Peter turned to face her. "Could you do me a favor?" he said. "I need something like, umm ... lipstick! Have you got any?"

"Ja ..." Larissa said curiously, "why?"

"Could you fetch it for me quickly?" said Peter. "And on your way back, could you try find out where Phillip is?"

Larissa gave him a doubtful look, but went to get the lipstick.

"Oh, wait!" said Peter. "Could you also bring that photo down? The one with the R.M.S. *Durham*."

Larissa nodded and carried on out the door.

As soon as she was gone, Peter turned back to the wine cabinet in a hurry; someone could come in at any moment. He started taking the bottles out and checking them two at a time, until he found one that was only about half-full and put it to one side.

He then looked around the room. He tried the next cabinet but, annoyingly, found that it was also filled with bottles. And not just wine, either. He took some out and read the labels: *Port, Sherry, Brandy, Whiskey, Peach Schnapps* ... This complicated things.

He hastily looked around the room for any other hiding places, but nothing was coming to mind. Gazing at the gray skies through the window and the heavy drizzle coming down, the idea suddenly came to him: nobody would be going outside in this weather! He rushed over to the window, opened it and stuck his head out to look at the ground below. There was a row of hydrangeas up against the wall in the flowerbed beneath the window—perfect!

He quickly grabbed some bottles and, leaning out of the window, lowered them as far as he could before dropping them gently onto the soil below. He got some more bottles to drop out the window, then some more, and carried on with the rest of the wine bottles, then with the whiskey and brandy bottles, until he couldn't drop any more out or he would be dropping bottles on top of each other. He didn't think he would need to worry about the peach schnapps and some of the other liqueurs, but there were still a few bottles of sherry and port that he thought he should hide. He rushed over to the next window, flung it open, and was about to start dropping bottles out when he suddenly recoiled and hid back inside—Tony van der Westhuizen was having a cigarette on the patio and almost saw him! Peter waited anxiously, taking a peek every now and then to see if Tony was still there, wishing he would hurry up and leave. Every moment he waited was another moment someone might walk in and find him with a handful of bottles and two empty cabinets.

Eventually he peeked out and saw Tony dropping his cigarette butt onto the ground and squashing it with his foot before going back inside. As soon as he was out of sight, Peter quickly dropped the last few bottles out the window. There were now two conspicuous piles of bottles in the flowerbed, but that was a problem for later. He closed the windows and was busy closing the cabinets when he heard the dining-room door open and jumped with fright!

"What's got you so jumpy?" Larissa said as she came into the room.

Peter sighed with relief. "Did you find Phillip?" he asked.

"Yes, he's in the sitting room," said Larissa. "Now, could you *please* tell me what we're doing?"

"We're going to go have a drink with him," said Peter, trying to sound confident. "Was there anyone else there?"

"No, everyone else is watching *Frozen*."

"Perfect!"

He went over to fetch the half bottle of wine he had kept to one side, and grabbed two wine glasses while he was there.

"Oh," he remembered, "did you bring it?"

Larissa took a stick of lipstick out of her pocket and threw it to him.

"Thanks!"

"And the photo?" she asked.

"Oh, just put that down for now," said Peter.

He opened the lipstick and started applying it to the back of the cabinet door handles.

"What on earth are you doing?" said Larissa.

"Sorry," said Peter as he handed the lipstick back to her, then started leading her out of the dining room and toward the sitting room. "Now, I reckon we go sit near him but not right next to him. We just have a glass of wine and a chat, and I'm pretty sure he'll want to join us. Our first objective is to find out about the men from the R.M.S. *Durham*, but I don't want him to feel like we came to find him. And that's because our second objective is to find out about the secret passage, which I'm hoping he'll end up showing us if everything goes according to plan. We mustn't bring it up."

They passed through the narrow passage under the stairs and started whispering as they got closer to the sitting-room door.

"You think he's just going to show us the secret passage?" Larissa asked quietly.

"Not intentionally," said Peter.

He took a deep breath and reached for the door handle, but Larissa stopped him.

"Wait!" she whispered. "We have to pretend we were already talking when we go in. Like this ..." She opened the door and at the same time, with a bit of dramatic flair, started speaking. "Well, it's an old photo, so I'm not surprised he doesn't know them."

Peter caught on and followed her lead. "Ja, I guess you're right," he said as he went in and put the glasses down. "And I don't think many of the family actually stayed in this area, so there probably aren't any others who know them either."

He started pouring the wine while Larissa flopped down on the couch and made herself comfortable, then pretended to see Phillip for the first time.

"Oh, I'm sorry, Mr. D'Arcy, we're not disturbing you, are we?"

"Oh, no, not at all!" said Phillip in his posh English accent. "Please, you're more than welcome."

"We were just having a glass of wine," said Larissa. "Care to join us?"

"I ... uh ... yes, I suppose I might as well." He sprang up surprisingly quickly for someone his age and fetched himself a glass from a little cabinet behind him.

"This is actually a cognac glass, but it should do the trick!"

He helped himself to about double the amount of wine that Peter and Larissa had in their glasses and sat down on the chair next to them.

"And to what are we drinking?" he asked, raising his glass.

"How about to Patricia?" said Larissa.

"Ah, yes," said Phillip, "to Patricia indeed!"

Peter raised his glass as well. "Patricia."

They all clinked their glasses together and took a sip of wine.

Phillip's sip was a particularly healthy one, and Larissa had to wait for him to put his glass down before she spoke again.

"Oh, Mr. D'Arcy—" she began.

"Please, it's Phillip."

"I'm sorry; Phillip," said Larissa. "You've lived here for a while, haven't you?"

"I haven't just lived here for a while, my dear girl, I grew up here! Mixed blessing, to tell you the truth. Mostly fond memories, of course, but certainly some dark ones as well."

"Oh, um ... why's that?" Larissa asked, trying to work out how she could bring the photo into the discussion.

"Well, my father and my mother's father never really got along, you see, and it made life quite difficult for the rest of us at times. Eventually, we moved to the Cape to escape all the drama."

"You were all living together in this house?" Larissa asked.

"Indeed," said Phillip, pausing to take a sip of wine. "When my father married my mother, you see, he had arranged with her father, Harold Woodwright, that they would live here and he would help to manage the farm. My sister and I were born here, and we lived here until about 1945, or 46. But it was a mistake from the start, from what I gather."

"You mean because your father and grandfather didn't get along?" Larissa asked.

"Yes, precisely," said Phillip. "You see, my father was a lot more, say ... 'progressive' than my grandfather Harold. My father didn't agree with the ways in which Harold treated the farm workers. Harold saw the workers as beneath him—they were his subjects, and he ruled with an iron fist. My father did not like that; they fought often. I sometimes found myself caught in the middle of it because I was friends with a boy on the farm named Sam. Samkhela Msimang. His father was one of the workers. May I top you up?" Phillip had almost finished his glass of wine and started to pour himself some more.

"Yes, please," said Peter, holding his glass out for a top-up. He gave Larissa a look.

"Oh, um, yes please," she said, sliding her almost-untouched glass over the table to Phillip.

"So," Phillip continued as he poured their wine, "whenever my father would say anything against Harold and how he was treating the workers, Harold liked to show that he was the boss by punishing the workers even more. They began to detest my father for his efforts, because he was ultimately making it worse for them. Sam used to tell me that my father must just leave them be. He would even get angry with *me*, as though *I* had something to do with it."

He paused to take a sip of wine.

"Let me tell you," he went on, "it's not a pleasant thing, seeing your friends being mistreated when you know you can't do anything about it without making it worse. You can't help but feel useless."

He was silent for a moment, then took another long sip of wine.

"Samkhela Msimang," Larissa said. "He wouldn't happen to be related to Thulani, would he?"

"Why, yes," Phillip smiled, "he was Thulani's father."

"Wow," said Larissa, "so their family has been around here for a very long time?"

"They've certainly been here longer than our family has," said Phillip.

"How long *has* our family been here?" Peter asked, seeing his opportunity. "Because they originally came from England, didn't they?"

"Indeed, they did," said Phillip. "I believe it would have been around the 1870s, or possibly even early 1880s when they first moved to South Africa."

"You know quite a lot about our family's history, don't you?" said Peter. "I remember you telling me about ... was it your great-grandfather who used to know the Royal Family?"

"Yes, that's right!" said Phillip. "Yes, Charles Woodwright used to be a very prominent member of society—on account of his wealth, mostly. In particular, I think he was quite good friends with Prince Alfred, the Duke of Edinburgh, and they would occasionally meet for tea."

"We were actually looking at a photo earlier," said Peter. "It's of two men who I presume were from England. I wonder if you might be able to tell us who they were?"

"I would have to see the photo," said Phillip.

"I'll go fetch it!"

Peter got up and quickly ran to fetch the photo they had left in the dining room.

"Here," he said, passing the photo to Phillip as he sat back down. "Do you recognize them?"

Phillip looked over the photo. "They do look familiar," he said as he squinted down at the photo, "but I can't be sure. What makes you think they're from England?"

"The ship," said Peter. "R.M.S. *Durham Castle*. 'R.M.S.' is Royal Mail Ship, which is English. That must be where they were from."

Phillip looked at the ship in the photo and raised his eyebrows slightly as he read the name. "Ah, yes," he said, "right you are, my dear boy."

"Why do you think they were here?" Peter asked. "Do you think they might have been carrying something?"

"I'm afraid I have no idea," said Phillip. "Although ..." He turned the frame over and looked at the back. "There's a small chance we might be able to find out. People often used to write on the back of photographs, like a postcard."

He delicately undid the latch on the back of the frame and carefully removed the photo. On the back, in black ink, was a short inscription. Peter and Larissa glanced at each other; Phillip read it aloud.

A kindly Indian fellow took this photograph of us in Durban when we arrived; we thought you might like to keep it as something by which to remember us. Once again, we're sorry for all that happened. M. and H. Jefferson.

Peter and Larissa watched Phillip as the realization washed over him.

"Oh ..." he said slowly as he leaned back and looked at the photo again as if in a new light. "I *do* remember these men! These are Mark and Henry Jefferson. They were the cousins of Harold Woodwright. They came to visit once when I was very young."

"What are they apologizing for?" Larissa asked.

"That story," said Phillip with an intriguing smile as he emptied the last few drops of wine into his glass, "begins with their uncle Charles. But I think we might need some more wine before we get into that."

"Yes!" said Peter, a little too enthusiastically. "Let's get another bottle!"

He quickly downed the rest of the wine in his glass, and instantly regretted it. He turned away as his whole face screwed up, and for a few seconds he thought he might throw up. Larissa pressed her lips together, trying her hardest not to react, but he could see in her eyes she was laughing at him.

Luckily, Phillip didn't seem to notice.

"Brian doesn't like it when I drink from the cabinet during the day," he said, more to himself than to Peter and Larissa. "But, I suppose, given present company—"

"Ja, I wouldn't mind some more," Larissa said casually, swirling her wine around in her glass as she watched Peter with a huge grin.

"Yes, let's see what else there is," Phillip finally decided.

He got up and led them out of the sitting room and into the dining room, where he went across to the alcohol cabinet. When he opened the doors, he stared in stunned silence at the empty wine racks.

"Where is all the wine?" he said in disbelief.

He looked around the room as though he might see where it had gone, then tried the next cabinet. Again, he stared in silence at the few remaining liqueur bottles at the bottom.

"What the devil is going on?" he said, looking around the room again.

"What's the matter?" said Larissa.

"I could've sworn these were filled just the other day," said Phillip, looking very confused. He furrowed his brows in thought. "Maybe this is Brian's doing …" he said to himself.

Larissa looked at Peter with a wide-eyed expression as if to say "what have you done?!" but Peter didn't react. "Is there none left?" he asked.

"Well, we could have these," said Phillip, picking up two bottles and reading the labels. "Cherry liqueur; peach schnapps ..."

"That's a bit heavy," said Peter. "Are you sure there's no more wine?"

"My dear boy, you can see as well as I can that the cabinet is empty," said Phillip.

"Is this the only place where wine is kept," Larissa asked innocently.

Phillip was silent, clearly in a quandary.

"Pity," said Larissa, "I think Peter really wanted some more." She gave Peter a cheeky glance.

"Well ..." Phillip began, but he hesitated.

"Ja, I was enjoying myself," said Peter.

"Alright," Phillip finally said in a low voice, "you two stay here and I'll go and fetch some more wine. But you need to promise not to tell anyone else about this; Brian doesn't know about my little hiding spot, and I'd prefer to keep it that way."

"Of course!" said Peter.

"We promise," said Larissa.

Phillip gave them each one last look, as though deciding

whether he should trust them, and then turned to leave. As soon as he was out of the room, they both ran to the door to watch where he was going. They got there just in time to catch him going back through the narrow passage, and then he was out of sight.

"In the living room?" said Larissa, perplexed. "Surely not."

"Do you think there's a secret passage in there?" said Peter. "Or just a well-hidden stash?"

"I don't know, but your lipstick idea worked a charm," said Larissa, pointing to the door handle. Smudged in dark red lipstick were Phillip's fingerprints. "He's going to leave a trace of lipstick everywhere he goes now."

Peter smiled.

"Yes, I thought it would," he said as he licked his thumb and wiped the lipstick off.

"Come on," said Larissa, "let's go sit down before he comes back."

They went to wipe the lipstick off the cabinet door handle and then sat at the table to wait for Phillip to come back.

"So, what did you do with all the wine?" Larissa asked.

"Flowerbed outside the window," said Peter.

Larissa looked over to the window, then back at Peter.

"I'm impressed," she said after a short silence. "This turned out to be a really good plan."

Peter nodded. "It did," he said. "But I didn't think about how we're going to get all the wine back before dinner tonight."

Larissa didn't have an answer.

Soon Phillip came back and stood in the doorway holding a bottle in each hand.

"Shall we return to the lounge?" he asked.

They followed him back into the sitting room, and Peter surreptitiously wiped the lipstick from the door handles as they passed.

"Would you prefer a Merlot or a Shiraz?" Phillip asked once they were sitting back down.

Peter had no idea what the difference was.

"I'll have the Shiraz, please," said Larissa.

"Um, ja, same," said Peter.

"Shiraz it is!" Phillip popped the cork off with a corkscrew he obviously kept on his person for such occasions as these. "Forgive me," he said as he started pouring the wine, "where did we leave off?"

"You were going to tell us about the men in that photograph," said Peter.

"Ah, yes!" said Phillip. "Mark and Henry Jefferson!"

He made himself comfortable in his chair and took a big gulp of wine before he continued. "Now, you may have heard rumors that the Woodwrights were once a family of immense wealth. If and how it was all lost, nobody knows for sure, though I daresay I can venture a guess. But if you've ever wondered how the Woodwrights came into such great wealth in the first place, it was thanks to Charles Woodwright.

"Charles Woodwright was my great-grandfather, which would make him your ... well, I'm not sure precisely what that would make him to you, but, suffice to say, you are also a descendant of his. He was born into a rather well-to-do family in London, along with a few brothers and sisters. One of his sisters was Charlotte Woodwright.

"Now the story goes that Charles was something of an academic. As was fashionable among the intelligentsia of that time, he took up the study of Geology, and acquired the habit of looking at rocks as he wandered through farmlands and over hillsides. On one such stroll through the countryside of North Wales, purely by chance, he happened across a small rock, about the size of a clenched fist, with a streak of gold in it! You must understand: many men spent their lives panning rivers in search of gold with very little to show for it, and here was Charles on a leisurely walk, not even looking for it when he found this little hunk of treasure!

Well, this should have been the discovery of a lifetime, surely? Not for Charles, as it turned out; it only sparked a fire inside of him. The geologist in him wanted to know where the gold had come from, and the man in him wanted to find it.

"And find it he did. He had been prospecting for less than a year when he discovered a substantial network of gold deposits in North Wales, not far from where he had found his initial gold rock. He teamed up with a man named Rodney Jefferson, and together they created the Woodwright-Jefferson Mining Company, one of the most successful gold mines in the United Kingdom.

"Well, as you can imagine, Charles became filthy rich at a fairly young age; but he never trusted money. Instead, he placed his trust in gold. Maybe he knew that the value of gold would only increase over time, or maybe it had just become an obsession. Whatever the reason, Charles invested a lot of his wealth into the acquisition of solid gold. They used what was called the 'Gold Standard' at the time, you see, so one could easily exchange money for gold at the central bank. And this is how Charles stored his wealth; he might have sold one here and traded one there, but it was certain that, at any given time, he had a hoard of gold bars safely locked away somewhere. Some say that he never even parted with his first gold find—the fist-sized rock with a single gold streak.

"But Charles's knowledge of Geology was not forgotten, and the apparent ease with which he found the gold did not go unnoticed. In about the late 1870s, possibly even the early 1880s, when the British were vying for control of South Africa, there were whispers of gold to be found in Zululand. The English, of course, wanted to control any raw materials in the land, so they wanted the gold to be found by an Englishman. They arranged for Charles to come to South Africa to take up the role of Surveyor-General of Natal, with the explicit aim of finding any gold in the region. So, Charles intended to come to South Africa for some years, fulfil his role as Surveyor-General, and then return to England."

"But hang on," said Peter, "I've never heard of gold in Zululand?"

"Well, precisely," said Phillip. "Things did not go at all as planned. I'm not sure if he ever claimed the title of Surveyor-General, but if he did it wasn't for long. I think he had no interest in the other duties of the position—mapping the area, road laying and what have you. He also, as you say, never found any more gold. There actually were one or two small findings, and I think he might have even floated a mining operation, but the rumors of gold turned out to be rather fruitless.

"Of course, around that same time, there was a great discovery in the Witwatersrand. Gold fever gripped half of the country, and everybody rushed north to make their fortunes.

"Charles, however, had had enough of hunting for gold. He had no intention of rushing north, nor indeed of even returning to England yet. He had met a young lady, you see—Mary Findlay—and didn't want to go anywhere until he had married her, which he eventually did. Her father was a missionary and had built the chapel up on the hill. Charles then bought the land to keep the chapel for Mary, and he took up farming and built this very manor in which we now sit almost a century and a half later."

"And what happened to the mining company?" Peter asked. "The one in Wales; what was it called? The Woodwright-Jefferson Company or something?"

"Oh, that carried on for quite some time," said Phillip. "Like I said, his initial plan was to only spend a few years in South Africa until his duty was done, and then go back to England. He still owned half of the company. In fact, he still owned property in England as well, I believe, to which he intended to return."

"So, what happened to all of it?" asked Peter. "What happened to the mining company and his property in England and everything?"

"I'm getting there, I'm getting there!" said Phillip, and he held the suspense as he took another long sip of wine.

"Firstly, Rodney Jefferson ended up marrying Charles's sister, Charlotte, in England. They had two sons, Mark and Henry Jefferson, and those are the two people you see in this picture, all grown up. I think Charles had some vague notion of one day returning to England, but he never did. When he eventually died, Harold, his first-born, inherited almost everything: Woodwright Manor, the property in England, and all his shares in the Woodwright-Jefferson Mining Company. Well, Harold had no intention of going to England, and by this time the amount of gold being extracted had started to dwindle; so he sold his shares in the company, sold the property in England, and arranged for most of their belongings to be auctioned off."

Phillip smiled as he took another sip of wine.

"Now this is where the story becomes somewhat mysterious," he went on. "It seems—though nobody is entirely sure—that Charles never brought any of the gold with him on his initial voyage to South Africa. Most people say it was just auctioned off with the rest of the belongings in England when Harold sold everything. But I think something else happened."

Phillip leaned forward in his chair.

"Not many people know this, but when Harold arranged for their belongings to be auctioned off, he also discreetly arranged for some of the more valuable and sentimental items to be brought to South Africa—and that's what Mark and Henry Jefferson were doing on their trip to South Africa, under the guise of a family visit. But something happened. I was only about five years old at the time, so I don't remember anything of it, other than all of the commotion with police and what have you, but I was told about it in later years. On their way from Pietermaritzburg to Woodwright Manor, the Jeffersons were hijacked and everything they had was taken. All of Charles's old belongings were lost. That's what they were apologizing for in this note on the photograph.

"But the peculiar thing was that they were strangely unforthcoming with the police when it came to detailing what had been taken. My own opinion, for what it's worth, is that among the items they were carrying was all of Charles's gold. I think it was taken along with everything else, and they didn't want the world to know that millions of pounds' worth of gold was up for grabs to anyone who could get to the hijackers before they did."

He leaned back in his chair.

"And that, at least in my opinion, is how the Woodwright fortune was lost."

He took one last conclusive sip of wine.

Peter couldn't believe it. Everything made perfect sense now! He desperately wanted to discuss it with Larissa, but they had to maintain the facade and act cool until they were alone again. He could see by the way Larissa was gripping the side of her chair that she was thinking exactly the same thing.

Her face, however, was as calm as ever. "Wow, that's amazing," she said, as though it was nothing more than an interesting story. "And none of it was ever found, was it? The hijacked car or the gold or any of it?"

"I have a sneaking suspicion that the car did eventually turn up," said Phillip. "Some years later, perhaps; I can't remember precisely. But, no, the gold was never found."

"That is a fascinating story," said Larissa, and she turned to Peter. "Imagine, you could've inherited some gold if it wasn't stolen."

"It would have to go through about four generations before I saw any of it," Peter said, remembering what his mom had told him.

"What would happen if the gold did turn up?" Larissa asked Phillip.

"Well," said Phillip, "if you could prove it was the gold that once belonged to Charles Woodwright, then I'd imagine it would legally belong to Patricia, because everything was ultimately left to her. And now it would go to the lucky soul to whom she's left her inheritance. More wine?"

"Oh, no thanks," said Larissa. "If I have any more I think it'll put me straight to sleep."

"Peter?" Phillip said hopefully. "More wine?"

"No, thank you," said Peter, "I've also had enough for now."

"Alright," Phillip said, disappointed. "I guess we'd better put this away then."

Not before he had poured himself one more glass, Peter noticed; but then Phillip did eventually push the cork back into the bottle and put the bottle to one side.

"Actually," said Larissa, "it's been lovely chatting with you, Phillip, but I think I'm going to need a nap before dinner. Would you like us to put that wine away on our way out?"

"Oh, um ... yes, I suppose," said Phillip, reluctantly handing her the two bottles.

"This was great," Larissa said. "Thank you for chatting to us."

"Not at all," said Phillip, "the pleasure was certainly mine! Thank you for giving an old man some company!"

Peter and Larissa left Phillip and took the bottles back to the dining room.

"Are you thinking what I'm thinking?" Larissa asked as soon as they were alone.

"You mean that Phillip's right and they *were* carrying the gold?" said Peter.

"And *that's* what Patricia took from them when she rode out to meet them!" said Larissa. "She and Mandla were going to take the gold and run away together!"

"Only they never realized she took it because they assumed it was taken by the hijackers!" said Peter.

"Exactly!" said Larissa. "She must have hidden it somewhere around here; and she never ended up running away with Mandla, so it could still be here somewhere!"

"*That's* what the person in the chapel was looking for!" said Peter. "*That's* what's hidden in the secret passage!"

"Ja," Larissa began, but hesitated. "Only ... if that is where Phillip keeps his stash, he's been in and out of there loads of times, and he doesn't seem to know anything about where it could be ... so maybe not."

Peter's excitement faded. "That's a good point. So maybe it's not hidden there."

"Or maybe that's not where he keeps his stash," said Larissa. "Either way, I think we need to take a look for ourselves. Tonight. Same plan as last night."

"Agreed," said Peter as he opened the wine cabinet to put the half-empty bottles away.

"On a separate note," said Larissa, looking at the empty cabinet, "what's your plan to get all the bottles back?"

"Haven't really thought about it," said Peter.

"I think there's an outside chance they might realize at dinner tonight that all the wine is gone."

"Yes, I'm aware of that."

"Even if we put it all back now, Phillip will know something's up."

"And if we don't, someone else will find it in the garden."

"Bit of a catch twenty-two you've got us into here," said Larissa. "Great plan."

"You thought it was a good plan when we saw where Phillip was getting the wine from."

Before they could decide what to do, the door opened and Thulani came through on his way to the kitchen.

"Good afternoon, you two," he said pleasantly.

Peter hastily shut the cabinet doors. "Hi, Thulani!" he said quickly.

"Hi, Thulani," said Larissa, doing a much better job of sounding casual.

Thulani stopped. "What's going on here?" he asked.

Peter and Larissa both glanced at each other. "Um ... nothing," said Larissa.

"Nothing," Peter repeated.

Thulani looked from one to the other, then a cheeky smile came over him. "Hawu, niyaqabulana?" he laughed, wagging a playful finger at them. "Heheyi!"

"Cha! Asiqabulana, mkhulu!" Larissa protested.

Thulani left them, still shaking his head and laughing to himself.

"What did he say?" Peter asked once Thulani was out of the room.

Larissa glanced at Peter but quickly looked away again, with a sheepish smile on her face.

"Don't worry," she said. "Come on, let's get out of here."

Chapter 14

Larissa kept her word about taking a nap before dinner, which turned out to be quite convenient: when the movie finished and the other girls found her in her bed, nobody bothered to ask where she had been. Peter, on the other hand, had returned to watch the end of the movie, but the wine also took its toll on him and he fell asleep in the TV room. Ellen woke him up afterwards and was the only one who suspected anything.

"You weren't sneaking off with Larissa again, were you?" she asked with a grin.

"I have no idea what you're talking about," Peter yawned.

"Where do you guys go?" Ellen asked. "What are you getting up to?"

For a moment, Peter considered telling Ellen everything: about the old letters from Patricia's love affair, the mystery of the intercepted letter to her executor, the person in the chapel, and everything Phillip had just told them … but it turned out Ellen's mind was somewhere else entirely.

"Have you kissed her yet?" she asked.

"What? No!" said Peter.

"Really?" said Ellen, her surprise both flattering and slightly humiliating. "You spend enough time together. I would get a move on if I were you; I don't think Daniel is going to wait around for your blessing before he makes a move."

"Daniel can do whatever he wants," said Peter. He really didn't want to think about it.

"Mmhm," Ellen said skeptically.

At dinner that evening, everyone was talking about the mystery of the missing wine. From the time Peter entered the dining room to the time he sat down, he overheard at least three conversations with people saying things like "It was filled only a few days ago," and "Surely it can't be finished already." Larissa, he noticed, was looking down at the table while everybody around her was discussing what could have happened.

His own parents were no different. "I think everybody just drinks a lot more than they realize," his dad was saying as Peter sat down. "You know, Phillip gets a bad rap, but he hardly drinks more than the rest of these lot. There must be fifty people at this table—I'm not surprised it's finished!"

Phillip was retelling the enthralling tale to those around him of how he opened the wine cabinet and found it to be empty. Thulani was shrugging and shaking his head as he explained to a concerned-looking Brian that he had no idea where the wine had gone. The butlers were looking flustered, checking the cabinets in the room, then checking them all again just to make sure they hadn't missed twenty bottles of wine the first time round.

Peter was very quiet while all of this was going on—quieter than usual. He did exactly what Larissa was doing and looked down at the table to avoid making eye contact with anyone. He glanced up to the other end of the table where Larissa was, and in the same moment she glanced up at him. She had been looking very somber until then, and Peter could only imagine he must have looked the same; but as soon as they made eye contact she cracked and started giggling. She quickly looked back down at the table and covered her mouth, but the damage was done: Peter also started giggling. He tried to cover his mouth as well, but his bobbing shoulders gave him away.

"What's got you in such hysterics?" his mom asked.

Peter tried to compose himself before he was able to say "nothing."

He and Larissa then made the mistake of glancing up at each other again and were both sent into another fit of giggles.

Ellen must have seen them as well, because when she passed Peter at the serving table, she stopped and eyed him closely. "Do you and Larissa know something we don't?" she asked.

"What do you mean?"

"Well," said Ellen, "the two of you snuck off again, then you stumbled back into the TV room and passed out, then we come to dinner, the wine is all gone, and you two are giggling away like children. *Slightly* suspicious."

"I mean, when you say it like *that* it does sound suspicious ..." Peter started saying.

"Also, I heard Phillip saying he was having wine with the two of you," said Ellen.

Peter didn't know how he was going to get out of this one. "Alright," he said, "but promise you won't tell anyone?"

"Obviously."

"It's all in the flowerbed outside the windows," said Peter.

"What?" Ellen said a little too loudly and immediately looked at the window.

"Don't look!" said Peter.

She quickly looked back at him. "Why?" she asked.

"We wanted Phillip to think it was finished."

Ellen stared at him. "Why?" she asked again.

"Because ... he drinks too much."

Ellen raised an eyebrow at him.

"Don't tell anyone!" he said, and hurried back to his seat.

After dinner they all moved through to the sitting room, where Vuyo lit a fire. Brian assigned Jesse and Daniel to fire-watching duty, and the rest of the kids all congregated around them next to the fireplace. Michelle and Ellen looked through an old chest that Brian had pointed out full of board games, puzzles, and playing cards, and after some digging around they pulled out Clue. Despite the duty being assigned to Jesse and Daniel, Austen and Katie were the ones who kept feeding logs onto the fire to keep the flames dancing in the fireplace, and in teams of two and three, they passed the evening arguing over where, with what, and by whom Mr. Boddy had been killed. Peter was on a team with the highly enthusiastic Steven and the highly-opinionated-though-not-so-strategically-minded Megan.

"I think it was Miss Scarlett in the Dining Room with the Rope."

"It can't be; look, we already have that one."

Peter tried to casually glance around the room during the game for any more signs of red lipstick that might tell them where Phillip had gone earlier, but he didn't see any. He had hoped Larissa might do the same, but she was too busy giggling with Daniel. They were the only ones who spent more time laughing than arguing, and Ellen's words from earlier rang in Peter's head.

Jesse, Ellen, and Austen found that it was Reverend Green in the Library with the Candle Stick, and once the game had been packed away and all the arguments forgotten, they made their way upstairs to bed. As had become customary, Jesse waited for everyone to settle down and switched the light off. Peter pulled the duvet up to his shoulders and waited for everyone else to fall asleep.

He awoke with a start when someone poked him. It took him a few moments in the complete darkness to realize it was Larissa hanging onto the side of his bed. He had dosed off. He couldn't really see her, but he could tell she was scowling at him.

As quietly as he could, he climbed down from his bed and followed her from the room.

"You were supposed to meet me out here," she whispered as Peter followed her down the passage. "I waited for almost fifteen minutes!"

"I'm really sorry," said Peter. "I fell asleep."

"No kidding!"

They began inching their way down the stairs, feeling very exposed. Every sound they made seemed to echo around the very big hall, amplified by the darkness. Peter would've almost preferred climbing down the balcony from the library again, where they could at least turn a light on and speak a bit more freely. Creeping down the stairs in the middle of the house where anyone could pass them was a lot more nerve-wracking. He just hoped that everyone was in bed and asleep by now.

But not everyone was in bed and asleep. When they reached the first floor, they could hear voices coming from the direction of the sitting room—the direction they needed to go.

They crept along to the edge of the narrow passage and peeked around the corner: luckily the door was closed, but there was a faint glow coming through the small gap below the door. They tiptoed through the passage and, peering through the keyhole, Peter could see a single table lamp illuminating the room in a dim light. The logs that were alight earlier with flickering orange flames had been reduced to glowing red embers, slowly breaking apart in the fireplace.

Two people spoke softly together, facing the fire. He couldn't really see them—they were just profiles against the dim light—but then one of them raised a cigarette to his mouth: Tony van der Westhuizen.

The other man was speaking in a low voice, barely audible through the door. "... very strange indeed, I agree. And who was it who requested it? Must have been Brian, I suppose?"

"No, actually Brian was opposed to the autopsy," Tony said, staring into the fire. "Said it was unnecessary and would just create drama. And he was right, of course; nothing conclusive when the results were in."

"So who then?"

"It was Phillip, actually; but I reckon someone else might have put him up to it."

"You think so? Who?"

Tony shrugged. "Thulani, maybe."

"Very interesting!" the other man said. "Now, dare I ask; you heard about the will?"

Tony suddenly looked up, startled by the question. "Um, yes, I heard about it," he said, shifting in his chair.

"You're an attorney, aren't you? So answer me this: if a will is missing, but the person had written another will before that, then would the first will stand?"

"In a lot of cases, yes," said Tony. "If there is a valid document in existence, it normally takes preference."

"I see, I see ..."

Larissa tapped Peter on the shoulder. "Come on," she whispered, "we can't check tonight. We'll have to try tomorrow."

Peter agreed, and they turned to leave. "Actually, hang on ..." He got out his phone flashlight and checked the closet door Thulani had taken him through to get towels. Nothing.

He then checked the door opposite. Phillip's lipstick-smudged fingerprints were on the handle.

"Here we go," he said. "Not in the living room after all."

Peter slowly turned the handle while Larissa stood by and clenched her teeth, both very aware of every creak the door made.

They found themselves staring into another walk-in closet, this one with shelves of duvets, blankets, sleeping bags, and a whole assortment of camping gear, but no sign of a secret passageway. Shutting the door behind them, they began to have a look around for any more lipstick smudges that might give away the entrance.

"No, it won't be there," Peter whispered as Larissa started

perusing the shelves on the right. "The sitting room is behind there. I think it'll be somewhere here below the stairs."

"Joke's on you," said Larissa, and she held up an old flashlight.

Peter looked at it and saw lipstick smeared over the switch.

"Good spot," he said. "I still don't think the passageway is behind there, though."

He went to the back of the closet and shone his phone up and down the shelves on the left.

"Here, I've got something," he said as his light found another unmistakable red smudge on the box of a camping stove.

He picked the box up to have a look at it, but, apart from the lipstick smudge, there was nothing special about it.

"There!" Larissa said, pointing to behind where the box had been.

"Shh!" Peter whispered. "There are still people next door!"

It was hardly visible against the dark wood, but she was right; there was another smudge of lipstick on the wall at the back of the shelf. At first it was unclear why there would be a smudge there—it almost looked like Phillip might have just touched the side by accident while he was moving the box. But as they leaned down to inspect it, they noticed a very thin groove in a square around it!

Larissa reached out to press it. Sure enough, the little square gave way like a button. There was a soft *click!* and the entire rack of shelves swung slowly and gracefully open as one big door. They were now shining their lights down a staircase into a dark passageway below.

Larissa flung her arms around Peter's neck and squeezed him in a tight hug just as she had done when they found the tin under the tree. "You can actually be quite smart at times," she said with a huge grin.

"You were the one who found it," said Peter.

"No, the whole lipstick thing was your idea!"

She used the flashlight to lead them down the stairs into the secret passage. The air was stale, the stone walls damp and moldy. As far as they could tell, there were no lights.

At the bottom of the stairs the passage opened up to a wider room, with a few old wooden crates and barrels lying here and there and a small pile of loose bricks in one corner. At the far end of the room was a small archway where the passage carried on. Wine racks lined the wall on either side, reaching up to the ceiling of the passageway not much higher than their heads. The rack in the middle seemed newer than the others and had a few bottles of wine, whiskey and the odd rum, but the rest seemed to have more cobwebs and dust than actual bottles. Their wood was slowly rotting; the bottles looked ancient: all different shapes and sizes, some of them without labels, the liquid inside looked more like dam water than drinkable liquor.

Peter picked out an old dust-covered bottle whose contents were a murky brown with a layer of sediment at the bottom. "Look at this stuff," he said, speaking freely now that there was a solid layer of stone between them and the house above. "What do you reckon this is?"

"Give it a taste," Larissa teased.

Peter considered it for a moment, just to impress her, but quickly gave up when he couldn't even remove the cork.

They investigated all the crates and barrels, but most of them turned out to be empty. A few crates were filled with empty bottles, and in one of the barrels they found an old shovel, a pickaxe, and a plastering trowel, which, judging from the layer of dust and cobwebs, had all been there for decades.

"I must say," said Larissa, shining the flashlight around the room, "I was expecting to find more down here."

"Look at this," said Peter, inspecting the wine racks.

On the side of the middle wine rack was a metallic lion's face. It was just like the knockers on the front door except smaller, and its mouth was empty. Larissa ran her hand over it, wiping the dust off, revealing it to be a dull golden color.

"What do you think it is?" she asked.

"No idea," said Peter, shaking his head.

Larissa shone the flashlight down the archway. "Come on," she said, "let's see where it goes."

She once again led the way as they continued along the passage. After the room with the wine racks, there wasn't much to see—stone ceiling above them, stone walls to their sides, and stone floor beneath them, which had started sloping gradually upward.

"Who were the people in the sitting room, by the way?" Larissa asked.

"Tony van der Westhuizen and someone else," said Peter. "It sounded like Tony knows a bit about the autopsy, and he didn't look very comfortable when it was brought up."

"Are you saying you think he's got something to do with it?" Larissa asked.

"I'm saying he knows something," said Peter. "I don't know what, or how."

They came to another staircase, which ascended to what looked like a dead-end. When they got to the top, however, they found that the dead-end had a circle in the stone wall that looked like it could be turned, with a handle right in the center of it. They looked at each other.

"I think we should turn off the flashlight," said Peter.

Larissa turned it off, and they were thrown into complete darkness. Peter took hold of the handle, turned it slowly with the sound of stone grating against stone, and carefully pushed the door open.

They were greeted by cool, fresh air and a starry night sky above them—the clouds had all lifted and the waning moon was visible. But no sooner had they noticed the stars than they noticed big shapes all around them in the dark, casting shadows in the moonlight.

"We're in the graveyard!" Larissa said as they slowly stepped out of the passageway onto the wet grass.

As their eyes slowly adjusted to the dim moonlight, Peter looked back to see where they had come from: the passageway emerged from under the chapel. The door was the gravestone with the lion's face that he had leaned against during Patricia's committal.

"No wonder they couldn't find this place!" he said, examining the front of the gravestone for some telltale sign that it was in fact a door.

"Can it even be opened from this side?" Larissa asked.

He tried the inside handle again, and as it turned he watched the lion's face on the opposite side turn in unison.

"Yup, looks like it can."

He tested it again to make sure, then looked around the graveyard. A few paces from him, Larissa was staring solemnly at Patricia's grave.

Peter went to stand beside her.

"I wonder what she would've thought about what we're doing," Larissa said.

"Did you know her?" Peter asked.

"Ja, I met her a few times. She was always very kind."

"Exceptionally wise, I found," said Peter.

"Yes, she was," Larissa smiled.

She hooked her arms through Peter's arm and rested her head on his shoulder, and for a while they stood looking at the grave in silence.

Peter was getting cold, and not entirely comfortable being out in the graveyard, but he wanted the moment to last for as long as possible.

"Okay," Larissa finally said, lifting her head off his shoulder.

"Time to go back?" said Peter.

"Not quite," said Larissa. "I want to see what they were doing here last night."

"They were looking for this," said Peter, pointing to the gravestone with the lion's face. "They thought it would be in the chapel. Whoever told them where to look only gave them half the story."

"It won't hurt to take a look anyway," said Larissa, and without waiting for Peter she went round to the chapel entrance.

Peter had to jog to catch up with her just as she tried the door.

"Locked," she said.

She carried on round to the other side of the chapel with Peter just behind her.

"This is where we were hiding last night," she said as they got to the window where they had been watching the man inside, and she leaned on it to try to take a look, her hand pressed against the glass. "Can't see a thing ..."

Peter stepped on something that felt weird under his foot, and bent down to pick it up. "Cigarette butt," he said.

But there was something else on the ground as well, a few of what looked like small pebbles. He couldn't make out what they were in the dark, but when he picked one up it was smooth to the touch.

"What's that?" asked Larissa.

"Not sure," said Peter.

He got his phone out again and, carefully shielding the side so nobody from the house might see the light, turned on the flashlight.

They were beans of some kind: bigger than ordinary beans, a mottled light and dark brown. As they both peered over them, they noticed more beans that had been thrown out into the grass below them.

"What on earth are they?" said Larissa.

Peter shook his head and shrugged. "No idea. Whoever that guy was must have chucked them out."

They examined the beans for a moment, and Peter turned the flashlight off.

"Okay, now let's get back," he said.

They went back through the graveyard and into the secret passage, keeping an eye out for anything they might have missed the first time—like a secret lever or hidden door handle that could lead somewhere else. They had another look around the wine racks as well, but they still couldn't find anything.

"I think we need to accept that we may have been wrong about this," said Larissa.

Peter sighed. "I was so sure we would find something down here," he said. "What could that person have been looking for?"

"Maybe they're also wrong about it."

Peter wasn't happy, but eventually they were forced to admit defeat and head back out of the secret passage. The two men who had been in the sitting room were no longer there, and the house was completely quiet.

Larissa had just opened the door of the closet when Peter, trying to close the secret passage, knocked the camping stove off the shelf and sent it crashing to the floor. The noise echoed through the entire house. They both froze as they waited for the sound to stop. But then another noise erupted from down the passage—a man was screaming! They heard doors open and saw lights come on down the passage.

Larissa's first instinct was to run down the passage toward the screaming, but Peter managed to catch her and pull her into the TV room.

"What are you doing?!" said Larissa. "They might need help!"

"Shhh!" Peter insisted. "Whatever's going on, the adults can deal with it. There's nothing we can do that they can't do on their own, and we don't need people asking why we're out of bed at this time of night."

They fell silent as they heard footsteps run past and a voice saying, "What is it? What's the matter?"

They both pressed their ears to the door to listen to what was happening at the end of the passage.

"He tried to smother me!" the man cried, almost incomprehensibly. "He tried to smother me!"

"It's okay, you were dreaming! You're alright, it was just a dream!"

The man's cries were getting softer. "He tried to smother me! He tried to smother me!"

"What's going on?"

"Oh, Gideon, he's just had a bad dream. Would you fetch his medication for me? I think it's in the kitchen."

Footsteps passed again the other way, and the cries died down.

"It's alright; you're alright."

Larissa and Peter looked at each other.

"Was that Phillip screaming?" said Larissa.

"I think so," said Peter. "And it sounds like Brian speaking to him."

A few moments later the footsteps came back.

"I have his medication here."

"Thank you! Here you go, Phil, take those."

"Is he going to be alright?"

"Oh, yes, he'll be fine. Surely he didn't wake you all the way on the second floor? Were you already up?"

"Oh, yes, no, I was just coming back from the bathroom when I heard him."

"Let's just close the door so we don't wake any others."

They heard the door close and looked at each other again.

"I think now's our chance to get back," said Peter.

They cautiously opened the door and snuck back along the passage and up the stairs. When they reached the girls' room, Larissa turned to Peter. "I don't think that was just a bad dream," she said.

"You think someone was actually trying to smother Phillip in his sleep?"

"The message we saw earlier said something about 'the old man'; something like 'force it out of the old man.' Maybe they're past that and have moved onto 'destroying the evidence.'"

Peter felt a chill down his spine.

"We'd better get to bed," Larissa said. She reached up and hugged Peter tightly. "See you tomorrow."

Again she lingered for a moment before she let go.

"See you tomorrow," said Peter.

Chapter 15

The next morning presented the clearest blue skies they had seen since arriving at Woodwright. The air was crisp and fresh. The mountains soaked up the morning sun, their shadows pooled at their feet, and their crests cut cleanly through the sky. The dam was calm and still but for a pair of geese drifting along slowly, and the gentle swaying of a few leaves gave away a light breeze in the air.

Peter was the last of the boys to wake up—all these late nights were starting to take their toll on him. He was still lying in bed when Jesse and Kyle came into the room.

"Last night? Are you serious?"

"Ja, bru, he woke everyone up with his screaming."

"And they've taken him to hospital? What's wrong with him?"

"I don't know; I think he hasn't been taking his meds or something."

They both started digging in their bags and took out swim trunks and towels.

"Are you taking your rugby ball?"

"Ja, definitely, bru!"

"Where's Daniel?" Kyle asked as they were leaving.

Jesse grinned. "He's preparing a little picnic."

"A picnic? For what?"

They disappeared out of the room and Peter didn't get to hear what the picnic was all about. He eventually got up and made his way down to breakfast, where he found Larissa sitting alone at the table.

"Morning, Pete," she said with an attempt at a smile. "Slept in a bit, did we?"

Peter put his plate down next to hers. "Why, what's the time?" he asked.

"After ten," she said, eyeing the amount of food on his plate with mild concern. "And it's our last full day at Woodwright."

"After ten? Wow," Peter yawned.

"It's good," said Larissa, "I think we both needed the sleep."

Peter lowered his voice. "Has Phillip been taken to hospital?" he asked.

Larissa nodded with a grim look on her face. "They're saying it's his medication, and he's losing the plot. Everyone's acting like it's not a big deal."

"And no one has any clue that someone actually *did* this to him?" Peter asked.

Larissa shook her head. "Someone who's still here."

Brian stuck his head through the door. "Morning, you two!" he said cheerfully. "I'm heading into town to drop off the videos and get a few cases of wine—I could use some hands. Would either of you care to join me?"

Larissa looked at Peter expectantly and he knew what she was thinking.

"What time?" he asked.

"Oh, there's no rush," said Brian. "Probably in the next hour. Let me know!" With a wave of his hand he turned and left.

"I had forgotten about that," said Peter. "I feel like we have bigger problems right now. What should we do?"

"*We* shouldn't do anything," said Larissa. "This is a *you* problem."

"Don't pretend you weren't part of it!"

"I was just doing what I was told," said Larissa. "I had no idea about the wine."

"Should we go with Brian?" Peter asked as he watched her finish her food and push her cutlery together. "Might make us look less guilty."

"Can't," said Larissa. She stood up and downed the last bit of orange juice in her glass. "I'm going for a walk with Daniel."

"A walk with Daniel?" Peter repeated dumbly.

"Ja, I think he's organized a picnic or something."

"A picnic?" said Peter. "Why?"

Larissa gave Peter a flat look to convey that they both knew perfectly well why. She then gathered up her dishes and turned to take them to the kitchen, leaving Peter alone at the table.

Peter couldn't eat anymore. He could feel a great big pit in his stomach. Everything that happened during the night was forgotten; all he could think about was what Ellen had said to him the day before and the way Larissa had just looked at him. Was it apologetic? What was with all those tight, lingering hugs if she liked Daniel?

"Cheers, Pete," Larissa said casually on her way back from the kitchen.

Peter didn't even look up. He was fuming. Before now he hadn't really admitted to himself that he liked her, but the jealousy he felt now was undeniable. How could she think it was okay to lead him on all this time, and then casually brush him off for Daniel?

Larissa stopped at the door. "Pete?" she said. "Are you okay?"

Peter composed himself and looked up with a fake smile.

"Hundreds," he said.

Larissa nodded. She looked concerned, which frustrated Peter even more.

"I'll see you later?" she said.

"See you later," said Peter. He got up and turned his back on her to take his far-from-empty plate to the kitchen. When he came back, she was gone.

By the time he had got dressed, brushed his teeth and had come back downstairs to find his parents on the patio, he was a lot calmer, and rational thought had started to take over. Were a few lingering hugs really enough to say she was leading him on, or was he reading too much into it? He had started believing what he wanted to believe. From her side, she was just being friendly. And if he wasn't imagining it and there *was* something there, why hadn't he done anything about it? Maybe Ellen was right: he had taken too long and now he had missed his chance. Either way, it wasn't Larissa's fault; he had no real reason to be angry with her.

But that didn't make him feel any better about the fact that she was now spending the day on some kind of romantic walk with Daniel.

He had to take his mind off it. "Where's Becca?" he asked his parents.

"She's with the Le Rouxs," said his mom. "They're going down to the dam. We might join them later—want to come?"

"I'll see," said Peter.

It was a beautiful day, perfect for the dam, but he wasn't in the mood for sunshine and frolicking. He wasn't in the mood for happiness in general.

"Good morning, Mr. and Mrs. Brewer!"

They looked up to see Ellen coming through from the sitting room, smiling brightly at them.

"Good morning, Ellen," said Gill, returning the smile.

"Pete," Ellen said, "Michelle and I are going with Brian into town. Wanna come with?"

"I don't know," Peter said in a very lazy, noncommittal tone.

"Let me rephrase that," said Ellen. "Michelle and I are going with Brian into town, and you should come with."

Peter remembered that he had told her about the wine. "Fair enough," he said. "Let me grab some shoes."

Ellen and Michelle met him outside where Brian was waiting with the bakkie—a single-cab with a canopy over the back.

"Anybody going to ride up front with me?" Brian asked.

"No thanks, Uncle Brian, we're going to ride in the back," Ellen said.

Peter would have rather sat up front in a proper seat, but he figured Ellen probably wanted them to sit in the back so they could all talk without Brian overhearing. The three of them piled in and Brian closed the hatch behind them. They attempted the impossible task of getting comfortable, and soon they were bumping up and down as Brian took off down the gravel driveway.

"How you doing, Pete?" Ellen asked.

"I'm fine, thanks," Peter said skeptically. "You?"

"I'm good, I'm good," Ellen nodded, and she looked down at the floor.

There was a pause, filled with the wheels rumbling over the gravel.

"So ... do you know where Larissa is this morning?" Ellen said after careful consideration.

Peter looked up at her with a raised eyebrow. "Why you asking me?" he said. "I have a feeling you know exactly where she is."

Ellen nodded again.

"I do," she said.

Michelle looked from Ellen to Peter, puzzled. "Why?" she asked. "Where is Larissa?"

"You might not have noticed," said Ellen, "but Peter and Larissa have been spending a lot of time together."

"Okay ..." Michelle said, starting to guess what this was about.

"You might also have noticed that Daniel has been flirting with her since we got here."

Michelle laughed. "Ja, I think everyone's noticed that."

"Well, the two of them went for a walk this morning," Ellen told her.

"A walk?"

"Ja, Daniel prepared a little picnic and everything. That's where they are now."

"Oof!" Michelle looked at Peter with a sorry-for-you kind of expression.

"It's fine!" said Peter, as though he had explained this a hundred times. "There's nothing between us! She can go walking with whomever she likes."

"Oh, please!" Ellen scoffed. "I think every guy here secretly has a crush on her. But you at least had a chance."

Peter felt the blood rushing to his cheeks. He liked hearing that he had a chance. He was, however, very aware of the way she said it in the past tense.

"Clearly not *much* of a chance," he said, still trying to act like it wasn't a big deal.

"No, I don't know," said Ellen. "I think she liked you."

"Then why's she off walking with Daniel?"

"Because at some point you need to make a move, dude!" Michelle cut in. "She's not gonna wait around for you forever. We're leaving tomorrow, and she'd rather go home and tell her mates that she hooked up with a first-team rugby player than go home and tell her mates she *didn't* hook up with a first-team rugby player because she liked someone else, but nothing happened with him either."

Her words stung. It was like he had known all along but had chosen to ignore it. He looked to Ellen for some reassurance, but her soft, apologetic eyes only confirmed that Michelle's words were harsh but true.

"Well, I guess it's too late now," said Peter.

Both girls looked away and didn't say anything, letting the rumbling of the wheels beneath them fill the silence once more.

"How long is this driveway?" Michelle said irritably, peering out the window. "It's so bumpy!"

"Should we go to the dam when we get back?" Ellen suggested, trying to sound chirpy.

Peter shrugged. "Ja, why not."

"How about you, Michelle?" said Ellen.

Michelle sighed. "Not if my mom and Kim are both there," she said. "I'm just not in the mood for their judgy looks and under-their-breath comments."

"Why, what's their deal?" Ellen asked.

Michelle spent the rest of the car ride telling them about how her mother and Kim don't get on, and how petty they can be with each other.

Eventually they pulled up at the supermarket in Underberg, and Brian came round to let them out the back. He sent Michelle across the road to return the DVDs, and asked Peter and Ellen to help him with the wine. He had obviously phoned ahead, because a man was waiting for them at the door with six crates of wine and other assorted bottles of liquor at his side. Brian greeted the man like an old buddy and the two of them chatted away merrily while Peter and Ellen walked to and from the bakkie, carrying the crates of wine and stacking them in the back.

With all the crates of bottles in the back there wasn't space for the three of them anymore, so Peter sat up front with Brian on the way back.

"So, have you had a reasonably good week here at Woodwright?" Brian asked as they were leaving Underberg. "Getting along with all your cousins?"

"Ja, it's been good," said Peter. "I haven't seen that much of them before now, so it's been cool getting to know them."

"You seem to have made good friends with Ellen?" said Brian. "You two get on, do you?"

Peter smiled. "Ja, Ellen's great," he said.

"And Larissa?" said Brian. "You two have also been spending some time together?"

Peter didn't answer. He started to feel the pit in his stomach again.

"Shame, I was worried she wouldn't know anyone and she might feel like a bit of an outsider," Brian went on when Peter didn't say anything, "but she's fit right in with you lot! Seems to get along with everyone."

"Yes, she does," said Peter, thinking that there was more truth to that than Brian probably realized.

Brian must have picked up on his tone because he immediately changed the subject.

"Are you all going to head down to the dam when we get back?" he asked.

"Ja, probably," said Peter. "Except Michelle wasn't too keen."

"Why not?" said Brian. "It's a beautiful day!"

"I don't know; I think because she doesn't want to have to put up with her mom and Kim in the same place."

Brian sighed. "It's always the same with those two," he said.

"Why'd it get so much worse after Walter died?" Peter asked.

"I'd love to know!" Brian said, shaking his head. "I would say you should ask them, except you'd probably just cause a stir."

"I think Megan said it had to do with what Walter told them about the missing fortune."

"Who knows ..." said Brian. "I suppose you could ask Gideon; I don't think he's too concerned about it all."

"Gideon?" said Peter. "Remind me who that is?"

"Gideon!" said Brian. "You know—Father Ian."

"Father Ian?" said Peter. "What does he have to do with it?"

"He's also Walter's son—Karen's brother; didn't you know? Walter was the one who gave him the nickname 'Ian.'"

Peter hadn't actually thought about it, but he guessed it made sense.

"Anyway, probably best to just let sleeping dogs lie," said Brian.

By the time they got back to Woodwright and Trixy had come to greet them with her tail wagging (the ridgebacks didn't bother getting up), Michelle had decided that she would join them at the dam after all. More accurately, she realized she would probably be the only person *not* at the dam if she stayed behind, and that didn't appeal to her.

They fetched their swimsuits and towels and went down to find Jesse, Kyle, Austen, and Steven passing the rugby ball around beside Katie reading her book, and Megan sunbathing on her towel. Rebecca and the other younger kids were all giggling and splashing in the dam, with their parents supposedly keeping an eye on them while they chatted on the side. Peter looked around but couldn't see Larissa anywhere—nor Daniel. He didn't know what he had been expecting, but he felt his heart sink.

Austen threw him the rugby ball which, thankfully, he managed to catch and throw back. He joined their circle; at least this would help to take his mind off everything.

"We should make a WhatsApp group with all the cousins before everyone leaves tomorrow," Steven said.

"Ja, to share some pictures from this week," said Austen.

"And just to stay in touch," said Steven.

"Have you actually got some pictures?" Jesse asked.

"Ja, I've got a few from Monday."

"What about from the Drakensberg?"

"I think Katie has."

"He's asking if you've got any pictures of him without a shirt," said Kyle.

"Bru, trust me, if you're in *any* pictures, you won't be wearing a shirt."

"Ja, Jesse, I think I've seen you wearing a shirt maybe twice this week."

"Megan has pictures from the braai as well, so you're covered."

"Enough profile picture material for the next few months."

Jesse laughed. "Whatever, man; I'm not as bad as Daniel!"

"Ja, Daniel *never* wears a shirt."

"Does he even own a shirt?"

"Hey, speak of the devil!"

They all turned to see Larissa and Daniel walking down the track from the house—and not, as Peter had been hoping, with Daniel chasing helplessly after a disinterested Larissa. They were side by side, chatting and laughing, which could only mean the date had been successful.

"Hi, everyone!" Larissa greeted them with a big smile on her face, looking at almost everyone except Peter as she lay down on the grass next to Katie.

Daniel was more coy, only giving the boys a quick eyebrow raise and a "Howzit" as he joined the circle to pass the ball around.

Everyone eyed the two of them with very obvious grins.

"So how was your 'walk'?" Kyle asked with finger quotations.

"It was lovely!" said Larissa, and she smiled up at Daniel. "It was a wonderful morning!"

"Is it, hey?" Kyle laughed.

Daniel just nodded and gave a bit of a shy smile.

Peter really didn't want to hear about their romantic little picnic. Looking around, he noticed that almost everyone was at the dam—which meant nobody would be up at the house. Now would be a good time to double-check the secret passage. He excused himself from the circle of rugby-ball passing with a feeble mention of needing to do something, and made his way back up to the house.

The house was almost perfectly quiet but for the soft ticking of the grandfather clock in the foyer. He first went upstairs to fetch his phone from the boys' bedroom, then came back down to the narrow passage. He opened the closet door, expecting to find the flashlight on the shelf to his right, but it wasn't there. He gazed around the closet but couldn't see it anywhere. Where had Larissa put it?

"Peter?"

Peter quickly shut the door. Ellen had just come through the foyer.

"Are you okay?" she asked.

"I'm fine!" said Peter.

"What are you doing?" she asked.

"Um ... nothing."

She looked skeptically at the closet door for a moment but quickly lost interest. "Listen, I think I owe you an apology," she said, "for what I said about Larissa."

"No, you don't, Ellen," said Peter. "Honestly, it's alright."

"Why don't you come back to the dam?" she said.

Peter sighed. "Look, Ellen, it's not that I don't appreciate you looking out for me and everything, but I'm actually quite busy right now."

Her eyes narrowed and she glanced at the closet door again. "Doing what?" she asked.

"I'm ... looking for something," said Peter.

"What are you looking for?"

"It's hard to explain."

Ellen nodded, still eyeing Peter suspiciously. "Can I give you a hand?" she asked.

"No, thank you."

"Okie dokie. See you later."

She turned and walked away, and Peter pretended to start heading for the stairs until she was out of sight, then quickly went into the closet and shut the door. He still couldn't see the flashlight anywhere, so he got out his phone to look for the little button to open the secret passage. After feeling around on the wall behind the camping-stove box, his fingers eventually ran over the faint groove in the wood. He pressed it and the door swung open.

He went in, closed the door quietly behind him, and had nearly reached the room at the bottom when he noticed that his phone was not the only light.

He suddenly realized why he couldn't find the flashlight in the closet—someone else was already down here! He stopped and tried to turn to go back up the stairs, but it was too late.

The flashlight was in his eyes.

For a while they stood in silence, the light on Peter, and Peter waiting for the consequences.

Finally they broke the silence.

"What are you doing here?"

Thulani's voice. It was a slight relief, but there was a sternness in his voice that didn't put Peter entirely at ease.

"Thulani!" he said. "I'm sorry! I, uh ... I was just—"

"How do you know about this place?"

Peter decided that honesty would be the best way to go. "We, um ... we followed Phillip down here yesterday," he said, feeling ashamed now that he was saying it out loud.

"*We*?" said Thulani. "You and Larissa?"

Peter wanted to kick himself. He had just sold out Larissa for no reason. "Yes," he said, hanging his head.

"And why are you here now?" Thulani asked.

"I ... well ..."

"Have you come to steal alcohol?" Thulani said sharply. "You and Larissa want to drink, hey? You think it will be fun for two sixteen-year-olds to get drunk?"

"No!" said Peter, startled. "No, I don't even like alcohol!"

"Then why are you here?"

"Well ... because we heard about the missing gold, and we thought it would be hidden down here."

There was a short pause, the light still in Peter's eyes. Then Thulani burst out laughing. He finally lowered the flashlight and Peter could see his face with a huge grin.

"Gold?" said Thulani. "You mean Walter Kingsbury's old tale? That was just a myth!"

"How do you know?" said Peter.

"How do I know? Because I've lived here for most of my life! There has never been any gold!"

Thulani turned back to the wine rack, still laughing to himself. "Why don't you make yourself useful now that you are here," he said. "Help me stack some of these wine bottles."

At least Thulani wasn't angry with him, but he had come to convince himself that the gold must be real, and it was disheartening to hear so definitively that it wasn't. Feeling foolish, he took a few bottles out from the crate at Thulani's feet and started stacking them in the wine rack.

"I'm not the only one," he said after a moment. "Someone else was also trying to find this place."

"Someone else?" said Thulani. "Who?"

"I don't know," said Peter, "but we saw someone trying to find the exit by the chapel."

Thulani was silent. When he finally spoke the humor had gone from his voice. "Whoever they were, I don't think they were looking for gold," he said. "Everybody knows the gold was a myth. Not even Kim or Karen believe in it anymore. But I was of the impression that nobody but myself and Phillip knew about this place."

"I don't think they found it," said Peter. "They had just heard about it."

Thulani didn't answer. Peter got the sense that this news made him uneasy.

"If you don't mind me asking," Peter said, "how do you know about it?"

Thulani looked at him and smiled. "This wine rack," he said, giving the wood a pat with his hand. "My father made this. He also made the door at the top. I was just a boy at the time." He had a chuckle. "We used to keep the good wine down here, and the cheaper wine in the dining room whenever people were staying over. Now Phillip and I just use it to make sure we've always got some when we want, because Brian ... well, let's just say he likes to think he makes the rules around here."

Thulani put the last two bottles onto the rack, and Peter was trying to decide if he should bring up one more thing while they were in private.

"Thulani," he said, "you told us about the letter that Aunty Pat asked you to give to her executor—the one that somebody took ... did you ever find out anything more about it? Or who took it?"

"No, I'm afraid not," Thulani said with a sigh as he picked up the now empty crate and placed it on top of one of the other empty crates. "But there has been a development: it appears that Patricia's will has gone missing."

"Missing? You mean it's been lost?"

"Or someone took it," said Thulani. "Both copies—Ms. O'Sullivan's *and* Patricia's."

"I think ..." Peter hesitated, "I think the person who took the letter might the same person we saw trying to find the entrance to this passage by the chapel."

Thulani frowned at him. "Peter, I don't know what you've heard, but I advise you not to get involved," he said sternly. "I have a feeling that Patricia did not die entirely of natural causes, and now Phillip's in hospital ... This person might be dangerous."

"You think someone did this to Phillip?" said Peter. "You don't think it's his medication?"

"We are investigating," said Thulani. "We are telling everyone the medication story so we do not start a panic, but I think everything that has been going on is very strange. We might have a criminal among us."

Peter thought about what Larissa had said the night before when they heard Phillip screaming, and he felt the same chill down his spine. He was reminded of seeing the person through the chapel window, and running for their lives down the hill.

"But, come," said Thulani in a more relaxed voice, "let's go back up."

They went up the stairs into the closet, and as Thulani closed the secret-passage door, Peter opened the closet door.

"Wait—" Thulani started saying, but Peter was already stepping out into the narrow passage and almost bumped into Father Ian.

"Whoops! Sorry, my boy, I didn't see you there!"

Father Ian stepped around Peter and carried on through the hall and up the stairs.

Thulani sighed. "You need to check that it's clear before you go opening doors," he said, and he moved a box over on a shelf next to the door to reveal a small crack in the wood that one could look through into the passage.

"Oh, I see ..." said Peter. "Sorry."

Thulani gave him a pat on his shoulder. "Coming to the dam?"

"Maybe later," said Peter.

But Peter had no intention of returning to the dam, where Larissa and Daniel were probably holding hands and who knows what else. He made his way upstairs and passed his parents on their way back from the dam.

"Oh, by the way, Pete," his mom said, "tomorrow once everyone else has left, we're going to stay behind to help clean up."

"What? How come?" said Peter.

"Because it's the right thing to do," his mom said. "They've had to host everyone for a week, and there's going to be a lot to do once everyone has left."

"Why should we have to stay and help when everybody else leaves?"

"We don't *have* to; it would just be polite. Everybody else has a long way to drive, or a plane to catch; we're just down the road, so we're in no rush."

"Just down the road?" said Peter. "It took us three hours to get here!"

"Yes, well, for the people driving back to Joburg it's more than five hours. So think of that as an extra two hours that you can help clean."

"Let's just hope it's a short will so everybody can leave quickly," said Martin.

"Actually," said Gill, lowering her voice, "it sounds like there might not be a will."

"Really?" said Martin. "How so?"

"I don't know," said Gill. "Ms. O'Sullivan is going to come and explain everything tomorrow."

Martin laughed ironically. "Shame, some people have put in a lot of hard work to be written into Patricia's will. They're going to be very annoyed to find out it's just being shared between everyone."

Shared between everyone? That gave Peter a thought. He went upstairs to the library where he looked for the book Larissa had been reading the night after the funeral. But everything had been packed away. He paged through a few books at random, but had no idea what he was looking for. Larissa would have to find it.

On his way back through the piano room, he sat down at the piano. Playing the piano always helped him to clear his head. He could let his mind zone out completely while his fingers played from memory.

He didn't know how long he had been playing when he heard the door open behind him. He carried on playing to the end of the piece before he turned round to see who it was.

Larissa was leaning with her elbows on the table and her chin in her hands; she'd been watching him play.

She stood up. "Hey, Pete," she said nervously.

Peter gave her a nod and turned back to the piano. He didn't start playing anything specific, just tinkered on the keys.

"Is everything alright?" Larissa asked.

"Why wouldn't it be?"

"I don't know ... you left kind of suddenly from the dam earlier."

"I needed to go do something."

Larissa was silent for a moment while Peter kept on tinkering.

"Have I upset you?" she asked.

Peter gave an ironic breath of laughter, shaking his head. "No, you haven't upset me," he said. "Everything's fine."

"I ... chatted to Ellen," Larissa said. "I, umm ... well ... I don't really know how to say this ..."

Peter stopped playing. "Then don't! Honestly, Larissa, you don't need to say anything. It's fine. I don't care."

Suddenly Larissa got angry. "I don't know what you think you're talking about, but clearly it's *not* fine and you *do* care!"

"No, I don't," he said, getting up. "I don't know what Ellen told you, but she needs to mind her own business."

He pushed past Larissa and left the room. Frustrated with her for leading him on, frustrated with himself for falling for it, frustrated with Ellen for getting involved, and frustrated with himself again for how he had just dealt with the situation. He knew he had been rude, and it wasn't called for. The more he thought about it, the worse he felt.

To make matters worse, he marched into the boys' room hoping to be alone and bury his face in his pillow, but found everyone already there, chatting and laughing as they got ready to go shower.

"Ay, Austen, lemme see some of your pictures?"

"Bru, you're obsessed! Just take a few selfies."

"Nah, it needs to be authentic. Can't look like I'm trying too hard."

Peter got onto his bed and stared at the ceiling, waiting for it all to quieten down. He had already resigned himself to showering last and was forced to just listen to everyone else while he waited.

"Can't believe we're leaving tomorrow!"

"Ja, this week's gone so quickly!"

"Ay, and it's been a productive week for some of us ..."

There were sniggers in Daniel's direction from all the boys.

"So, what did you guys get up to today, Dan?"

"Nothing," Daniel said with his back to them as he busied himself with his bag.

"Come on, Dan, it's just the boys now; tell us what happened!"

"Ja, Dan, it's just the lads here! Spill the beans!"

"Did you guys hook up?"

"Surely?"

"I told you; nothing happened!" said Daniel, his face bright red. "Not everything's about hooking up all the time! We're just friends!"

There was a shocked silence as they all stared at Daniel. Even Peter stuck his head up.

"Oh, damn, she rejected you?"

"She gave you bat!"

"She didn't give me bat! We're just friends!"

"You got friend-zoned?"

"Waaalala!"

Everyone laughed and Daniel stormed out of the room. For the first time, Peter actually felt sorry for him.

Mostly, though, his mind was on Larissa and how he hadn't let her say what she was trying to say. Feeling like a tool, he jumped down from his bed and ran across to the girls' room. He peered in but couldn't see Larissa. Instead, Ellen's head appeared round the door.

"Ellen," he said, suddenly remembering how he had spoken to her earlier. "I owe you an apology."

Ellen had a slightly amused grin. "Yes, you do."

"I'm really sorry," Peter said earnestly. "I was a jerk. It was really uncalled for."

Ellen's smile spread across her face. "No worries," she said happily.

Peter felt the relief wash over him and he couldn't help smiling. "Listen ..." he said, glancing into the room again.

"I'm afraid she's not here," said Ellen. "I think she's with her parents. You probably won't see her before dinner."

"Oh, okay, thanks," said Peter. He was about to walk away, but stopped. "Actually, could you just tell her that I, umm ..."

"I'll tell her you were looking for her."

"Great, thanks!"

Chapter 16

Peter joined his parents at the table for their last dinner. There was now an empty seat where Phillip usually sat. He looked at everyone around the table, smiling and laughing.

The butlers went round with the new wine and poured everyone a glass. Miraculously, no one had seen the pile of wine bottles in the garden yet. Peter had glanced at them when he was walking up from the dam, but they were well hidden.

Once everyone had something in their glass, Brian stood up. The noise slowly died down as they all turned to face him.

"Good evening, all," he said loudly. "It's our last night here together, and I just wanted to once again thank everyone for coming. It was lovely having all the family together again, and I think it would've made Patricia happy. Despite the solemn circumstances, it really has been a great week; Patricia would have had it no other way.

"The last order of business before we get stuck into our meal is that Patricia's executor, Ms. O'Sullivan, will be coming tomorrow morning at around ten o'clock to read the, umm ... to talk us through what is going to happen with the estate and all of Patricia's belongings. If we could all just gather in the guest hall ahead of time, that would help things to go smoothly. I know some of you are driving back to Joburg and others have flights to catch, so we want to be wrapped up as quickly as possible."

Brian then picked up his glass of wine.

"I think it's fair to say that things are going to be different now without Patricia, who has been the cornerstone of this family for as long as most of us have been alive, but she will forever be cherished in our memories." He raised his glass. "To Patricia!"

Everybody raised their glasses. Peter felt like it had new meaning now that he knew so much more about her life, and they were no longer just words when he joined in the chorus with everyone else: "To Patricia!"

Once dinner was underway, Peter almost by habit glanced at the other end of the table. Larissa was talking with big eyes and loud expressions and had everybody around her engrossed—except for Daniel, who was looking down at his food and eating in silence.

Peter happily turned back to his parents' conversation with Frank Greenacre across the table.

"... It's not as bad as some other places, but they could definitely be doing a better job of getting rid of some of the exotic species around here," Frank was saying. "I mean things like the *babylonica* I wouldn't get too tense about, but—"

"I'm sorry, the what?" Gill cut in.

"Oh, *Salix babylonica*—the weeping willow," said Frank.

"Are those exotic?" asked Gill.

"Oh, ja!" said Frank. "They're quite a big problem. But they're aesthetic and quite a mission to get rid of, so it's understandable to leave them be. But walking around this garden I've seen a few species that are inexcusable—"

"I think they are starting to change that, though," said Peter. "Thulani pointed out a few exotics he wants to get rid of. And we chatted to a gardener the other day who was removing a whole lot of castor bean plants to replace them with something indigenous."

"Oh, well that's good!" said Frank with a laugh. "Castor beans aren't just exotic, they're highly poisonous!"

"Oh, really?" said Martin. "Are they dangerous to have in a garden?"

"Not very dangerous, no," said Frank. "They're actually quite common ornamental plants. You'd need a lot of them to actually kill someone. But people have died from ricin poisoning."

Peter surreptitiously pulled his phone out under the table and googled "castor bean poisoning." He almost gasped when he saw the results. The beans in the pictures that came up looked exactly like the beans they had found outside the chapel the night before! He looked up the symptoms of castor bean poisoning, and it confirmed what he had already guessed: fluid in the lungs, hemorrhages in the organs, but nothing conclusive that would show up in an autopsy ...

Patricia had been poisoned.

After dinner, Peter desperately wanted to tell Larissa about the castor beans, but he hadn't even been able to apologize to her yet. They all gathered in the sitting room again for one last round of pre-bedtime board games, and Larissa barely even looked at him. She seemed her usual bubbly self, completely unperturbed by anything, but did a great job of paying him no attention unless she absolutely had to. At least she wasn't giggling away with Daniel this time. In fact, there was a slightly tense atmosphere now that everyone knew what had actually happened between them, but were all pretending not to.

Eventually, once almost all the adults had turned in, they wrapped up the games and started to amble slowly out of the sitting room. Larissa stuck very close to Megan and Katie so Peter didn't get a chance to talk to her. He went to the room with the other boys, and once most of them had got into bed he resorted to messaging her.

I need to speak to you

He anxiously stared at his screen, waiting for a response.

Peter, I'm tired. Let's just talk tomorrow.

She didn't get it. He quickly typed another message.

I think I know why they stole the letter that Patricia sent to her executor. And I know how they poisoned her.

He waited a little more, but soon enough the door opened and a wide-eyed Larissa stepped out, closing the door behind her.

"Are you serious?" she said.

Peter nodded. "Come on," he said, "let's go talk in the library."

She followed him down the passage and past the stairs, round the corner of the next passage and then through the piano room into the library. As soon as Larissa had closed the door behind them, she spun round to face Peter.

"She was poisoned?"

"Remember when we were in the garden and you were speaking to the gardener, and he said he was removing the castor bean plants because they had been chopped down?"

"Ja?"

"Well, we were chatting to Frank Greenacre at dinner and he reckoned castor beans are really poisonous. So I googled them. Look at this ..."

He took his phone out and showed Larisa the pictures that came up.

Larissa gasped. "Those are the beans we saw outside the chapel!"

"Exactly," said Peter. "And then I googled the symptoms of castor bean poisoning, and the results of the autopsy match up."

"I don't believe it!" said Larissa. "But ... why did they have the beans at the chapel then?"

Peter shook his head. "I'm not sure ..." he said.

"Okay, what about the letter?"

"Oh, ja," said Peter, "where's that law book you were reading?"

"The what?"

"Remember the first time we came into the library, you started reading that law book that was on the desk?"

Larissa looked around at the tidied study area. "Yoh, Peter … It could be anywhere. What do you want it for?"

"Didn't it say something about what happens if there isn't a will?"

"Ja, it did!" said Larissa. With renewed motivation she checked the shelves for books on law, glancing over the titles. She found the law section and ran her finger across the spines. "No … no … no … Here it is!" She pulled it out and leafed through a few pages until she found the passage that had been underlined. "Here we go: 'In this case, the entire estate will be inherited by the descendants of the parents. The descendants inherit *per stirpes* by representation.'" She looked up at Peter. "What does 'per stirpes' mean?"

Peter didn't know, but Larissa already had her phone out and was typing it into Google.

"Okay, I get it," she said. "Because she doesn't have any children, it'll be divided equally between her siblings, and then those amounts will be divided equally between *their* children if they're deceased, and then *their* children, and so on. That makes sense."

"Okay, wait ..." said Peter, "so that means ... anyone with no living predecessors will get a share of the inheritance?"

"Ja, that sounds about right," said Larissa. "But what does this all have to do with the stolen letter?"

"What if the person who stole the letter *wants* there to be no will?" said Peter. "What if they weren't in the will, so they'll only inherit something if there isn't one? And what if that's what the letter is about, and that's why they don't want anyone to see it?"

"Oh, my gosh, you could be right," said Larissa. "So, who stands to gain from the will being missing? Who's in line?"

“Off hand, I have no idea,” said Peter. “But there’s that family tree in the secret study ...”

They looked at each other.

“Should we—?”

“Yup!”

They quickly left the library, peeked down the passage, then hurried through to Patricia’s room and into the secret study. They went straight over to the family tree on the wall and had a look.

“There’re actually a few people who are in line ...” said Peter.

“Which of them were here when the letter went missing?”

“Well, Phillip and Brian are always here … I have no idea about the Croxfords or the Le Rouxs … Karen and Kim are both in line! They’ve been fighting since we got here. I think they were both here at the time.”

“We need to tell someone!” said Larissa. “Thulani, or someone. Before Ms. O’Sullivan gets here tomorrow morning.”

“Agreed,” said Peter.

They left the secret study, closing the door behind them, and Peter was about to open the door to leave the bedroom when Larissa grabbed his arm and he stopped; she had her finger to her lips. She pointed to her ear and then toward the passage. Peter listened, but couldn’t make out for certain what she had heard. He crouched down to look through the keyhole, and saw the legs of a person coming toward them.

“Too late!” he whispered urgently. “Someone’s coming! Quick! Hide!”

Without thinking, they hurried back into the secret study.

“What if they come in here!” said Peter.

“Get in the cupboard!” said Larissa. “Quick!”

She pulled open the door of the small cupboard next to the desk. Peter wasn’t sure this would work, but he didn’t have any other ideas, so he quickly got in. Larissa followed, but they didn’t both fit and she was struggling to close the cupboard door behind them.

They heard the bedroom door open.

Larissa put her arm around Peter's neck and pressed her body tightly against him so she could squeeze the door closed behind her. Her face was almost touching his. Peter put one arm around her waist to help support her so she wouldn't press back against the door.

"Don't. Make. A sound," Larissa whispered in the darkness. Peter could feel her breath on his cheeks.

The secret door creaked open. They tried to hold their breath.

Footsteps came into the room and stopped at the desk, right next to where they were hiding. They kept absolutely still. They could just see the faintest glint of each other's eyes in the darkness only inches apart.

The footsteps started pacing slowly up and down the room. Then, in a hushed voice that was little more than a whisper, the person spoke.

"McKenzie? Ja, it's me. Are you nearly here?"

He was on the phone. Peter tried to think who the voice belonged to, but it really could have been anyone.

"Ja, I just had to come to a place where nobody would overhear me."

Peter's arm around Larissa was starting to go numb, but he couldn't move without making noise, and if he let go, Larissa would go tumbling out of the cupboard. He tightened his grip around her, and he felt her tighten her arm around him as well and press herself against him.

"Are you sure about this? Why don't we just stick to the original plan? ... No, I know, I'm just saying, it seems like a risk; this letter has already complicated everything so much … okay, no, it's fine … ja, just leave it at the gate and I can come to collect it ... Yes, I know; but if anybody comes, I'm going to burn it immediately. And look, the paper is either going to make it obvious or it's not. If I can't find it straight away, I'll just burn the letter anyway ...

Okay, yes, I think I can do that ... No, I'll head out now. I don't think anyone else is still up. I'll call you again tomorrow once she's come to tell us what's happening ... Ja, I think I know who one of the kids at the window was, but I don't think he'll be a problem, I can sort him out … No, we'll be long gone by then. But regardless, I'll be glad to get rid of the letter, just to put my mind at ease ... Alright, cheers."

Once the man had hung up the phone, he let out a long, deep sigh. Then there was silence. Peter could feel Larissa's heart beating pressed against his chest. His arm was beginning to ache; he knew he couldn't hold on forever.

Finally, the footsteps left the room. They heard the secret door open and close, then the bedroom door after that. They hung onto each other for a little while longer, just to be safe, then collapsed out of the cupboard.

Larissa looked up at Peter with wide eyes. "What do we do?"

"We have to stop him!" said Peter.

"How?"

"Balcony!" said Peter. "Stables!"

Larissa didn't have time to ask what Peter was talking about; he was already rushing out of the room and checking through the keyhole. She followed him down the passage, almost at a run, back into the piano room and through to the library. Peter quickly unlocked the doors to the balcony and basically jumped over the balustrade.

"Peter, be careful!" Larissa called, but he was already climbing down the gutter at a pace. She quickly climbed over and followed him down.

They ran through the garden in the dark, around the house toward the stables. Peter took his phone flashlight out and went straight into the tack room, with Larissa right behind him.

"Peter, what are we doing?" she gasped, out of breath.

"We need to get to the gate before him," Peter said as he frantically shone his phone around the room. “Dammit, I don’t remember any of this ...”

“We’re not going to *ride* there?!” exclaimed Larissa.

“That’s exactly what we’re going to do,” Peter said as he grabbed a saddle, a bridle and some reins.

He ran across to Rusty’s stable.

“Hey, Rusty, how’s it going,” he said as he flung the saddle over Rusty’s back. Rusty was getting excited. “Easy, boy, let me just put this on ...” Peter said, struggling to put on the bridle and reins. “Good enough!”

He used the side of the stable to hoist himself up onto Rusty’s back.

“Alright, come on,” he said to Larissa, holding his hand out.

“Peter, I don’t know ...” Larissa started saying, but just then a car engine started up near the garage.

“Come on, Larissa! We have to go *now*!”

Larissa took his hand and he pulled her up onto the horse. She wrapped both arms around him and held on tightly.

“Do you know how to ride a horse?” she asked.

“Nope, not a clue,” said Peter. “Come on, Rusty, let’s go!”

He gave a kick with his heels, and Rusty shot off out of the stables!

They caught a glimpse of the car’s headlights lighting up the trees in front of it before they disappeared behind the hill. After that Peter couldn’t see anything, except for the dark shape of the chapel up on the hill. He just trusted that Rusty would take them where they needed to go. The wind rushed past their faces as they galloped at full speed around the hill, Larissa holding onto Peter and Peter holding onto the reins.

“Peter, I’m slipping!” Larissa cried, and she hugged his body as tightly as she could. “Peter, I’m gonna fall!”

Peter could feel the saddle slowly slipping to one side. He knew he hadn’t done it properly.

"Just hold on a bit longer!" Peter shouted back over his shoulder. "We're almost there!"

The saddle was slipping further and further; they were leaning heavily on one side. Peter could tell it was about to fall off any minute now when finally he saw the gates looming up just ahead. He pulled on the reins and Rusty slowed down to a stop just as the saddle slipped off. They both jumped off and tumbled into the grass.

Peter quickly helped Larissa up. "You alright?"

"I'm fine," said Larissa. "Go get the letter; I'll try keep the horse out of sight!"

Peter ran to the gate. He shone his phone up and down the gate, around the sides, looking everywhere for the letter but he couldn't see it. He spotted a little mailbox, but he checked inside and there was no letter there either.

Suddenly the trees near the bend in the road lit up and he could hear the wheels of the car over the gravel. He frantically double checked everywhere. He finally spotted a white envelope peeking out of the lion's mouth on top of the far wall.

The car was about to come round the corner.

Peter climbed up onto the gate, stretched as far as he could and just managed to grip the letter before he heard the car rounding the bend. He quickly jumped off the gate and rolled behind a tree as the headlights came beaming down the road, illuminating the gate and everything around it. Peter pressed himself up against the tree, hoping against all odds that he hadn't been seen, and that Larissa and Rusty had managed to hide themselves.

The car pulled up to the gate, between Peter and wherever Larissa and Rusty had got to. He heard the door open and someone step out onto the gravel, with the engine still running and the whole area flooded with light. Listening to the footsteps, Peter slowly edged his way round the tree as they approached the gate.

When he was sure that they were at the gate, facing the other way, Peter finally allowed himself a peek: Was it ...? No, surely not ... But it was! Father Ian was standing on the gate, stretching his hand up to the lion's mouth as Peter had just done.

"Bloody hell, McKenzie, where have you put this thing ..." He jumped down and went across to try the lion on the other side.

Peter looked across the road to see Larissa hiding in a bush, beckoning him over as she nervously looked to and from Father Ian at the gate. Rusty was behind the bush, not very well hidden, and starting to get restless. They had to hurry.

Glancing at Father Ian again, who was standing on the gate and reaching up toward the second lion, Peter crept out from behind the tree and tiptoed as quickly as he could to behind the car; luckily the growling of the engine muffled his footsteps. He ducked down suddenly when he heard Father Ian jump down from the gate. After trying to listen for signs of what was going on, he peeked through the window. Father Ian was looking down at his phone, facing Peter's general direction. He ducked down again.

"McKenzie, where the hell did you put this letter? ... No, I looked in the lion's mouth; it's not there ... I've checked both of them ... I don't think so, I don't see it on the ground anywhere; unless the wind blew it ... Okay, hang on, let me double check ..."

Peter risked another glance through the window: Father Ian was facing the other way again, going back to the first lion.

He seized the opportunity and quickly crept across to where Larissa was. Without a word, they quietly started leading Rusty away.

"Let's try get on," Peter whispered, tightening the saddle. "I'll give you a foot-up."

He knelt and held his hands out on his knee, which Larissa used as a step to get on Rusty's back.

"No, I'm telling you man, it's not here ..." they heard Father Ian saying as Peter tried to hoist himself up.

While Peter was struggling to get up, Rusty gave a little neigh. Father Ian immediately turned round to see them.

"What the ... HEY! HEY, YOU, COME BACK HERE! COME BACK HERE RIGHT NOW!"

But Rusty was off! Peter was on his stomach on Rusty's back, his legs dangling off the side, barely hanging on as Rusty galloped away. Behind them they heard the car door slam, the engine rev, and gravel being kicked up everywhere as the car spun round and raced off back down the driveway.

"He's going to get there before us!" Larissa shouted over her shoulder.

The saddle was slipping again. Peter knew they weren't going to make it. "Stop!" he shouted at Larissa. "Pull the reins!"

Larissa pulled the reins and Rusty came to a stop, sending Peter tumbling into the grass once more.

"Are you okay?" Larissa said as she jumped down.

"Fine," said Peter, getting up and dusting himself off.

"What are we going to do?" said Larissa. "He'll be waiting for us at the house!"

Peter pointed up at the chapel. "Secret passage," he said.

"Yes! Brilliant!"

"I'm just worried about Rusty," said Peter.

"He'll survive the night," said Larissa, grabbing Peter's hand and pulling him.

They could still hear the car tearing down the gravel road as they climbed the hill up to the chapel, then went through the graveyard to the gravestone in the wall with the lion face.

Peter turned it to open the door to the secret passage. They jogged down the stairs and along the passageway until they got to the room with the wine racks.

"Hold up," said Larissa, and she stopped to catch her breath.

Peter stopped running and looked at her, also breathing heavily.

"Let's have a look at that letter," said Larissa.

Peter had forgotten he was even carrying the letter. He pulled the envelope out from his pocket. It had a wax seal that had already been opened. Inside was a folded piece of old college-ruled paper with patches of extra lines ruled across it, torn on one side as though it had been ripped out from a book. When he unfolded it, they recognized Patricia's handwriting, which hadn't changed since she used to write letters to Mandla from school.

4 December 2015
Dear Olivia

I have some grave news. I recently overheard a very disturbing conversation that somebody was having on the telephone, though I could not see who it was. All I know is that it was one of my own family. They had planned to destroy my will—both your copy and mine—so that they would receive a share of the inheritance. They then spoke of "bumping me off" to prevent me from changing anything.

To be frank, Olivia, I am not afraid to die. But I'll be damned if my estate falls into the hands of someone so greedy they would turn on their own family!

I fear they may already have destroyed the will, but this might not be a problem. You may recall, when you came to me all those years ago to convince me to write a will, I initially wanted something very different to happen with my estate, but you informed me it was not possible and I had to settle for something a little more conventional. What I did not tell you was that I had in fact already written a will, signed by myself and two witnesses, that I think you will find to be legally binding. Moreover, what wasn't possible thirty years ago is now perfectly legitimate.

This document not only reflects my true intentions for the destiny of my estate, but also sheds some light on a long-held secret of mine to which very few people have been privy. I think it is finally time that everyone knew.

I therefore kindly request that you come to see me at Woodwright Manor to discuss this, and so that I can give you the document. In case these culprits succeed in their attempts to "bump me off" before I can give you the document, I have hidden it somewhere only you will know—you might recognize the paper that this is written on. You will find it if you look Under the Willow Tree. Pay attention to every minor detail, and you shouldn't have any Major problems.

I hope to see you soon.

Sincerely,
Patricia Jane Woodwright

Peter and Larissa looked at each other.

"A long-held secret?" said Larissa. "She must be talking about the gold!"

"*That's* what they were talking about when they mentioned finding the will!" said Peter. "They meant her *old* will! I'll bet it says where the gold is!"

"Under the willow tree ..." said Larissa. "You don't think it's the willow tree where we found the letter?"

Peter frowned in thought.

"That sounds right," he said, "but we never found anything else when we looked there?"

"We didn't look very thoroughly, though, did we?" said Larissa. "She says *pay attention to every minor detail*—we basically just pulled out the tin and left!"

"You've got a point," said Peter. He turned the paper over to examine it. "This paper is also meant to be significant. It's got hand-drawn lines on it. Where have I seen this before?"

"Let's worry about that later; right now, we need to get this to Brian or someone!"

They ran up the stairs, opened the secret door into the closet, and almost ran into what looked like a long pipe in the darkness, pointing right at them. They skidded to a halt and a flashlight lit up in their faces.

"Back down you go," came Father Ian's cold voice. He was holding a rifle.

Chapter 17

They both instinctively put their hands up and started backing slowly down the stairs. Father Ian followed them and closed the door behind him, then marched them all the way to the wine cellar at the bottom.

They stared at each other in silence, Peter and Larissa still with their hands up and the light in their eyes, Father Ian still pointing the gun at them.

"You were the ones who saw me through the chapel window, weren't you?" he said. His voice was on edge.

Neither of them said anything.

"I was trying to find this place," he went on, glancing anxiously around the room now. "But then I saw you coming out of the closet today, and I knew that that must be where the entrance is."

Again, they both remained silent.

"Alright," he said. "There's a solid layer of stone above us, so if you even *think* of doing anything, no one will hear the gun go off and no one will hear you call for help. So, for now, I'm going to need you to tie yourselves up." He quickly reached into his pocket as he held the gun and the flashlight in one hand, threw some cable ties on the floor in front of them and hastily took up the gun again. "Girl, pick them up."

Larissa reluctantly bent down and picked up the cable ties.

"First, hand over the letter. Just throw it toward me."

Peter did as he was told and threw the envelope with the letter onto the ground in front of Father Ian.

"Good. Now tie his hands together. No, no, behind his back. There we go. Now, boy, sit down against the wall. Good. Alright, girl, hands behind your back and walk slowly backwards toward me."

When Larissa was near enough, he grabbed her hands and tied them together.

"Now you can sit next to your friend," he said.

Larissa sat down next to Peter. Father Ian took out the letter. He studied it for a short time, turned it over to look at the back, and sighed.

"I think we can safely say that no one is going to find the will," he said. He pulled a lighter out from his pocket. "And now no one will ever know it exists."

He lit a corner of the letter and dropped it to the floor. Peter and Larissa watched helplessly as it was engulfed by flames and Patricia's dying wishes turned to ash.

Once the last of the flames flickered out, Father Ian pressed the ashes with his foot. The only evidence that the letter ever existed was a dark mark on the already dark floor.

Now that Peter and Larissa were tied up, Father Ian seemed to relax a little. He walked slowly around the room, shining the light this way and that.

"So *this* is where Phillip keeps his stash," he said.

Peter remembered seeing the castor beans outside the chapel. "You wanted to poison him!" Peter suddenly realized. "You wanted to poison his wine to kill him!"

"Well, I didn't, did I?" Father Ian spat back at him.

"And when you couldn't find the wine, you tried to smother him in his sleep!"

"That is not true!" he said defensively. "I just wanted to keep him quiet, but he wouldn't stop screaming!"

"Well, why was he screaming?" said Larissa. "Why were you even in his room?"

"I thought he might have a key to this place!" said Father Ian. "And you know what," he went on, raising the gun, "it's actually none of your business. Now sit still and be quiet!"

Peter and Larissa both leaned back and fell silent. They watched him carry on looking around the room, peering into various crates and barrels.

"The gold isn't down here," said Peter. "It doesn't exist."

"My father wasn't a liar," said Father Ian. "Everyone said he was lying about the secret wine cellar, but here we are. Patricia even said she had a secret to reveal."

Peter didn't answer as Father Ian continued with his search. He rested the gun against the side of a barrel to free up his hands, clearly not sure what exactly he was looking for and where he might find it, but intent on searching the whole room nonetheless. When he was scratching around at the other end of the room, Peter leaned over to whisper to Larissa.

"I think the gun is fake," he said as quietly as possible.

"It doesn't look fake," Larissa whispered back.

"I think it's Patricia's old rifle, from that storeroom. If it is, it doesn't work."

"And if it isn't?"

They both suddenly fell silent as Father Ian stopped rummaging around in one of the crates and stood up, looked around the room, then spotted another crate to investigate.

"We need to get out of here," said Peter. "He knows that we know too much. I don't think he's just going to let us go."

Peter propped himself up against the wall and tried to get his hands underneath him. Larissa tried to do the same. She quite easily managed to slip her hands out, then looked at Peter.

"Hurry up," she whispered.

"I can't," said Peter.

No matter how hard he tried, his arms just weren't long enough.

"But I think I can snap the cable tie if you help me," he said.

"Then he'll definitely hear us."

"Doesn't matter. I'll distract him; you run and get help."

Larissa slipped her fingers into the cable tie around Peter's hands and they both pulled.

"What's going on there?" Father Ian said, shining the light on them. "HEY! STOP THAT!"

Peter and Larissa pulled as hard as they could. The tie snapped and Peter jumped to his feet just as Father Ian snatched up the gun.

"I swear to God," Father Ian shouted, "If you move—"

Peter didn't wait to hear what would happen if he moved; he sprinted at Father Ian and rugby tackled him into the wine racks, sending bottles of who-knows-what crashing to the ground and shattering all around them. The flashlight tumbled out of Father Ian's hands and spun across the floor, its light shining in all directions. Larissa stood frozen in shock for only a second before her mind kicked into gear and she started running up the stairs. Father Ian pushed Peter off with a lot more strength than Peter had anticipated, then swung the gun at him and caught him across the cheek with the butt of the rifle, sending him to the floor in a daze. As blood started gushing from his face, Peter saw him immediately turn to chase Larissa up the stairs. Without thinking, Peter reached out and grabbed his ankle to trip him up, and he fell face-first onto the stone floor. He kicked Peter's hand off, but, as he scrambled to get up, Peter jumped on him and wrestled him back to the ground. Once again, though, Father Ian was too strong for Peter, and Peter couldn't hold him down. He caught Peter with an elbow, threw him off, and kicked him down again as he tried to get up. Peter, already exhausted and in so much pain, his face covered in blood, was beginning to realize he had maybe bitten off more than he could chew; this might not have been the best idea ...

"Lay one more hand on him and your life ends tonight," came an intimidating voice from the top of the stairs.

They both stopped and looked up to see Thulani glaring down at them, the silhouette of his large figure so menacing that Father Ian just dropped the gun and put his hands up.

"Thulani," he said slowly, "let's not jump to conclusions here; the boy attacked *me*!"

"Step away from him," said Thulani, his voice ice cold.

Father Ian didn't even attempt to argue, but slowly stepped away from Peter.

"Peter, are you alright?" Thulani asked.

Lying on his back on the ground, panting, blood still dripping from his face, Peter stuck a thumb in the air.

Thulani came down the stairs and picked up the gun and the flashlight, then held a hand out for Peter.

"Thulani, listen to me!" said Father Ian. "This is not what it looks like."

"It's exactly what it looks like!" said Peter as he pulled himself up.

"I haven't done anything wrong. It isn't even a real gun!"

"You can explain everything upstairs," said Thulani.

"No, you know what, I don't need this!" Father Ian said indignantly, and he started rushing up the stairs while Thulani's back was turned.

"Gideon!" Thulani called after him.

"You'll hear from my lawyers!"

He left the passageway and ran out. Peter looked to Thulani, open-mouthed.

"Let him go," said Thulani. "Come, let us get you upstairs."

He helped Peter up the stairs and into the lounge, where he turned on a light and Peter flopped down onto a couch, holding the side of his face where he had been hit. They heard a car start up outside.

"Where's Larissa?" Peter asked.

"I don't know," said Thulani. "I haven't seen her."

"How did you know where to find me?"

"After we spoke this afternoon, I thought I should stay up to keep an eye on things, just in case something happened. When I saw the car speeding down the driveway, I came as quickly as I could. The door to the wine cellar was open and I heard you fighting down there."

"Quickly, over here!" they heard Larissa's voice coming from the hall. "Oh, wait, I think they're in the lounge …"

Larissa came rushing in. "Thulani, thank goodness you're here!" she said. "Where's Father Ian?"

Brian came in after her, confused and dazed from having just been woken up.

"He fled," said Peter.

Larissa noticed the state of Peter's face and rushed over to him. "Oh, my word, are you alright?" She knelt on the floor next to him and inspected the gash in his cheek.

"I'm fine," said Peter.

"Will somebody please explain what's going on?" said Brian.

"It was Father Ian," Larissa said. "He was the one who stole the letter that Thulani was supposed to deliver to Ms. O'Sullivan."

"He poisoned Patricia and tried to smother Phillip in his sleep," said Peter.

"No …" Brian couldn't believe it.

"But he had an accomplice," said Larissa. "We heard them on the phone, and the other person was going to come and drop off the letter so we raced out to get there first. And we did! We got the letter and we were bringing it back but he caught us. He had a gun so we just did what he said, and he took the letter back and burned it."

Brian looked at Thulani, who held up the gun.

"Patricia's old rifle …" he said.

"So, what about the letter?" said Brian. "Did you read it? What did it say?"

Peter took his hand from his face and looked at the blood before responding. "Basically, Patricia said she had written another will a long time ago that apparently reflects her true intentions for her estate. She knew someone had destroyed her more recent will and was going to try to destroy this one as well, so she hid it somewhere where they wouldn't find it. I think she knew that they might try to intercept the letter, so she didn't say where it was. She just gave some kind of cryptic clue that was specifically for Ms. O'Sullivan, so nobody else would find it. But the letter's gone now, and the clue along with it. Father Ian burned it. He didn't want there to be any evidence of the will or what he had done."

Brain still looked puzzled. "I'm not sure I understand," he said. "Why did Gideon destroy the will?"

"Because if there's no will, everything Patricia owns gets divided … what's it called?"

He looked to Larissa.

"*Per stirpes*," she said.

"That one," said Peter. "And then he's in line to receive a portion of it, which he wouldn't be otherwise. He's convinced Walter wasn't lying about the missing fortune, so he thinks it'll be worth a lot."

"And then he poisoned Patricia so she wouldn't be able to change her will," said Larissa.

"So why was he so intent on finding the other will as well?" Brian asked. "The original one. If he doesn't want a will, why not just leave it hidden?"

"I think that is exactly what he intended," said Peter. "Except, in the letter they intercepted, Patricia said her original will also reveals a long-held secret."

The realization crept into Brian's widening eyes. "The missing fortune?"

Peter shrugged. "That's definitely what Father Ian thought. And then I think the plan changed from receiving a portion of it to finding all of it before anyone else."

Thulani's expression remained unchanged throughout their telling of the story, thoughtful and reserved. "It looks like he's going to get his wish," he said. "They must have done a very good job of getting rid of Patricia's will, because there is no trace of it at all. After chatting with Ms. O'Sullivan at length, Patricia's estate will be divided intestate—*per stirpes*, as you say."

"No, it can't be!" said Larissa. "That's exactly what he wanted!"

"I'm afraid there isn't much that we can do about it," Brian sighed. "Patricia is no longer here to tell us what she wanted, nor do we have any documents on record that do so. This is literally the definition of 'intestate'. I'm afraid it's just the way the law works."

"But what about her old will?" said Larissa. "We can still look for that?"

Thulani nodded. "It's true," he said. "If we found her old will, I'm sure that it would stand up in court."

Larissa's eyes lit up, but Brian was quick to quash her spirits. "But," he said, "nobody has any idea where it is, and since the letter was burned there is no evidence of its existence—other than the word of two over-involved teenagers, which won't hold the courts for very long."

"Except ... we might have some idea where it is," Larissa said, and she looked at Peter to back her up.

Brian and Thulani both looked expectantly at Peter. Peter wasn't so sure, and the reserved look he gave Larissa showed it.

"We should at least check!" said Larissa. "It's worth a shot!"

"What is?" said Brian.

"The letter said to look under a willow tree," she said. "We think we might know which willow tree she's talking about."

Wide-eyed, they both turned to Peter again.

Peter sighed. "It's true," he said, "we do know of *a* willow tree that does seem like it could be the one Patricia was referring to. Only thing is, we've already looked there. We didn't find any old will."

"The letter said to look carefully," said Larissa. "We didn't look carefully. It's worth double checking."

Brian nodded. "If there is a chance it could be there, it's worth another look."

"Agreed," said Thulani. "Where is it?"

"The other side of the dam," said Peter. "Near the stream. Where you can only get to by boat."

Brian looked to Thulani, who took a moment to consider it. "So be it," said Thulani. "We will go by boat."

Thulani fetched the flashlight and they left out the front door, which was still standing open after Father Ian had run out. In single file they passed through the little garden gate and onto the track down to the dam. Trixy came bounding up to them again, very excited to be going for another walk in the dark, and the five of them marched to the dam's edge.

"We won't all fit," said Peter. "The boat only takes two."

Brian immediately stepped back.

"No trouble, I can wait right here!" he said, relieved for the excuse.

Peter looked at Larissa.

"Thulani's the one who needs to see it," she said. "I think you and he should go."

Peter stepped into the boat, which was all the affirmation Trixy needed to jump in after him. Thulani then stepped in cautiously, and the boat rocked. He was much bigger than Larissa, and they didn't feel quite as stable as when they'd gone the last time. Thulani helped to push them off from the jetty and Peter began rowing with all his strength, the boat swaying with every stroke.

"How do you know about this place?" Thulani asked.

"I just found it," said Peter. "The day we had the braai, I took the boat out to get away from everyone and I stumbled across it."

Thulani nodded silently in the dark.

"And how does Larissa know about it?" he asked.

"I, um …"

"You don't have to answer that," Thulani said, with a hint of a chuckle in his voice. He clearly had the completely wrong idea about why they had come here, but Peter was happy to let him think whatever he wanted.

They pulled up onto the bank, and Trixy immediately jumped out with a splash. Thulani was too heavy for Peter to pull him further up the bank, so they both stepped out into the water.

"Which way?" said Thulani.

"Just follow Trixy."

With the flashlight still in hand, Thulani followed the Dalmatian up the stream. He took longer than Peter to pick his way over the rocks, but he managed just fine. Soon Peter was directing him to turn off onto the overgrown path. They came to the glade and Thulani shone the flashlight all around before focusing on the tree.

"I can see how this would be the tree she was talking about," he said.

"Actually, this is why we think it's the tree," said Peter, and he led Thulani to the side of the tree where *M + P* had been engraved into the bark.

"M and P?" Thulani said curiously.

"Mandla and Patricia," said Peter. He reached into the hole and pulled out the tin.

"And this?" Thulani was becoming more and more astonished at everything he saw.

"You remember you told us the story about how Mandla was

arrested?" said Peter. "But before he was arrested, he sent a shoebox of letters with your father to Patricia?"

Thulani nodded.

"This is how they would send letters to each other," said Peter. "They used to leave them in this tin under the tree."

Thulani crouched down and ran his fingers over the engraved bark.

"So, when Patricia said 'under the willow tree,' we thought she could well be talking about this one," Peter concluded.

Thulani took a moment to take in the weight of all the history the tree symbolized. "Let's see if we can find it then," he said.

First, they checked the tin. It opened easily this time, not having been rusted into place for decades. After going through the loose papers that had been left in it—there was no sign of a will—they shone the light into the hole and checked it thoroughly. Thulani even stuck a hand in and felt around inside. When that didn't yield any results, they started to dig: in the hole, outside the hole; even Trixy was sniffing around. Nothing. Eventually they both sat back, defeated.

"You're sure it said 'under a willow tree'?" Thulani asked.

"Definitely," said Peter. "It also said to pay attention to every minor detail."

They both looked around as though something might reveal itself. They checked the hole again, and the tin, looking for any small detail they may have missed the first time. Still, they found nothing.

"Perhaps," Thulani said with a sigh, "when she wrote the letter, she had not yet hidden the will here. Perhaps she had only intended to."

They left the glade empty-handed.

Brian and Larissa stood on the edge of the jetty as Peter rowed Thulani and Trixy closer.

"So?" Brian called out to them before they had docked. "Any luck?"

They grabbed hold of the jetty to steady themselves. "Nothing," Thulani said as he pulled himself out of the boat.

Open-mouthed, they turned to Peter as though hoping for a different outcome. Peter shook his head.

"Sorry."

Larissa's face fell. She had been holding on to this one glimmer of hope, and now everything they had worked for was for nothing.

"So Father Ian wins?" she said. She looked up at Brian. "But surely he isn't going to get anything? After what he did?"

Brian sighed.

"I don't know," he said. "I hope not. But there's no evidence that he's done anything illegal, so if he gets lawyers involved it might be difficult to discredit him."

"But we saw the letter!" said Larissa. "We watched him burn it! We're eyewitnesses!"

Brian shrugged. "Your word against his."

It was a somber walk back to the house. Nobody said a word. Trixy was the only one happy with how the evening had turned out and bid them farewell with a wag of her tail as they went through the little garden gate. In the hall under the stairs, they all stopped and looked at each other for a silent moment of shared dejection.

"Alright," Brian eventually said, "you're both safe, and that's the most important thing." He then looked at Peter's face where the blood had dried around the gash in his cheek. "Do we need to get you to a doctor?"

"No, I reckon a Band-Aid and a painkiller and I'll be okay," said Peter.

"Good lad," said Brian. "Larissa, will you be able to help him out?"

"Yes, of course!"

"Good. Let's all get some sleep, I'll get hold of Ms. O'Sullivan first thing in the morning so we can sort all of this out."

Once they had all said their goodnights, Brian headed back to his room down the passage, Thulani left to go back to his house, and Peter and Larissa headed up the stairs.

"I can't believe he's going to get his way," Larissa said. "After everything."

"It's not fair," Peter agreed.

"You're positive there was nothing under the tree?"

"Positive," said Peter. "Thulani was saying it's possible that she planned to hide it there but never got the chance."

"That's true; I never thought of that," said Larissa.

She led Peter into the girls' bathroom, and Peter sat down on the side of the bath. She gently held his face with her hand as she inspected the wound. "That was a hell of a thing you did earlier," she said.

"Ja, I didn't really think it through," said Peter. "If Thulani hadn't come when he did, it might not have worked out too well for me."

"I didn't know what we were going to do," said Larissa, wetting a cloth in the basin. "I thought the gun was real. Now hold still; this might hurt a little."

She carefully wiped the blood from his face, softly dabbing over the cut across his cheek. Now that the adrenalin had worn off, it was even more painful than before; Peter gritted his teeth and tried not to wince.

"All done," Larissa eventually said. "I think I saw some Band-Aids in this cabinet ..."

She gently put one over the cut on his cheek, then another one over a cut on his forehead that he didn't even know he had.

"There you go," she smiled. "Good as new."

"Thanks, Larissa," said Peter.

They stood looking into each other's eyes.

Larissa was glancing from one eye to the other, and it gave Peter butterflies in his stomach. He was suddenly incredibly nervous. He glanced at the door, then back at Larissa.

"We should probably go to bed," he said.

"Ja, we should," said Larissa.

But she didn't move. She just stayed staring at him. Peter's heart was beating even faster than before.

"Alright," Larissa finally sighed. "Goodnight, Peter."

She put her arms around him and gave him a tight hug.

"Night," said Peter, with the distinct feeling that he was blowing this.

She let go; her hands slid down his arms and her fingers just hooked onto his for a moment as she started pulling away.

Without thinking about it, Peter pulled her back. He put his arms round her waist, she put hers round his neck, and suddenly her lips were pressed against his and he was kissing her and she was kissing him and for a brief moment Peter forgot about everything that had happened that night.

When they eventually broke apart, Larissa giggled softly, her arms still hanging around Peter's neck.

"I wondered if that was ever going to happen," she said.

"I'll be honest, I've been wondering about it a lot," said Peter.

She giggled again, and pulled him toward her to carry on kissing him.

But their kissing was cut short by the sound of the boys' bathroom door closing at the other end of the passage.

"Okay, we really do need to go to bed now," said Larissa.

She led him by the hand down the passage to the girls' room.

"See you tomorrow," she said, and she gave him one more kiss goodnight before disappearing into her room.

Chapter 18

"Okay, boys, up you get!"

Carol van der Westhuizen marched in and flung the curtains open. "You all need to be packed up before Ms. O'Sullivan gets here so you're ready to leave straight afterwards."

The boys all started moaning and slowly sitting up in their beds.

Peter, however, woke up with a smile on his face. He had to think about it for a moment to convince himself that it hadn't just been a dream ... but it wasn't: Larissa had kissed him. He didn't know what it meant for them going forward—was it a once-off? Were they going to carry on seeing each other? He had no idea. But it made him both nervous and excited to see her again.

He hopped down from the top bunk. It was only then, as he landed with a heavy thud, that a sharp pain reminded him of the gash across his cheek. The memories from the night came flooding back: hiding in the cupboard, riding out to retrieve the letter, fighting with Father Ian, and rowing to the other side of the dam. The other boys were only starting to rouse themselves, none of them any the wiser. He turned away from them to hide his face as he got dressed and left the room in a hurry.

"Morning, Pete!" Ellen greeted him as she came round the corner on her way back from breakfast. "Brian sent me to ... Jeepers, what happened to you?"

She looked from his face all the way down to his knees, which Peter hadn't even realized were also grazed from falling off the horse.

"Is it that obvious?" he asked.

"Peter, you look like you fell out of a tree and hit every branch on the way down! What happened last night?"

"It's a long story," said Peter. "I promise I'll tell you the whole thing later, but you were going to tell me something about Brian?"

Ellen folded her arms and narrowed her eyes at him. "Just that he wants to talk to you," she said. "I'm assuming it's related?"

"Indirectly," said Peter. "Where is he?"

"Guest hall."

"Thanks!"

He left Ellen still looking suspicious and rushed down the stairs to the guest hall.

"Oh, Peter, there you are!" said Brian and he ushered Peter back out the door into the foyer. "I've called Ms. O'Sullivan. She should be here any minute now. Have you seen—ah, Larissa, there you are!"

Larissa had just come down the stairs. Peter glanced at her and their eyes met for a brief moment before she looked at Brian.

"Ellen said you were looking for me?" she said.

"Yes, I've just told Peter that Ms. O'Sullivan is going to be here soon," said Brian. "Would you mind waiting with him? Probably better if you're both there to tell her everything that happened. I don't think it will change anything, but she needs to know the full story."

"Of course," she said. For once, her voice gave away a hint of awkwardness.

"Great," said Brian. "I'm going to carry on setting up—get some breakfast in the meantime and listen out for the door!"

He left the two of them in a delicate silence. Finally, they had to look at each other.

"Good morning," Larissa said. Her head was tilted down

slightly, and she was looking up at Peter with uncharacteristically shy eyes.

Peter didn't know what to do. He had entirely expected Larissa to take the lead on this. "Morning," he replied.

He held eye contact for a moment, but soon looked down.

"So … does Brian want us to tell her what happened last night?" Larissa said.

"Ja, I think so," said Peter. "Just so she's aware of everything and has all the information, you know?"

"Ja, no, makes sense," said Larissa.

Peter nodded. For an uncomfortable moment they both looked anywhere but at each other.

"Should we, umm …"

"Get breakfast?"

"Yes!"

They went into the dining hall together and each grabbed a bowl of cereal. A few people were busy having breakfast, and Peter found his parents in their usual spot. Larissa looked around but couldn't see her parents anywhere.

"Can I …?"

"Ja, of course!"

She followed Peter to sit with his parents and Rebecca, greeting them politely as they sat down.

"Hey, Larissa!" Rebecca said with a huge smile.

"My heavens, Pete!" his mom exclaimed. "What happened to you?"

"It turns out your son is quite a hero," said Larissa.

Peter's parents both looked perplexed. "Please do tell?"

"I'll tell you the whole story on the drive home," said Peter.

"Although I have a feeling you might hear about it sooner than that," said Larissa, looking at Carol who had just walked in.

Before they had finished their cereal, they heard the knocker on the front door.

"That's for us," said Larissa, standing up and pushing her plate forward.

"What do you mean that's for you?" said Martin.

"I'll explain everything later," said Peter, also standing up, and they left his parents looking completely baffled.

Larissa answered the door. "Hi! You must be Ms. O'Sullivan?"

Ms. O'Sullivan, with her gray hair and spectacles, stood away from the door as though she had no immediate intention to enter. She eyed Larissa from behind her glasses, nodded, and said, "Indeed. And you must be Larissa. Pleasure to meet you."

She gave Larissa the same no-nonsense handshake Peter had come to expect from her, before turning to Peter.

"Good to see you, Peter. I trust you're well."

Given his appearance, Peter took that to mean that she was here to talk business and a few cuts and bruises did not warrant a mention.

"Good morning, Ms. O'Sullivan," he said.

Her demeanor suggested that business was to be conducted outside. Once Peter had closed the door, she led them down the front steps to the lawn in the sun.

"I'm told you have information for me," she said. "Spare no details."

Peter and Larissa looked at each other, trying to decide where to start.

"It started that day my dad and I came to your firm," said Peter. "The day Thulani delivered the letter."

"Yes, I've already had this conversation with Thulani," she said. "We are still in the process of figuring out who could've taken it."

"We think he goes by the name 'McKenzie,'" said Peter.

Her eyes narrowed and she nodded.

"We'll look into that," she said. "Tell me what happened after that."

Peter and Larissa dived into the entire story about Father Ian, how they think he poisoned Patricia, destroyed the will, and intercepted the letter. They told her about hearing him on the phone and racing out to the gate to get the letter.

"Tell me about the letter," she said. "What does it say?"

"It said she knew someone was plotting to destroy the will and kill her," Peter explained, "but she didn't know who. It said she had actually written another will a long time ago; apparently you had told her that what she wanted wasn't possible back then, but she says it is now. She says that *that* will, the original one she wrote, reflects her true intentions for her estate. But she knew the person would try to find it so she didn't say where it was; she just gave a cryptic clue that only you would be able to understand. It said something about under a willow tree …"

They watched her for a reaction to the willow tree, but her expression was unchanged.

"We thought we might know which willow tree she was talking about, but we looked there and didn't find anything."

"Do you still have the letter?"

"No, Father Ian took it back and burned it so there wouldn't be any evidence."

They told her about how Father Ian had caught them, and Peter had fought him off.

"And where is this 'Father Ian' now?" she asked.

"He ran out while Thulani's back was turned, saying we would hear from his lawyers. And then he drove off," said Peter.

"And you're sure Father Ian was the only conspirator from within the family?" Ms. O'Sullivan asked. "He's not the only person who stands to gain from the will being missing. No one else was involved?"

"Well, we … um …"

Ms. O'Sullivan eyed them both and could see from the mild panic in the way they looked at each other that they hadn't considered the possibility of someone else from the family being involved.

"Ah, Ms. O'Sullivan!" came Brian's voice from the door. "My apologies! I didn't hear you arrive!"

Ms. O'Sullivan glanced at Brian as he began down the steps, then leaned in toward Peter and Larissa and spoke in a low voice. "Let's assume for now that there could be someone else who was working with Father Ian—so don't let anyone know what you're up to. I don't know about any willow tree, but I doubt whether Patricia would have made her way outside to bury a document—she was too old, and it would have drawn too much attention. It must be in the house somewhere. Find it."

She looked up with a smile just as Brian reached them. "Good morning, Mr. Kingsbury. Peter and Larissa here have just filled me in on everything that happened."

"Did they tell you about Gideon?"

She only looked puzzled for a brief second. "Father Ian's proper name, I presume? Yes, they told me everything." She looked at them purposefully. "You two have been very helpful. You can go now," she said with a very subtle raise of her eyebrows.

"Alright, let us know if you have any more questions," Larissa said, and the two of them turned to leave.

"My own nephew, can you believe it!" they heard Brian saying as they left.

As soon as they were through the doors, they turned to face each other.

"Of course she didn't bury it under an actual willow tree!" Larissa said. "We were being so stupid! The clue was meant for Ms. O'Sullivan—she would never have known about that tree on the other side of the dam."

"Exactly!" said Peter. "And—" He cut his sentence short when Kim walked into the foyer.

"Morning, you two," she said pleasantly, then hesitated when she saw the looks on their faces. "Everything alright?"

Thank goodness for Larissa.

"Everything's great," she said effortlessly. "That's a lovely hat—where'd you get it?"

"Oh, this? I had it made, actually, by a friend in Cape Town. She does all my accessories."

"I'm going to have to get her number from you," Larissa said, feigning just the right amount of jealousy.

"Of course!" said Kim. "I can give it to you after ol' what's-her-name comes to read the will."

"That'd be great!"

"Lovely, I'll chat to you then. Cheerio!"

Kim went into the guest hall and Larissa looked at Peter and rolled her eyes. "Come on," she said.

They immediately headed up the stairs. "Aunty Pat used to be Ms. O'Sullivan's music teacher," said Peter. "Whatever the clue means, I'll bet it has something to do with that."

They reached the top of the stairs and headed toward the piano room, but just before they turned the corner into the passage, they heard Ellen's voice behind them.

"Where are you two off to?" she asked in a playfully suggestive tone.

They both spun round, looking about as guilty as two people who were doing exactly what she was insinuating.

"No, we're not …" Larissa began. She and Peter exchanged an awkward glance.

Ellen's smirk quickly turned into a frown. "Wait, what's going on?" she said.

Even Larissa was slow to answer. But the voices of Daniel and some other boys coming down the passageway hurried her up.

"Come with us," she said. She grabbed Ellen by the hand and pulled her with them round the corner and into the piano room.

"Oh, a piano!" she said. "Peter, didn't you say you …"

Her voice trailed off as Larissa glared at her with a finger on her lips. They waited in silence until the boys' voices had disappeared down the stairs.

"Okay, seriously, guys, what's going on?" Ellen asked.

Larissa took a deep breath.

"Peter and I have to find something," she said. "We have no idea where it is, or even what it is, and we have no idea how long it will take us. But nobody else must know what we're doing."

Ellen could see on their faces that this was serious. "How can I help?" she asked.

"Keep this a secret," said Larissa. "Nobody can know. Not your parents, not my parents. Nobody."

"If anyone asks where we are, lie," said Peter. "If they ask where Larissa is, say she's in the bedroom or something. Or the bathroom. If they ask where I am, say you saw me two minutes ago, but you have no idea. Don't give anyone the impression that we've been gone for a long time, or that we might be together."

"And let us know if anyone is being persistent about it," said Larissa. "You have my number, just message me."

"Also let us know if anyone is coming this way," said Peter. "Anyone whose bedroom is on the first or second floor has no business coming up here—so tell us if you see someone going up the stairs."

Ellen looked at each of them in turn and nodded. "Got it."

She left the room and Larissa turned to Peter. "Where do we start?" she said.

"No idea," said Peter, already flicking through books on the shelves. "I guess I'm just hoping something will stand out."

Larissa joined in the hunt, and for a while they both leafed through books, turned them upside down, looked behind them on the shelves … Peter went through a stack of old vinyl records, Larissa checked the cupboards of the cabinet the record player was sitting on ... Nothing.

"This is hopeless," Larissa said as she sat back against a bookshelf, ready to give up. "Father Ian's been doing this for a week, and we're expecting to just come in here and find it in five minutes."

"You're right," said Peter, also sitting back. "We have to be cleverer than that."

Larissa's phone buzzed, and she took it out to look at it.

"Ellen says she overheard Brian asking two different people where we are." She looked at Peter. "That's not necessarily suspicious, though, is it? He probably just wants to know what we told Ms. O'Sullivan."

Peter shrugged. "I don't even know anymore."

Larissa looked back at her phone. "Everyone's getting ready in the guest hall for Ms. O'Sullivan. Soon it'll be pretty obvious that neither of us is there."

"Right," said Peter, "we have to hurry."

"Hurry how? What are we supposed to be looking for?"

"Well, let's think about it. What did the clue say?"

"It said it's under the willow tree, but we have to look carefully."

"No, it didn't say look carefully," said Peter, "it said something like 'pay attention to minor details.' Remember that riddle in those letters she wrote to Mandla—the wording will be important."

"She also made it sound like the paper itself was part of the clue," said Larissa. "That must be why they dropped the letter off here for Father Ian."

"Yes, that's right!" said Peter. "It's something she would've recognized ..." He suddenly sat up. "That book!" he said. "The one she had written her own music in! Ms. O'Sullivan was the other person who had written in it!"

He urgently looked around, trying to think where the book was. He checked to see if it was still on the rack of the piano, but then he remembered. "The stool!"

He rushed over to the piano stool and pulled it open. On top of a pile of other old music books was the one he had dropped in there after sight-reading some of Patricia's music.

"This is it!" he said as he picked up the book and opened it. "And this is the paper, look!"

It was the same college-ruled paper with the extra lines that the letter had been written on. He fanned through the pages until his thumb stopped at a small gap, and he opened at that point.

"That's obviously where she took the page from," said Larissa, looking at the tear where a page was missing.

"But why is this point significant?" said Peter, scanning the next page for anything of interest. It had Olivia O'Sullivan's name on it, but, as Peter flipped through some more pages, so did a few of them. Larissa then turned the pages back to where the tear was, and then a few pages before that to the beginning of the previous piece.

Peter exhaled deeply, and Larissa grinned. The piece they were now looking at was the one Peter had played that night: "Under the Willow Tree."

"She must have written this for Mandla," said Larissa. "For their spot under the willow tree where they used to read together and left notes for each other."

Peter pointed at the date on the top of the page.

"This was written long after he died," he said. "This is in memory of him."

They stared at the page.

"Okay, so … what are we looking for?" said Larissa.

"I don't know," said Peter.

They scanned the page, looking for clues. The first thing Peter checked was if the letters of the notes spelled anything, but that was a dead end.

"These look like they were written with a different pencil," said Larissa, pointing at the chord symbols. "B, C, D … they don't spell anything. Why do the Bs all have a lower-case b next to them?"

"That's not a lower-case b, that means flat. Those are B-flat. But these majors and minors are wrong …" He looked up. "Majors and minors! The letter said pay attention to every *minor* detail and you won't have any *major* problems! That was the clue—she was saying to look at the minor and major chords!"

Larissa was excited by Peter being excited, but she didn't really understand. Peter looked at the chords again.

"What do they say?" she asked.

"They're chords, Larissa; they don't *say* anything."

"Okay … so … what's the clue?"

Peter pored over the chords. "I'm not sure …" he mumbled.

Larissa was silent for a moment while Peter tried to figure it out.

"Maybe it's Morse code?" she said optimistically.

"Larissa, these are chords. How could it be—" He went silent as he gazed over the notation. "Wait a minute … you might be on to something!"

"Really?"

"If minors are dots, and majors are dashes …" he inspected the music further. "Each line is a different letter. Look, sometimes the chord isn't even written, or there's an extra chord, just to make it work!"

He pointed at the music, and Larissa nodded along eagerly despite having no idea what he was on about.

"Let's test it," he said. "We need to decipher it."

"On it," said Larissa. She pulled her phone out and found an online Morse code translator. "Give it to me."

"Okay: dash, dot, dash, dot …"

He looked up at Larissa as she typed it in.

"C."

Peter looked back to the music. "Dot, dash."

"A."

"Dot, dot, dot."

"S."

"Dot."

"E."

They looked at each other.

"So far so good," said Larissa. "What's next?"

"Dot—" Peter began, but he was interrupted by Larissa's phone vibrating.

"Ellen says almost everyone is waiting in the guest hall and a few people are wondering where we are now."

"We need to step this up," said Peter.

"Let's do it."

"Okay: dot, dot, dash, space, dash, dot, space …" Peter raced through the entire piece of music, narrating dots and dashes while Larissa hurriedly typed them in. Finally, he reached the end and turned to see Larissa's phone. "Alright, what do we have?"

Larissa held the phone out. What they had was a long string of letters:

CASEUNDERBEDCODEYEARYOUBEGANLESSONS

It took them a moment to make sense of it.

"Caseund … something cod eye, are you … no, wait …"

"Case under bed, code year you began lessons," said Peter.

"That's it!" Larissa gasped. She flung her arms around Peter and squeezed him. "We did it!"

"Not yet," said Peter. "We still have to find it."

She let go awkwardly. "Surely she means her own bed?" she said.

"Must be. Let's go have a look."

They opened the door cautiously and peeked round before rushing out and down the passage to Patricia's bedroom. They went in, closed the door in a hurry, then paused as they looked at the bed: the base was solid, with no space underneath for anything. Peter's first thought was that some kind of trap door was hidden beneath the bed … only, the bed was an old, Victorian-style four poster, complete with tasseled curtains and an elaborate headboard, and the solid base sat flush to the ground. Intricate patterns in the dark wood suggested it was dense and immensely heavy, near impossible to move.

Larissa had a different thought. She went up to the bed and gave the base a knock to confirm that it was in fact hollow and immediately began searching around the sides for a way to open it. She soon found a concealed latch near the headboard, unfastened it, and the side of the base folded down on hinges.

"Yoh, I thought we would have to try move the bed," said Peter. He knelt next to Larissa to look inside.

At first all they saw were a few old boxes, but then they noticed a briefcase, and Peter reached in to pull it out. It had a latch on either side, both of which needed a combination to unlock.

"What year did Ms. O'Sullivan start lessons?" said Larissa. "Do you know?"

"I don't. But it would've been nineteen-something so we can start there."

Just as he began turning the combination dials to nineteen, Larissa's phone buzzed again.

"Ellen says someone's coming up the stairs!"

"Okay, scratch that idea; let's get out of here!"

They quickly closed the latch under the bed and left with the briefcase. As they were about to round the corner, they heard footsteps coming up the stairs and froze.

"What are we going to do with this briefcase?" said Larissa. "How do we explain this?"

Peter slid it into the piano room. He then grabbed Larissa, pressed her against the wall and began kissing her. She was taken by surprise, but kissed him back fiercely, wrapping her arms around him …

"Ahem!" Brian's not-so-polite cough interrupted them.

They broke apart, looking sheepish and awkward. Larissa smacked her lips and tried to hide her grin.

Brian looked annoyed. "Everyone's waiting to start," he said, "and you two are hiding away up here …"

He gestured at them to fill in for what he was unwilling to verbalize.

"Sorry," said Larissa. "We'll come right away."

"Quickly," said Brian with a stern frown.

He led them down the stairs. Peter and Larissa glanced at each other behind him like two naughty school children being marched to the principal's office.

When they came to the bottom, Thulani was busy helping Phillip through the door.

"Oh, Phillip! Are you alright?" said Brian. "I was so worried about you!"

"And you said I was dreaming!" said Phillip.

"I'm so sorry! I just couldn't believe that someone in the family would do something like that!"

"He was quite traumatized," said Thulani. "But he'll be fine."

"Nothing a strong drink can't fix," said Phillip.

Peter saw his opportunity. "Stall them!" he whispered to Larissa.

He ducked into the guest hall, where everyone was sitting in rows facing the lectern that had been brought in from the chapel, waiting restlessly for something to happen. He spotted Ms. O'Sullivan busy typing on her phone and rushed over to her.

"It's in the piano room!" he said. "There's a briefcase with a combination lock—the combination is the year you began lessons."

She looked up, startled, then caught on to what he was saying and stood up.

"Brian and some others are just outside," he warned as she started leaving without a word.

She clearly received the message because as she passed them in the foyer she said, "I'm terribly sorry, I have to take this," her hand over the mouthpiece of her phone as though she were on a call, and then she disappeared.

"What's going on?"

Peter turned around—Ellen had found him and was looking both concerned and curious.

"Did you find whatever you were looking for?" she asked. "Where's Ms. O'Sullivan gone? Was it a success?"

"Hard to say. I guess we'll find out soon enough."

Thulani and Brian helped Phillip in, and the hum of voices swelled with murmurs throughout the room; Karen even got up to help, as though they needed a third person. Larissa came in after them and joined Peter and Ellen.

"I saw Ms. O'Sullivan heading up the stairs," she said; "You told her where it was?"

Peter nodded.

"Could either of you please tell me what's going on?" said Ellen.

"We found Patricia's true will."

"Her true will?" said Ellen. "What do you mean? What does it say?"

"We have no idea. But it's supposed to reveal some big secret that nobody knows about."

Brian then walked up to the lectern. The three of them quickly found seats at the back next to Thulani and Ngesihle, and the chatter in the room started dying down.

"Family and friends, thank you for your patience. We apologize for the delay—recent findings may have potentially changed the verdict on Patricia's final wishes. Ms. O'Sullivan has been in discussions with her team all morning to try to sort everything out, but she will explain everything shortly. For now, please just—ah, Ms. O'Sullivan!"

Right on cue, Ms. O'Sullivan entered the room. A sense of finality in her expression sent a flutter of whispers around the room as Brain made way for her and she assumed control of the lectern. She placed a sheet of paper down, cleared her throat, and looked up at everyone.

The room became perfectly still.

"Good morning," she said. "My name is Olivia O'Sullivan, and I am the executor of Patricia Woodwright's estate, appointed by Patricia herself. I have come here this morning to read her last will and testament." She paused to look at the document and shift her glasses. "In 1962," she continued, "Patricia wrote her Last Will and Testament, unbeknown to me or anyone else. In 1985, I approached her about drawing up a will, but what she wanted to have happen to her estate was unfortunately not feasible at the time and so we drew up a new will. However, this will was stolen and destroyed. Therefore, the first will, which she wrote by herself, which was not feasible at the time but is now, is the document that will be followed regarding the distribution of her estate. I have it on good authority that she wanted this to be the case. I will say now that I still need to examine this and other documents to determine its legality, but it is my opinion at present that it is indeed legitimate."

She held up the piece of paper for everyone to see. "I have with me the original will of Patricia Jane Woodwright, which I will read to you now."

She placed it back down on the lectern, shifted her glasses and began reading.

I, Patricia Jane Woodwright, being of sound mind and body on this day the 24th of July in the year of our Lord 1962, do hereby declare this as my last will and testament.

I loved a man named Mandla Sithole. The two of us were in a secret relationship and would have spent our lives together, but he was taken from me when he was shot and killed by the police because of the color of his skin. I was denied a most basic human right—to share my life with somebody whom I love—while he was denied the most basic human right of all: the right to exist in this world.

My heart has always belonged to Mandla. In a just world with any manner of virtue, we would have lived on this land together and, when the time came, the land would be inherited by our children who were raised on it. Therefore, because his ancestors inhabited the land long before mine did, I bequeath, bestow, and devise, with full fiduciary entitlement, my entire estate, including Woodwright Manor and all possessions therein as well as any other assets I may own, to Jabu Msimang, Mandla's sister and closest relative, or to the eldest of her descendants in the case that she is predeceased at the time of my death.

Ms. O'Sullivan looked up at the crowd of people all gaping at her in stunned silence.

"I believe," she said, addressing everyone, "that Thulani Msimang is Jabu Msimang's eldest living descendant."

She raised a hand to gesture toward Thulani at the back. Everybody turned round to look at him. Thulani was staring at her as though he was still trying to piece together what she had said.

Peter looked around the room; the only other person not staring in disbelief was Phillip, who had a little chuckle to himself and took a quick sip from his hipflask.

After the initial shock, the room erupted with a buzz of commotion. Larissa's dad was the first to congratulate Thulani, and others followed. Ngesihle was in tears. Thulani shook everyone's hands in a daze, still not having fully grasped what Ms. O'Sullivan had said. Karen and Kim looked irate, and were both harassing Ms. O'Sullivan for explanations, their differences forgotten. Others tried to make sense of the new information.

"... a secret love affair? ..."

"… the will got destroyed? …"

Larissa and Peter turned to each other.

"That was all us," Larissa beamed.

"We actually did it," said Peter.

"No gold, though," said Larissa.

"We should've known," said Peter. "The big reveal was Mandla."

"I'm so happy it's all over and everything turned out okay!" said Larissa.

She gave Peter a tight hug, and Ellen eyed them suspiciously. She might have said something, but Ms. O'Sullivan came over and saved them from interrogation.

"Peter and Larissa, I wanted to personally thank you," she said. "Patricia was a very dear friend of mine, and because of you two she has been properly honored. I gave her my word that her final wishes would be seen to, but I must say that without you, I don't think I would have been able to keep that promise. It means a lot to me that I could, so I thank you.

"I don't know how much of what happened Brian and Thulani will choose to disclose, and there is a chance that your efforts may be forever unknown to the rest of the family. But you stopped a criminal and helped justice prevail. You can always be proud of that."

Peter and Larissa both nodded awkwardly, not knowing what to say.

"Now, as I'm sure you can imagine, I have a lot of work to do. You will most likely be contacted in due course for official statements. Until then, thank you again, and I bid the two of you farewell."

She turned to leave, but Larissa stopped her. "Sorry, Ms. O'Sullivan," she said. "The whole reason Patricia had to write a new will with you was because you said her original one wasn't feasible—why not? What was wrong with it? Why couldn't she have left everything to Mandla's family?"

"Because until 1991, black people could not legally own land in South Africa," she said matter-of-factly.

She nodded to confirm they were satisfied, then turned and left.

"'Stopped a criminal,'" Ellen quoted once she was gone. "What on earth was she on about?"

"Father Ian was up to some seriously sinister stuff," said Larissa. She and Peter recounted the entire story for Ellen, from the night after the funeral when Peter played "Under the Willow Tree" and they found Patricia's and Mandla's old letters, right up until finding the case under the bed an hour or so earlier.

"And that's when you messaged to say someone was coming," said Larissa.

"Ja, we owe you," said Peter. "I don't know if we would've done it without your help."

"So what did you do with the case?" Ellen asked.

"Peter hid it in the piano room, just as Brian came up the stairs."

"Wait, you don't think ..." she looked around and lowered her voice. "You don't think *Brian* was in on it with Father Ian?"

"We honestly have no idea," said Peter.

"So, wasn't Brian suspicious that you guys were up there?"

"Well ..." Peter and Larissa exchanged a glance. "He found us, but we managed to get away with it."

"And then I came and told Ms. O'Sullivan where it was."

"I can't believe this was going on the whole time and I had no idea."

"No one did," said Peter. "I think we, Thulani, and Brian were the only ones who knew about it."

Larissa looked round at her dad, who was busy laughing with Thulani, jabbing him with his elbow. "Alright," she said, "I need to finish packing. I'll see you soon."

She got up and left Peter and Ellen in silence.

"So …" Ellen said, now that it was just the two of them, "I couldn't help but notice …"

Peter could tell just from her tone where she was going with this. He started blushing.

"Did you guys …?"

He broke a smile. "We did."

"Good for you!" Ellen laughed, and she punched him playfully on the arm. "Took you long enough; she was practically begging you."

"Whatever, man."

"So what's the story now? Are you going to carry on seeing each other?"

"I … don't know," said Peter. "It happened last night, and to be honest it's been quite awkward this morning. I don't know what's happening."

"You should talk to her."

Peter nodded. "You're probably right."

The guest hall started emptying out as everyone went to fetch their suitcases from upstairs and bring them out to the parking area, getting ready to leave. Steven followed through on setting up a WhatsApp group and was asking everyone for their numbers. Soon they were all exchanging numbers and saying their goodbyes.

"Cheers, mate!"

"Cheers, bru, we must make plans Jozi side!"

"Hundred percent!"

Jesse came over to Peter and offered a handshake. "Cheers, Peter, was lekker to be able to spend some time with you."

"It was," said Peter. "Cheers, Jesse."

"Ja, cheers, Peter," said Austen. "Let me know if you're ever in Joburg!"

"Cheers, Austen, will do!"

He shook hands with Kyle and Steven, gave Megan and Katie a hug, and got a lukewarm "cheers" from Daniel.

Ellen was the last to say goodbye, and gave him a tight squeeze. "Don't be a stranger, okay? Let me know how you're doing from time to time."

"I definitely will," said Peter. "Was great spending time with you!"

She caught him glancing over at Larissa saying goodbye to Katie's parents.

"And talk to her," she said. "Don't leave things awkward."

"I will, I will."

One by one, the cars started to leave. Peter hadn't even packed yet. Once he had said goodbye to everyone, he slowly made his way back inside. The house was perfectly quiet but for the old grandfather clock and felt completely empty as he ambled up the stairs. At the top of the stairs, he remembered about the briefcase that he had left in the piano room for Ms. O'Sullivan. Instead of going straight to the bedroom, he decided to quickly check if it was still there.

Sure enough, the briefcase was sitting on the piano stool. The lid was closed, but not latched. Naturally, he opened it to have a look inside.

It was mostly old documents, all type-written, the paper an old, dusty yellow. They contained confirmations of times, meeting places, prices, some for transportation like trains and carriages, some for accommodation, one for agreeing a buying price for gold—and all with an undercurrent of discretion and secrecy. These were their plans to run away. They had it all mapped out, ready to go, if it weren't for Mandla being arrested and killed.

At the bottom of the briefcase, underneath all the documents, was a bunch of old black-and-white photographs. He picked them up and looked at each one: they had all been taken at Woodwright Manor, and a couple of them were of Patricia and her friend, Alice. But the rest were all of Patricia and a tall man who at first glance Peter thought was Thulani. But these were pictures of Mandla. In some of the photos they were looking at the camera, in some of them they were looking at each other, and in others Mandla was either holding her up in the air or they were in an embrace; in every photo, they both looked perfectly happy.

Peter noticed something else in the pictures; something he had seen before. Around Mandla's neck was a string with a key tied onto it, like a necklace. Peter recognized it.

He grabbed the briefcase and ran out of the piano room, down the passage to Patricia's room. He threw the briefcase on the bed and went straight into Patricia's secret study, to the box of trinkets, and emptied it out on the desk. After a moment of shifting things around on the desk, he found what he was looking for: a key that he and Larissa had once said looked like a flame. He held up the picture to compare: it was definitely the same key, and it wasn't a flame at all!

He raced out of the secret study and out of Patricia's bedroom, sprinted down the passage and leaped down the stairs two at a time. He ran out through the foyer and toward the parking area as fast as he could.

"Peter, there you are," said Larissa. "I've been looking for—Hey, what's going on?"

Without explaining, Peter grabbed her hand and pulled her back toward the house.

"Alright, alright, I'm coming!"

She followed him through the foyer once more, then through the narrow passageway and into the closet on the left.

"What are we doing?" she asked as Peter shoved aside the camping stove and pushed the button for the secret door to open.

"Why was Walter convinced that he had seen treasure down here, but then he could never find it again?" said Peter as he led her down the stairs. "And why did Patricia suddenly want Thulani's father to build this secret door and a new wine rack?"

They finally came to a stop next to the new wine rack and Peter held out the key.

"It's not a flame," he said; "it's a lion's tail."

Larissa gasped.

"The tail in the lion's mouth ..." she whispered, and she looked down at the metallic lion face on the side of the wooden wine rack.

Slowly, she took the key from Peter and tried it in the lion's mouth. A perfect fit. She turned it until there was a loud *click!* The entire wine rack creaked as it swung open.

Behind it was a small chamber. On the floor, in neat piles, were bars of solid gold that had once belonged to Charles Woodwright.

On top of the piles of gold: a rock about the size of a clenched fist with a single streak of gold in it.

Glossary of South African terms

asiqabulana: *(isiZulu/isiXhosa)* "we are not kissing."
aweh: *(South African slang)* an informal greeting or expression of agreement: "hey," "okay," "what's up."
bakkie: *(Afrikaans; South African English)* a pickup truck; a small open-backed utility vehicle used for transporting goods or people.
boet: *(Afrikaans)* literally "brother;" an informal term for a male friend or companion.
braaimaster: *(from Afrikaans)* the person in charge of cooking meat at a braai; the "grill master."
hawu: exclamation of surprise, like "OMG."
mkhulu: *(isiZulu/isiXhosa)* "grandfather;" also used as a respectful form of address for an elderly man.
ngicela: *(isiZulu)* "please;" literally "I ask," used to introduce a polite request.
niyaqabulana: *(isiZulu/isiXhosa)* "you are kissing."
oupa: *(Afrikaans)* "grandfather;" an affectionate term, commonly used in South African English.
ous: *(Afrikaans)*; colloquial term meaning "you guys."
San: *(anthropological/historical term)* the indigenous hunter-gatherer peoples of southern Africa; a collective name for several related groups. Some groups contest the term.
umhlabana: *(isiZulu/isiXhosa)* the isiZulu name of the aloe plant.

unamanga: *(isiZulu/isiXhosa)* "you are lying;" literally "you have lies," a direct accusation whose force depends on context.

Mason O'Connor co-wrote the graphic novel *Shaka Rising: A Legend of the Warrior Prince*. He grew up in KwaZulu-Natal, South Africa, studied Mathematics at Stellenbosch University, and works as a data analyst in Cape Town. His passion for storytelling, music, games, puzzles, and the outdoors inspires his writing.

www.ingramcontent.com/pod-product-compliance
Lightning Source LLC
LaVergne TN
LVHW091108080826
845145LV00008B/1849

* 9 7 8 1 9 6 0 8 0 3 2 6 9 *